THE NEW ROAD

NEIL MUNRO was born in 1863, the illegitimate son of an Inveraray kitchen-maid. After leaving school, he worked for a time in a lawyer's office, before leaving the Highlands for a career in journalism, eventually editing the *Glasgow Evening News*. However, it was his work as a poet and novelist that established Munro as one of Scotland's finest writers. His historical novels, such as *John Splendid*, were acknowledged as masterpieces of the genre; but he also achieved great success with the *Para Handy* tales and other light-hearted stories he wrote under the pseudonym Hugh Foulis. *The New Road* was Munro's last, and most accomplished, historical novel. Neil Munro died in 1930.

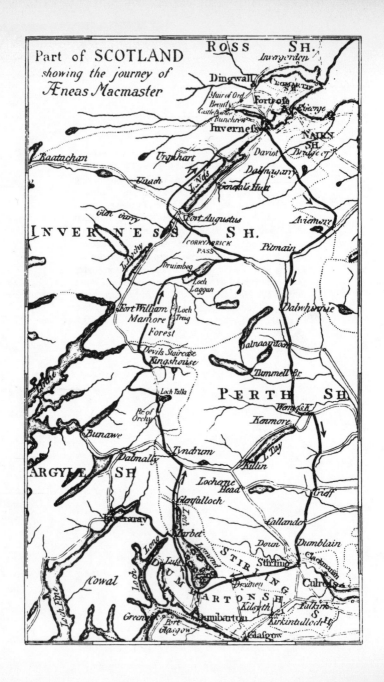

Part of SCOTLAND
showing the journey of
Æneas Macmaster

THE NEW ROAD

NEIL MUNRO

Introduced by Brian D Osborne

EDINBURGH
B & W PUBLISHING
1994

First published 1914
This edition published 1994
by B&W Publishing, Edinburgh
Introduction © Brian D Osborne 1994
ISBN 1 873631 34 0
All Rights Reserved.
No part of this publication may be reproduced
or transmitted in any form or by any means
without the prior permission of B&W Publishing

The publisher acknowledges subsidy
from the Scottish Arts Council towards
the publication of this volume.

British Library Cataloguing in Publication Data:
A catalogue record for this book is available
from the British Library

Cover design by *Alexander Duncanson & Co*

Cover illustration:
Detail from *Portrait of Edward Harvey* (1747)
by Allan Ramsay, reproduced by kind permission
of Dundee Museums & Art Galleries

Printed by Werner Söderström

CONTENTS

Introduction by Brian D Osborne   vii

    I   THE DOVECOTE TOWER   1

   II   AT THE OUTPOST   13

  III   NINIAN MACGREGOR CAMPBELL   25

 IV   DRIMDORRAN   35

   V   A CALL TO THE NORTH   42

 VI   THE ANGLER   56

VII   THE INN AT BUACHAILLE ETIVE   67

VIII   COL-OF-THE-TRICKS   76

 IX   BARISDALE'S MART   88

   X   THE WICKED BOUNDS   95

 XI   ÆNEAS-OF-THE-PISTOL   104

XII   CORRYARRICK PASS   113

XIII   IN THE WAY OF TRADE   122

XIV   INVERNESS   131

XV   THE DEN   142

XVI   DEAD MEN'S BONES   153

XVII   CASTLE DOUNIE AGAIN   163

XVIII   A HANK UNRAVELLED   174

XIX	THE TRAMMEL NET	184
XX	TO THE WOODS	192
XXI	JANET	203
XXII	BY BUNCHREW BURN	212
XXIII	NIGHT-LADS	220
XXIV	AT THE EBB-TIDE	230
XXV	THE *WAYWARD LASS*	237
XXVI	THE ESCAPE	247
XXVII	THE ADVOCATE COMMANDS	257
XXVIII	THE RETURN	266
XXIX	CANDLE-LIGHT	273
XXX	A SEARCH	284
XXXI	THE MAN FROM GUNNA	294
XXXII	CONFESSIONS	302
XXXIII	NIGHT-WANDERING	309
XXXIV	CONTENTS OF A BARREL	317
XXXV	THE PORTRAIT	326
XXXVI	THE COBBLER'S SONG	335
XXXVII	DIRK	342

INTRODUCTION

Brian D Osborne

"Red, level, sixteen feet to twenty wide, and thrown across the country like a string . . ." the great military roads of General Wade were built through Highland Scotland in response to the Jacobite rising of 1715. Linking the Highland garrisons with the south and intended to facilitate the movement of troops to control the unruly North the roads run as a pervading theme through *The New Road*, Neil Munro's exploration of the process of change in the Highlands. The adventures of Æneas Macmaster and Ninian Macgregor Campbell are the mechanism by which this process is explored and revealed.

This oddly matched pair, whose partnership is reminiscent of that of David Balfour and Alan Breck Stewart in Robert Louis Stevenson's *Kidnapped*, travel north in the Autumn of 1733 and find themselves doing battle with the forces of the old Highlands. Æneas and Ninian fight on the side of those determined to end the romantic, picturesque but unruly world of arbitrary power.

The forces of progress are an unlikely alliance. Wade's road-building Captain Leggatt who sees his task as having ". . . helped put a light up here." Æneas's uncle, an Inveraray merchant, sees the coming of ". . . Wade and his bonny Road" as the force to ". . . make the North a land for decent folk to live in . . ." and knows that "Once the New Road is finished, and the troopers and the guns and my carts on it, it's an end to the dominion o' the chiefs." Ninian travels from Inveraray to Inverness in the service of the Duke of Argyll and his brother, Lord Islay, who attempt to rule the Highlands on behalf of the Government. John Campbell, 2nd Duke of Argyll, (1680-1743), "Red John of the Battles" as he was known in the Highlands, was at one and the same time a soldier, politician and statesman on the British and international stage and *MacCailein Mór*, chief of Clan Campbell and the dominant force on the Whig and Protestant side of the great Highland divide.

His brother Islay, the day to day ruler of the Highlands operates, in the novel, through his secretary and "doer" the treacherous Alexander Duncanson and the shrewd Ninian Macgregor Campbell, the *beachdair* or scout, a Messenger at Arms and confidential intelligence agent in the service of the House of Argyll. The Northern branch of this alliance is represented by Duncan Forbes of Culloden, His Majesty's Lord Advocate and the chief law officer in Scotland.

Arrayed against them are the Jacobite chiefs and those, like Col Macdonnell, determined to maintain the status quo, the rule of force, their power, influence and opportunity for ill-gotten gains. Pre-eminent among these is the graphically drawn villain of the novel, Simon Fraser, Lord Lovat. Lovat's career was indeed quite as chequered and bloody as Munro paints it. Outlawed for abducting and forcibly marrying his first wife he brought his clan out for the Government in the 1715 rising. Implicated in the notorious kidnapping and unlawful imprisonment of Lady Grange in 1731 he backed the Jacobite side in the '45 and paid the penalty with his head on Tower Hill in 1747. In one of the most memorable scenes in the novel Æneas has the last vestiges of romantic illusion about the old Highlands stripped away from him. He and Ninian are at Fraser's seat of Castle Dounie and hear Lovat denouncing trade, roads, education and all that such progress would bring: "My people always have what fits them best in their condi-tion—schooling of the winter and the blast, rough fare, the hills to strive wi', and the soil to break. They need no more, except their swords and skill to use them.... Æneas, looking at the face thrust close up to his own, saw in it everything for which he had contempt—unscrupulous craft, and cruelty, and greed."

The New Road, first published in 1914, was Neil Munro's last, and perhaps most accomplished, historical novel. With it, and earlier explorations of Highland life in transition, such as

John Splendid and *Doom Castle* he achieved a reputation as the heir to Scott and Stevenson in the field of historical romance.

The New Road displays an imaginative combination of historical fact and real characters with the fictional foreground characters such as Æneas, Ninian and Duncanson. Munro did not slavishly adhere to accurate chronology and historical accuracy. The action, we are told several times, is set fourteen years after the abortive Jacobite rising of 1719 and the Battle of Glenshiel, where Æneas's father was believed to have been killed. This would set it in 1733 but other references, for example to the kidnapping of Lady Grange "lifted near a twelvemonth since" would suggest 1732 while the reference to Lovat's second marriage to Primrose Campbell, which in fact took place in 1733, as being a year past when Æneas and Ninian visit Castle Dounie, suggests a date for the action of 1734. All the characters refer to George Wade, the Commander in Chief in Scotland, and architect of the network of military roads as 'Marshal Wade'—in fact he did not attain the rank of Field Marshal until 1743. Munro took what he needed from history and applied it to his creative needs. One would hesitate to cite *The New Road* as an accurate work of reference, but as an insight into the Highlands between the '15 and the '45 and the varied and conflicting cross-currents of Highland life it stands high in Scottish historical fiction.

There are many memorable passages in the book—the exposure and downfall of the double-dealing Duncanson who had cheated Æneas out of his inheritance; the warm portrait of Forbes of Culloden—"a man as deep's a well and clean as crystal"; the portrayal of the black Castle Dounie and its sinister master, *MacShimi*, Simon Fraser, sitting at the centre of a web of intrigue and corruption.

Neil Munro's own roots were in the Inveraray and Argyll of Æneas, Ninian and *MacCailein Mór*. Born in 1863, the illegitimate son of an Inveraray kitchen maid, rumour persistently identified his father as a member of the ducal house of Argyll. Educated in Inveraray, he worked for a time in a lawyer's office there before leaving the Highlands for a career in the Lowlands. In Munro's case this was to be in journalism, in and around Glasgow. This career was a distinguished one and ended with his editing the *Glasgow Evening News*. However Munro's commitment to journalism was never strong and his heart always lay in his work as a poet and novelist.

His emotional involvement with the Highlands remained strong throughout his exile in the Lowlands and influenced and informed all his writing. When The New Road was published a reviewer in the *Glasgow Herald* observed that it was "... the best novel Mr Munro has yet given us. More than that it is the sort of novel to which his admirers have long been looking forward to." When Munro died in 1930 one commentator described him as "the greatest Scottish novelist since Sir Walter Scott, and in the matter of Celtic story and character he excelled Sir Walter because of his more deeply intimate knowledge of that elusive mystery." His contribution to Scottish literature was recognised by the award of Honorary Doctorates from Glasgow University, in 1908, and Edinburgh, in 1930, and by the Freedom of Inveraray in 1909.

With such a reputation and such recognition it is ironic that to modern readers he is chiefly known as the author of *Para Handy*—a light-hearted series of sketches of the adventures of a West Coast puffer *The Vital Spark* and her crew. While these stories are, as their survival in print for 90 years and their adaptation for television and theatre amply testifies, classics of Scottish humour they were very much a product of Munro's journalistic career. Like the other sketches produced for his newspaper column, *Erchie, My Droll Friend* and *Jimmy Swan, The Joy Traveller*, Munro distanced himself from them and distinguished such journalism from his serious work by publishing them under the pseudonym of "Hugh Foulis".

This edition of *The New Road* not only brings back into print an important and thoroughly enjoyable Scottish novel but allows a fairer and more balanced assessment to be made of Munro's role in Scottish literature. The adventures of Æneas and Ninian do indeed arouse comparisons with *Kidnapped*. *The New Road* is in some respects the more complex and rewarding work because the clash of personalities and backgrounds which Stevenson engineers by bringing together the Lowland Whig, David Balfour, and the Highland Jacobite, Alan Breck Stewart, is managed by Munro with a purely Highland cast. The complexity and contradictions of the Highlands and Munro's own personality are echoed in those of his characters: Forbes, reluctant to see evil in his neighbour Fraser, committed to the rule of law but nostalgic for the old ways and the glitter of the sword; Æneas and his uncle, bitterly opposed to the Jacobite cause Æneas's father had given his life for; Ninian, a Macgregor, one of the proscribed "children of the mist", who has turned his back on the bloody past of his clan to take the Campbell name and serve the Campbell cause; and above all the road itself, the New Road "which means the end of many things, I doubt, not all to be despised,—the last stand of Scotland, and she destroyed. And yet—and yet, this New Road will some day be the Old Road, too, with ghosts on it and memories".

THE NEW ROAD

I

The Dovecote Tower

With the down for the first time shaved from his face, young
Æneas stood in the draughty passage, turning his cocked hat in
his hands till the nap had a cow's-lick on it. Chagrin it was that
kept the tutor fidgeting outside the door of the study, where at
this hour he ought by rights to have a couple of pupils on the
march with him and Cæsar's sturdy lads through Gaul. It is one
of the solemn days in life for a man when he starts to use a razor:
now that the curly down was gone, and Æneas had seen in his
glass a youth as boyish as he always shamefully felt himself to
be, he rued the rash act that seemed to rob him in a moment of
his manhood. He had come for the evening lesson with his
pupils, feeling somewhat like a man half-naked in a dream, but,
like the usual dreamer in these circumstances, hopeful no one
might observe his own confusion at the absence of a beard—a
small one at the best: he had come prepared at most for the
bantering of Margaret Duncanson, eager to have it past; and
now the skirmish was postponed! That was to make a double
call upon his courage, and the supply he had flogged up for this
rencounter was already vanished—gone from the field in a
shameful rout, and the enemy not yet in sight.

Feeling that new-recovered velvet chin of his with nervous
fingers, he stood in the dark of the lobby swithering what he
should do next. The house was full of the smell of celery;
Drimdorran had some curious Lowland whims, and dined at the
hour of four from the first day he became a laird; faint rumours
of the kitchen wafted up the stairs at times, to hang about all
evening like the mists upon Glen Aray. At the lobby-end—far-
off, for the house was long and the passage stretched from wing
to wing of it—a voice was booming from Drimdorran's closet
room; Drimdorran never boomed with greater satisfaction to

1

himself than after waking from the noisy doze which always followed on his dinner. Some one was in his room with him— not Margaret, his daughter, nor his ward, young Campbell, Æneas' other pupil; at times a grown man's voice broke in on a different key on the laird's delivery; he had an outside visitor.

Except for this familiar sound from old Drimdorran's business quarters, that night the passage might have been a gully of the wood abandoned to the dark, and vegetable odours; the quiet that held the dwelling was the quiet of suspense and expectation even though Drimdorran boomed.

"They have gone out; I wonder where they are?" thought Æneas, and walked along the passage. It had upon its flags a runner carpet—yet another of Drimdorran's Sassenach concessions,—and his footsteps made no sound. At the top of the service stair which led from the underworld of stanchioned windows where Drimdorran's celery soup was cooked, a man stepped out with a lighted candle and drew back, alarmed, when he ran against the tutor.

"King of the Elements, Master Æneas, but I got there the start!" he gasped. "You have chased the breath of me into my breast! This is a house that frightens me—so full of things in waiting. Shadows! Sounds! My loss that I ever left the Islands! In the name of the Good Being now, what did you on your face? I did not know one bit of you, and you before with such a noble whisker!"

"*Coma leat sin!*—Never mind that, just man!" said Æneas, also in the Gaelic. "What am I but looking for two rangers? Didst thou by chance see any sight of my scholars and they a-wandering?"

The Muileach, as they called him from the isle of Mull he came from, was Drimdorran's man, and had learned in that employ to be discreet in seeing anything. He shook his head, a hand about the candle for the draughts, and said: "I have put no eye on them since dinner, Master Æneas"—but there he stopped, being friendly with the tutor, threw a glance across his shoulder to be sure they were alone, gave a pull at his nose and whispered in the loof of his hand, "It might be them, when I think of it, I

2

saw at the mouth of evening down beside the river."

Some dash of the conspirator, a twinkle in his eye, annoyed the tutor. "So?" said he shortly; "I'll take a turn that road and maybe come on them," and he walked out at the porch into the darkness.

It was little more than a step to the clean, cool night from the celery-scented lobby of Drimdorran House, but every step in life has its own particular fate attending it, and Æneas Macmaster, though he could not guess it, gave a twist to his seeming destiny on the moment he had crossed the threshold.

He was fairly launched upon the great adventure of his life.

Drimdorran House, with two or three hundred years of weather in its bones, stood on the slope that rose to the north above the river. Immediately about it lay its garden, sheltered from the east by clumps of high-grown firs and a belt of holly round them. From the windows of the house its owner, at a glance, could see his whole estate—not great, but snug and compact, tucked in a warm fold of the valley, in the very bosom of MacCailein's land, with finest grazing of the parish stretched for half a mile along the river bank and on the other side two profitable farms. Upon that green expanse of arable and pasture land a single tree had never been encouraged, save a scrog of beech and alder Duncanson the laird had put as a kind of screen between his outlook and the dovecote tower, which stood, three stories high, more like a place of ancient strength than a pigeon-house, upon the river's brim. As yet the planting was too young to hide the tower in any sense, except, as it might seem, from its former tenants. Never a bird was harboured now in the dovecote, where, in the time of Paul Macmaster, Æneas' father, they had swarmed. No one rued their absence less than the laird himself, who had made great ado with them and helped to breed some droll fantastic kinds of them with ruffs and pouter bosoms when Paul was still the laird, and he was Paul's commissioner. Many an hour they spent there in the dovecote loft; the little lower-story window would be lit till midnight sometimes, when these two were waiting for a pigeon-post; on the leg of a homer-pigeon came to Duncanson the news of Sheriffmuir. The fancy for them must have been most strong in Paul Macmaster, for, when he was dead, and Duncanson became the laird, he counted what it cost in grain upon the stalk to feed them, and could never thole the cooing of a dove again. So he locked the dovecote up, and set the beech and alder round it, yet even in its abandonment its presence someway marked the glen more palpably than did the mansion-house.

So much for the place by daylight, but this was a September night when Æneas Macmaster stepped out on the lawn of what should have been the house of his inheritance, from the sound of the usurper's booming and the smell of his celery soup, and early though the night was yet, it was as black as a porridge-pot. There had been rain all day, so that the Aray roared at the cataracts below Carlunan Mill, but now the night was dry; a wind, most melancholy, burdened, to his bookish fancy, with the griefs of time and change, mourned in the fir plantation; to the east, beyond MacCailein's castle policies, he could hear the sea billow thundering.

No light was in the glen except from the house he quitted, where some windows, looked back on from a little distance when he reached the garden foot, appeared as yellow squares stuck high up on the arch of night. One of them he knew to be the window of Drimdorran's closet; none of them was Margaret's. He felt that the best thing he could do would be to walk into the town and wait for an explanation of the truancy until the morrow's morning, but at two-and-twenty years of age it is always something else than the best in policy that commands our acts, and Æneas, with one hand feeling at his chin and the other at times thrust out before him till he had come to his second eyes, passed through the fringe of shrubbery about the garden limits, and out across the fields to the riverside. By the time he reached it he had got a little of the howlet's vision, and the dovecote and its scraggy thicket were to be perceived as bodies massive, blacker than the night.

It was with something like dismay he saw, for the first time in his life, a light in the little window on the ground floor of the tower!

There was nothing, based on thinking, beyond the Muileach's crafty hint, to make Æneas ascribe the disappearance of his pupils and the lighted window to one common chain of circumstances, but that notion instantly took full command of all his movements. For the first time, since he quitted his uncle's house in the town an hour ago, he lost the uncomfortable sense of nakedness, and felt more like the man he was before he shaved. This recovery exhibited itself in a feeling of moral indignation that he should waste his time on a ninny like young Campbell and a girl with so little self-respect as to skip the march through Gaul with Cæsar for the sake of a clandestine hour in an abandoned pigeon-house.

At first his inclination was to leave the scraggy grove that drew the night wind through its rustling tops with the swishing sound of a tide on sand, and made a pattering among the alder leaves, but the chance of discounting Margaret's anticipated bantering on his changed appearance—once again remembered with a twinge—by breaking with tutorial dignity upon her hiding, was too precious to be resisted. On an impulse that a moment of reflection would have quelled, he strode across the river gravel laid a score of years ago so thick on the path that led to the dovecote that even yet the grass had not won through it, and he hammered loudly on the door.

There was no answer from within, nor the slightest sound of movement.

A wild-bird with a doleful whistle rose a little way off by the waterside, and swept across the valley towards Drimdorran House, whose windows seemed more unbelievably aloft in space than ever. All the other watery windy voices of the night were blent for the moment in a deep sonorous hum, as if Glen Aray had become a bagpipe drone to which this searcher in the darkness had his ear; a gust of rising wind was blowing from Dunchuach.

Æneas stood back a pace, and, lifting up his head, peered at the tower, whose rounded form stretched high above him like a lighthouse. A just conception of its size had never been conveyed to him before; it was the first time he had stood close up beside its white-harled walls, and in the gloom they looked immense, mysterious, invested with some immaterial essence as of ancient secrecy and dead men's frustrate plans. It had been immemorially old when his own folk owned Drimdorran, yet it showed no symptom of decay, or Duncanson, no doubt, had long since made an end of it with a blast of powder, for its useless presence roused his visitors to curiosity and speculation.

A second time he rapped in vain, then groped to find the sneck. His thumb fell on it as by custom, and he pushed the door, to find, with some astonishment, the place all dark within. All dark and tenantless! He could not doubt that he had seen a light a minute or two ago from the little window, and he assumed that whosoever used it had ascended to the upper flights, but the thought immediately gave way before the sure conviction that in the circle of the chamber he was now encroached on there was apprehension cowering, and a lantern or a candle in its hand.

Distinctly he could smell the greasy odour of a tallow wick!

It was ever Æneas Macmaster's singular conviction that he was a hopeless coward, since a property inherent in his blood gave startling meanings to events which, when approached with trepidation, were disclosed as trivialities that should not fright a child; and it seemed to him, as he stood on the flags of the dovecote floor, that it was time to be taking his feet with him (in the Gaelic phrase of it), and putting the door between him and this mystery.

Nevertheless he bided, fumbled through his short-tailed coat, and got a tinder-box wherefrom he struck a light that wanly glowed on the pallid face of Margaret Duncanson. She stood in agitation by a seed-bin, with an open lantern in one hand and the key of the dovecote in the other.

"I guessed it would be you," said Æneas quietly, taking the lantern from her hand and lighting it anew. "You have six-and-thirty ways of being foolish, and every one of them's more idiotic than the other: what puts you on an escapade like this, and I to be waiting for you yonder with the *Commentarii*?"

She was a littlish woman, black-avised, a year or two perhaps his junior, with eyes like sloes, not strictly speaking by the letter beautiful, but beautiful enough to be going on with, as Roderick said about his first shape at a fishing-skiff. Her head was bare, as if she had just run over from the house.

"Oh!" she gasped, with a hand on her heaving chest, "you have given me two horrible experiences! I thought at first you were my father, and then when you struck the light I thought you were a stranger! I went almost into a swound; if I live to a hundred years I'll never be nearer one. How did you think of coming here?"

Æneas pointed to the window sunk in a five-feet depth of wall, she saw at once how it had betrayed her, looked about her hurriedly, picked up some empty sacks and stuffed them in the opening.

"What a fool I was not to think of that!" said she with agitation. "Nothing would have quicker brought my father down upon me!"

"And what, if I may ask, are you doing here?" said Æneas.

"Looking about me, only," she replied, recovering a pertness that was obviously her nature. "I was determined to see the inside of the doocot. Here have I been staring at it every day since my infancy, and this is the first occasion I have put a foot inside the door."

"It's surely a fancy that could be gratified at a more convenient season," said the tutor gravely, "and with less of the clandestine element. Any day, I'm sure your father would have given you the key."

She made a grimace which brought an unbroken coal-black line across her face by the joining of her eyebrows. "I had to find it for myself," she answered. "He had mislaid it. In any case, he said he was not going to have me break my neck on these rotten steps. And now that I am here, I find it was hardly worth my trouble, there's nothing wonderful to see, and in the last half-hour I have ransacked the place from top to bottom."

Æneas cast an inquiring glance at the wooden steps which led to the hatch above them.

"They're not so bad," said she.

7

"You would get the wind about you, anyway," said Æneas. "It must be cold up there, blowing through a hundred pigeon-holes."

"Not it! As snug as a cellar; every pigeon-hole in the tower is boarded up inside."

With the lantern dangling from a finger, he surveyed the kind of cell to which Miss Margaret's escapade had led him. It must have been the storeroom of the dovecote in its active period; the great corn-bin filled up a part of it; there was a pile of sacks half-filled with mildewed grain, and others wholly empty; creels, spades, and other tools were flung about, the lantern, too, he found was to be included in the plenishing—Margaret had found it hanging on a staple. Upon the chamber and its properties the dust of years was thickly settled; to stir in the trash of the floor was to raise a cloud that floated like a smoke in the lantern's beams. He felt begrimed, uncomfortable; some repugnance of the place came over him, he wanted to be gone.

Most of all he thought of the place as an inappropriate setting for the personality of Margaret Duncanson, whose airy summer gown demanded something finer in the way of background; whose sprightliness ill accorded with the sombre air of this forsaken vault, that somehow made her less attractive than she was for usual. He had lost the consciousness of the change on his appearance, and was only brought back to an uneasy apprehension of her mockery by the interest with which she stared at him, now that her fears were past. There was a glint of mischief in her eyes, but she cunningly said not a word on the topic he had expected her to make much of; that was Margaret's most disconcerting power to mortify—she always chose some different way from what he had expected.

"That's a night lost!" he said at last. "You're accounted for, but where is William?"

She flushed, and laughed uneasily. "And is he truant too?" she asked. "Never mind! I have something here of interest to show you; I found it with the doocot key,—isn't that the ravishing creature?"

It was a little silver snuffbox, which she opened with the

pressure of a finger so that he could see inside the lid of it the miniature of a girl. Indeed the portrait justified Margaret's admiration; it pleased the casual glance immediately, and opened up some curious charms to the more intent examination. Holding it up to the lantern lozen, Æneas devoured its every feature—the little tilted chin, the lips a bit apart in what might either be a smile or an inward breath of something on the verge of tears, the forehead swept by waves of auburn hair that had in parts the copper hue of winter breckans, the throat that seemed even in the paint to have the animation of a voice that would be sweet, the gradual white shoulders just escaping from the shelter of a crimson cloak. What hit most strongly at the sentiment of Æneas was a kind of pause in the expression; in some moment of suspended eagerness the woman had been taken, and something of rebellion cried from her parted lips and in her lifted eyes.

"My goodness!" he cried out, "it is a jewel! The heart of me is half divided between the fellow who could paint it and the darling who could give him such a chance. It's Holbein, honest man! with something of the mountain breeze in him, and it puts me out of taste with all yon round fat faces that they have in Amsterdam! Where on earth did you get it?"

"Do you think she is beautiful?" Margaret said, paying no attention to his question.

"Beautiful," said he, "is but a word; I could not rightly tell you what she is unless I played the fiddle."

"What raptures! And I'll swear she's dead a hundred years!"

"No, nor fifty, by the execution," said the tutor. . . . "What is that?"

He straightened up with a jerk, as if he had been stabbed between the shoulders. He turned his head to the side a little. He listened with suspended breath. Not the most trivial sound was to be heard within the tower in which the stillness of the grave was reigning, nor anything outside beyond the dry clash of the beech-tops, whelmed in the hum that came at intervals from every twig and leaf together when a fresh gust struck the planting.

"I could swear I heard the scuffle of a step," he whispered.

9

"Did you?"

Margaret shook her head. She was as grey as sleet, and terror was in her eyes. The tip of her tongue played nervously between her lips.

"You should not have been here! You should never have come here!" she gasped in an under-breath. "I hate the very look of you! If my father finds us here he'll kill me! O Lord! haven't I been the silly woman!"

"Listen, Margaret; listen!" he enjoined her, slipping the snuffbox into his pocket and clutching her arm. "I'm certain I heard someone outside!"

She began to weep in a singular way that puckered up her face and sent the tear-drops down her cheeks and all without a sound, like a woman dumb.

"There! There it is again! There's someone walking round the doocot," said Æneas.

There was no mistake about it; plainly they could hear the footsteps on the gravel, appallingly deliberate and stealthy.

"It's you! It's you!" she charged him, gulping sobs. "You came here like a fool, and somebody's following you."

"Nonsense!" he whispered. "Nobody, I'm sure, saw me—the night's like pitch;" and he was shaken not a little at the pickle in which his being there involved her. "I'll tell you who it is," he hurried on with a comforting inspiration, "it's Will."

She moaned. "Whoever it is," she said, "it's certainly not Will; he couldn't possibly be here. I know in every vein of me it's father, and oh! how on earth could he discover?"

"The light in the window," whispered Æneas.

"Aren't we the fools!" she exclaimed. "He'll be in this moment! Blow out the candle!"

It went out at a puff from Æneas just as a hand began to fumble with the iron door-latch.

The door itself came slowly inward, they could hear the hinges creak, and the cold wind fanned them. The darkness of the chamber and the dark outside were one in hue, and whoever stood in the doorway was invisible, but they heard the breathing and it was a man's. He never said a word, but stood for half a

10

minute on the threshold, once only uttering a sigh. It was, of all the strange experience, the most dauntening of things, that sigh, which seemed to gush up from the depth of misery. Margaret's fingers sunk into the flesh of her companion's arm till he winced with the pain of it. He could hear the beating of her heart—or could it be his own, so stormy?

A moment later and she would have screamed, but the figure in the doorway turned; the hinges squealed again; the iron latch fell into its catch with a clatter, and the footsteps crunched across the gravel, this time less deliberate. Then the wind resumed its prevalence.

Still greatly dashed, the tutor took to flint and steel again and lit the lantern when it seemed the visitor had no intention of returning, and found a great relief imprinted upon Margaret's countenance.

"Thank God he didn't speak!" said she. "That would have finished me."

"Strange!" said Æneas musingly, like one apart; "I would have better liked to have a voice to him."

"No! no!" she said, "not I! I dreaded it! Do you think he suspected any one was here?"

"He knew it perfectly!" said Æneas ruefully,—"if he had a nose upon the face of him. What way did I not think of pinching out the candle! This one fairly stinks."

They stood for twenty minutes more imprisoned in their cell, deliberating on a score of possibilities about tha baffling visitation. No vagrant reputation of the neighbourhood was overlooked—the chance of gangrels, thieves or spies—but always they came back upon that disconcerting sigh which gave some tone to the experience not in key with any theory they could advance. One thing Margaret was blissfully convinced of—that it had not been her father. "Had it been he," said she, "and knew that any one was here, nothing under heaven would have turned him back!"

Æneas at last went out, leaving her the lantern, muffled till the door was closed behind him. He circled round the tower; traversed the path a little, questioned the night with every sense,

11

and then returned to tell her that the way was clear. They could not flee the place too quickly!—When the door was locked behind them, over her head she drew her cloak and ran across the grass like one demented. Before he could decide what next to do the dark had swallowed her.

"Fair wind to her!" said he; and turned about, and started for his lodging. He had not gone a hundred yards when a reflection stopped him—he had still the snuffbox! Five minutes later he was in her father's house again, to find her speaking with the Muileach in the lobby at whose end Drimdorran still was booming.

Without a word for him she snatched the snuffbox from his hand and dashed upstairs.

II

At The Outpost

A mile of distance from Drimdorran House and from the glen, from whose tail-end it was shut off by old high woods, there was, at the time, what might be properly regarded as the strongest outpost of invasive influences which by sap and contravallation were, in God's good providence, to destroy the ancient Highland world. Already it was shaken to its mountain roots, save in the farther North. Whole tribes, that not so long ago were ill to meddle with as any bike of wasps, were now as little to be feared as butterflies; packmen from the Lowlands sometimes travelled through the worst-reputed valleys selling specs and ribbons. Here and there in the Garbh-chrioch—the Rugged Bounds,—and even as near at hand as on the fringes of Breadalbane, there was still an orra chief with a ferocious gang about him, struggling—unsubdued, defiant, doomed—against some force that was more hateful and alarming since so often it assumed the insubstantial shape of alien ideas, not of arms: they roved, these fellows, still, in an always lessening area, demanding for themselves a savage liberty, holding the sword as the only tool and charter fit for the *duineuasail*, the Gaelic gentleman, and they ever grew more desperate as they felt the squeeze of this encroaching civilisation. Beyond the confines of their native glens they knew themselves for outlaws. Their people followed them from custom, born with the conviction that the clan must stick together and go out upon the old road when Himself required: Himself, with a handful of savage virtues, made the clan the instrument of his every selfish inspiration, spoon-fed them with the flattery of blood equality, and in return extorted blind submission to his whims.

Perhaps at the spring of things no loftier motives influenced the invasion, but the assault at least was carried on with a

13

superficial elegance, and nowhere with a more unflagging zeal than from the outpost of Argyll, settled, itself, for more than a hundred years, its capital become a Lowland town in all except the language, with a philabeg or weapon scarcely to be seen upon its causeway, save on a fair or market day. Here was the destiny of the clans decided; crafty policies inimical to lawless folk and broken men were hatched; the Duke, *MacCailein Mór*,—Red John of Battles, as they called him,—held the fate of Gaeldom in the hollow of his hands. He had never seen the Uist machar-lands, so fine, so sorrowful, nor even but afar the great brave peaks of Skye, but he had widely seen the world, and no one living better knew the Gaelic people. Nor more was he familiar in the flesh to the scattered folks who spoke of him in fashions roundabout—as of a man inscrutable, invisible, and to be feared, directly named as cautiously as possible, much better indicated as the "Red One," with a fidget of the shoulder.

Even Inveraray saw but little of him; from the age of seventeen, when he was colonel, he had fought in all the wars and sieges; more than once he was the Regent in his sovereign's absence; half his days were spent in London. And yet it was upon his flying visits to Loch Fyne that, with his brother Islay, he concerted every plan to tame the clans above the Grampians. The strings of Hanoverian policy for Gaeldom ended there, in him, and yet in manner he was simple as a child. For him and Islay (who was most at home, though also something of a wanderer), messengers and spies continually were plying through the troubled shires, in which, likewise, he filled a thousand offices with his nominees.

In island crofts and mainland clachans that knew him not but as a fabulous being, the castle of MacCailein Mór, in which they somehow learned their destinies were handled and arranged, was pictured in the people's fireside winter *ceilidhs* as enormous, filled with regiments of Campbells; no other way, they thought, could he maintain the power which even their chiefs confessed. They figured him as misty and Fingalian, night and day in an iron coat, and brooding, without sleep, upon their harrying.

14

And the droll thing was, if they had only known it, that though he loved and mastered Gaeldom, it engaged his mind but casually when he was in its bounds; he spent himself more lavishly on greater things. Though the strings might come together in his castle, some one else was usually at their pulling—his brother Islay, Keeper of the Privy Seal, who, in his absence, left them to a man whose name was never heard outside the confines of his parish—Alexander Duncanson, Black Sandy.

Great men may plot and rule, but always there is some one inconspicuous who executes; for nine months of the year—in unvexed periods at all events—Black Sandy was as good as Duke, and ruled the Highlands, in so far as they were capable of rule, from the closet in Drimdorran House. He was, officially, MacCailein's Baron-Bailie, also Islay's business man or "doer," ward of his lordship's natural son, and private secretary; but all his neighbours knew this did not limit his authority. Had but the clansmen only guessed what common being ruled their destinies, instead of that fantastic monster they imagined; had they any proper notion of MacCailein's castle, dark through half the winter, undefended, they would certainly have swarmed across the passes!

The castle was a keep of insignificant extent, and jostled on the shore-side by the town, the smoke of which in certain winds blew in upon MacCailein's very dinner-table. It was a burgh of no great proportions, vilely overcrowded, far too often with the tar-pot burning for its fevers, only half the houses slated, these the winter domiciles of landed gentry having dwellings elsewhere, or of thriving merchants. No rational plan was in the town's arrangement; it lay all heads and thraws in a nook at an angle of the river and the loch, with crooked, narrow, broken lanes with all the gable-ends of the abutting buildings frontaging the thoroughfare, cold-shouldering the passers-by. In the hour of the meridian dram it did a thriving business in a score of inns or taverns; it was the briskest period of the day for this metropolis which did the best part of its work in furtive ways in writers' chambers, since, now that steel was going out of fashion, people did their quarrelling before the Sheriff or the

Lords. Near the quay, however, there were profitable booths and market-stances; the shipping trade was always growing.

Æneas' uncle—Alan-Iain-Alain Og, as he was styled before they made him Bailie—had a store beside the quay, below his dwelling-house; although he never lowered himself to put his belly to a counter or put on a brattie he maintained a prosperous merchant business, due in no small measure to the influence of MacCailein. Three ships he had that traded with the islands and the North, and even to the coast of France and up the Baltic; in busy seasons he kept half a dozen coopers going. From Ayrshire he bought oatmeal cargoes that were sent about the Mull to the shire of Inverness and to the Hebrides, along with herring, salt, and timber, but the bulk of the merchandise he brought from London, Dantzic, Rotterdam, Stockholm, Cadiz, or the Mediterranean was stored and packeted at Inveraray in the sheds which smelt of lemons, spices, smoked salmon, or Archangel tar, according to the season.

"That's right!" the Duke would say to him, with a jaunty step into the store among the coopers packing powdered sugar, tea, and hops, silk cloths, tobacco-rolls and looking-glasses,—"that's right, Bailie! keep tickling them with luxuries, and I'll guarantee you'll help to subjugate my savage Hielandmen far quicker than we'll do it with their Watches and dragoons."

Such was MacCailein's humour—that the spirit of the mountains could be pacified if once the people got a taste for something more than brose and tartan; he looked upon the Bailie as a pioneer, and gave him every help to send his merchandise in safety, even to Clan Campbell's bitterest enemies. The Duke secured for him a share of the commissariat of the garrisons at Fort William, Bernera in Glenelg, and Duart, Mull; on two or three occasions he had got for him a convoy of the troops to run a thousand bolls of meal by horse through troubled country to Kilchuimin Fort, fed usually from Inverness.

And the Bailie, too, had a kind of vanity in his part in Highland politics; he would give a chuckle when he got the bills of chiefs like Keppoch or Glengarry, all payable at Crieff, and, waving them like trophies, would say to his spouse, who was a lowland woman, "Annabel, *a' ghalaid*, here's another hem on Donald's shroud! I'm getting all the papists in the North for customers!"

"Perhaps they'll not can pay ye when it comes to Michaelmas!" would she say anxiously, for Annabel was never sure of any Hielandman except her own.

And there would her husband laugh at her: on Gaelic probity—for all the cattle-lifting—no small part of his business had been founded, and he knew his money would be sure at Crieff, even if the man who owed it had to seek the tryst with a hundred claymores round him.

He was a sturdy-built, broad-shouldered chunk of a man who had at one time been the champion hammer-thrower of the shire and a great hand with the gun, but that was five-and-twenty years ago. Mercantile prosperity would seem to have an ill effect upon the trunk, in which the energy and elegance of men and women mainly centre, as they say, and he was grown a little heavy and deliberate in his movements. Never again the white hare on the hill for Alan-Iain-Alain Og! Never again the mountain-tops! Himself, he was a notable example of the Highlandman as altered by the progress of the times—no spark of the adventurer nor any natural wildness left in him, as one might think to see him in the kirk; devoted to his wife and bairnless fireside, going no farther off from them than once a year to Crieff or Glasgow, all his business in the North and in the Islands being done for him by agents or his skippers. Indeed it took him all his time to handle things at Inveraray, where he was for ever on the quay at which a boat of his was certain to be warped, or in the store where he broke his bulk and made up packages.

He had been busy all that day at the unloading of a freight of cod and kipper salmon sent through his agent, Zachary Macaulay, in the Lews, by his *Good Intent*, a vessel of 50 tons; the work of the day was over, and he was wearily going up the outside stair to his house above the store when Æneas, with a lighter step, came up behind him.

17

"You're surely early home!" said the uncle as they were passing into the house together.

"There was no evening lesson," answered Æneas. "The young fellow was amissing and Miss Margaret—" He was on the point of saying something that he realised might lead to questioning and involve exposure of the lady's escapade, and that, he felt, would not be fair to her, so he checked himself in the middle of his sentence.

Bailie Macmaster noticed the check in his nephew's speech, and slyly glanced at him as he shut the outer door. Annabel had put a cruisie in the porch. No little part of Alan-Iain-Alain Og's prosperity was due to the fact that he could put two and two together and not make five of them; he caught his nephew by the shoulder before they left the porch to go in where sat the mistress, and he said in Gaelic, which is capable of searching personal examination framed in words of no offence, "Angus, lad, art in any way concerned with yon young woman?"

"What should make you think it?" Æneas asked him.

"The thing, my shorn young lad, that made the roebuck sniff and not a hunter to be seen—a bit of a smell to windward! I never knew a man of two-over-twenty start at shaving if there was not something in the thicket. Let thou make a fool of thyself with old Drimdorran's lass and the tune is through the fiddle! He will crush ye like a biscuit."

"I'm as good a man as he!" said Æneas, not greatly put about.

"Indeed and ye are, and better! Sandy has not got the blood, our kin were in Drimdorran when his ancestors were feeding pigs in Coll. But that is not the bit of it! Let him get it into yon brindled head of his that ye're like to mar his plan for getting Islay's son for his daughter Margaret and ye'll find it not a healthy climate here in Inveraray."

"To the dev—"

"At thy leisure, lad!" said the Bailie, back to his English, warningly, for his nephew's tone was getting high. "Not a word of this to herself in-by; I kent before ye mentioned it that the schooling had been off this evening; Will Campbell was on the quay and told me; that's the reason for the roebuck sniffing." He

18

chuckled slyly, pinching his nephew's arm. "Keep a dog's bark distance from Drimdorran's kennel, when business does not bring ye there!" and they went in together to the room where Annabel was spinning, with a supper ready on the board.

The room, lit by a girandole, had an iron grate, a glass above the chimney-brace, a wainscot table, rosewood chairs with water-tabby bottoms, and a floorcloth made of tapestry, all plenishing that marked it as the room of a thriving gentleman, for the Bailie liked to see things tosh and cosy round about him, and brought many a bit of plenishing from London in his barques: still Annabel would aye be at the spinning in the midst of all that grandeur, with the *rollagan*—the carded wool—in a creel beside her feet. On the top of a large 'scritoire were the books of Æneas that he had brought from Utrecht with him; they were his aunt's delight to look at, though she could not read a word of them, as they were mainly in the Latin.

Annabel was a clever body,—*geur*, as her husband called her, which is sharp, and sly, and gently mocking in an Ayrshire country fashion, and implies the tartish quality which judges like in sappy Ayrshire apples. A good deal younger than her man, it was her humour to maintain a sort of playful coquetry with Æneas, as she said herself, to keep her hand in at the gallivanting. The same good madame had not altogether lost the art of it; she still could fleech and tease the laddie like a young one! Perhaps the game was not judicious, for it had one consequence she never bargained for—it made her nephew clever far too cheaply and too soon at a sport that properly should have a stiff apprenticeship, and not with aunties.

Her husband, he would laugh at her betraying all the tricks that won himself in a fortnight's courtship down at Girvan, but sometimes he would ask her if the thing was altogether wise; there was a risk that Æneas might find this sham philandering grow stale, and all the sooner try his hand on game with uncut feathers.

"No fear o' that!" said Annabel on these occasions; "the mair he kens o' his auntie's wiles the better he's set up to come unscathed through others; it's what I would do wi' a son o' my ain if I wasna a'thegither doited. Laitin doesna learn ye how to meet designin' women."

"*Ubh! Ubh!* that's an awful character ye're giving to your sex, mem."

"Man! Alan, do ye think the Lord intended men to hae the whole o' the manoeuverin'?" would Annabel say, with pity smiling on him. "But ye canna say I ran after *you!*" she added quickly, to preserve a married woman's last illusion.

"Oh no!" says he, "I'll no' say that of ye; ye just went on ahead and dragged a hook. But I'm no' complaining, whatever."

"And a bonny fish I caught!—a ragin' Hielandman!" quo' Annabel.

"All the same, *a' ghalaid!* it is time ye had your draglines in. It's my belief ye're keepin' up the practice wi' some end in view, and lookin' at your carry-on wi' Æneas I feel I would be hooked again mysel' if ye happened to be my widow."

And there she would laugh at that, fair like to end herself, and tell him to put it in the Gaelic for himself and see what sense it made.

That night when Æneas and her man came in where her wheel was purring she was in a merry key. By, on the instant, went the wheel and *rollagan*. Never before, since Æneas had been a lodger, had he managed to get back from his evening task in time to join them at their supper; she was so pleased with this unusual experience that she never asked its reason.

Down on a stool plumped Æneas and took off his spatterdashes. "Never mind the leggin's i' the now," said she impatiently. "Sit in, my dear, and take your supper; I'm sure ye're needin' it. . . . Unless your appetite is gone," she added, twinkling, "wi' broodin' on your trouble."

"The only trouble I have," said Æneas, "is a right sore head,"—the fusty dovecote air had made him really ache a little.

"Oh, that!" said Annabel. "Distemper! I ettled there was something wrong when I saw ye shaved this mornin'. For puppy ailments there's naething beats the auld cure—butter and brunstane. I thought it might be something mair alarmin'. Alan, sit ye in, and pass the bannocks."

20

The Bailie did as he was told, then loosened several buttons. Something in her manner told him that she was at her old pranks in a quickened spirit; and still he was bound to laugh within himself at her play-acting with the youth—the way she bobbed her ringlets, and languished on him with her eyes and hung on his most trivial utterance. Annabel Loudoun, in her Girvan days, for a lass bred in a manse, was wonderfully acquainted with the worldly arts; in twenty years of married life she had forgotten none of them, and she was helped in them by having still a jimp and girlish figure and a dauntless grip of youth.

"*Thoire an aire!*—Watch thyself! she's up to mischief!" Alan warned his nephew in the Gaelic, which they seldom spoke before her for good manners' sake.

"There ye are!" she cried with an affected anger. "Tak' to your savage language when ye're plottin', baith o' ye, for my deceivin'."

"Ye should have learned it then, and been upsides with us," rallied her man.

"I had mair to do," was her retort, "and I didna do sae badly wi' ye wi' my lalland Scots. A bonny pair ye are—the jeely man, for Æneas!—keepin' me in the dark about the cairry-ons wi' silly glaikit lassies!"

This hit so close on Æneas' last experience that he started, whereupon she laughed with mock bitterness, and made a great pretence at wounded vanity. "Oh!" she cried, throwing up her hands in comical resignation, "I ken fine I'm gettin' auld: it wasna to be expected I could keep my joe. Ye needna glower, Alan, sittin' there like a craw in the mist! I'll have it out wi' the young rapscallion."

"Tuts! there's no' the lady in the parish I would even wi' ye, auntie," said the nephew. "I doubt there's no' another, neither, who could bake as good a scone," and he helped himself to one of those proofs of her housewifery.

"I didna say she was a lady, did I? Just a hoyden lass 'that's bidin' wi' her daddie O!' as the sang says. She daesna ken the schemin' rascal that she's ta'en the fancy for. My scones, quo' he! I might have kent it was the press and what was in it kept ye in the house at night, it wasna Annabel Loudoun's charms, fair fa' them! I clean forgot ye were just a laddie till I saw ye shaved."

That touched Æneas on the tender side of his assurance; the youth, which for her was something not to be relinquished without a gallant struggle, was for him a mortifying burden, and he reddened at her confirmation of a feeling that had lately grown upon himself. She was quick to see where she had pricked him, and at once her manner changed; there is a point where friskiness in mellow ladies becomes grotesque and pitiful, but Annabel was far too shrewd to push her humour such a length. She changed her key immediately.

"There now!" said she, "amn't I the haiverin' body! Just put it down to a done auld auntie's jealousy! But I'll say this for the lass—she might be waur; indeed she's just the kind I would pick for mysel' if I had breeks."

"What's this lass ye're bletherin' about?" her husband asked, surprised that so soon she should, like himself, have got upon the scent of Margaret.

"A figment of the mind," said Æneas, smiling, though uneasy; the dovecote business was assuming more significance than ever.

"That's what a young man's view of any woman is if he's fond enough," said Annabel. "But I'm no' gaun to say another word about your infidelity; that would be cruel to yoursel' and hardly fair to the lass whose secret I discovered this afternoon. Your name, I can assure ye was never mentioned, at least *she* never mentioned it, but every time I did, I saw her give a hotch upon her chair."

"I wish I knew who it was!" said Æneas with resignation.

"Mercy on us, Lothario! Bluebeard!" cried Annabel. "There are so many o' them about him that when I charge him wi' his perfidy he canna guess the particular one I mean! Was ever such a monster! Let me tell ye this Æneas, this one's secret is safe wi' your auntie Annabel, I'll put her at no disadvantage next time that ye meet her."

"I told ye, Æneas," said his uncle gravely, "that the roebuck had his head up, though I didna think the hind had got the scent o' anything."

There was never less excuse for sniffing, then," said Æneas dryly. "I never changed ten words outside her father's door with that one since I started teaching in Drimdorran—well, until tonight. And that's the last I hope to hear of her in this connection, flattering though you may consider it to mix her name with mine, Aunt Annabel. If you want to know—the lady's much too interested in Willie Campbell to bother her head about me."

Annabel stared at him, astonished. "Nonsense!" she exclaimed. "I think I have my wits about me, and she sat this very afternoon on that chair you're on, fidgetin' at every step in the lane—"

"What, Margaret!" says he, and at that his aunt gave a gasp and began to laugh. "Ye perfect villain!" she cried, "is Maggie Duncanson a victim too? 'Faith it wouldna be a bad way for ye to get back your father's property—to marry Maggie; but na, na, I couldna thole Drimdorran in the family;" and not a word more, good or bad, would she say about the topic, though her husband, now curious himself, made sly attempts at drawing her.

"Who were ye talkin' of?" he asked, when Æneas had gone out a little later, leaving them to their evening game of dambrod.

She bustled at the clearing of the table. "I'm no' gaun to tell ye that!" said she. "If women are to have a chance at a', they must be loyal to each other."

"I thought at first like Æneas," said he, "that ye were on the track o' Margaret."

Annabel slyly smiled. "I think," said she, "I have spoiled *her* chance wi' him, if ever she had any; there's no a quirk in Margaret's wee black heid I havena put him up to wi' my actin' o' the lovesick lass. To tell the truth to ye that was the object o' my philanderin' wi' him. When he came back from Holland he was just a greenhorn; he couldna look at a short-gown dryin' on a line but aff his hat went to it, and his face went red. Any rubbish a woman liked to utter to him he would listen to wi'

23

reverence. I mind o' him wi' Bella Vicar—she had been talkin' some poetic nonsense to him, wi' yon dark, eerie, Hielan eyes o' hers in the proper shape to hint at a soul as deep as a loch behind them, and when she was gone says he to me, 'There's something fascinatin' in that girl; I feel I could never quite understand her; wonderfu' depth o' character!' 'Heaven help me, is it Bella!' says I. 'Ye muckle calf! she's just as shallow as that ashet! Yon meltin' voice and swimmin' e'e were a' put on for your beguilement, and she didna understand the half o' what ye said about your Mr Milton, though she let on she did.' 'A certain kind o' mystery,'—says he, and at that I fairly lost my patience wi' him. 'The mystery's all in your imagination,' I tell't him. 'There's no' as much mystery in Bella as would keep ye gaun for a week wi' her.' "

"She's a fine, big, bouncin' girl, whatever of it," said the Bailie, putting out the dambrod men.

"Just that! That's all you saw in her, you wicked monster; poor Æneas, on the ither hand, wi' a heid fu' o' Laitin poetry and nae experience, saw naething but the mystery. There's a mystery about a pig in a poke, and it's aye the innocents that's maist ta'en up wi't. I saw my nephew had a lot to learn afore he could be trusted anywhere awa' frae men and aunties and the books o' that 'scritoire; I was just in mortal terror Maggie Duncanson would glamour him between her tasks; he was like a ripe plum ready to drop into her pinny. That's the way I started makin' a parade o' tender interest in him. Losh! Alan, do you mind the fright he got at first when he thocht I maybe was in earnest!"

"I was put about to think it might be Margaret," said the Bailie. "Everybody kens that her father has an eye on Islay's son for her; that's the way he clapped her in wi' William for the lessons, though Æneas was only hired by Islay for the lad."

"Margaret's a very clever lass wi' no' much sense, and she'll be better suited wi' Will Campbell," said Annabel. "But I doubt my practice wi' him hasna made him proof against attack in other quarters; a lass was sittin' in that very chair ye're on, twa hours ago, and she's the very kind to lead him on a halter made o' snow."

III

Ninian Macgregor Campbell

Æneas had left his uncle's house with an intention to go up the glen again and make a search about the dovecote neighbourhood; it hovered in his mind that possibly some wastrel band of cairds was harbouring near Carlunan, and might have among them the intruder on the tower. Yet he had hardly reached the causeway when there flashed on him the popular repute of Ninian Campbell, who had, earlier in the day, been asking for him. That curious man, for whom the darkness of a strath, the sleep of towns, could hide no secret, might, in a sentence, dissipate the mystery!

Ninian was a Campbell only for expedience—his father was Macgregor of Dalvoulin in Balwhidder, who, when the Gregorach were shaken out of all their ancient holds like weevils from a seaman's biscuit, and their very name proscribed, had found protection with MacCailein and a home in Shira Glen. This clemency was not without design; Macgregor of Dalvoulin paid for his security in wits. He wore the myrtle badge at Sheriffmuir, but also plied a craftier war, and long-sustained, by night and day, and disconcerting, with Clan Campbell's enemies, most of whom were now his own. In the place of his adoption he was known as "Iain Beachdair"—John the Scout. He throve amazingly, and had a tack of some extent between Glen Shira and the braes of Cladich. Ninian, when his father died, took up the *beachdair* business, but dignified and cloaked a little by the sounding name of Messenger-at-Arms, though such a thing as a citation never soiled his hands. He was Macgregor to the bone—a gentleman with curious toleration for the broken lawless folk whose fortunes as a laddie he had shared—the scurry in the mist, the night-long watches, skulkings in the heather; even in his burgess days he could not see a drove of

25

cattle passing but his eye would lift. Many a time Lord Islay got him on the hill with the gun below his oxter, only to shake a finger at him with "Ah, Ninian! ye'll never lose your taste for venison!" "Indeed," would Ninian say, no more abashed than if he had been stalking weasels, "here's a man that never yet turned his back to a haunch of that same nourishment. Good sport, Islay, for the day with both of us!"

Such a man as Ninian was worth his weight in gold as an instrument of governmental strategy. He knew the Highlands as he knew his pocket; below Loch Ness, at least, there was no pass or cave or clachan where he had not as a boy been wet and cold and weary, or sat about a fir-wood fire, or cried out the triple hoot of the *cailleach-oidhche*—the night-hag owl—to warn his folk of something dangerous stirring. As Messenger-at-Arms, with a badge he never showed, he was for ever on the road upon MacCailein's business, gathering hints and tracking rumours; the jealousies and pacts of clans, the private character of chiefs and chieftains, were better known to him than anybody; his was the skill that foiled them often in their plans.

It was his habit to be always out at night. "That is the time," he would say, "for people of my name and occupation. It is in the night that things worthwhile will aye be happening in the Highlands. There's nothing to be learned in daylight except that the girl is beautiful or otherwise, and people all mean well." The dark for him was full of meanings, intimations; things dim in daytime, tangled and confused, assumed a rational order then.

This curious faculty in Ninian it was that, coming to Æneas' recollection, sent him in a hurry to the house the *beachdair* occupied in town from harvest-end till spring. So keen he was to have his curiosity assuaged that he forgot, to start with, that no matter how he put the case, there was a danger that Miss Margaret's escapade would be revealed: when this occurred to him, the purpose of his call on Ninian seemed scarcely wise. Nevertheless, he followed out his inclination, which, to tell the truth of it, was influenced in a measure, though he did not let his mind dwell on it, by the fact that Ninian had a daughter!

She was in the house alone when he was shown into it by a

servant-lass—a piece of luck, as he first esteemed it, which he had not looked for, though it soon took on a different complexion. Her father, earlier in the evening, had been summoned out on business, and she expected his return at any moment.

Æneas waited willingly; there could not be a better chance to improve an acquaintance with the lady who, since he had left her at her door three weeks ago at two o'clock on a moonlight morning, had occupied his mind much more than he himself was well aware of, and all the more remarkably since in the interval she had been unusually invisible. There was a reason why the parting in the moonlight morning should engage his mind and make him now uneasy as he took the seat she proffered; harmless practice with a merry aunt had had exactly that result his uncle looked for,—Æneas some time ago had learned that women were not quite so terribly austere as he had thought at first and that even a frolic interchange of gallantries had a good deal more of spice in it when exercised with others than with Annabel. It was not a quite unpractised hand who, as the convoy from a ball, for Janet Campbell, boldly sought a Highland convoy's fee in the shape of a parting salutation in the moonlight, and got her palm across his cheek!

The tingle of that buffet stayed with him for days; he felt it now as he sat in her parlour-room, and all his puzzling about the dovecote incident was swamped in a flood of new sensations.

It was the first time he had seen her in her own surroundings, which conferred upon her all the charm of novelty. She seemed a different being from the wide-hooped, tightly-bodiced partner he had sailed with down Macglashan's room, so simply dressed now, so demure and purpose-like, as if the house were meant to be her natural setting, that he took a new disgust at his own effrontery.

Not a word, of course, was said about that lamentable error, but her face, for usual pale, had a flush that spoke of some commotion, though she quickly took to her tambouring-girr, and stitching wildly, dashed into a conversation miles remote from the topic of the unlucky ball. He felt he was not forgiven, and he cursed anew his folly, seeing, as he fancied, half alarm and half reproof in her grey eyes, however level and unflinching, placed upon him.

He did not see her in detail so much as, in a fashion, take her presence in by other senses—the sound of her voice with its tang of Gaelic lending softness to her careful English sentences, all trimly finished even to the "g's" his lowland aunt could not be bothered with; the little scratchings that her needle made upon her thimble; her breathing, which, in awkward pauses in their conference, seemed to indicate an agitation that he felt himself; a perfume, fugitive and pleasant, as of cool spring wells, that hung about her garments.

This hint of wells, and mornings cool and fragrant, all at once began to give to her a character which he had never thought before was shared by human beings with the landscape he delighted in—surprise, variety and stimulation; she was like a day upon the wild high moors in spring, and when she spoke it was the creamy gurgle of the April burns.

He took a look at her again, enchanted, when her eyes were on her occupation, hardly knowing what he talked of.

"I haven't seen you for so long!" he said with recklessness. "You have been busy? Do you never come out?"

"Oh yes!" she answered, "every day. I was at your uncle's house this afternoon."

His face went crimson! The visitor his aunt had spoken of was not imaginary; Janet was the girl!

He felt abashed, remembering Annabel's interpretation of her caller's fidgeting, though fidgeting was none of Janet's traits tonight, however much they were his own. The calm was all with her, with him the gale of agitation, and now it swelled into a whirlwind blast in which his wits seemed blown away like perished leaves and swirling in the air. It is, indeed, a staggering hour when youth with no experience of these tempests of the breast is lifted from its feet by powers invisible with which it has been playing, thinking them no stronger than a woman's breath. That squall upon the instant levelled every dyke of self-possession, took him from himself, and gave him to the force that rules the world!

Like a man that grabs a hat blown down the road before him, he groped, one moment, wildly, for that splendid confidence he had but recently,—no use! the storm had swallowed it! And not without some warnings, premonitions—he had shut his eyes to them deliberately, but now he knew the very razor was compelled by a dangerous interest in Janet Campbell, though he had been too timorous to admit it to himself!

Commingled with a great elation, such as always comes to healthy youth when thrown in battle with the elements, was mixed a sense of shame that he should have the girl at an advantage through that revelation of his aunt. And still he was terrified to think that Annabel might be mistaken!

All this commotion filled some moments only, if one counted passion-hurricanes by time, which would be folly: he was much older when he spoke again without a quiver in his voice, to show the girl that she was separated only by about the thickness of a waistcoat from the stress of weather.

"I did not know you had been calling," was all he said, and to himself it sounded very thin. "And oh!" he thought, "I had the daring to put arms about her!"

"Yes," she said, "I called," and suddenly grew very red again as she bent above her work.

His education had not quite cleared out the rustic lout in him; a silly boldness took the hold of him again, and "I'm vexed I was not in," said he.

"And I was almost glad you weren't," she rejoined, and showed confusion in her manner.

"Why not?" he asked. "And I had almost kissed her!" he reflected with amazement to himself.

"For a private reason," she replied soberly. "It is of no consequence! I think I hear my father."

To Æneas, even, this relief was opportune; so many doubts and guesses seized him at the evidence of her perturbation that her father's entrance was welcome, though immediately it roused the awkward thought that even the discreetest reference to the dovecote and its problem was become impossible. In Janet's presence it would feel indecent to pursue the subject, which had someway lost importance in the last few minutes.

Ninian came in upon them bustling, like a man full-charged with news, and only pulled himself together when he found he had a visitor.

He was, in a way, a young man still, to have a grown-up daughter; hardly over forty, with a step like a dancing-master, and a swing about his every movement betokening that he had some fancy of his limbs, whereof so many people at that time of life appear to lose the relish. The movement of his members seemed a pleasure to himself, as to a mountain cat or stag; it looked as if he never would be weary. A little under middle height, and lean about the flanks to which his square-cut coat was closely shaped, he had, withal, a frame that looked exceedingly robust, and even powerful—a square deep chest, and a leg with a tumble-home (as the sailor says) above the rounded brawn. A charge of horse, it might appear, would scarcely stagger him; he was a cliff.

In his face that was weathered to the hue of nuts, clean shorn, and slightly pitted, there was manifest a bold and confident sagacity; his hair, dark red, was drawn back from his temples, and knotted with a ribbon at the nape; his eyes appeared to have a living of their own apart from all the rest of him—deep-set, and keen, and black, they were his most conspicuous feature; nothing could escape, as it might seem, their penetration.

"What! is it thyself that is in it, Æneas?" he cried in the phrase of Gaelic though he spoke in English, an oddity of speech that always gave his utterance a foreign sound. "Did I not say to myself in the street, out-by, 'There is some one waiting on me!' I knew it by my feet! Stop you, till I throw off my gentleman!" and plucking at the belt about his middle, he loosed a slim dress sword that on his coming in had poked its nose between his skirts.

"Now lie ye there, my lad!" said he, and flung it in below the table. "As sure as death, my dear, I canna stand their slender ones, their point-and-parry ones, their Sunday swords; give me a good broad leaf and a basket to it, or a snedded stick of oak!"

"But still you would have it on this evening—you that never

30

wears a sword except for a bravado," said his daughter quietly, and still at stitching.

"That was for Drimdorran's eye," said he, with a laugh. "He hates the very look of weapons; it seems to put him aye at disadvantage, perhaps because it shows him that he's dealing with a gentleman. That's the gentleman of me for Duncanson!" and he kicked the tool below the table, till it snarled back, clattering.

"Did ye bring yon, Æneas?" he asked, with a sudden turn upon his guest.

"Did I bring what?" asked Æneas.

Ninian wheeled round upon his daughter: "Did you not go for it, *m'eudail*, as you promised?" he implored.

"I went," she answered, "but Æneas was not in, and I felt so foolish upon such a message that I came away without a word to his aunt about it."

"What was it?" Æneas asked, much damped at the suggestion in the daughter's speech that the cause of her agitation in his uncle's house was something that her father understood. He would have liked it otherwise.

"I'll not be long in telling you that," said Ninian, standing to his feet and throwing out a chest of resolution as if to give him courage for a task he felt ridiculous. "It's yon Molucca bean."

"Molucca bean?" repeated Æneas, perplexed.

"Ye know, yourself,—your father's—peace be wi' him! Yon Molucca bean—the Virgin nut that came from Barra to your family. With the silver clasps, ye mind?—the plump, round, brown fellow that would lie, like, in the loof of a hand. For God's sake, Æneas, do not tell me ye have gone and lost it! I'm sorely needin' it."

"I have you now!" said Æneas. "Of course! the bean my father had."

"The same!" said Ninian. "My grief! that your father had not got it with him in Glenshiel! It would have been a different story yonder!"

"I think," said Æneas, "that I have it somewhere," and Ninian, clapping on a chair in front of him, leaned in, and fixing

31

him with a glance that defied amusement, said, coaxing, "Ye will give me the loan of it, *loachain?* What am I but going on a journey to the North? I said to herself that's sewing there, 'If it's the bens and the mountain moors for me again among yon devilish clans, I must have a backing with me, and the very best I ken is Paul Macmaster's Virgin nut.' Did I not this very evening send this lady over to your house to ask you for it? But her courage faltered, and the half of her Macgregor too! *Mo nàire!*—my shame upon you, daughter!"

"You can have it with all goodwill," said Æneas; "but what is the good of it?"

At that was Ninian embarrassed; he puckered up his lips, as if to whistle, drew down his lids a bit to hide for once unsteady eyes. The man was plainly feeling shame to tell his purpose with the bean; he started once or twice a stammering word, and stopped, and hummed and hawed and finally with a "pshaw!" turned round upon his girl with a blameful aspect, charging her with having botched his errand.

"No wonder you are black affronted, like myself," said Janet soberly. "Æneas must think you daft to put your trust in *giseagachd*—in freits and talismans. In front of his Lowland aunt I could not say a word about your Virgin nut, it seemed so foolish."

She turned to Æneas. "What my father wants it for," she said, "is for an amulet. He thinks there will no harm come to him on his business in the North if he has that thing about him."

"Neither there will! Neither there will!" her father burst out confidently. "I don't believe, myself, there's anything at all in it, except some old wife's story, but there's aye a chance. And I would be the better for it in my pocket in among the rogues of Badenoch."

At this display of superstition Æneas could have burst out laughing, any other place than here in Janet's presence and in her father's room, but not a blink of his amusement did he show. He had forgotten all about this wizard property in the bean from Barra.

Ninian was delighted to be promised that the charm would

be handed to him on the morrow, and to cover his confusion at having been discovered with such a weakness broke into a voluble account of a commission he was just about to start upon. 'Twas he who had been in Drimdorran's closet whence Æneas had heard the booming; he had been getting his instructions for a journey to the North. There had been trouble with some lawless clans. Arms were being smuggled in from Spain and Holland. The Highland Watches were considered in some quarters dubious servants of the king. Blackmail was rife as ever. Worst of all, there was the opposition to the Road.

"George Wade's red sodgers, as ye ken," said Ninian, "have been for years at the makin' o' the Big Road that is goin' to put the branks upon the Hielanman—a bonny job for sodgers! It's killin', as ye might say, the goose that lays the golden eggs, for, wi' this road across Druim-Albyn, fighting will be by wi't in the Hielands and the trade o' war will stop. But that's the way of it— the Road is cut already through from Crieff to nearly Lovat's country; I trudged a bit o' the lower part o' it myself last summer; most deplorable!—the look o' things completely spoiled and walkin' levelled to a thing that even cripples could enjoy. A body might as well be on the streets! I'm tellin' you that Road is goin' to be a rut that, once it's hammered deep enough, will be the poor Gael's grave! There's plenty o' them wide-awake to see it; from the start they hindered Geordie's shovellin' brigade. But now the Road's goin' through Clan Chattan country, the devil himsel's to pay! Every now and then there is a skirmish wi' the sodgers. A bit of a bridge or a culvert that is finished clean and ready on the Saturday is all to smash between the kirks on Sunday. Boulders like a house for size come stottin' down the hillside, landin' on the road. The very rivers take a fancy, through the night, to start stravaigin', and where do ye think should they stravaig but over the brawest parts o' Geordie's track? Oh yes, they're clever fellows yonder! clever fellows!"

He smacked his lips upon his admiration for their cleverness, and then became the Messenger-at-Arms.

"The Government is fair distracted, and of course it has to fall back on Himsel'—MacCailein. It's his idea that the trouble on

33

the Road is not the wanton capers o' a lot o' unconnected gangs, but managed by a bond, wi' someone cunning at the head, and indeed I wouldna say mysel' but something's in that notion. All for your private ear, this! Not a word to nobody! Whatever o't, Drimdorran sends for me this mornin', and claps me down a letter from Lord Islay. He was himsel' so much against the tenour o't that he wouldna even read it to me. I'm to go North and take a look about me. . . . Nothing more or less than *beachdair* business—you understand yourself!" and he gave a sly grin to Æneas. "I can see it's no wi' old Drimdorran's will I'm goin'; it's too much of the Royal recognition for his lordship, but he daren't go against his master. But here am I, whatever of it, takin' to the hills for it on Monday; I wish I had a smart young fellow wi' me, like yoursel', to keep an eye behind me, but anyway you'll not forget yon nut!"

"You'll have it, sure!" said Æneas. "I'm thinking that I have so much of luck just now I can afford to give a lend of it," and thereupon the other gave a disconcerting start and took to pacing on the floor with his hands plunged deep in his great wide waistcoat pockets.

"I'm not so sure of that," said he. "Ye're in the black books of Drimdorran, someway; that's a thing I found this very evening. A ruddy fury's on him; he could twist your neck!"

"In heaven's name, for what!" cried Æneas, astonished.

A disconcerting pause in her father's manner instantly sent Janet from the room, and Æneas, too, got on his feet, alarmed at something in the other's manner. "At any rate, ye've put his birse up!" Ninian said. "What made ye miss your evening lesson?"

"I was there at the usual time," said Æneas; "it was my pupils who failed me."

Ninian looked sharply at him out of half-shut eyes and changed the conversation. It was with thankfulness his visitor went with the object of his call untouched on.

IV

Drimdorran

From sound sleeping Æneas was wakened at a dark hour of the morning by the rattling of sand on glass. He jumped from bed; threw up the window; stuck his head out; saw a figure standing in the gutter of the lane.

"He's wanting you this instant, Master Æneas," said the Muileach hoarsely. "Take my excuse for wakening you with a fistful of the gravel."

"Who wants me?" said Æneas, and still with some of his sleep upon him.

"Who but Himself—Drimdorran? My loss! but we have had the night of it! He's yonder like a man that would be in the horrors, tramping the boards, Master Æneas, tramping the boards! And not a drop of drink in him, no more than's in myself, though cold's the morning and I all trembling."

"What hour is it?" asked Æneas, shivering; indeed the morn was bitter cold.

"Five hours of the clock," said the messenger. "Sorry am I to turn ye out like this before the bird has drunk the waters, but the man is raging for ye, and when it comes to the bit with him, there is no one in the leeward or in the windward, or in the four brown boundaries of the deep, can hold a candle to him!"

Æneas drew in; threw on his clothes, and having given to the man a glass of morning bitters, left a sleeping house and took to the road with him, benumbed with wonder. Not one word of satisfaction could he get from the excited messenger, only that Drimdorran House was not yet bedded and the master clamant for his presence. They went up by the brawling river through the woods that roared with wind. In the sky was not one twinkle of a star, but when they reached the open glen, upon the dark as high as ever was the light of half a dozen windows.

At the sight of them, high-hanging, something struck Drimdorran's man; he stopped upon the road and slapped himself upon the haunch with an exclamation. "Men and love!" says he, "if I have not clean forgot the lady's letter till I saw her window yonder."

"What is't?" said Æneas, and had a billet thrust into his hand.

"Margaret gave it to me," said the Muileach. "She followed me like the wind through half the grounds, and put it on to me as spells and charms and crosses that I was to give it to yourself, and oh! the *burraidh* that I am, did I not clean forget it in my thirst down yonder!"

"She's not up at this hour?" said Æneas, unbelieving.

"She has not put her wee round head to pillow!" said the Muileach.

Æneas had just one moment in the lobby of the house to turn the billet outside in and read one frantic line: "For God's sake not a word to him about the dovecote!" when Duncanson, with a flannel wrapped about him, sodden-eyed for the want of sleep, and a cheek on him like rusted bone, came out upon him from the closet.

"You're there," said he harshly, with a girn upon his face; "come this way!" and Æneas, shaking in his shoes, went in behind him, looking at the back of the old one's neck, for every hair was bristling on it.

The room was like an oven, from a fire piled high above the hobs with sizzling timber; it was lit as for a wake with a dozen candles, three upon the mantle, three upon the desk, the rest on brackets. For ordinar that business-room, as Æneas saw it once a month when he came in to get his wages, was as cold as charity, and as prim's a vestry; now was it all disorder, and bestrewn with papers that had sluiced across the open desk-flap to the floor. Duncanson, slipshod, ungartered, shut the door with calculated thoroughness, swished through the mess himself apparently had made by tearing out the desk's contents in some impatient frantic search, and on the hearthstone turned upon Æneas a granite visage.

"I want an explanation, sir," said he in a voice that choked with passion. "What is this my daughter tells me of your taking William to the town upon a gowk's errand?"

Æneas would have hardly known the man in any other situation! It was not only that the sloven dress, the bald high head without its periwig, with turgid veins upon the temples, the brindled tufts above the ears, were new to him, but that the manner and the voice were so transformed. Drimdorran hitherto in all their meetings, that were rare indeed and formal, ever was the sleek well-mannered gentleman (a bit aloof) who boomed in magisterial tones with an averted absent eye, as if his eloquence was strengthened by an inward contemplation of the sort of man he thought he was: his very post with Islay was maintained in measure by his reputation for a gentlemanly presence and a suave though confident address.

And now he was a bubblyjock—a frenzied turkey, gobbling his words; a chin like to an adze, and the high points of his parchment face like rust!

"Well, sir! Well, sir!" he cried out, clenching his fists and stamping, "I'm waiting for your story!" for not a word at first could the tutor say to him.

A moment since, and Æneas was in a panic, but this bullying approach called up his pride and self-possession. At once he understood, in part at least, the situation—Margaret had sacrificed him, and it was for him to take the blame for her misdoing. But as yet he was not clear about the nature of her story to her father; caution must be exercised. He blandly took a chair.

"The thing can be explained," said he, and wondered where on earth the explanation was to come from.

"I warrant it will take explaining!" screamed Drimdorran. "You make my daughter, sir, the instrument of some scheme of yours, and got her to send off my ward on a pretence that you desire his presence somewhere else at eight o'clock than here, where you are paid to come and learn him. He went to the town in search of you by her instructions: you were not there—"

"I missed him by ten minutes," broke in Æneas, now seeing the way more clear before him.

"You did sir, did ye! Where was ye?" shot Drimdorran

at him.

"At Ninian Campbell's house," said Æneas, too quick for caution.

"At Ninian's—was Ninian there?"

"Most of the time, sir," answered Æneas; and the old man thrust a finger at him. "Ye are a liar, sir!" he shouted. "Ninian was here, in this room, at the very hour for which you trysted William in the town."

"I know," said Æneas. "All the same, I met him in his house later."

Drimdorran twitched the flannel wrap with nervous fingers, fumbled in some inner pocket, and produced a horn from which he ladled snuff into his nostrils like a man who hardly knew what he was doing. It seemed to calm him somewhat; in a tone more settled yet with something crafty in his eye, he put the very question that the tutor had been dreading.

"Was you, by any chance, with Margaret?"

"With Margaret! Not I!" said Æneas boldly, surprised to find so critical a stage in his examination could so easily be passed by simply lying. He looked for some sign of relief at this on the father's countenance, but on the contrary he found dismay. It looked as if the man was on the point of whimpering!

"You will not bamboozle me, sir!" he protested furiously. "I am not so blind! You were in this house, I learn, at the usual hour you meet your pupils; you went out when you found they were not here—as no doubt you had been aware,—and you were back again. What were you doing, sir, in the interregnum?"

"I was on some strictly private matters of my own," said Æneas, no longer even anxious to be civil, and at that Drimdorran made three scuffling steps from the hearthstone to him with the squeal of a rabbit trapped, as if to catch him by the throat.

Up started Æneas with a front of resolution, and the nostrils of him flaring, which perceiving, Duncanson stopped short and stood a moment swaying on his feet like one that had a stroke. The notion came to Æneas as he stood looking at him, he had never rightly seen the man before, but always in a mask or a veneer, made up of clothes and studied manners; this creature,

38

stripped of all that gave to him the semblance of a person schooled and prudent, stood stark-nakedly revealed a savage, club or dagger only wanting to give murder to his passion. Under eaves as coarse as heather were his eyes recessed and glinting like an adder's.

With a dry gulp of the throat he pulled himself together, turned sudden on his heel, and sought his desk to scrabble with a hand among the papers. He brought one out of a pigeon-hole and ran a finger down its lines.

"The term of your engagement as young Campbell's tutor ends next week," said he—"to be precise, on Thursday the twenty-fifth. I have had no instructions from his lordship to extend—so far as I am concerned, it is an end to your incumbency,—it is neither for his son's advantage nor for mine that you should any longer come about my house. I will report to his lordship, and you need not put yourself to the trouble of coming back to implement the week that is to run of your engagement. Your money will be sent."

"My terms," said Æneas, as cool as ice, "were made with Islay."

"They were," said Duncanson, sneering, "and much against my will. But I was here to keep an eye on your deportment, and it does not please me."

"I'll write to him in the first instance," said Æneas. "This sudden stoppage of my office calls for more explanation."

Drimdorran turned on him with a voice that was hoarse with fury. "If it comes to that," said he, "there will be several other points demanding explanation. I have made no charge against ye on another matter that I would be loth to lay before his lordship,—I found last night that some one had been tampering with my keys and with this desk," and he slapped an open hand upon it. "No, no! I make no charges, mind!" he cried as Æneas started blurting out denials. "I'm only telling you; you'll see at once it looks gey bad against you! My keys were lifted from a room upstairs; my private desk was rummaged, to what purpose detrimental to his lordship's private interests I canna say. They were replaced, I found, about the very time that you came back."

"It seems a small affair to make so much ado about," said Æneas, with more composure than he felt, and realising now how justified was Margaret's terror lest her escapade should be revealed.

"Ado! Ado!" Drimdorran shouted, jumping to his feet. "By God, sir, I could have ye jyled for less. It's not a small affair to pry in lockfast places, I'll assure you!"

"Small enough, being only a supposition, to haul a man from bed at this hour of morning," Æneas retorted, and now he fairly sweated in the suffocating heat to which the old man's fury seemed contributory. He turned to leave the room. "The matter can be settled in a better air and at a wiser hour," he said, upon the threshold. "I'll see you when I talk it over with my uncle."

He got outside the door with Duncanson behind him pressing so close he felt his breathing.

"If I were you," said Duncanson, "I would consider about consulting any one regarding such a thing. I make no public charge against you, mind, except that you have been neglectful of your duties in this instance, and have tricked your pupils."

"That's a point, sir, that I'll ask you to remit to my own judgment," said Æneas quietly

"Please yourself," said the old man, "only I'll advise you not to say too much about it to the mealmonger," and with a bang he shut the closet door.

The tutor groped his way along the passage, more furious within himself at this last insult to his uncle than with all that had preceded. He had just got to the exit from the house when he heard light running steps behind him; stopped, and found his elbow grasped by Margaret.

"Oh, Æneas!" she whispered in a voice of the greatest tribulation, "what happened?"

It was the first time she had ever called him by his Christian name, and that, in some way, instantly dispelled the angry feeling that he had to be her victim. He was sorry for her—that she should be child to such a man.

"Do not vex yourself," he said to her softly. "You are quite

40

secure. He does not know."

"But he is furious; I heard him shouting to you! And what a night we have passed! He has been like one deranged. Oh, Æneas! I meant to tell him everything, but when I saw his state I daren't."

"Indeed," said Æneas ruefully, "it is a pickle we are into. You have put back the keys?"

"The keys, but not the box," she answered. "I had the keys restored before you came that last time, and since then I have not had a chance to put the box back."

"I think he has not missed it yet," said Æneas. "At all events, he has not charged me with it; that's about the only insult that he spared me. Upon my word the man is crazy! And now I'm on my warning; my tutoring is at an end."

On hearing this she fell to silent weeping, hanging to his arm. The fanlight of the door let in the break of morning, and they were revealed to one another something like to phantoms grey and bloodless.

"Oh!" she said with passion, "you must think me an abandoned wretch! It was because I could not rid myself of William any other way, and I was keen to see the doocot, that I told him you were waiting for him in the town. And now my father thinks the thing was planned between us to get rid of Will. It is not fair to you—I'll tell him everything."

"Margaret!" her father's voice came bawling from the lobby, "are ye there?"

"Tell him nothing," Æneas whispered; he could see that shout already shake her resolution. "I can thole his anger: what's the odds to me?"

V

A Call to The North

The morning bell was ringing when he reached the town. Salt
airs from sea were blowing through the lanes. Men at the
harbour, dragging ropes, cried cheerfully. Oh, the bold, cold,
hard, beautiful world! He felt like one that had come out from
fever-rooms among the hearty bustle of the quay to which he
went immediately to seek his uncle, who was there already at the
loading of the *Good Intent* with timber baulks for Skye.

In half a dozen sentences he told his story, only keeping back
Miss Margaret's prank with the forbidden keys, the meeting in
the dovecote, and the shameful charge against himself to which
her subterfuge had made him liable. Now that it was daylight,
which brings caution and cools down the ardours of the night,
he saw quite clearly that the girl was much to blame, deserving
of no shelter, but he would be the very last to punish her. Rather
would he stay silent, suffering Duncanson's suspicions if they
went no further. The situation as presented to his uncle, too, was
just in keeping with that gentleman's predictions.

"I told ye!" he declared when Æneas reported that the
tutoring was ended, and that Drimdorran had some fancy that
the pupil and her tutor had, between them, planned the missing
of the evening lesson, "I saw it coming! That girl a while ago was
daft about ye; any one could see it in the kirk on Sundays! I
would be much surprised if old Drimdorran didna notice. And
that doesna fall in wi' his plans at all; he's set on having her for
Campbell."

"He's welcome so far as I am concerned," said Æneas.

"Are ye sure, man?" said his uncle. "Till last night I thought
different. I didna tell your aunt nor say to you that Will's being
on the quay at the hour he should be at his tasks looked gey and
curious. For he was asking about you. He said he had been sent

by Margaret to meet ye here, and that I couldna fathom, seeing you were gone as usual to Drimdorran House."

"That was some caprice of Margaret's," said Æneas. "She herself had shirked the lesson."

"Ye werena with her somewhere?" said the uncle drily, and Æneas looked blank to have the very keystone of his secret tapped so soon. He did not answer.

"Man!" cried his uncle, comprehending, as he fancied, "ye have put your foot in it wi' Sandy! I knew if ye gave him the slightest reason to think ye were trifling wi' his girl and spoiling sport with Campbell, he would squeal. The man is fairly cankered wi' ambeetion; all his body's hoved wi' vanity since he became a laird and stepped into the property that should be yours. It's six-and-twenty years since he came here, no better than a packman, to be clerk to old Macgibbon. He played cuckoo wi' poor Macgibbon, and secured the factorship wi' Islay. Then he trafficked with your father, managing for him when he was off upon his silly escapades among the Jacobites, much against my will, and God be wi' him! No one better knew than old Drimdorran what your father was conniving at in France, and in the North wi' Glendaruel, and the damned old rogue, I'll swear, encouraged him, well knowing what the end would be. He leased Drimdorran from your father who could never stay at home after your mother died and got him in his debt for loans, the size of which gave me the horrors when I saw the bills. What your father did with all that money God Almighty knows! unless, like Glendaruel, he scattered it among the disaffected clans. I couldna pay them off, whatever o't, when your father died; I wasna then in the position. When your father's name was plastered at the cross a rebel at the horn and outlawed—him a corp up yonder in Kintail,—I went and saw the man that he had supped and drank wi', played the cartes and fished and worked at pigeons wi', and he was rowtin' like a bull about his loss. Not the loss o' his friend, ye'll mind! but of the money he had lent him. He staggered me by bringing out a deed in which your father pledged Drimdorran as the bond for Duncanson's accommodations, but he doubted, by his way o't, if the deed would hold against a property in danger of escheat for treason. Sly devil! Well he kent MacCailein could put that all right! And there he sits, this fourteen years,—a son of Para-na-muic of Gunna—the Gentleman from Coll, and bonny on the gentleman! What will please him now but that Lord Islay's boy should get him grandsons! If it werena for Lord Islay—honest man!—ye wouldna dare have put a foot within Drimdorran's door! And on my soul, I'm glad ye're bye wi' him and his; I've something better for ye!"

For some time past the tutoring engagement had appeared scarcely worthy of his nephew to the Bailie. Æneas, to tell the truth, was something of a disappointment to his uncle who had reared him, sent him to the college with Lord knew what object, though the Law was mentioned, and some study of the same had sent him later on to Holland, where he met with Islay. But Æneas no more regarded Law than cutting breckans; his heart was all in pictures and poetry,—very pretty things, no doubt, but scarcely with a living in them.

Many a time, since he came back, the Bailie spoke to Annabel about the possibility of giving him an interest in the business. She liked the notion well enough in some ways, but she had a hankering to keep the lad a gentleman,—a gentleman to her idea being one who lived in some ambiguous way without a shop or vulgar occupation.

"Do ye think, *a' ghalaid!* I'm no gentleman?" her man would ask.

"Ah! but you're different," she would tell him. "Æneas, by rights, should be Drimdorran, and nae Drimdorran ever fyled his hands wi' merchandise."

"A sight better if they did, my dear," said Alan-Iain-Alain Og, far sundered from his family traditions. "It was better for Paul if he had dealt in stots and queys that's very good for folk, and profitable, rather than be scampering about the country herdin' French recruits and breeding trouble. What did he make of it, poor man? He's yonder in Kintail, and Duncanson, the man o' business, sleeping in his blankets. And as for me, myself, I'm proud to be a merchant! I owe no man a penny, and your gentlemen are in my books. There's some of the finest family gentlemen, as ye think them, canna sleep at night for thinking what I'm thinking o' their bills, and all the time I'm sleeping sound and never bothering. It's quite enough for me that they're harassed."

The sudden termination, then, of Æneas' office gave the very opportunity the Bailie wished for. It was so opportune that the occasion of it never caused him any feeling of annoyance; at the hour of breakfast he was full of schemes for launching Æneas on a career as merchant.

The Bailie's schemes had their dependence on the great New Road that Marshal Wade was cutting through the mountains. Hitherto the peaceful Lowland world—the machar of the Gall, the plains town-crowded, bartering with England, making money—was, in a fashion, sundered wholly from the world above the Forth. The Grampians, like ramparts, stood between two ages, one of paper, one of steel; on either side were peoples foreign to each other. Since roads had been in Scotland they had reached to Stirling, but at Stirling they had stopped, and on the castle rock the sentinel at nightfall saw the mists go down upon a distant land of bens and glens on which a cannon or a carriage wheel had never yet intruded. Only the bridle-paths to kirk and market, the drove-track on the shoulders of the hills!

Now was the furrow being made, as Ninian said, on which to drive the Gael like bridled oxen—smooth, street-wide, a soldier's road, cut straight across the country through the thickest-populated valleys, till it reached the shores of Moray and the forts that stretched from sea to sea.

In this New Road the merchant saw his opportunity. Always to the inner parts of Inverness it had been ill to get his goods in winter time with vessels weather-bound among the isles or staggering round Cape Wrath. Now he saw a chance of opening communication by a route as safe as the King's highway to London, and already was MacCailein talking of a branch into Argyll.

Annabel, in the nerves about her nephew's sudden stop as

tutor, that day at least got little satisfaction for her curiosity; the big grey map of Blaeu that hung in the lobby was spread out upon the table; and her husband, stretched across it like a sailor, marked the track the New Road took through country in the chart set down without a line to break its rough ferocity.

"It may be a sodger's road," he cried to Æneas, "but it's just the very thing for merchant waggons. It's true we're off the line a bit, but I have the Red One's word that there's a lot of roads in view across the country, and in the meantime I could send my wintering straight from Leith to Stirling. And then what have I on the either hand of me for a hundred miles or more but the very pick o' people—Menzies, Robertsons, Stewarts, the Athole men, Clan Chattan, and the Frasers!"

"A bonny lot!" said Annabel. "No' a pair o' breeks among them!"

"We'll soon put breeks on them, the Duke and me, *a' ghalaid!*" said her husband cheerily, plucking up the waistband of his trousers. "Stop you!"

"It's not so much at first what I'll put into them," he said to Æneas, "it's only meal, eight merk the eight stone boll, and salt perhaps to start with; herring maybe, and an anker now and then of brandy for the gentry, but it's what I'll lift from them in beef. It's just a great big breeding-ground for stots! And look at all them Great Glen lochs and rivers—full o' salmon! There's a man in Inverness called Stuart has the pick just now of all their kippered fish, but I'll be learning him!"

"The only thing," said Æneas, "I know about it is that there's a lot of trouble on the Road at present." And he told of Ninian's mission.

"Ye tell me Ninian's going!" cried his uncle. "That is better still! My notion was to send ye round by Crieff, but what's to hinder ye to go with him?—ye may be sure he'll take the nearest way for it: for all that he is tainted in his name, the man's an education."

He dashed more heatedly than ever into Æneas' immediate occupation. If Ninian would take Æneas in his company they might be in the North by Michaelmas, or at the very latest by St

Martin's Day, when lairds and tenantry alike were desperate for money. Æneas, in Inverness, would have the money, in *buinn oir* and bank notes—three hundred pounds of it, enough to make the Hielandmen run wild; the Bailie, for a wonder, had the cash that moment at his hand. Mackay, his correspondent in the town of Inverness, would give the lad an insight to the market situation, go about with him, and show him where to look for freights and either come to terms for barter or buy stuff for money down.

"Ye'll find a lot of them will want the money," said his uncle in the Gaelic. "Money is the boy in Gaeldom! It's seldom that they hear the cheery chink of it."

Chinking his coin, then, Æneas was to spend a while in bargaining for salmon crops from Beauly, timber from Glen-Moriston; if occasion offered, herring, cod, or mackerel for Spain. But what his uncle most insisted on was careful study of the Road, and what there might be in it for his trade.

It was but ruefully at first that Æneas spent that morning with the map and Alan-Iain-Alain Og's commercial dreams. It seemed to him a sad comedown in life from Cæsar and the bards, but what was he to do? He looked across his uncle's back, and through the window, at the seagulls swooping in the wind above the ferry, and felt that what was here proposed was shackles for the spirit, mean engagements.

But one word of the Bailie's cleared away his vapours, and it was the word Adventure.

"It's just a bit of an adventure," said the Bailie. "That's the thing wi' me in business, otherwise it wasna worth a docken leaf!"

At that word Æneas took another look at Blaeu, and there at last he saw the marvel of the North as Blaeu had figured it—the mountains heaped like billows of the sea, the ranging bens, the glens with rivers coiling in them; great inland lochs and forests. He saw high-sounding names like Athole, Badenoch, and Brae Lochaber, Lorn and Spey; they moved him like a story. All his days had they been known to him, but mistily and more as things of fable than of actual nature—lands of the fancy only, like the lands of Ossian, figuring in winter songs and tales of old revenge.

Now, to his uncle's great astonishment, he leapt on Blaeu, and with his chest upon the parts he knew, he peered, transported, on that legendary region of the boisterous clans, still in the state of ancient Gaul, and with Gaul's customs. The very names of castles, passes, straths, misspelled, entranced him: everything was strange and beckoning. Moreover, it had been the country of his father's wanderings, somewhere there his father had been slain, somewhere there was buried. The reflection shook him.

"Where does it lie," he asked in his mother tongue, "the place of my father's changing? I do not see its name." And someway all at once he felt the climate of his mind had altered, and the North was plucking at his bosom.

The other answered solemnly. "Of what blood art thou, young Angus, that cannot hear the name cry grievously upon the paper! There it is—Kintail! Black be the end of that Kintail that finished him!" Not the merchant spoke but kinship; on the forehead of Macmaster swept the dark cloud of undying hate. His visage was convulsed; he smote upon the map; he seemed that moment like a man a million miles remote from the world of ledgers.

"Dear me!" cried Annabel, "ye shouldna swear like that before a lady, even in the Gaelic."

"I wasna swearing, *m'eudail*," he assured her, scarcely cooling. "I was only speaking of my brother Paul." He turned again to Æneas. "I'm not forgetting, mind," says he, with bitterness. "For me the claymore's by wi't but I'm fighting wi' MacCailein. These blackguards in the North brought out your father—the very men I'm selling meal and wine to; many a time I wish to heaven it would choke them! Do you think it's what I make of it in siller that's the pleasure of my trading wi' the North? If it was only siller I would never seek to sell an ounce beyond Loch Fyne. Na! na! there's more than that in it—*I'm smashing them*, the very men that led my brother Paul astray. MacCailein and me! MacCailein and me! And now there's Marshal Wade and his bonny Road that's going to make the North a land for decent folk to live in! I have the bills o' men like Keppoch and Glengarry flourishing about the Lowlands in the place o' paper money; they're aye gettin' a' the dreicher at the payin', but whatever comes o't I have got them in my grasp. It's no' the common people, mind!—the poor and faithful clansmen—but their lairds and chiefs I'm after, them your father marched wi' in his folly, blind to their self-interest, thinking they were only out for James."

"I'll go!" cried Æneas, almost lifted from his feet; the soul of him seemed filled with some dread pleasure.

"Of course ye'll go! That's what the Road's for—you and me and vengeance. Look at it!"—with a piece of keel he drew a line from Stirling far north on the map to Lovat's country. "That's the Road the harrow is to go to level down the Hielands, and I have put a lot of seed in there already that is bound to come to crop. Once the New Road is finished, and the troopers and the guns and my carts on it, it's an end to the dominion o' the chiefs! The North, just now, might be in Africa, for all we ken about it; nobody dare venture there except wi' arms."

"Does the law not run there?" Æneas asked.

"Law run!" the Bailie cried with mockery. "It runs like fury—and the clansmen at its heels. Ask you Ninian! I'll no' say that he ever ran himsel', but many a time he had a smart bit step for it! Of course ye'll take a weapon, if it is nothing better than a wee Doune pistol, and at any rate it canna be so bad upon the Road,—there's always sodgers back and forward from the barracks."

"It's no' wi' my consent ye're goin', but I hope ye'll walk wi' caution," said his aunt.

"Six years ago I darena send ye," said his uncle. "Ye might lie and rot for years in Castle Dounie dungeons and nobody would ken your fate except old Simon Lovat and his warders. That's the head and front of them—the fox! I ken him, and I've bought his fish—a double-dealing rogue that's married on a decent woman, Primrose Campbell, daughter of Mamore."

"Poor Prim!" said Annabel, "I'm vexed for her; I don't know

49

what on earth possessed her to take up wi' such a man!"

"Nor I," said the Bailie. "Nor what on earth it was that made MacCailein and Lord Islay let her marry him. That's the sort o' man the Road's to put an end to; some day yet, if he is spared, ye'll see his head upon a stob and it no' very bonny! Mind I'm telling ye! There's no' a roguery in the North for forty years he hasna had a hand in—one day wi' the Jacobites, the next day wi' the others. Many an honest man he hanged before his windows or sent to the plantations. God knows who he has in yon bastille o' his in irons! It's the only quarrel that I have with Himself here that he maintains a correspondence wi' the fellow. 'Policy,' says MacCailein wi' a cough, but any one that plays at politics wi' Lovat has a tarry stick to hold. And still, were it not for Simon's runners coming here wi' letters for Himself so often, we would ken no more about what's happening in the shire of Inverness than if it was Jerusalem, though every messenger he sends, as Ninian tells me, is as sly's himself. Far is the cry to Castle Dounie, and it's steep on Corryarrick! Not a whisper will come over Corryarrick that he doesna want. But the Road's going over Corryarrick, and the end of Sim's at hand, and of his kind! Perhaps when it is finished we will hear what happened to Lady Grange; since she was lifted near a twelvemonth since in Edinburgh nobody has found her whereabouts, and Lovat gets the blame for her trepanning. I wouldna put it past him! He's a dirty brock!"

The tutor's stipend came that afternoon to him from Duncanson, and with it came a little scrape of letter that confirmed his liberation from an office that had all at once become repugnant. It looked as if Drimdorran meant to have a plausible excuse for his suspension; the story, later in the day, went round that Islay's son was going to the college of St Andrews.

Æneas at once went to the Messenger-at-Arms to ask him when he meant to set out for the North.

"I'll soon can tell ye that!" said Ninian, and showed to him a knapsack. He turned it out upon a form. It held a shirt or two, some hose, a pair of brogues, a shagreen case of razors, a pot of salve, a Bible, and a dirk. "The Bible," he explained with gravity, "is for the thing that is within us all, but the dirk is for my own particular skin; what else would any man be needing but his wits about him and a coin or two? Have ye the nut, my hero?"

Æneas had the nut.

"And now I'm all complete!" said Ninian, quite contented.

"It would be better, would it not, with a companion?" Æneas said to him.

"Ha, ha! You may be sure I thought of that," said Ninian, "and I've got him—there he is, the brave grey lad, and he not slender!" and with a movement of the haunch he brought to view the basket of a claymore, tucked away so sly below the skirts of him, its presence hitherto had been invisible.

"That's him," he said,—"Grey Colin, sober as a wife and sharper in the tongue."

"I was thinking of a man with you," said Æneas.

"Another man's legs are no use for my travelling," said Ninian; "I'm better with my three fine comrades—courage, sense, and foresight."

"What I thought," said Æneas, "was you might take me: I'm finished with the tutoring, and my uncle wants me to go North on business."

"Oh ho!" cried Ninian, sharp-looking at him. "That's the way the wind blows, is it? I'll take the last thing in my mind the first, and tell ye this, that I'm the man that's willing, if you can have your pack made up tomorrow morning. I'm starting at the skirl of day myself, but whether you're to leave the town with me or not will have to be considered. Now for the first thing in my mind, and most important—what ails Drimdorran at ye?"

"Young Campbell's going to St Andrews," said Æneas uneasily, and Ninian's eyes half shut.

He placed the plenishing of his knapsack back with some deliberation, whistling to himself the tune of "Monymusk," then put the Molucca bean with care in a pouch he had inside his coat below his elbow, where was a small black knife; but all

51

without a word, and Æneas felt mightily uncomfortable.

"What's in my mind," at last said Ninian, turning on him quickly, "is that if you're going with me, you'll need to be as open as the day. I'm deep enough for two of us whatever—that's my trade, and I want nothing muffled in my comrade. Stop, stop!"—for Æneas was about to blurt the truth—"I'm asking nothing, mind! But at the very start ye try to blind me with this story of young Campbell going to St Andrews, and I'm not so easy blinded. *I asked what ailed Drimdorran at ye!* Last night the man was in a fury. What's more, he never put his head to pillow, and he sent for ye this morning at an hour when gentlemen are snoring. It's not for nothing that the falcon whistles—is he blaming ye for Margaret?"

"That's the truth," admitted Æneas. "I thought for her sake it was better not to mention it. But the man's mistaken; there is nothing in it."

"Just that!" said Ninian dryly. "Whether there is or not is none of my affair at all, at all; but it makes a difference in the way we'll have to start for Inverness. It would never do in the circumstances for the two of us to leave this town together like a cow and a veal at her tail. Myself I'm going by Glen Aray and the Orchy. I might have tried Glen Lochy, but I want to see some salmon in a linn that's close to Arichastlich, and forbye, I ken the folk that's in Glenorchy—decent people though they're no' Macgregors! It would not hinder you, now, to start on a road of your own. It might be that you would be going to the Lowlands, like," and he gave a wink of great significance, and stuck his tongue out in the corner of his mouth. "There's not a finer glen in Albyn than Glen Croe, and you would, let us be saying, take the track across Glen Croe down to Loch Lomond. But you would kind of shift your mind about the Lowlands when ye got to that fine water, and start up Glen Falloch, and who would I be seeing in the evening at the Bridge of Orchy change but young Macmaster! My welcome to him, I'll can swear, would be in grandeur and in splendour!"

"Very well; so be it!" said Æneas. "You are riding?"

"Indeed and I'm not!" said Ninian firmly. "Only to the length of Bridge of Orchy, just to show my friends upon the road I'm not a man that needs to wear shoe-leather. From there I'm sending back the horse by a man that's coming that length with me. After that I'll stretch out like a warrior and take my shanks to it. Ye'll need a horse, so far, yourself, or else I'll have to wait a day for ye."

"I'll take a horse to Bridge of Orchy too," said Æneas, "and send it back or sell it as my uncle may advise."

"You see, a horse is not much use on my affairs," said Ninian. "It's something like two extra pair of legs—an awkward thing to have about ye; it looks too much like business in a hurry, and I like to give the notion that I'm daundering at my ease. Ye canna hide a horse behind a bush of juniper nor take it crawling wi' ye up a burn, and it's aye another thing to run the risk of losing. Nothing better than the shanks, my hero! and ye'll see a good deal more on them than cocked upon a saddle. Ye'll need a pickle money."

"In that I'm likely to be well enough provided," answered Æneas. "I'll have three hundred pound about me."

"What!" cried Ninian. "Through Lochaber! God be about us! am I to travel wi' a banker's vault? Ye havena robbed Drimdorran, have ye?"

"No," said Æneas, laughing, and explained the nature of his mission to the North.

"Not a word about it then!" said Ninian. "It's not that stealing money is a habit with the folk we're going among, poor bodies! They never touch a thing but bestial, and perhaps, at whiles, a web of clothing, but at this time o' the year, wi' Crieff Tryst comin' on, there's many a droll stravaiger stopping at the inns and changes we'll be sleeping in, if sleeping's going to be a thing we're going to waste much time on, and a man wi' all that money on him would be smelling like a spirit keg for their temptation."

In the midst of their discussion, further, on the preparations for the journey, Janet entered, and at the sight of her, for Æneas the zest of the adventure flattened. It was not frosty wells she was today but ice itself, until her father told her Æneas was going with him, when she brightened.

"But why not all the way together?" she inquired, surprised to learn they were to take such devious ways into Breadalbane.

"Because, my lass, our friend here's leaving not in the friendliest trim with Mr Duncanson," said Ninian, "and I've no mind to vex that bonny gentleman until we have the width of two good parishes between us. He seems so little taken up, himself, with my bit jaunt on Islay's business, that he might be glad of any excuse to put it off. And indeed, forbye, it is a splendid chance for Æneas here to see Glen Falloch. It's a place I'm very fond of."

"It seems a queer-like start," she said with puzzled brows, "but anyway I'm glad my father is to have your company." She turned upon the young man rather warmer. "You will find him," she said, "a kind of crooked stick to take the road with on the forests and the mountain moors."

"It's ill to take the crook out of an old stick," said Ninian blythly, "but sometimes it's as good as any other for the business."

"I hope you'll see that he will not go wandering about too much at night; that will always be the time when I'm most anxious for this man—this wild young dad of mine."

"And that's the very time when I am surest of myself," cried Ninian. "My name's Macgregor and the fog's my friend! I'm thinking, too, you couldna send a better man wi' me to watch me in the night; he has that turn himsel'!" And there he gave a nudge to Æneas.

Æneas flushed before the level glance she gave him upon this.

"There's one thing I hope," she said, "and that is that you are not in a desperate hurry to get North or to get back again, for my father is a man who makes little speed through any country where there is a fish to catch."

"I'll do my best," said Æneas, "to keep him from his angling."

"It will be hard," she said. "A rod and a riverside for father, and the day slips by! It is like life itself and us, poor things! at playing."

With a breast tumultuous Æneas went home, and with the help of Annabel prepared for a departure so precipitous she almost wept about it.

VI

The Angler

A better day for travel never shone, and Æneas rode through it till the gloaming with uplifted spirit on a track that, till he reached Loch Lomond, gave no trouble to his riding, for, so far, it was the trail to Lowland markets, and the very rock of it was stripped by feet of men and beast. The way was new to him; he saw the wild abyss below Ben Arthur and Ben Ime with wonder, gladdened in the salt breeze of the yellow beaches of Loch Long, and, having come to Tarbet, rested. His way was rougher in the afternoon—along Loch Lomond-side and through Glen Falloch, where Macfarlane crofts were thick upon the braes, and folks were harvesting, and it was not yet dusk when he passed through Tyndrum. There was he on the main route of the Appin drovers and the men from Skye; a change-house by the wayside hummed like a skep of bees with voices, and a field beside the change was occupied by big-horned shaggy cattle bellowing.

Two or three men came out and looked at him when he rode past, themselves no gentler-looking than their herds,—thick, hairy fellows, wearing tartan, one of them at least in fier of war with a target on his back and a leather coat.

Æneas gave a wave in by-going.

"You're surely at the start of fortune, trim young lad, to be at the riding for't," cried out the fellow of the targe: "come in and drop your weariness!" and Æneas looked at him again—he was so like a Roman, with bare knees!

But he went on, unheeding them, and by-and-by his track rose up among the heather for a bit above a plain all strewn with shingle of the winter storms, and there he saw the sun go down upon the wild turmoil of bens they called the Black Mount of Breadalbane. The dark was on when he came to the Bridge of Orchy, and the sky all shivering with stars.

There, too, were droves of cattle round the inn; no sooner had he clattered in upon the hamlet than a score of men were out upon him, even shaggier than the fellows of Tyndrum, and only reassured about the safety of their charges when they found he was a gentleman alone.

The inn was shabby to the point of scandal, no better than a common tavern, smoke-blackened, smelling of the reek of peat and mordants used in dyeing cloth; lit by cruisies, going like a fair with traffic. In the kitchen of it men were supping broth with spoons chained to the tables, and a lad with his head to the side as if in raptures at his own performance stood among the ashes with a set of braying bagpipes.

"*Failte!*" said the landlord courteously to Æneas. "Stick your horse in anywhere, just man, and what's your will for supper?"

"Cook for me a bannock and roast a cock," said Æneas, like a traveller of the hero stories.

The landlord had the hue of drink upon him, and seemed in a merry key.

"Son," said he (and he, too, thinking of the story), "wouldst thou prefer the big bannock of my anger or the little wee bannock and my blessing?" and Æneas laughed. He took a squint at the baking-board upon the dresser, and said he, more wisely—

"I think we will not mind the bannock, big or little, but I have a friend who should be here by this time from Glen Orchy, and the bird will do between us."

He had hardly put his horse into a stall when the company burst out again upon the house-front at a clack of hooves, and going out himself he heard the voice of Ninian. Before he could address him, Ninian was off the saddle at a jump, had ordered his attendant to put up the horses for the night, and dashed into the inn without the slightest notice of his friend.

"What is wrong?" asked Æneas, following him.

"Nothing at all," said Ninian cautiously in English, with a look about him at the drovers. "But ye'll be better in your bed before the man that's with me there puts bye the beasts. I wouldn't for the world that he would see us here together."

"I'm sorry to be such a bother to you," said Æneas stiffly. "I thought the width of two good parishes between you and Drimdorran made you master of yourself!"

"That's the best word ever I heard from ye!" said Ninian heartily. "I'm glad to see ye have your tongue and I'm thinking we'll get on no' bad together. But still-and-on I'm serious about that fellow with me, and if we can get a chamber by ourselves I'll tell ye what's my reason."

The only chamber they could get was that in which they were to sleep, and that not stately. Thither were they led by the landlord's wife, who said the fowl was now at plucking for their supper, and when the door was shut on her, Ninian turned on Æneas and looked him firmly in the eye.

"Ye didna tell me all, my lad," says he, "about Drimdorran's anger. I'm doubting you're a close one!"

"What else have you been hearing now?" asked Æneas, greatly downed.

"When I was coming up the glen this morning he was out upon the road with letters for my man to leave round here, but I was not long of learning that he knew you were away from Inveraray, and what he really wanted was to know if I could tell your destination. That, I'll assure ye, put me in a corner. But I was able for his lordship! 'By all accounts,' says I, 'he is riding to the Lowlands.' Then what in all the earth should happen but Drimdorran burst upon you for a thief—"

"Now is not that the swine!" cried Æneas, furious.

"Stop you! I knew the man was talking nonsense, and I was right, for in a bit the only thing he had against you was a snuffbox. But a body more concerned about a snuffbox never breathed the morning air of Scotland! He swore he would be even with you if ye ever set a foot again within the barony. You will see yourself, now, the position I was in—I had myself to think about as well as you, and if I was kent to be tramping through the North in company with the gentleman who stole the snuffbox, after telling Old Drimdorran yon about the Lowlands road, it would not look respectable."

"Good God!" cried Æneas, "you're surely not believing that

I have the body's snuffbox!"

"Tach! What's the odds about a paltry snuffbox?" Ninian said lightly.

"But, man! I haven't got it! It's yonder in his house," cried Æneas. "Will you not believe me?"

"I believe every word of you," said Ninian, "but if there's not a snuffbox missing, what's the cause of yon one's tirravee?"

"I'll tell you that," said Æneas, and straightway laid before him all his tale without a word of reservation. Away from Janet Campbell's presence the dovecote incident now appeared quite innocent; he did not even baulk to tell Drimdorran's charge about the desk.

"If ye had told me this before," said Ninian, "I could have cleared the air for you. It's droll that my girl Janet should jalouse the truth before myself. She didna know, of course, about the doocot, but she guessed ye were with Margaret somewhere when ye should have been at your tasks whenever I said that Drimdorran had been angry looking for ye. Now I can tell ye something. When I was there colloguing with Drimdorran in his closet, he turned him from the window once as he was walking up and down the room, and with a changed complexion made a dash to look his desk; he went out of the room and in again like lightning. 'Ye havena seen the young folk?' he inquired of me, and I had not but thought ye would be at your lessons. Ye werena there, he said, and out again and left me cooling twenty minutes, by my lone. I started wondering in the Gaelic what was bothering him, and walking to the window saw a thing that put me to my calculations. The window of his room, you may have noticed, shows the window of the doocot in between the branches of the thicket, and a light was there, the first time I have ever seen it. I watched it six or seven minutes, then the light went out."

"Then after all it was her father!" cried out Æneas, "and he knew that we were there."

"Not a bit of doubt of it! I can see that now, although I thought when he came back he had not left the house, because he still had on his slippers. But there was something in his manner curious; he was a troubled man who found it hard to keep his mind upon our business. He asked me just the once again if I had seen you anywhere, and in a key that showed ye werena in his graces, and all the time was I not thinking it was just because of the neglected lessons?"

"There's no doubt it was he," said Æneas. "We thought at first it was, and then I was led astray by thinking he and you had been together all the time."

"He had plenty of time to reach the doocot and be back," said Ninian.

"But what," said Æneas, "was he lamenting for?"

"I would lament myself if I had any thought a girl of mine was yonder," answered Ninian. "It's aye a chancy thing a buzzard in a doocot. The difference with me is that the neck of ye would likely have been twisted. He's so keen on Campbell for the girl he wouldna risk that scandal. But that's all bye wi't; there's this business of the snuffbox; it's a handy story to give colour to his putting ye away without entangling the reputation of his daughter, and it's maybe just a pity that we're on the march together after that bit tale of mine about the Lowlands road. If this man with me takes the story back tomorrow that ye met me here, the tune is through the fiddle, and that's the way I want ye in your bed, or out of sight at least till he is gone."

So Æneas took his supper in the bedded room, and Ninian kept his man engaged till he too went to bed, and in the morning got him off at break of day.

"All clear now; we'll have a bite of breakfast, and take our feet to it ourselves," he said to Æneas, who had not slept a wink.

"First of all I have to send my horse back," mentioned Æneas, and the other started.

"No other horse goes back from here!" he said with firmness. "The man ye would send back wi't couldna hold his tongue. No, no, ye'll have to sell it. Some of these men there for the Tryst at Crieff will buy it from ye."

To this was Æneas willing, since he had his uncle's consent to do what he thought best with the horse, and Ninian soon found among the drovers one who had a fancy for a bargain.

They went together to the stable, and no sooner had the Messenger beheld the pony, dapple-grey, that carried Æneas from Inveraray, than he gave a cry.

"My grief! we're done for't now!" says he, and backed out of the stable, Æneas behind him.

"What's the use of me telling lies if ye go and bring a horse like that with ye?" he asked, dejected. "Ye might as well go round the country with a drum, to call attention. That speckled one is known to everybody in the seven parishes, and my man's off to Inveraray with the story that it's here. He couldna well mistake it, and in the stall next to his own! I thought there was something droll about his manner when we parted."

For a while this new misfortune daunted Ninian, but he was not a man to nurse despair: they sold the horse, between them, for a sum of fifteen pounds shaken out of as many sporrans. They humped their pokes in which they put some cakes and cheese; Æneas cut for himself a hazel stick, to be upsides with Ninian who bore a curious thick rattan, and it seemed as if the world would fly below them till the dusk as they took up the waterside.

It was a mountain step that Ninian had—spanged out and supple, and the burgess of him left behind. He sniffed the air of gale and heather with applause, and searched the mounts before them and their corries with the eyes of birds that have come far from wandering and know their home. Now would he run upon a hillock with droll sounds of pleasure like a whinny, now leap the boulders and stretch flat among the thyme and thrift to peer into the dark, small pools of stream. "Ah, now," thought Æneas, "I have here with me but a child," and yet it was, himself, a boy he felt, so bland and pleasant was the morning and his heart so strong, so sweet the thinking of the North before him, and the things that might befall. So he, too, stretched brave legs, and in the great wide moorland hollow of the upper Orchy looked ardently upon the massing clouds that floated silverly about the confines of the world.

They had walked but half an hour when Ninian all at once stopped short, and staring at a pool saw salmon leaping.

"*Mo chreach!*" said he, "Look yonder!" and began to fidget with his stick. "I was just thinking what two daft fellows we are to be taking the world for our pillow like this, as the saying goes, without first making up our minds together what's to be the tack we'll steer on." And aye the corner of his eye was on the leaping fish.

"The nearest way is the best as far as I am concerned," said Æneas.

"I would never take the nearest way anywhere," said Ninian. "Half the sport of life is starting and the other half is getting on the way, and everything is finished when it's done," and he almost jumped as another fellow in the water splashed. "Put we down our packs just here and be considering cautiously what airts we are to follow, for, thank God, there's many ways before us, every one as splendid as the other, like MacVurich's songs. To save the time when we're considering, I'll try a cast," and in a second he had whipped the ferrule off his sturdy cane and out of it there came three parts, at sight of which the other smiled to have Miss Janet's reading of her father proved so soon.

Off went the poke from Ninian's back, and out of it he fetched some tackle ready busked with flies. He put the rod together, trembling with excitation, keeping up the while a constant chatter on their plans as if no other thing engaged his mind, and still and on his eye was aye upon the bonny fish.

"What we'll do, lad," he said, "is to put the night bye in a change-house yonder close on Buachaille Etive. It's only four-teen miles or thereabouts, but it's the only one between us and the Spean, and that is twice as far again. For a gentleman on my business there's many a bit of information to be picked up on a night in that inn beside the Moor of Rannoch. It's close enough on Glen Coe to learn what's stirring there among MacIan's folk I darena venture in among; forbye there's lochs beside it on the moor that's full of fish."

"If it's fish we're out for it is not soon we will be at Inverness," said Æneas ruefully, sitting down upon his pack and looking at the other stepping out already on the stones.

"Men and love! look at yon fellow!" cried Ninian in Gaelic

over his shoulder. "God's splendour! is he not the heavy gentleman! And me with this bit trifle of a stick not better than a wand." All his wind seemed fighting in his breast; his very voice was changed with agitation. But still he kept up for a moment longer the pretence of interest in their route, and cried back to the lad upon the bank, "Up Loch Laggan-side or through Glen Roy. . . . Oh, Mary! is not that the red one!"

For half an hour was not another word from him; he was a man bewitched, that crawled among the rushes of the bank and crouched in shadows of the boulders, and threw the lures across the linn among the playing fish, with eyes that seemed to grudge each moment that they were not on the water.

Æneas lay back and crushed the mint and thyme that gave the day a scent for ever after in his memory: fishing had never been a sport of his, and he but wondered at his comrade's patience. For long it looked as if the fisher worked in vain; great fishes surged and leaped about his hair-lines and his feathers, but they never touched them.

"Aren't they the frightened dirt!" cried Ninian at last. "Not a bit of gallant spirit in them! And me so honest, striving wi' them! Stop you, though!" and he fixed another lure.

And Æneas, lying in his hollow, fell asleep. When he awoke the sun was straight above them, and his friend was still bent on the water-edge and whipping in the eddies where the fish still lay. An ear of Æneas was on the ground; he rather felt than heard a horseman galloping upon the track a little way above the river. Such furious haste was in the rider's manner that Æneas walked up the brae to watch him, and hailed him as he galloped past.

He got no answer. The horseman never even raised a hand, but swept upon his way as if some fiend were after him—a boorish fellow with a head like a two-boll bag of meal and a plaid upon him.

"We are in the land of poor manners, surely," thought Æneas, and went down again beside his friend, and just as he got to him, saw him give a twitch. Ninian, crouched knee-deep now in the water, turned as he came nigh him with an aspect that astonished Æneas. All his face was puckered up with exaltation; in his eyes a curious glitter, proud and savage.

"*Tha e agam, a bhruide!*—I have him, the brute!" he screamed, and slowly backed out of the stream with his rod-point bent. Æneas watched him, fascinated, play the fish. It threw itself into the air, and fell with great commotion in the middle of the pool, and then the line went whirling out of the wooden pirn the whole length of the pool, which ended in a shallow narrow channel. Ninian, with his teeth clenched and his lips drawn back from them, all in a kind of a glorious agony, strained lightly on the rod and span the reel at every yard he gained upon his quarry. Repeatedly it burst away again and leaped until the pool was boiling with its fury.

"If I had only just a decent stick instead of this child's playock!" said the angler in anguish. "I never had it in my mind to touch such big ones!"

He fought with it for near an hour; at last he had it close upon the bank; they saw it rolling at their feet blue-backed, and Æneas stretched a hand to grasp the line and lift it.

"Put a finger upon a hair of that and there is not a timber of your body but I'll break!" roared Ninian. "I will take him to this stone and you must tail him. Catch him by the small and grip as if it were the very bars of heaven and you by God rejected!"

Æneas gripped. The fish moved mightily within his hand, writhed with extraordinary power, and breaking slimy from his grasp, snapped Ninian's line. It slowly turned a moment, and Ninian with a yell dropped rod, plucked out the knife below his elbow, threw himself upon the fish, and stabbed it through the gills.

"*Sin thu!*" he roared, and heaved it high upon the bank. "Oh, Æneas!" he cried with brimming eyes, and, all dripping, put his arms about his friend and squeezed him to his breast. He skipped then, like a child, about the fish, and fondled it like one that loved it, saying the most beautiful things in death were a child, a salmon, and a woodcock. Then broke he into a curious Gaelic brag about his prey,—he spoke of it as if it were leviathan.

"It is not so very big a fish as all that!" said Æneas, and at that the other looked again upon his prize, and his jaw fell.

"By the Books and you're right!" said he with some vexation. "It's just a middling one, and red at that! And that is mighty droll, for I was sure this moment that he was a monster, and the side of him like a silver ship. But I think you'll must agree I played him pretty! Look you at this stick, that's only meant for catching trouts! But now we must be stretching. You were sleeping yonder like a headstone and I hadna the heart to waken you."

With two slashes of the small black knife he ripped the ends from off the salmon, and he shoved its middle, wrapped with ferns, into his knapsack.

"Whatever comes of it we have our dinner," he exclaimed.

"That was a surly dog who passed," said Æneas, as they turned to leave the river.

"Where? When?" cried Ninian, surprised; so keen had he been on the fish he had not heard nor seen the horseman.

"That's gey droll!" he said, when Æneas told him what had happened. "A gentleman might pass like that without the word of day to you but not a common man in all Argyll; there's something curious in it—something curious! He wasna, was he, like a man in drink?"

"I think not," answered Æneas.

"There's two or three things only sends a man at gallop through Breadalbane when he's sober—the ailment of bairns in women and the need for knee-wives; a bit of mischief in the rear to run away from, or a scheme ahead."

"He might be just a man who went with letters," said Æneas.

"Letters don't go at the gallop through this country yet," said Ninian, "whatever they may do when the Road is finished. They crawl. But still-and-on there's something in the notion; it might well be that the man had letters. And I don't like letters. They make trouble. They're sly and underhand. They may be going past ye in broad daylight and you not know. I never write a letter myself if I can help it; it's putting words in jail, and it's not the man alone who puts them in can get them out again; too many have the keys. I wish I had seen the fellow; there would certainly be something in him that you did not notice that would mean a lot to me."

It seemed to Æneas that this was making far too much of what was, after all, a commonplace affair, but he was soon to find that everything that happened, night or day, set up this curious kind of speculation in his friend.

VII

The Inn At Buachaille Etive

Ninian's notion was to save some miles of walking round Loch Tulla by a kind of ferry which he knew could always be procured across it at the middle, where there was a boatman's hut upon the other side that could be signalled. This ferry, hitherto upon his missions through Breadalbane, never failed him, and when they reached the loch and stood below its fir-trees they could see the hut was reeking and the boat was on the shore. The day was warm, and they were not in haste; they sat upon a knoll of berries, ate with them their bread and cheese, and only now and then would shout and whistle to the other side. The wind had fallen and the loch was like a glass, with every tree and every blade of grass reflected. Red deer were moving on the shoulders of the lower hills, which Ninian thought a thing portending change of weather, though the heavens looked as if they never more would frown—so blue, so clear, with only rolling clouds like drifts of snow upon the edges. The corries of the mountains sent a sound of running waters; the red-pine tops, as old as Scotland, bent above them, hushed and dark; the air was heavy with the tang of myrtle and of heath. From where they sat there was no sign of human life in all the country they could see, except the smoking house upon the other shore, and the man who once came out of it upon their whistling and went in again.

"No doubt it's very pleasant this," said Ninian, "but the boat is what I'm wanting, and I never saw a boat more dour. I'm sure he saw us!"

They fired a pistol; waited twenty minutes longer; then they made a smoke with withered bracken and some greenwood twigs. The reek rose like a pillar in the air, and more than once they saw the ferryman come out and look at it, but still he never made a move to come across for them.

"Now isn't that the caird!" cried Ninian, amazed. "Just laziness! Pure laziness! Even for the money he will not take oars for't! There is nothing for it but for us to go about the end of the loch, and that's a great vexation, for there's a river there I never had a line on, and I didna want to venture near it,—it's a great temptation."

"You can shut your eyes when you're passing it," said Æneas, jocular, as they took their packs again.

"And what would my ears be for but hearing her go gluck-gluck?" said Ninian.

It took them nigh an hour to walk around the loch and reach the neighbourhood of the reluctant ferry. Although it lay far below their track along the shoulder of the hills, so furious was Ninian that he must go down and storm upon its tenant—a fellow with a sullen eye, a falling lip, and little conversation.

"I heard you, and I saw your smoke," he admitted, "but my boat is like a sieve; she had been staved since I took over peats a month ago, and put her on a craig in stormy weather."

Ninian without a word walked down to where the boat was lying, and came back more furious than ever, for it was as hale as Haco's galley.

The man scratched his head at this discovery of his lies, and then at last informed them he had acted on commands. He had been told he was to give no help to two long-coated men who would reach the loch that afternoon and likely want the ferry. But more than that he would not say. The source of his instructions he would not reveal. "All I know," he said, "is that the coats of the both of ye are long."

"It was the man who passed upon a horse some hours ago gave you your orders, I'm aware," said Ninian at last, and though the man denied it, it was plainly true.

"I don't like the look of things one bit," was Ninian's confession when they left the fellow. "There's something in the air. I don't like yon one galloping past without one word in his head for you, nor I don't like this brose-brained, sulky fellow and his story of commands. 'Long-tailed coats,' quo' he. In faith they have the measure of us! in a place like this our coats fair cry out 'Inveraray'! But I must have a skirt to hide my hilt; a claymore swinging plainly at my hurdies would look ridiculous in a Messenger-at-Arms, and still I darena march without Grey Colin."

He hung, uncertain, on the track they had reached again, and looked ahead upon it with suspicion and distaste. At last he fairly turned upon his heel, and said the horseman's way was not the way for them.

"There's miles and miles of it," said he, "upon the edge of Rannoch Moor, the bleakest place in Albyn, if it wasna for the fishing, and we couldna move a yard but what the world would see us. There's not the shelter of a berry bush upon it."

"What are ye frightened for?" asked Æneas.

"I'm a man that never yet was frightened," Ninian cried stoutly, "but I have my calling to consider. If I'm to be of any use at all on this affair I'm out on I must not be too kenspeckle in my movements. Forbye, I'm not at ease at all about your horseman, and I'm wishing that you had not all that money on you. There is not a corrie opening on the moor that might not have a band of ruffians in it, though I say't who shouldna, since the country is, or was, my own—Macgregors, and it's just a bit too soon for me to start disputing: that's a thing perhaps I'll have to do in earnest nearer Corryarrick. Now I'm thinking this is not the way we will go at all; we'll make, instead, up Shira-side and past Loch Dochard through a pass that's yonder namely for its goats, and down upon Glen Etive. About the dark we should be close on Buachaille Etive and the inn I mentioned. Whether we stop there for the night or slumber in the heather like our fathers, who were men, will be a thing to settle when we see what like the place is. Didst ever lie on heather, lad? and waken in the mist of morning with the plover whistling?"

"I would not mind a bit," said Æneas, quite hearty, and the other smiled.

"I'm all for beds myself," said he. "That's age and wisdom. I've lain too often on the hill and a devil of a root below my middle, but it may be that we'll have to couch among the deer this night. Anyway, it is a crooked road we're going—crooked as the fool's furrow and he at ploughing. Let us be going, merry, light, and tuneful."

And so it was with them; they turned and went gay-hearted to the west for miles beside a stream which Ninian all the way looked at with longing, whistling to himself as if to keep his feet from lagging. It was an old drove-track from Appin; something like a score of low black houses belching peat-smoke from their doors were in a swampy plain on which high peaks that Ninian had a name for frowned. They skirted past a mile-long loch where seagulls screamed and ravens croaked among some stunted thickets of the rowan; then left the waterside, and going north, went up a corrie where a stream came pouring down as white as milk. High parts they reached, and at the highest, where it seemed a world of barren mounts, the weather changed. Black clouds came from the west, and thunder rumbled on a peak that Ninian called Stob Gabhar. Before the rain came down upon them they could see into Glen Etive, lying green below them; they could hear its stream.

And then it was, as they were on the summit of the pass and looking down, they saw a strange appearance. It was a human figure, naked to the skin, and running hard across a hollow of the glen.

"The devil's in it if that is not a fellow stark!" cried Ninian, astonished.

They watched him for a little, but the thunder broke upon them, and the rain came on so thick it drew a veil across the prospect. It looked as if they occupied the very nesting-place of storms; each peak and corrie cried; the lightning stabbed; the slopes they stood on seemed to shiver.

Drenched now in every stitch of them, they dropped down hurriedly upon Glen Etive, and were hardly at the level when the sun came out again and every pebble glinted. When they had reached about the place where they had seen the naked figure, there was sitting eating bread composedly beside a well, a man in dark-blue flannel clothing even to the kilt. A great flat bonnet with a tuft of heather on it cocked upon his head; he tugged it

70

down upon his brow at sight of Ninian and Æneas coming down the hill.

"You're sitting, good man, behind the wind and before the sun and beaking of yourself," said Ninian to him gaily, and looked round about, and there was neither house nor ember, tree nor bush for shelter to a wren. "What now are you, if a body dare to ask?"

"I am," said the man with the bonnet, as he fidged himself, "a hunter of wandering game, and it but scanty in this quarter."

"That's what I was thinking to myself," said Ninian blithely. "Are you going west?"

Long the fellow thought upon this question, and said at last his way was through the Lairig Eilde.

"And where do you come from?" said Ninian. "We, ourselves, are from the Bridge of Orchy."

"I came from a good bit off," the other said, with eyes upon the hills, and very short and dry.

They sat a while together on a stone beside the well and talked of hunting and of marriage, till the man said he would have to go, and up he got upon his feet and took his leave.

"Good journeying to you!" said Ninian, and clapped him friendly on the back. They sat beside the well a little longer, and watched him cross the glen and pass into a hollow on the other side. They lost him for a while, and then they saw him running like a deer upon a knoll.

"He's in a hurry, yon one!" Æneas said; and Ninian, who had all the time been pondering, began to put some questions to him. Had he noticed that the man was of Clan Tyre, judging by his garters and his heather badge? That he had no gun with him and could not therefore be a-hunting? That he was curious about the route they meant to follow and reserved about his own? None of these things had struck Æneas, and Ninian began to mock him.

"That's the worst of schooling," he declared; "it spoils the eyesight. Pity on ye if ye were by yourself and me not thinking for ye! Your blindness would make a stirk laugh!—oh no! ye need not bristle at me, little hero; the scolding of friends and the peace of enemies are two things not to be regarded. But ye never said a word about the naked man?"

"No," said Æneas, "I left that to you, and I thought you had your reason for not mentioning it."

"Good!" cried Ninian; "I'm pleased to find ye had that much in ye! Did ye notice anything more than I have mentioned in this curious hunter that goes hunting without a gun? The clothes that he has on him are as dry's a peat, and look at us, all dripping!"

"Impossible!" cried Æneas. "There's not a place in sight where he could shelter, and the ground is soaked."

"That's just the bit!" said Ninian. "There's not a place here he could put his head below, and still he's dry's a whistle. I clapped him on the back to make it certain. That's the very gentleman we saw a while ago when we were on the hill and he the way his mother saw him first."

He got up from the stone he sat on and went searching round about the hollow, and came at last upon a boulder with a hole below it where a man might pack his clothes.

"There," said he, "is where our friend made certain of his dryness," and he plucked out from the hole a bunch of shelisters with which the naked man had closed his curious wardrobe.

"It's a strange way to keep dry," said Æneas.

"Indeed and it would not do every place," said Ninian. "There are only two things in the world a man would take the trouble for in Gaeldom, and one of them is going to see a lass. But that man from Glen Strae—for now I ken the cut of him and whence he came—is on the hunt for neither deer nor maiden."

"You are very sure of it!" said Æneas.

"He is a married man: you'll mind I asked him. The other reason that a man would have for stripping to keep dry ye would not think of for a month, for all your Latin, and still it's almost just the same as going to court a lass. It's self-respect. No man could carry himself courageously before a girl or an important gentleman if he was seeping-wet the way we are ourselves, and yon one skipping over to Glen Coe is after business where he wants to look his best. I'm doubting, Æneas, they're on my track already."

Æneas now could think of half a score of other things that might account for the uncivil horseman and the disappointment of the ferry, but a likelier explanation of the MacIntyre's stripping than the one now given him by Ninian fairly beat him. And Ninian backed it up with many arguments. It was not altogether vanity which made him think himself conspicuous in Breadalbane, nor the cause of some anxiety to lawless folk upon its borders. As *beachdair* for Argyll he had many times made visitations to the neighbourhood they now were in, and always followed up by some vexatious check or levy from the law at Inveraray. It might be that the object of his going to the North was guessed, and they were drawing close upon some glens where troubles often hatched: he had his own suspicions that the Camerons and Macdonalds had a hand in these assaults upon the Road.

"You and your money," said he, "would maybe be much better trudging through the country by yourselves without my reputation tacked to them, but now we've started we will have to stick together. One thing's plain in all these gentry turning up in such a desperate hurry to get on before us, and that is that the best way for us is aye the back way and the moon our lamp."

It was a lonely valley that they went through for another hour or two; at dusk they stood below the Herdsman of the Etive and in the only dwelling on the riverside they heard a woman singing.

"That's the change-house," Ninian said, "and there's meat and music in it, as the fox said when he ate the bagpipes."

The tavern crouched, low-eaved and black, beside a pack-horse bridge on Rannoch edge, and not another light except its own in all the evening. When they went in, they found its only tenant seemed to be the sweetest, jaunty, russet girl at baking, singing at "Crodh Chailein" with a voice to put the birds to trees.

"You are far too merry on it; you should marry," said Ninian to her, throwing down his poke.

"God of Grace!" she cried, "are you Macgregor Campbell?"

Ninian ducked his head as if a shot were passing over him. "It has been so suspected sometimes," he made answer. "But the name, brave girl, is not for shouting in a change. What's of me that was once Macgregor now is in the mist and best forgotten. Ask them in Balwhidder! I did not think that you would ken me. You are John Maclaren's daughter, peace be with him!"

"Yes," she said, "I am John Maclaren's daughter, and you and I will not fall out together in a hurry, for my father liked you well. I saw you last time when I was a lump of a girl, and it was at a wedding in Glen Lyon. Weren't we merry yonder, ochanie! And you are the last man I would like to see in these parts with your friend—this comely fellow—for there's people looking for you."

"I said it!" cried Ninian.

"This very afternoon, a man called Niall Roy from Succoth passed here on a horse and stopped for meat. Some men from Kinlochrannoch were about, and he got to the talking with them. His talk was all about two gentlemen, and one of them yourself by name. They went away together on the moor, the horse between them, and I did not like their friendship, not one bit! I knew that they were studying something. And I said to my mother, who is now gone to her bed, 'It will be well for Ninian Campbell to be not about when Niall Roy of Succoth and these men are on the moor.' "

"Niall Roy!" said Ninian. "Now that is droll! I never did the man an injury. What way did he set out, *a ghalaid*?"

"They went," she said, "along the Cruach on the track that is on the hillside yonder."

"Fair wind to them on that line then!" said Ninian contentedly, and put his bit of salmon out for her. He then went out of doors and looked about the house and smelt the evening wind and listened.

The girl began to lay a table, with a smiling face, for Æneas. "What will you have for supper?" she inquired, and her voice, he thought, was sweeter than the thrush.

"I am starving," he told her. "Not a bite to speak of since the morning at the Bridge of Orchy. There is fish for broiling, but

I want some meat. If you will give to me a steak so thick,"—he showed the thickness on a finger,—"not too fat nor yet too lean, well beat and tender; not cooked too sore and yet not lukewarm at the middle; well spiced and salted—"

She burst out laughing. "O my young heart and it broken!" cried she. "It's not food you want at all but feasting. If there was a miraculous steak like that to be had in all Breadalbane you would not get it, for I would eat it myself."

"Treasure of all women of the world," said Æneas, "I will take whatever you will give me and eat it with a relish if you will only look at me while I am at it," and he warmed himself before a fire of peats on which she had the girdle swung for baking.

"Now are you not the bold one!" said the girl, her teeth like newborn lambs, her eyes all dancing wickedly. "Your mother must have been a pretty woman. Will you kiss me?" But she ran away and woke her mother as she said it.

They fed like soldiers, cracking blithely with the women, and at the end of eating and of talk, "I want to lay my head," said Ninian, "where I'll find it in the morning; where will we be sleeping?"

They took them to the best room of the house, and Æneas heard a door-bar run in channels of the masonry, a murmuring from Ninian in a bed across the room, the scream of birds upon the moor, and that was all.

His head was hardly on the pillow when he was asleep.

VIII

Col-Of-The-Tricks

What had one time looked a night of winter, and the dark clouds surly, took a change about the threshold of the morning, and the moon came out and stared. The mountains seemed to lift, the glens to deepen; everywhere were shadows dark as ink, inhabited by creatures drowsy or alert—the creeping ones, the squeaking ones, the swooping ones, and in the grassy nooks the big red stags at stamping, roaring on their queens. Glen Coe was loud with running waters falling down the gashes of the bens, the curlew whistling and the echoes of MacTala, son of earth, who taunts. From out its lower end among the clachans and the trees there came a company of men behind a fellow on a horse, all belted, bearing weapons, walking one behind another.

Their track was by a little lochan where the sedges hissed, and one wild swan took wing for it and flew across the water. They climbed the steep, steel jingling, so high the voices of the glen they left behind were muffled to them, and they heard, instead, the fresh commotion of the spilling burns of Buachaille Etive. About them here were fragments of the mountain roots high-piled, great rocks that seemed to clang as they went through the gorges of them; chambers of the fox, and chanters of the wind.

A little while upon the saddle of the glen they rested, gathered round the man upon the horse. It was about the hour of two.

No word was said among them louder than a whisper; it might seem the night commanded reverence, but one who stood a bit apart came suddenly among them with the story that between the rocks he heard a sound of cracking nuts.

"Nuts!" jeering said the man upon the horse. "Thou art the champion for hearing! Nuts will not be ripe till Hallowmas!"

"It was most desperate like nuts, then, Barisdale," said the other earnestly. "Every now and then they will be cracking, if

76

you come and listen."

They gathered, some of them, about the riven boulder where he led them, and no sound of cracking nuts was there but only squeaking from some beast that tenanted the cranny.

"Oh, Calum!" said his comrades, mocking him, "green nuts in the foumart's lair! Put down your hand for him, brave fellow!"

"*Air t-adhart!*—feet for it, lads!" cried Barisdale, "our cracking of nuts is still before us," and they took up again their tramping. The wind was now upon their faces very cold. Their captain he was humming something French, well off to be upon a saddle, for the track was boggy. Behind them was a night-hag hooting in a place without a single tree; it was, they said, a sign of dirty weather.

Æneas heard the owl too, later on; it mingled in a dream he had of dancing with the russet girl upon a doocot floor, and sometimes would the eyebrows of her meet, deep-black, and sometimes she was Ninian Campbell's daughter gutting fish. The fish fell from her hands and clashed as one would shut a door, and he sat up in bed and heard again the bar run into channels of the walls.

"Waken, lad!" said Ninian, entering, with his breath short-panting. "Here's a Watch upon us, and it's not the hour for sleep."

"Were ye out?" asked Æneas, jumping to the floor, astonished.

"I have been but little in," said Ninian hastily, "and you there like a winter badger. I knew it in my flesh that something threatened from Glen Coe, and out I went whenever you were sleeping, and went in between the jaws of Buachaille Mór and Crulaist. A bonnier night for mischief never fell, so far as I'm concerned; the moon is shining— Not a stitch of that on ye!" he broke in suddenly, as Æneas began to dress. "It's not the time nor place for breeks nor for the bonny coat of ye: stop you! and I will get ye something like the business."

He went and beat upon another door to waken up the

women, and asked if they had Highland clothes for two. The need for them, he cried, was desperate; a Watch was coming from the glen.

"Would a dead man's clothes be any use to you?" cried out the mother. "Yes," said he, "even if the man himself was in them!"

He came to Æneas with clothes of John Maclaren. "There," said he, and threw them down. "I kent she had no son to wear them; that's one mercy in short families. Back to blankets, lad, the pair of us, and never mudge;" and gathering their proper garments thrust them in below the bed. Once more he sought the women and communed with them, and back again to Æneas, and stripped, and into bed with cold Grey Colin stretched beside him.

"Now," said he, "we're ready for them! Here we are—two honest men from Lorn on the road for Appin."

"How did you come across them?" Æneas asked, bewildered at it all.

"When you went to your bed," said Ninian, "it was like falling in a hole for you. You just played 'plop!' and there you were back where mankind came from, *Tir a' chadail*—Land of Sleep. Myself, I could not sleep a wink for listening to the river mourning and the moor-birds, and the less because I saw, before I put the candle out, a pillowslip of nuts there in the corner. Now, I'm a sort of man who cannot go to sleep in any place where something's to be eaten; I get hungry. So up I got—it was not at the run, but jumping—and made to get the pillow-slip, when all at once I took it for an omen that this wasn't meant to be a night of sleep, and something was to crack. Yon fidging fellow with the bonnet, slashing for it over to Glen Coe, stuck in my mind, and I would aye be wondering what it was he wanted there. I put my clothes on, and a fistful of the nuts into my pocket, and went out without a sound. In the throat of the glen I heard the hammering of a horse's feet, and I got in a craggy bit beside the track that smelt deplorably of polecats. Who came climbing up but half a hundred musket men and one tall fellow riding!

" 'There you are, my night-lads! trim and ready!' I said to myself, and wondered who the fellow was upon the horse, for not a word was passed that I could hear between them. Thinks I, 'If I could make some noise to make them wonder, but scarcely loud enough to make them look, I might learn something of them,' so I started cracking nuts, and every nut I cracked was rotten. But they did the business—the man who heard me first called out the rider's name, and who could you imagine it would be but Barisdale!"

"Col Macdonnell!" said Æneas: the name was often on his uncle's tongue.

"That same! Col-of-the-tricks—a shifty lad! The last man I would want to see at this stage of my journey, for he's nothing but a robber. I thought for a little yonder that they had me, for they came quite close beside my crevice, listening, but I gave a polecat squeak and they went off.

He sat up in his bed and in another voice said, "Oh, Æneas! when I was lying on my belly yonder cracking nuts, and saw the moon glint on their muskets, I had a feeling that I was a boy and watching for my father's people. I rose when they were gone, and thinking I was young again I gave the warning of the *cailleach oidhche*. There is no need for that for John Macgregor now; the hooting of the owl will not wake him that's on the sod of truth now yonder, sound and careless, in the kirkyard of Balwhidder."

"Are they far behind you?" Æneas asked.

"Not more than twenty minutes: I cut through the rough and got before them,—there they go, man! there they go!"

The sound of many feet and voices came about the inn, and some one hailed it. Æneas and Ninian got up and looked out through a porthole in the shutter of their window. They could see the Watch already drawn about the house, the moonlight shining on their weapons, and Barisdale dismount, walk to the door and hammer on it loudly. He looked enormous, tall and heavy, all the taller for a wing that jutted at a slant above his bonnet, all the broader for a plaid rolled round his chest.

"By the Books and he's a burly one!" said Ninian. "I never

saw you, Col, before this night, though well I ken your history."

Few, indeed, above the Highland border did not know the history of Barisdale. The name of him was in the very mouths of bairns, not mentioned in the dark, he was their mother's goblin. "Big Col will catch thee!" would they say, the women, and the little ones with trembling legs would pelt for home. He roved the mountains, heedless of the marches, like a hart, and with a tail of thirty men would flash down through the glens demanding tribute. His den was in a strath of Knoydart, where he had a wadset from Glengarry who was cousin-germain to him. A small estate that he had married in the shire of Ross could raise for him two hundred of his clan, and so he played the chief. No doubt the man had parts; the bonnet off him, and the target from his back, and he could be the dulcet gentleman. He had the name of dancing like a prince at lowland balls, though always with a dozen gillies waiting for him in the close lest he be dirked; his swords had graved on them Virgilian tags, and he could roll out bits of French and Latin that were thought by all except the country ministers exceeding fine.

That was Barisdale abroad—at home he was a kite, and trembling things went clapping in the heather when he hovered. He was among the earliest of the chiefs to raise a Watch—a company of men that scoured in name of honesty and order, from the Monadh Liath to Flanders Moss, a check on forays and the cattle thefts of unclanned men. "Give me a halter and I'll soon pick up a horse to fit it," was his boast; he captured many a *creach* upon the hoof from rifled townships on the Gaelic border, but they never were restored to those who owned them. Blackmail he lifted like a rent on quarter-day, and made five hundred pounds a year from it, not counting what some ruffian folk he banded with in Badenoch and Rannoch picked up at his commands, from such as would or could not pay his tribute.

The door was opened to him, and Æneas and Ninian heard the widow parley. He talked her plausibly; he wanted roof and stretching-space for sixty men, and for himself a bedded room.

"There you are!" said Æneas; "it has nothing to do with us at all, his coming here;" but Ninian shook his head.

80

"It's a little too soon to say," he answered. "Col is a pretty deep one, if all tales be true."

It seemed that half the men at least could get rough bedding in an outhouse. "Very well," said Barisdale, "the rest will have to make a shift among the fern."

His company sought round the gable-end among the wooden houses, all but two or three who hung about the front, and Barisdale was inside now and talking very calmly to the women. The inn was known to him, it seemed, in every nook; no other chamber than the best would please his lordship.

"Sly dog!" said Ninian; "that's the way he'll get a sight of us. He kens we're here! On with the kilts, my hero! and remember that my name's your own—Macmaster. For you, you're just a kind of gentleman, and we are on the road from Lorn to Upper Appin. You had best be dour on it, and I will do the talking."

The voice of Barisdale grew louder; he would have the fire room or none, if all the honest travellers of Lorn were bedded in it, and their galley with them.

"Hurry with the kilt, lad!" Ninian said, and stuck his small black knife against the door that had no snib or lock upon it.

Next moment Barisdale was pounding on it with his claymore head. "That's my room," he cried, "I had it trysted. Sorry to disturb ye, gentlemen, but that's the long and short of it—I want my room!"

"My God!" said Ninian in a whisper, "if I had him on the hill I'd make of him a blackcock. I'd scatter the brains of him. I sore misdoubt I'm going to be angry, and oh, man! that's a great mistake! . . . At leisure, honest man! At leisure! At least let us be clad before we open for what seems a gentleman."

He drew the knife out of the jamb and stuck it in his stocking, opened up the door, and let in Col.

"Come, come, come, come! What's this of it?" cried Barisdale; then "prutt, prutt, prutt!" said he, in a bullying kind of trumpet, as he stepped into the room with his chest swelled out, his sword in one hand and a candle in the other—a tremendous sword that would perhaps have given Æneas qualms if he had not seen that the man who bore it was, for all his bellowing, and devouring eye, as hollow as a drum. All at once it came upon him that his glamoured notion of the North was just a kind of poetry in himself; it vexed him to reflect that, after all, the heroes of the *ceilidh* tales—the chiefs and caterans—were, like enough, but men of wind as this one seemed.

And yet it was a martial figure, almost six feet and a half, and brawny to the ankles, over which a pair of trews were closely fitted. He had a doublet made of buff that creaked and smelled like saddlery, a sun-discoloured plaid across his shoulders, pistols in his belt, a dagger at his hip, and on his back the grandest kind of shield, brass-studded, with a prong set in its navel. Down he clapped the candle on the table, and stood straddled on the floor, the feathers of his bonnet scraping on the ceiling.

If he had thought to find two cringing men in broadcloth in the room, he could not but be startled to behold a sturdy pair of Gaels in John Maclaren's garments.

"Did my ears deceive me now, or did I hear ye rap?" said Ninian, looking, in his kilt, as staunch as Castle Campbell, and a handsome leg upon him. He had Grey Colin naked in both hands across his body like a switch, and if the big one straddled he was straddled more.

"That ye did!" said Barisdale, and stuck out his lips to make a snout. "This room is mine at all times when I'm here on service," and his eye went roving round it. "I'm Captain Macdonnell of Barisdale."

And I am John Macmaster of the land of Lorn," said Ninian, sniffing. "Now we ken each other. It's droll to me ye did not think of bringing in your horse. Son of the world! but you're the long one! How do ye find out, now, when your feet are cold? If I was you, Sir Captain, I would take my bonnet off and not be spoiling feathers on the ceiling."

"*Habet!*" said Æneas, sitting on his bed and wishing the knees of him were not so white; he had not worn a kilt since he had gone to college.

Barisdale looked at him, and Æneas stared him back and felt that if this creature had a thousand swords behind his back he still would be a fool. But Barisdale maintained his bonnet.

He turned again to Ninian. "What are ye of?" said he.

"The Master," answered Ninian, "the sons of The Master; I thought I gave ye our name. And now, if I may ask, sir, what want ye in this room?"

"The Captain of a Watch has first command of every public room this side of Perth," said Barisdale; and stood upon his toes to make himself the bigger.

He cocked his bonnet more upon the side; and they could hear the women talking in the lobby. He "prutted" not so coarsely, laid a hand upon his pistol, swelled his chest, and tried to glower down Ninian.

But Ninian was not to be glowered down. "Man, I see ye!" cried he. "There's not so little of ye! Out ye go this room, or by the mass I'll spit ye!"

He beat Grey Colin's point upon the floor; he grew like sleet; a crinkle went across his face like curdling milk, and Barisdale drew back, put fingers in his mouth, and whistled.

In from the tavern front came his three sentinels and stood behind his back, and at the back of them the russet girl, barefooted. She pushed her way betwen them, stood upon the cold stone flagging of the floor, and turned on Barisdale.

"My loss!" says she, "that John Maclaren is not here to the fore, or ye would not dare, Barisdale, make strife with decent people sleeping in below his roof. I told ye they were gentlemen! There is a bed for ye upstairs."

He never let his eye rest on her, and his neck that lay in folds above the collar of his coat was purple.

"You have no right in this room, sir," said Ninian.

"Whether or not," said he, "I have the might, and Might is good enough to use till Right is ready," and he added something in the Latin. It was the Latin, which to Ninian meant nothing, and was like enough a taunt, that roused him most.

He turned in rage to Æneas. "What is he saying? What is he saying? You that kens, stand up and see me righted!"

"Oh yes, I ken," said Æneas quietly. "It's pitiful! But maybe that's the way they speak the Latin up in Knoydart-of-the-goats.

The line, most noble Captain, is so"—and he corrected Barisdale's citation. "With some pretence at scholarship it would become ye to keep mind of what is due to manners." He suddenly put up his hand and plucked the bonnet off the Captain's head and threw it on the floor. "Put your little feet in that," said he to the russet girl, "and keep them warm."

She did it, smiling on him, almost laughing. "Well done, lad!" cried Ninian, "Brother of my heart!" and Barisdale was, for the first time, sorely put about and humbled, for his head was bald!

At once the situation changed. "Pooh! Prutt! prutt!" said he, "we're in a stew about a trifle!" His speech was now entirely for Æneas, on whom he looked with something of respect. "I did not think I was disturbing folk who had the arts. Here in the hills it's seldom that we have the chance of meeting scholars like myself, and I'm vexed I claimed the right that lies with every Captain of a Watch."

"You're out of your country altogether," Ninian broke in. "Ye have no Watch rights that I ken of in Shire Argyll."

"Just that, good man! Just that!" said Barisdale. "It's true, it's not my quarter this, but I am here at present in connection with a tribe who are at mischief about Rannoch, and I'm acting for some gentlemen who pay me cess to watch their interests."

"I'm not under cess myself to you," said Ninian, "so what ye may be here on's none of my affair, and I'm a sleepy man. Good morning to ye!"

But nothing now could anger Barisdale; the russet girl was gone, he got his bonnet; sent his men away, and made, himself, to follow, but at the door he turned and said to Æneas, "Your friend is as cross as a thorn with me, I see, but he's a gallant fellow!"

"It is well known that I am," said Ninian, putting past Grey Colin.

"The women tell me you are on the road from Lorn to Appin," said the Captain. "You did not see two men in Lowland dress upon the way?"

"Plenty," broke in Ninian before Æneas could reply. "The country down-by is fairly hotching with them. The last we saw were two long-coated fellows fishing near the Bridge of Orchy."

Barisdale's eye lit up. "Just that!" said he. "I'm very keen to meet them," and all at once there was another kind of kindling in his manner as he looked at Æneas.

"By any chance," said he, "are you of the Macmasters of Drimdorran?"

"The last there was of them," said Æneas, "was my father," and had no sooner said it than he saw that Ninian was displeased.

"Put it there!" said Barisdale, and thrust his hand out. "I knew your father—peace be with him!—and he was a worthy man. Proud am I to see the son of Paul Macmaster! I met him only once—before he went abroad, when he was putting up with Lovat."

"He wasn't in the best of company when he was there," said Ninian, and Barisdale looked at him oddly.

"Indeed," said he, "he is a queer one, Simon, but there's maybe worse. Whatever o't Drimdorran was a bonny fencer; we had a bout of foils in Castle Dounie yonder, and he learned me one or two bit points, although his arm was in a sling.

"I'm thinking that was not Macmaster of Drimdorran, sir," said Ninian. "There's many of the name."

"Oh yes," said Barisdale, "it was himself, and you, sir, are his living image," and he shook the hand of Æneas again with warmth, picked up his candlestick and took his leave of them, as if his call had first and last been of the friendliest nature.

"The back of seven Saturdays to you!" said Ninian when the door was shut, and sat down upon a chest, his chin upon his hand, and fell in cogitation.

"If that," said Æneas, "is what the Road is going to put an end to in the North, good luck with it. The man is just a bully."

But not a word from Ninian, lost in contemplation.

Æneas began to strip again for bed and thereupon his friend awakened. "Wait a bit," said he. "We'll maybe need to take the road for't as we are. Without offence to you, you kind of put your foot in't when ye owned ye were of Drimdorran; up till then I think that Barisdale was off the scent of us; the clothes of John

Maclaren and the patness of the widow's tale about the nature of her lodgers did the trick. He couldna guess, ye see, that we were warned about his coming, and to get us in the short-clothes must have been a disappointment to him, if, as I'm inclined to think, he got the cut of us from yon one scudding through the Lairig Eilde. The fault's my own, perhaps; I should have picked some other name than yours, but how was I to guess that he had kent your father?"

"That seemed to make him rather friendly," said Æneas.

"Perhaps, so far as you're concerned," said Ninian, "but I'm afraid it may have made him dubious of myself; it's just a bit too close on Inveraray. I'm not so sure but now he kens he has his man. I wonder who's behind him? He daurna put his hand on me for anything that I ken of in name of law, but he might hang on to me and make my jaunt up to the North of little use, and I've a notion that is what he's after. I think ye'll see now that we're watched."

Again he stuck his chin upon his hand and fell to thinking.

"Tuts, man!" said Æneas, "don't let Barisdale bother ye; we'll surely manage to get quit of him in some way."

"That's not what bothers me at all," said Ninian, "although it's bad enough to have my passage hampered this way. I'm thinking about something else of more concern to you that wasna in my mind an hour ago. Later on I'll maybe tell ye what it is. And it makes me the more anxious to get up to Inverness with no delays."

"I know what you mean," said Æneas suddenly. "You're thinking of Drimdorran's snuffbox, and that they may be after me."

Ninian shrugged his shoulders. "It's not likely," said he, "that I would put off thinking that till this hour of the morning. Man! I thought of that whenever ye told me of the man upon the horse. I wouldna put it past Drimdorran in the key I left him in to put a hue and cry about the country for ye, but I threshed it out and saw he couldna guess that ye were coming this way. He's sure to know it now, but he has not had the time to stir up all Breadalbane since my man went back and told him, as I'm sure he did, about your dappled horse in Bridge of Orchy."

"It wouldna, think ye, be the money that I have about me?" said Æneas, with his hand upon his waist where it was hidden.

"I thought of that, man, too! I never travelled with such money in my life before, and it's a great confusion. I always think I hear it jingling. If you had been a fool and let some stranger know that you were travelling so rich I might have thought it risky, but I know it's not that: it's me they're after. My notion is to start upon the road again this moment if our friend will let us."

They could hear the Captain walking on the planching of the room above them; he had given a last look to his company and come in to bed.

But when they looked out through the shutter-hole they found his guards were on alert.

"It's what I feared," said Ninian. "Whether he knows or not, he's going to have us watched till daylight. We'll have to wait and see what happens in the morning."

IX

Barisdale's Mart

If Barisdale had any notion of the Messenger's identity he showed no indication of it at their common breakfast-board. The swaggering Captain was put off, and he was now the country gentleman, offering up a Latin grace before his viands. With Æneas he kept a blithe crack going upon books and travel, in both of which he had experience; to Ninian at times he threw a jovial Gaelic story. Their Lowland clothes were securely out of sight now; the women had disposed of them, and Æneas made no bad shape in John Maclaren's homespuns once Ninian had whipped his knees with nettles. Half the Watch at daybreak had gone off in pairs as if to reconnoitre round the country, but the other moiety remained about the inn with Barisdale, who gave no sign of an immediate departure. The morning seemed to take its key from little Etive plashing softly on the stones.

In all of Æneas' progress up till now, except among the corries, he had not, for very long at any time, been out of sight of human life or the things of human labour; the land was wild, but almost everywhere inhabited. In every glen that he had traversed there were huddled on the faces of the braes small hamlets thatched, from which gushed out a stream of bairns as he rode on, or single houses set apart in grassy bits between the rocks, themselves so green with moss they looked like fairy knolls, with smoke of fairy fires. Long strips of laboured soil ran up behind the clachans where were women singing as they wrought at oat and barley, and higher on the hills would men be herding cattle. It seemed to him he moved then through a land Sicilian, before the bards were vocal—wild Sicily of meal and honey, labour songs and unlocked doors.

But now that he could see whereto the last night's march had brought him, he was startled at the desolation of the scene. The inn stood on a desert edge; behind rose up the scowling mountains of Glen Coe, so high and steep that even heather failed them, and their gullies sent down streams of stones instead of foam. Eastward, where the inn-front looked, the moor stretched flat and naked as a Sound; three days' march from end to end they said were on it—all untracked and desert-melancholy. Its nearer parts were green with boggy grass, on which the cannoch tuft—the cotton-sedge—was strewn like flakes of snow; distantly its hue was sombre—grey like ashes, blackened here and there with holes of peat. The end of it was lost in mist from which there jutted, like a skerry of the sea, Schiehallion. God-forgotten, man-forsworn, wild Rannoch, with the birds above it screaming, was, to Æneas, the oddest thing, the eeriest in nature, he had ever seen. It charmed and it repelled him. He thought no wonder that the tribes who dwelt beside it should be wild, and envious of Lowland meadows. The very sight of it, so bleak and monstrous, filled even him with feelings of revolt against the snug and comfortable world.

Half a dozen times before the noon that day he walked up to the brae from which the moor was widest seen, and looked across it with uneasy breast, and drank, as one might say, the spirit of that wilderness, so strange and so forlorn. Once he ventured out a bit upon its surface, and he found an inland sea had likely once been there, and later, maybe, in the morn of time, a forest, for its old red fir-roots, like the ribs of cattle, stuck out from the slime of peat. One spot only—far off to the east, a silver glimmer plumed with woody little isles that seemed to float on air—relieved the dun perspective's desolation, and Ninian told him that it was Loch Ba, and gave it loud applause for fishing.

"I know every creek of that same loch," said he, "and every wee bit ealan on it. It is alive with fish, it is the nursery of Tummel and Tay,—it is the mother of floods; there is for me no fonder place in great Breadalbane, and many a day the ghost of me is standing there upon its shore, remembering, remembering!"

This was hours after it was plain that quitting the inn was not like to be so easy as coming to it. Ninian had slyly put it to the test, and blamed himself for one bad error he had made in giving even a fictitious hint to Barisdale of Appin as their destination. For Barisdale it seemed was going to Appin too, at least in that direction, and would be honoured by their company. Then Ninian declared he was not in a hurry to proceed, especially as the river seemed in ply for fishing after last night's storm. But Barisdale was in no hurry either; two of his men had spent the night in scouring through Strathfillan, and returned with tidings of a *creach* of cattle on the way from near Tyndrum; he only had to wait until the afternoon to have the rievers and their booty plump into his arms.

"That's the chance for us!" said Ninian to Æneas. "When Col is gathering in his winter mart from those poor lads, whoever they may be, who did the picking of it, we'll play the foot, my comrade, and go our ways. And, indeed, I'm just a little curious to see what way his lordship sets about his business of keeping law and honesty afloat; it's always something of an education just to see a rogue engaged."

Perhaps if Etive river had not been so close upon the door, the Messenger-at-Arms might earlier have slipped his tether. He spent the day fishing up and down the bank on which the inn was perched, and all the time, as he was well aware, with eyes upon him. Even Æneas could not take a step across the bridge but some one of the Watch was slouching after him. Barisdale would seem to have at least his doubts about them, and was determined not to let them out of sight. But ever he kept a bland and mannered attitude, and even joined them in a midday dram.

It was a singular situation—to be prisoners, as it were, and yet at large; to have no proof, indeed, that any obstacle was in the way of their departure, yet to see, in many things, a confirmation of their apprehensions. The three men sat together to a dinner of sheep's-head singed, and might, to any casual visitor upon the inn, have seemed upon the best of terms with one another, but no one came the way that day until the sun was filling up Glen Coe with evening fires.

It looked as if the folk on foray might have changed their route and cheated Col.

Ninian put up his rod at last and held communion with the women in their kitchen, to which he brought a decent string of fish.

"You're the best man ever put a switch upon that water in my time," said the goodwife with approval. "My man would aye be saying all the fish were down below Dalness, and there are you, good man, with plunder!"

"Half the fishing is to keep your hooks well wet," answered Ninian gaily; "and, indeed, the trout up here are dour and scanty. I was better on Loch Ba or Loch na Staing, if only my good friend that's out-by there would trust me on the heather," and he jerked a thumb across his shoulder.

"You should go away," said the russet girl hurriedly in a whisper. "No good in staying! I do not know what that one wants, but he is never here except for mischief. My mother got him in your room when you were out this morning."

Ninian went to the room at once, and came back to tell the girl that he and Æneas would leave that night.

"Ye needna mind about the door," said he; "keep it on the bar. I have a desperate fancy for a bonny little window yonder at the back, that looks upon the river."

"It's mine," said she.

"I knew it was a darling! Anyhow we must make use of it in case we spoil his lordship's sleep; the front is watched."

"And the back too," said the girl. "A man is on the bridge. He sat there all last night and blew his nose."

"I know," said Ninian. "That's the Knoydart way of singing to the girls; perhaps, like me, he had a fancy for your window. He has been planted there to watch the back as well as mind the bridge, but I will get him shifted some way at the time that suits us best. We'll drop from that bit window down upon the bank and then seek down the river. It wasna only fish I looked for all this day; I ken that burn now, even in the dark, a mile down, like a lighted street. If you will not be minding, we will keep these Gaelic clothes till we come back from—from where we're going. I have a great respect for breeches; there's pockets in them ye can put your hands in, out of mischief—different altogether from

91

the little kilt; but it's long-tailed coats and breeches, seemingly, the country's looking for, and we'll be less kenspeckle in the homespun. And now (said he) I'll pay the lawing."

The lassie flushed. "No, no," said she; "you were my father's friend. My father's friend, even if he had a dead man's head in his oxter, is welcome to his share of the night and shelter in this house at any time."

"Very good!" said Ninian, and snapped his sporran. "We'll look upon ourselves as in your reverence—at least till we come back, and that will make a pleasant journeying."

Outside there rose, as he was speaking, a commotion; the voice of Barisdale was heard in loud command above the eager chatter of his men, who gathered, at a whistle, from the brackens, where all day they seemed to snatch at sleep like foxes, storing up the night-time's power. They clustered for a moment round their captain on the road, and in another moment they were gone. They vanished. On the place a hush fell down.

"Mark fowl!" said Ninian, as Æneas came hurrying in. "There's something on the road, I'll wager!"

"Lowing cattle," answered Æneas. "They're coming round the turn, and the lads of Col are squatted in the fern."

"That's the spoil he's waiting for. Now we'll see what way he got such beef on him." He went and stuck his head out at the door, returned, and grimaced. "Two men on the bridge," said he, "and Col himself, full fig, even to the target on his back, is sitting on the dyke. It's what I thought—we'll have to make the night our friend. Come out and hear the parley, for the poor lads with the bestial will not can face a company."

The stolen cattle, to the number of a score, attended by a gang of fifteen rugged fellows, were quite close upon the inn when, from the ground, the Watch rose round them like a pen. A shot or two was fired; Col challenged, with his pistols flourished, and went strutting down beside the leader of the party.

"Good stuff!" said he, with a prod of his pistol barrel in a heifer's flanks. "Where now, if I may ask, have ye been lifting?"

"Glen Lyon," said the leader, "and it took us all our time; we left two pretty fellows yonder stretched." He was as black of visage as a whelk, a gaunt, small-hipped, tight-belted, desperate-looking man of middle age, without a coat, and like a wolf's for hair the chest of him seen through his open shirt.

"Who's folk are you?" asked Barisdale, and looked upon the man like dirt.

"God's own," replied the black one. "Too few of us here to prove it to you, but we're all well picked. My name's Macgregor," and Ninian, who, with his friend, stood by to hear the parley, looked on his namesake with compassion. His own folk he had seen in that same plight on many a time gone by.

"Stout man!" said he to Æneas, "he did not flinch to give his name! I wish he had a handful more of people with him; Barisdale will get his mart, this Michaelmas, too easy."

Too easily indeed; the Watch pushed back Macgregor and his men and drove the cattle to a little pasture by the riverside. In twenty minutes they had started filing horns to give the older beasts a look of youth.

"You see," said Ninian, jeering. "Col kens his trade; at heart the man's a Saxon drover. Not a word about the cattle going back to where they came from in Glen Lyon; he'll have them on the way to market somewhere in the morning. Glen Lyon is a place that pays no mail to him, I know, or he would take my namesake and his lads as prisoners. He's only anxious now to have them scatter I wonder where they came from?"

The rievers, spoiled in this way, in their turn, as they had spoiled Glen Lyon, hung about the inn. To Æneas the whole affair came as another revelation. Till now, the customs of the North, as he had heard of them, high-coloured with imagination, had appeared to have a kind of gallantry, and now the foray—most inspiring of them all, as having in it something of adventure and the risk of war—was shown as commonplace and mean. Macgregor and his men, outnumbered, seemed to take the situation almost meekly. For two days and a night they had not tasted food, they said, except one hurried meal for which they bled the cattle. In an onset with the sword, or seen, plaid-wrapped and singly on the hill, or peeping from the edge of some lone wood, they might have kept for him the spirit of his boyish fancy, but not as they were now.

Barisdale went down the waterside to see about the trimming of his booty, and Ninian took the chance to talk apart a little with Macgregor, who, he found, was on his way for Badenoch when this misfortune came to him. His men, he said, were *scalags*—landless folk of Cluny's country, and Barisdale he soundly cursed for robbing them of what had been a hard-won spoil.

"Ye're a bonny pair, as the crow said to his feet," cried Ninian. "But, man! I'm vexed for ye."

"Ye're not with him, then?" said Macgregor, looking first at him and then at Æneas curiously.

"I never saw the man between the eyes until he burst upon us here this morning on a search for a MacCailein man on his way from Inveraray."

"I heard of that one down at Bridge of Orchy," said Macgregor, with a shifty eye. "Some Big One—God knows who—has put the country up against him, and his name's my own—Macgregor—though he takes the Campbell like Rob Roy. I'm asking you, as of his race myself, and here in trouble, are you that very man?"

"You have me!" Ninian answered, and Æneas was astonished at his risking the confession. "I'm telling it to you because you are Macgregor like myself, and both of us a bit below the cloud. All the waters in the world will not wash out our kinship."

"Does Barisdale know ye?" asked the Gregorach.

"No," said Ninian, still more to Æneas' surprise. "But he is keener to keep me company than I am keen for his, and I doubt we'll have to flit for't early in the morning; we are going by Ben Alder. The trouble is to get a start without the long one knowing, and you're the very man to help me."

Thereupon he laid before the Gregorach a plan to stay about the neighbourhood till five o'clock the following morning. He and Æneas would then come out and join him and his fellows and go in their convoy as far as Badenoch, and he slipped a little money in Macgregor's hand.

X

The Wicked Bounds

"On foot!" said Ninian in the ear of Æneas, who stared from the bed he seemed that moment to have entered, and inquired the time.

"One o'clock," said Ninian, throwing on his kilt. "The bridge is clear."

"But we were not to start till five," said Æneas complainingly, and full of the dregs of sleep. "It was at five we were to join your namesake."

"Never you mind that! I'm done with him, and he can settle with his master. This is the hour for us, my hero; I have just been ben and warned the women."

They dressed in haste and darkness, and slung on the sacks without another word. No light was in the house, by Ninian's orders; even the women's chamber, opened to them by the russet girl, had not a blink in it except what came from the moon. A breeze of north-west wind was blowing through the ready open window; Etive splashed below.

"If luck is with us ye will hear us chapping at the door again before the badger's moon; I've left my fishing-rod," said Ninian to the girl whose mother lay in bed.

"Whist!" said she, "the man is sitting at the door; you cannot cross the bridge or he will see you. Here is a collop, cold, and oatcake, that will carry you to where there is another meal."

"That's my clever lass!" said Ninian, and put them in his knapsack. "We need not cross the bridge at all; our way is by the moor, we're going by Ben Alder."

"Success go with ye!" said the woman in the bed. "Ye have been welcome, gentlemen."

Ninian got through the window first and dropped upon the bank.

"Goodnight with thee!" said Æneas, and took the maiden's hand. Her hair was down in massy waves upon her shoulders; he could see the moon swim in her eyes.

"You are no man of your name," she said to him in English, where she had advantage of her mother. "My shame! that I should have to offer you my mouth!"

He gave to her a little squeeze, and kissed her softly; she was warm as milk.

"Ah!" she said, and shivered, "you will think me wild!" and she drew back. "But *coma leam!*—I do not care; look at this barren land about us and no gentle fellow to be kind! It was because I know you are in danger, and I'll maybe never see you more!"

He dropped upon the bank and sped with Ninian down the waterside without a word. The stolen cattle mourned among the grass where they were strangers; heavy dew was lying; far out on the moor the birds were still loud-crying; rose from off the banks the smell of mint. The house was out of sight when Ninian stopped at last and said, "We cross here; there's a shallow bit with sand, stick close to me," and waded over to the other side. The water took them to the knees, as cold as salted sleet.

"Surely, surely this is off our way!" said Æneas when they crossed.

"How's that?" asked Ninian.

"You said, this moment, to the girl, that we were going by the moor and by Ben Alder; that is to the east," and Ninian stopped and looked at him, astonished, with the full moon shining.

"My grief!" said he, "you are the simple one! It's me that wonders at you! Of course I said Ben Alder—the opposite of what I meant. If I was like yourself, Nathaniel, she would have had the truth from me and I would say Glen Roy, which is the place we're going to. Am I a fool to give my plans to women? Friendly folk, I'll not deny, the both of them, but only what a woman does not know she will not tell. That girl all day will have her eye upon the moor because ye kissed her and she thinks ye're somewhere there—"

"Kissed her!" Æneas cried; "what put the notion in your

96

head?"

"If ye didn't ye were daft! Just think of it!—Ye'll maybe never see the lass again! And I to give her such a moving tale of ye—the homeless wanderer and the foe behind! How better could I get a young one's favour for us? Whatever o't, she'll have an eye upon the moor in spite of her, and that will send his lordship with the feathers on a scent I wish him joy of. Better there than pelting up behind us."

"You told Macgregor, too—"

"Oh Lord!" cried Ninian, with a sudden stop, and shrugged himself, then started off again. "Come on! We have to climb the Devil's Staircase, and it's I, it's plain, have many a thing to think of for the pair of us."

Whatever were his thoughts, he kept them to himself and led the way across the rushes and the gale, high-stepping, for two miles. Within the portals of Glen Coe they came upon a track that climbed up steeply to the right, until the glen, all washed with yellow moonshine, could be seen far down below. They crushed the garlic in their stepping till the morning smelled of it; they heard the moorhen hoarsely croak. Hinds of the mountain, brave princesses, stood in troops and stared at them; the proud buck stamped, threw out his breast, and trotted softly to the mist. It was the Sabbath morn, the beasts were unaffrighted. "Go-back!-go-back!-go-back!" the cock-grouse cried that led the covey from their feet.

When dawn came they were on the topmost traverse of the steep, and saw it pale a mountain Ninian called Ben Bhreac. Below them, they could hear the waves plash on Lochleven.

"There," said Ninian, and pointed to the north, "is the start of what my father—peace be with him!—used to call the Wicked Bounds, where every man you'll meet has got a history, and a dagger in below his coat—Camerons, Clan Ranald's men, Clan Chattan, and the Frasers—it stretches to the Firth of Inverness for sixty miles the way a kite would fly."

The break of day was spreading fast. The mist, like sapple of the sea, was lying in the gullies of the hills that lifted up their heads above the night like to a herd of seals. To Æneas it looked a dreadful place, all heaved together in confusion. The mounts of it were giants.

"In fortune's name!" he cried, "are you acquainted with the tracks of it? It looks to me as if a man might go astray there till he died of age!"

"Not him!" said Ninian lightly, shrugging up his poke, and leading down the mountain-side. "And if he did, what odds?— the whole of us are only straying through the world at best of it. Be glad of it that we are men, and not the wild geese of the sky that know not whither. Ye may be sure that I'll not wander ye! But mind ye'll not get through it easy! If I were a frightened sheep, and put about too much concerning them that's after us, I would be making for the fort at Inverlochy where there's sodgers. But that would poorly serve my turn; no, lad, we'll keep the way we're on and make for Corryarrick."

The sun was high before they rested by a loch in what to Ninian was known as Mamore Forest, where the deer were belling in their season. There was no habitation to the view nor wood at first for kindling, but they fared like hunters, even to a fire, for Ninian got roots of candle-fir upon the water's edge, and slit them with his knife, and made a fire that warmed the widow's collop. Heather-tops he gathered and white hay, and made a couch for them they lay in sleeping till the afternoon. When they awoke it was with hunger. Not a thing was there to eat in Mamore Forest, and they walked for hours until at dark they stood beside the tumbling water of the Spean, where was one dwelling, stark alone, that had in it the clack of someone weaving. Ninian went to the door himself, and Æneas sat waiting for him by the river. The other came back in a little, hasty, with some barley-bread and a side of kippered salmon.

"I thought," said he, "of putting past the night here, but we'll have to spend it better getting on our way. This cursed country—and a plague on't!—'s roaring with the name of Ninian Campbell!"

"What is it now?" asked Æneas, and Ninian was hurrying them away while yet they ate their bread and fish.

"I went in there and I found a hag of a woman not joyous to

look on, weaving cloth. 'It's an hour ago,' said she, 'since men were here and asking for you. Your name is Ninian Campbell.' 'How ken ye that, just woman?' I inquired, astonished. 'Fine that!' croaked she; 'ye have the very poke upon the back of ye!' 'What poke?' said I, and she was busy spreading butter on the bread. 'The poke,' said she, 'ye plundered from the man ye slew beside Ben Alder. God's pity on ye, stranger, for to kill a man for that! They're waiting for ye on the road between here and Fort William.' "

"The thing's beyond belief!" cried Æneas, and Ninian was stretching out, up-water, till the sparks flew from his heels. "Who could have set about so wild a story?"

"Who could set about that story but the devil's son, himself?" cried Ninian in a fury. "Black death be on the brute! It's Barisdale! I sent him yonder chasing the cuckoo about Ben Alder side, but he has been too slippy for me; when he found the birds were not in that direction he made up his mind, and pretty cleverly, that we were maybe for Fort William."

"But the story of the murdered man—"

"Any story's good enough for Col to rouse the countryside against us. I wish to God I knew whose pay he's in in this affair."

"He must be well paid indeed, to leave his *creach* of stolen cows to come so hard in chase of us," said Æneas.

"You may be sure the cattle will be well looked after by my friend the hairy one, who picked them up to start with in Glen Lyon."

"Macgregor?" Æneas said, not understanding.

"No more Macgregor than yourself!" cried Ninian with disgust. "I could have laughed to end myself to see ye taken in with such a story. I thought by this time ye could put a thing or two together. Yon was a man of Col's—his own lieutenant. I ken the way Col lifts his mart now; he puts on a band of nameless men to do the stealing and comes up behind to take their plunder in the name of law. A bonny Watch! The devil's but a boy compared to him! If yon had been a decent band of any worthy name it would not be so meekly they gave up their prize."

"I was quite misled!" said Æneas, ashamed. "But what did ye

engage the black fellow for with all your story about five o'clock and going by Ben Alder? And ye told him who ye were: I thought myself, that very queer of you."

"I told him that," said Ninian, "to get the bridge clear of the fellow with the nose. When Col heard from my friend his rogue that we were safe till five o'clock he took away that sentry. Of course my friend went to his master, straight, and told him what we planned and who we were,—a thing his lordship knew quite well already."

"You weren't sure of that."

"As sure as that I walked on leather! The woman told me he had looked our knapsacks, and at first I thought there was no harm in that, but then I minded something—he would see my father's name upon the Book! There's noble reading in the Bible for our good, and many a turn I take at it when I have time, but Col, I'll wager, didna bother much with that; he found the name of John Macgregor there. But I wasna vexed; my knowing that he kent me gave me an advantage."

The land by now had donned the mantle of the night and buttoned it with stars. They sat, two hours, upon a stone when they had walked a mile or two, and there deliberated upon the situation. Glen Roy, that Ninian had thought to take through Keppoch's country, was now out of the question; Barisdale was pack with Keppoch's folk, and could depend on help from them in any hunt that had a Campbell for its quarry. To stop Glen Roy as well as scour the country to Fort William was sure to be his policy. From Corryarrick they were only some twelve miles of distance, but that meant across the hills, and in the dark it was not to be ventured. They fixed upon a longer route that followed up the Spean and skirted to the westward of Loch Laggan. Loch Laggan head was close upon the finished Road, although it was as far from Corryarrick as they were that moment. Once upon the Road, though, they were in a climate safer than the hills; all traffic of the soldiers working at its end went over it, and honest men were surely free from molestation.

This latter was the argument of Æneas, who felt he could not have his feet too soon upon a highway.

100

"I'm not so sure of that," said Ninian, however. "All this trouble since we left the Orchy is to keep me off the Road, and I've a notion that there's something special brewing there. You may be sure the Road itself is watched; we darena venture on't until we join the sodgers."

On Æneas had weariness come with an ache for every limb, and he was all for sleeping for a while upon the heather, but his friend said no; the night was made for them; although the moon was not yet up they had the light and guidance of the stars; it was about the hour of ten; the Plough was lying upside down upon the hills.

At midnight they were halfway up Loch Laggan-side, from which their track was sundered by a clump of firs, and Æneas was walking half asleep, when all at once they came upon a score of houses on a level at the foot of woody crags, and every one of them was lighted. The smell of burning peats was strong, and also something like the smell of melting rosen, but stronger was the smell of roasting meat, and Ninian was the first to speak of looking for a bed and supper.

The houses with stone-anchored thatch on them were laid in rows, with dungsteads piled before them and black stacks of peat; a score of dogs began to bark, and down upon the place the yellow moon of Michaelmas was glaring. Out the folk came rushing to their doors, and all of them were women. Not a man was to be seen!

"We've come on a night of *ceilidh* and the men from home," said Ninian. "Take the nearest door and in before they gather round."

A woman very dun of visage, and a bunch of children stretched across a bed, were in the house they stopped at, and by luck, or else by Ninian's judgment, they had got the very house where meat was cooking on a brander.

"In the name of the Good Being, what is't?" the woman cried, as Ninian and his friend stepped in and hailed her stately. She stood upon the floor in great alarm, and what was she engaged upon but dipping flambeaux in a pot of rosen?

"Will't give us leave to sit beside the fire till morning?"

Ninian asked. "For we have come a distance; in the dark we cannot make our way."

She was, as well as dun, a *biorach*, sharp-nosed woman, plainly mother of the flock stretched on the bed; the softness of his speech apparently assured her, but she lifted up a cruse that, hooked upon a cabar, lit the house, and coming up to him she held it close beside his breast.

"What clan art thou?" she asked, her eyes upon his clothing: it was not of tartan but a hodden brown.

"What clan," said he, "but of Clan Alpine, children of the mist and sorrow?" and to her face there came a yearning.

"Sit down," she said, at that. "My mother was Macgregor. Ye will at least get supper and a warming."

She gave them water, warmed, to bathe their feet, and brandered venison, and all the time the bairns stretched on the bed keeked from their bolster at the strangers. Druimbeg, she said to Æneas, was the township's name, and all the tenants were Macdonalds. About her guests she never asked a question.

"And where, goodwife, if I might ask, are all the lads?" said Ninian; and thereupon, in spite of her, she showed confusion, hinting at a small black pot they were engaged with on the hill. "It will be as well," she said, "if ye were not about on their returning," and she gave them both a dram of spirits, rank and reeked beyond description. But as for stopping for the night below her roof, she plainly made it out impossible.

"A shed itself would serve," said Æneas. "Any place at all to pass the night in."

"I know of no place, honest men; my shame to say it, and my melting!" she exclaimed with agitation.

They gave her thanks, and Æneas, with a joke, slipped in a coin below the children's bolster; then out he followed Ninian. The door was barred behind them instantly.

"That looks mighty droll," said Ninian—"barring up a door, and not a living soul between her and the Sound of Sleat but honest Gaelic people!"

And then they found that every glimmer in Druimbeg was out

and every door was barred. They rapped at two or three without
an answer.

XI

Æneas-Of-The-Pistol

The noble moon that ripes the corn was skulking in black clouds. A wind that seemed to sweep from every quarter, seeking harbours, as the saying goes, was whistling round the peats, and it was grown exceeding cold. Ninian led the way across the dung of fifty cattle, skirted through the weeds that bordered some tilled fields, went through a sandy patch encumbered with thick whins in which they got entangled, making for the clump of firs that they had noticed earlier, where they counted on a sleep within its umbrage. Owls were mourning there; it was the water's-edge of Laggan, and the waves were plashing on its fringe. The night seemed given up to all the ancient things. Never a word was passed between them till they reached the planting and got in upon its dust, and there, as they were standing in the dark, the muttering of the wood about them, Ninian smelled crumbled lime. "There's more than fir-trees here!" said he, and pushing farther in, they came with great surprise upon a building. What its nature was they could not solve; four-square it stood among the trees, too big for a domestic dwelling, still in human use, for glass was in its windows, and it had a door, but something in its spirit, cold and bleak, proclaimed it not a place acquaint with fires.

Twice they went about it in the darkness that was here intense, but could make nothing of it; then they found the door of it was only on an outer bar; Æneas, who came upon it, drew it back and gave them entrance to what seemed one single big apartment, like a barn, but floored with flags and smelling rank of grease. He would have struck a light, but Ninian forbade it, apprehensive that a glint of it might penetrate the wood and bring upon them some intruder. They stumbled round a while, and felt at walls unplastered, woodwork like to folded trestles

104

heaped up in the middle of the floor, some benches, and a crock of tallow. At one end was what seemed to feeling like a massive table with a great flat stone upon it.

Æneas, groping for some other clue to what the place was meant for, came at last upon a heap of hides, and had no sooner found them than he gave a cry.

"What now?" said Ninian eagerly.

"What do you make of this?" said Æneas, pulling at the skins. "Muskets! Here they are in scores, and smeared with tallow."

"My God, but we are in the kittle country!" said Ninian, with amazement, handling the guns that had been hidden in below the hides—in scores, as Æneas said. "I wouldna miss this night for any money! There's not supposed to be a gun in Badenoch since the Act was passed disarming Donald, but here they are in heaps like paling-stobs! I knew it! Fine I knew it! 'Only a weapon here and there among the thatch,' says Islay, but he doesna know the devils!"

Æneas was fumbling at the muskets. "Not much use in them," said he, "for half the cocks of them are broken. By the locks and length of them I take it they are Dutch."

"Good lad!" said Ninian, with surprise. "You have some observation, I will give you credit. We'll get on with one another nobly. Dutch they are, man!—ay, but here's a Spanish fellow; now what in all the world would they be doing here?"

"You told me there was smuggling of arms yourself," his friend reminded him; "the thing might mean another Rising."

"Tach!" cried Ninian disdainfully. "Wi' trash like this ye wouldna burn to boil a pot wi'! Na! na! they're never meant for serious business. But what's the reason of them being stored so snug and greased? . . . Oh man alive! I see it!" and he laughed until the roof was dirling.

But what it was he saw he would not tell; it was, he said, a drollery that would improve by keeping till they reached a barrack. "And then," said he to Æneas, "you'll laugh at the confusion that I'll put them in. I wish my father was alive this night to see this ploy with me, and what a lot of clever lads they are in Badenoch!"

They stretched themselves upon the hides; Æneas at least dog-wearied to the bone, and he was sound asleep when Ninian, twenty minutes later, jumped upon his feet on hearing somewhere on the confines of the wood the voice of women. He did not rouse his friend, but went out through the trees, and from the border of them witnessed what disclosed the reason for the dun wife's hurry to be quit of them.

Making through the whins that he and Æneas had tangled in, were close on thirty men well geared for fighting, in the middle of them four who carried upon spokes what first he took to be a coffin. They passed so close where he was standing in the timber he could see their very buttons, for although the moon was still in hiding, they were lit up in their going through the whins by flambeaux, two or three of which had been brought out to guide them by their wives. If spoil had been their object, none of it was with them, save perhaps the box, which Ninian now perceived was not a coffin but a chest well clamped with brass. A chest like that, thought he, was never built beside Loch Laggan.

When they had passed, he sought the hides again alongside Æneas, still asleep, and slept, himself, until above him clanged, tremendously, a bell!

At first he could not trust his ears; the sound came from the roof, outside, fantastic, like a belling in a dream, and only for a moment. Its echo died away upon the hills surrounding. Opening his eyes, he found white day was at the windows and Æneas, dumfounded, standing with a rope held in his hands.

"*Mo chreach!*" cried Ninian, jumping to his feet, "ye've done it now!"

"We're in a church!" said Æneas, bewildered.

"In faith we are! I might have kent it by the cheeping of your boots last night; ye sounded dreadful like an elder. And what is more, I ken the kind of kirk it is—it's one of the sly old chapels of that heather priest, Big John of Badenoch. And now, my grief! that ye have ca'd the bell, we're like to have a congregation."

"How was I to guess a bell was at the end of this accursed rope? I saw it there, and tugged it without thinking. What a

106

chapel!" Æneas looked round it with disgust.

"Good enough for keeping guns! Ye'll mind we're in among a lot of heathens, no' right sure yet whether they are Protestant or Papist till the chief of them comes round to tell them wi' a yellow stick. It's clear a Mass has not been said in it this Sunday, but now that ye have clinked I hope ye have your sermon ready. There's not a wakened body in Druimbeg that's not already putting on his hose for chapel. On the cheeping boots of ye!— we'll better jump!"

He turned, so saying, for the open air, slinging on his knapsack as he went, and Æneas soon after him, and through the wood they scurried to the waterside. They had not run for fifty yards along the shore, secure of observation from whatever hamlet folk the luckless ringing of the bell brought out on them, when in a little creek of shingle, very rough, they came upon a boat upturned with oars below her.

Loch Laggan here was narrow—little more than half a mile across; if they were on the other side they still were on their way to Corryarrick. So far as they could see, no other boat was visible than this which they threw over on her keel. Although a coble only, she was heavy as a barge, and took them long to launch, and then they found she had no tholpins.

Up the shore and to the wood ran Ninian with his small black knife to cut him pins, and he was gone some minutes out of sight behind a patch of hazel when his voice came to his friend.

"Stir ye, Æneas, or Ninian is done for!"

Four men, and two of them with guns, had burst out from the firs, and now came down upon the Messenger. The leader was a fellow clad in skins, and had an eye as clear and fiery as a cairngorm stone; his weapon was a *tuagh*, or halberd of Lochaber, and he looked like mischief.

"*Stad! stad!*" he bellowed. "Thou that got my supper, stop and get thy breakfast!"

Ninian, breast-high in the hazel brushwood, with the tholpins cut, his knife still in his hand, backed out and cleared Grey Colin. It was then he gave the cry that summoned Æneas.

They crowded down upon him cautiously as he fell back

107

along a kind of passage to the shore; close up on either hand of him the thicket screened his flanks, and so he had them all before him, hampered in the space so much they could not come at him but singly. He that had the axe was first to close upon him as he crept back, crouching from the houghs, Grey Colin glinting, and the knife along his other wrist. A shape more wicked, wildcat-like and venomous, was never seen at bay in brake or timber; the very teeth of him were bared; he gave a shout—"*Ardcoille!*"—ferociously, so loud the wood rang with it; the cry came to him without thinking from Balwhidder graves: he had not used, he had not heard, the slogan of Macgregor since he was a boy.

"Here for you, Gregorach!" said the man in skins, and swung his halberd high above his head.

Ninian, from his crouch, sprang in upon him like a salmon at a fall, and with the black knife stabbed him under the uplifted arm. "*Sin agad!*" said he: "there's for you!" and with his claymore head he smote him on the forehead. The man fell like an ox and grovelled. "Pick up thy dirt!" said Ninian to the rest, and turned about and ran.

The three were hard upon him when he reached the cove, and faced them for the second time with Æneas beside him. "My lad, ye'll not forget this day, whatever o't!" said Ninian, flourishing his sword, and Æneas had the small Doune pistol of his uncle ready in his hand. As he was standing on the shingle there at Ninian's shoulder, he was put about so much he dared not part his jaws a hair's-breadth lest his teeth should chatter.

A speckled man in trews, his white face patched with brown spots like the back of ferns, was first to make at Ninian. He had a sword ground almost to the thinness of a spit, light as a feather, and he walked on *courains*—slippers made of hide with hair outside of them, lashed on his feet with thongs. Of Ninian he had a head's advantage in the height and twenty years of youth.

"Black water on ye!" he cried out, and lunged.

Æneas for the first time cocked his pistol.

"No, no!" said Ninian to him quickly, falling back a bit and parrying, "leave it between us and the swords! Ye better mind the guns." His eyes were piercing on the speckled man's; he said no word, but like a strapper grooming horses hissed between his teeth and briskly plied his sword. He beat upon the other's weapon—ventured once or twice a thrust—broke ground.

At that the other screamed some taunt, mistaken of the movement, and came at him with his weapon back to cut. Grey Colin flashed and got him on the shoulder; he went down upon his knees and fell to crying loudly on the Virgin Mary, but the spit still in his grasp.

Ninian swithered, looking at him for a moment as he cried and with his bonnet dabbed upon his neck to stanch the blood, then turned to find a musket levelled at himself. It never fired. The small Doune pistol gave a crack, the man who held the musket fell grotesquely like a string of fish, and Æneas stood unbelieving that the crooking of a finger held such dreadful chance. He looked about him like a man come from a swound— at Ninian with his sword advancing on a lad who dashed into the wood, and at the others stricken. A bird cried out, "*Bi glic! Bi glic!* Be wise! be wise!" and flew across the creek.

"Better a good retreat than a bad stand!" said Ninian, panting; "you in the beak of the boat and me behind and pull like fury!"

They pushed the boat off, wading to the knees before they had her floating, boarded her and started rowing wildly. A very bedlam of distracted folk broke loose was coming through the wood with hunting cries.

"Can ye make any shape at the swimming?" Ninian asked across his shoulder as they tugged the oars.

"A bit," said Æneas.

"Good luck to ye! Ye'll maybe need it. Here's this bitch of a boat, and she's geyzing like a boyne. I doubt she'll not can stay afloat till we reach the other side."

So keen had Æneas been glowering back in a dreadful fascination at the crumpled figure of the man he shot, he had not noticed that the coble leaked; at Ninian's words he realised the water was above his ankles, and was gushing 'twixt the planks in half a dozen seams.

"We'll manage it!" said he, "I think we'll manage it!" but

doubted it within his soul. The wind was lifting up the waves white crested, the freeboard of the boat already looked appalling low, she moved but sluggishly.

At last a score of men broke through the planting, and ran down into the creek where lay their friends. "Easy all and jouk!" said Ninian quickly. "Grey lead's flying!"

He and Æneas ducked; some bullets whistled past; again they started rowing.

Twice again the grey lead flew, but wider of them.

"Not a gun in Badenoch!" quo' Ninian mockingly. "This, if I were spared, would make a pretty tale for Islay!"

The loch was in the boat and almost to their knees before they reached the opening of a burn, screened from the other side by sauch-trees growing on a spit of sand bent round the outlet like a shearing-hook. Out they jumped before the boat was grounded; Ninian threw the oars out in the current of the burn and thrust the boat herself out after. About them, all Loch Laggan-side was clothed in birch and hazel, wind was humming in the leafage and the boughs were waving; never was a bit of country bonnier, a morning air more sweet and peaceful.

But from the shore that they had fled from came a sound that filled the hearers with dismay—the cries of keening women. At that wild corranach the heart of Æneas filled with horror at his share of what had caused the lamentation; down he clapped upon a stone among the willows, with his head bent in his hands.

"Oh, Ninian!" said he, and rocked himself in anguish, "did I kill him? Did I kill him?"

"Devil the doubt! I knew the way he dropt he was as dead's a herring. And now ye are a man—full-grown, ye have been blooded. I'm proud of ye, Macmaster; stand you up!"

He drew Grey Colin with a flourish from the scabbard, and the clotted blood of him that he had struck was on it: with a Gaelic utterance he laid it lightly on the young man's head.

The flesh of Æneas grewed; he retched at such an accolade.

"What, man! are ye sick?" asked Ninian.

"Yes!" said he, "I'm sick!" and broke into a furious condemnation of this wretched country.

"What in Heaven's name did ye expect?" asked Ninian. "Dancing?"

"Everything's destroyed for me!" cried out the lad. "The stories have been lies, and we have aye been beasts, and cloak it up in poetry."

"We are what God has made us!" said his friend. "And we must make the best of it. All this belly-ache and bocking over one or two Macdonald thieves the world were happy rid of! *Mo naire* on ye, Macmaster! If I had not your father's Virgin nut upon me, it is you and I would have been yonder stretched. Stick your head and hands into the burn, and that will make ye better."

Æneas bathed as he was told, and rose from that lustration somewhat comforted to find the other with his shagreen case of razors out and started shaving.

"Were ye frightened yonder?" Æneas asked him.

"Not one bit!" said he.

"It's more than I could say! I was in terror!"

Ninian gave an oath and turned on him. "Let that not out of your mouth," he cried with spluttering passion. "A bonny-like thing it would be if we went bleating every time we were in fear. What better than the beasts ye speak about were we unless we hid our trembling from each other?"

"Ah yes!" said Æneas, "but you were yonder glowing like a flame; with you there was no flinching, and with me my very blood was ice."

"Was I?" cried his friend in Gaelic, with his face convulsed. "I was just yonder like thyself, and every drop of me was frightened for the death. Not till I took Ninian Campbell's body with my father's hands could I command the coward. 'Stand fast, thou, craven, there!' I said to him, 'for there is worse to come!' "

The face of Ninian lightened. "Was that the way of it with you?" he asked, quite understanding.

"Never ask me yon again if I was frightened! God help us if we were not better than our bodies' inclinations! Do you know the reason for my asking you if you could swim? Do you know the way your father died?"

"It would be strange if I did not know that," said Æneas. "He perished at Glenshiel."

"He did not! Not one bit of him!" said Ninian. "He died, poor man, by drowning, and he's in the deep. We always give to him the honour of Glenshiel, a battlefield, but, still-and-on, although he fought, he never fell there. When his side was scattered he and other two made over country for Loch Duich where there was a brig in waiting. They launched a coble, just the way we did ourselves there, and were scarce a cable-tow from shore when down upon them came the redcoats firing. The boat was swamped. . . . Near a month was passed before the story came to Inveraray wi' some straggling men of Glendaruel's. That's what I was thinking of when you and me were rowing; seldom will a thing be happening in a family once but it will happen twice, and if you couldna swim I would have given you the Virgin nut of Barra. Myself, I canna swim a stroke! . . . And now," said he, and put his razor back into the wallet, "I'm feeling fine; come on again the gallant pair of us. The splendid name I'll have for you in Scotland after this is Æneas-of-the-Pistol!"

And still, when they had walked a mile or two there came upon this valiant gentleman a mood as gloomy as his friend's. Now that the heat of war was out of him their skirmish took a different aspect. The people of Druimbeg, he said to Æneas, would learn, even if they did not know already, who had brought them such disaster; he dare not set a foot in Badenoch again, and that was awkward for his business. There even was a chance of some inquiry by the law—a power he feared the more because he was its nominal officer, and that at least would bring the fact of Æneas being in his company before the world, and raise some ugly questions with Drimdorran.

"The truth of it," he said at last, "is, we have made a perfect bauchle of the business going near Druimbeg at all and sleeping yonder. What day is this?—St Michael's. I'll never go to kirk again on Michaelmas."

112

XII

Corryarrick Pass

In a nook of the mountains where a loop of Spey and two deep
tributary burns served both to drain and to defend the situation,
if defence were called for, there was pitched the wooden camp
of Leggatt's men. It occupied about an acre of rough moorland
grass, bog-myrtle, yarrow herb, and heather; the huts were laid
out in a square upon a gentle slope; behind them lined some tents
with ditches for the rains. A bleaker prospect than was seen from
Leggatt's camp was difficult to fancy; save that the innumerable
streams, loud-bickering down the hillsides to the valley, took in
pools the colour of the sky or glitter of the sun, the landscape had
one universal hue of dull grey-green and purple, wearisome
beyond endurance sometimes to the eye of Wade's subaltern.
Not the colours only, but the dull monotony of shapes, afflicted
Leggatt and his lowland comrades; they were sick for trees, and
here not even a middling bush was visible: months had lapsed
since they had seen a mortared house or garden; every day they
rose to work at bugle-call they cursed that barren tableland on
which they were sequestered, prisoned in by gloomy mountain
walls.

Two hundred men were under Leggatt—redcoats mainly
from the Great Glen forts, a squad or two of tradesmen privates
picked from the blockhouse garrisons set here and there about
the country, and a score or more of native soldiers, wearing
tartan, from the Highland Companies. Three years had Leggatt
worked upon the Road on this particular section that started
from the gusset at Dalwhinnie; he had the brevet rank of
Captain, and was known among his men as Captain Trim, so
keen was his insistence on exact particulars and neatness in the
finish. He never added on a chain of road to what was made of
it already, till, like one that makes a song, he had gone back upon

113

the parts accomplished, seeking for fresh heart, and to maintain the key and harmony. Thirty miles a day, on horse or foot, he covered of the Road. Red, level, sixteen feet to twenty wide, and thrown across the country like a string, ascending lesser hills and sinking into hollows, floated on morasses over brushwood, or built up on them with timbers and fascines, it seemed (so far as it was made) to hurry to the North, impatient to be there, defying nature's quirks to lure it into roving. And yet, of all the men who built it, few looked on it otherwise than as a road worth going on but one way—that was to the end that lay far off in Stirling and the towns. Here, at the foot of Corryarrick Pass, this notion of it only as a road for home was maybe natural; high up in mist above the camp of Leggatt it came to a sudden end. Five-and-twenty hundred feet above the sea it tacked in eighteen sharply-angled steep traverses buttressed up with walls, and seemed, as Leggatt's humour put it, sorry to have climbed so high and with such labour just to find it must go down again.

Seven miles were yet to cut and build to Fort Augustus, and Leggatt hounded on his soldiery as if they had been slaves of Carolina. As yet the winds of autumn breathed, the floods had not begun, but days were shortening, and he meant to have the Pass accomplished ere the winter burst upon the land and took possession till the spring. His soldiers' sixpence extra pay each day was earned in sweat. The mattock and the spade were in their hands at daybreak; often through the night they wrought prodigiously by torchlight or the flare of brushwood fires, stemming the course of newborn torrents from the hills, strengthening the bridges, shattering or burying enormous boulders, patching up the damage done at times by natives, who, since the Road had come across Dalwhinnie, loathed it like a pest. Leggatt's section was the roadman's hell; each spring he had deserters to the numbers of a score; the half of them were Highlanders, the other half he feared were under Highland influence. In all the three years he had worked upon the Road as man of Wade's he had not seen a native walk on it a furlong, parallel beside it there were beaten down already, by the clansmen and the clansmen's cattle, trails that both preferred as easier for the feet. Often with amazement would he watch men plunging to the knees at icy fords below the very shadow of the bridges they looked on askance as meant for Sassenachs and women. But even their women waded.

Doubtless what affected them in some degree was a foreboding of the part the Road would play in times of trouble with the Gall. They saw it used continually, so far as it was finished, by the redcoats and the Watches; standing, wrapped, themselves, in plaids, on thicket verges or the slopes of hills in mist, like figures of some other clime and age, they watched, with gloomy brows, dragoons pass cantering, four abreast, or companies of footmen out of Ruthven Castle. Sometimes on it could be heard the roll of drums; up Blair of Athole once had come a house on wheels, glass-windowed, horses dragging it, a gentleman within it smoking, and a bigger gentleman they touched their caps to, driving. Never a day went past but someone could be seen upon the street (as Gaelic had it); here, in Badenoch, the world seemed coming to an end.

The night that followed Michaelmas was drawing in with something of a threat of rain in it. Low on the hills all day had mist gone trailing; westward were there black clouds gathering, and the wind was gone. In Leggatt's camp prevailed a Sabbath hush; upon the making Road the pick and spade lay idle; out of doors no living creature moved. It looked a place surrendered back to nature, man-abandoned. Since noon all work had been suspended, and the men were in their huts asleep; all night before they had been searching through the hills for robbers.

And now, as fell the night, came Leggatt—bearded like a Frenchman, with a coat bemired, and red soil to the knees, upon a horse: he had been on the hunt himself since early in the afternoon; had lurked in brake and spied from hilltops everywhere about the habitable country, but with no success. As he came into camp, and found it thus submitted to a kind of peace he grudged even on the Sabbath, he was filled with indignation. With him the Road itself was now become a boast although he loathed the country; every furlong added to its length appeared to him a personal triumph, every idle hour a crime. The half-a-crown a day he got of extra wages scarcely served to pay the added cost of rations brought laboriously by pack-horse once a month from Perth, but vanity got ampler pay in Wade's approval and a sense of pride in being instrument of that red hack cross the country. Every second Tuesday of the month the Marshal would appear upon his sheltie, with a staff about him soft and red and puffed with too fat life and too much drinking in some Lowland barrack; then it was that Leggatt, tanned and lean and dirty, had a task to keep his vanity in check when he displayed his latest victory over natural obstacle, streams vanquished, heights subdued.

No word would Wade say, but a clap upon the back for Captain Trim—that clap was the best of Leggatt's pay. He knew that he was beating old Macgillivray, who had the branch of Road across the Monadh Liath, and had not put a mile to it since June.

This night, then, he was vexed to find the work at pause, although there was excuse for it: he had not changed his boots or tasted supper when the bugle cried across the wooden village.

"Turn out!" he told the sergeants. "There's a day been lost! Rain will be on by morning, and that trenching must be finished now. Let them have the fires."

When he came out again from that rough shed that was his dwelling, pitched a bit apart from all the rest, a crimson pennon constant flapping on its roof, big fires of whin and heather, gathered on good days and stacked, were burning at the foot of Corryarrick Pass, and every soldier plied a tool. The scene looked scarcely human. Spread out half a mile along the red gash through the heath were vague forms moving in the crackling fire light, as in labours, and in tortures of perdition; iron clattered, block and tackle creaked, and through the night rose strange and melancholy cries.

He stayed but long enough to satisfy himself the work went on; conveyed some orders to the foremen, and went back to where the camp lay dark completely save for that one light that was his own.

He reached the hut and opened it; two native iron lamps with

116

wicks of rush were burning; pinned out on his table were some engineering plans. The place was starkly furnished, like a shipper's box, except that in it was a soldier's mattress. A soldier-servant at the moment when his master entered was engaged in turning down the bedclothes for the night.

"Waken me at four," said Leggatt, throwing off his great-coat; "that's to say, unless Maclean comes back with any news that's worth my rousing."

The man went out.

A little while—it scarce was quarter of an hour—did Leggatt with a compass work upon his plans, and then prepared for sleep. He sat upon a stool and bent to loose his boots; when suddenly, without a footstep to account for it, he heard a gentle tap upon his door.

"Come in!" he cried, and started to his feet at sight of two men clad in kilts and strange to him. His solitary situation flashed on him; he was the only man in camp except his orderly across the square. And one at least of these two men was armed; a hilt was at his hip. Instinctively did Leggatt give a glance behind him to a corner where his sword was hanging.

"No occasion! None whatever," said the elder of the two men quickly.

"You know it is forbidden to have arms about you in this country. Who are you?" said Leggatt.

"A poor place for the girls, I'm thinking!" was the answer. He dived a hand into his sporran and took out a paper which he passed to Leggatt. "That's my licence for my boy the grey one here," he said, and with a twinkle patted on his claymore.

Leggatt cast an eye upon the document and smiled. "The very man I want to see! By any chance have you a pinch of snuff on you?"

"I never had the practice; neither has my friend; it spoils the scent."

"That's most vexatious, Mr Campbell!" said the Captain. "I would give my whole month's pay for just one pinch. However, here you are, and snuff or no snuff, I am pleased to see you. Sit you down! The Marshal, last time he was here, let out a hint that

117

you were coming."

"That's a proof a Marshal shouldna know too much," said Ninian. "In this part of the world my trade was better served if nobody said nothing. I would come much better speed across the country if folk would not be clattering. How-and-ever, here I am, and here's my worthy friend Macmaster, umquhile of Drimdorran, of a namely family."

Leggatt spilled them out a dram and drank their healths himself, and was about to leave the hut when Ninian stopped him.

"Where are you for?" he asked.

"You're staying, surely, for the night?" said Leggatt. "I was going to see about your sleeping quarters."

"Not one step!" said Ninian hastily. "Keep shut that door! I would not, for the world, have any of your people ken that we were here."

"They must have seen you come into the camp," said Leggatt with surprise.

"Indeed they didn't; we took care o' that, the cunning pair of us! If you will let us stretch upon the floor here till the early morning, then we'll slip away, and nobody need be a bit the wiser that Macgregor Campbell ever was at Corryarrick."

Leggatt threw up his hands in dismay. "You cannot go like that!" said he. "There's urgent business for you. Last night we had some trouble here with a marauding gang of ruffians. They fell upon a small convoy from Stirling coming with the pay-chest for my fellows. A dirty business—several men were wounded in the scuffle."

"Did they get the kist?" asked Ninian eagerly.

"In faith they did! My men last night were scouring through the country for it; I've been out myself all day. Now you must wait and help me, Mr Campbell; I was lippening on your help. You see I know your reputation."

"Not all of it, I hope!" said Ninian with a grimace. "Have ye a bit of anything for us to eat? We havena touched a morsel since a meal-and-water drammock that I picked the oats for from a field at Garva."

As fortune had it, Leggatt had a piece of loin of deer upon a shelf: he set it down in front of them, and as they ate he talked to them about the Road and all his troubles. Æneas it was who talked the most with him; he had experienced some tremor of the soul when first he came across a hillock in the night and saw so many men far from their homes at work like creatures under judgment in the glare of Tophet fires.

"You like the work?" he asked.

"At times I hate it!" Leggatt cried with fervour. "Then, again, at times, and oftenest, on the whole, I wouldn't call the King my cousin; my work comes over me like drink! I like it, man!—to see my mark—John Leggatt's mark!—away back yonder, through the hill and heather, and feel a kind of glow to think it will be there for generations after I'm below the divots."

"I understand!" cried Æneas, generously uplifted. "I understand! The one thing I have seen since I left home that made me proud of humankind is this place on the hills. I think, myself, your task is noble!"

The Captain flushed; that spirit pleased him. "So I think, myself," he said. "I'm not like to be much the richer at the hinder-end, but still it is something to have helped to put a light up here." And then he looked at both of them, abruptly stopping in his speech, his glance peculiarly on their Gaelic clothing. "You are Highlanders yourselves," he added hurriedly, "but I can tell you this,—it is a dark country we are in this moment—dark, and deep, and cunning! It's come to this with me that I declare to you I'm sometimes frightened. Plots—schemes—roguery of some infernal kind in every slated house from here to Inverness, and I'm mistaken if the hatching's not done somewhere in that quarter."

"You're meaning Yon One?" Ninian remarked with interest.

"I'm mentioning no names, Mr Campbell. All I know is that some very cunning agent is behind a lot of things that's happened since Lovat's Highland company was taken from him. And now there's this affair about the chest; it puts the copestone on my troubles. If I cannot trace that chest and punish them that took it, Wade will roast me like a herring. Now, you that knows

119

the country and the people, Mr Campbell, could assist me greatly to discover where my chest has gone, and who they were who took it. I wish your friend and you would stay with me a little."

"As for myself, I'd like to stay some days and see the Road," said Æneas. "It's mainly what I came for."

Ninian shook his head. "Na, na!" said he; "we must be off! To let ye know the truth o't, Captain Leggatt, we were in a habble of our own last night on Laggan-side, and 'twixt a small Doune pistol and the pair of us we killed a man."

The countenance of Leggatt fell. "That's bad!" says he. "That's dooms bad!" and walked the floor.

"The thing was forced on us," said Æneas. "The shot was mine. He had a musket levelled at my friend, and I behove to act."

"And well ye did it, lad!" cried Ninian. "Whatever o't, the man was killed between us, not to mention other two that I gave *yon* with Gentle Colin," and he clapped his claymore's head that had its chin upon the table.

"I wish—I wish—" said Leggatt, stuttering; "I wish this hadn't happened. You see yourself it's awkward, Mr Campbell? I wish it had not been in my domain. About what place was the encounter?"

"Druimbeg," said Ninian. "Ye'll maybe ken it? Off and on, a score of wee black houses, no' a white among them."

"I know the place," said Leggatt. "All Macdonalds, and a gey bad lot! They're out of Keppoch's lands, but he'll make cause with them. There will be trouble."

"That's what I was thinking," Ninian said warmly. "And it will fairly spoil my reputation if the thing came out that I had any hand in such a business. Ye have some Hielandmen among your corps; I thought of that, and waited till the night before I came to ye; at any cost the name of Ninian Campbell must be dark. There's no one but yourself need know that we were here, or were the men in trouble at Loch Laggan."

"But if I'm asked," said Leggatt. "There's a point of duty. An officer. . . . It is the last place you should have come with such a story!"

Ninian stretched himself composedly and yawned. "*Naile!*" said he, "the fault, to start wi', was your own; ye should have put your kist in better hands. It was because we came athwart your kist the trouble happened. Do ye want it back?"

"I'd be your friend for life!" cried Leggatt.

"If ye can spare a couple of scores of wise-like men and send them off at once, they'll find it at Druimbeg, although I'm no' so sure they'll get much in it."

In half a dozen sentences he told what he had seen.

"By heavens!" said Leggatt, "I'll give them the lesson! I'll start myself, at once, and you stop here till morning; nobody will disturb you; I will lock the door."

He rose to leave them. "Give a glance," said Æneas, "at a kirk that's in the firwood on the shore."

"I clean forgot that!" Ninian said. "Ye'll need some creels and horses; there's a booty in the chapel yonder worth your while—a stack of splendid muskets!"

Leggatt, with some final words of caution for them, hurried out and locked the door behind him. They heard him in a little, bawling; by-and-by the bugle blew, assembling. Ninian turned to Æneas with a grin of satisfaction.

"I knew I had the size of him," said he. "He's just a Lanrig calf that wants to be a major, cocked up in his own conceit. Canna trust the Hielandmen, quo' he! 'Dark, and deep, and cunning,' are they? A fine-like thing to say to you and me, Macmaster! Now that he's got the kist and all yon guns, you'll never hear our names connected wi' the business; you'll see that all the credit after this will go to Captain Leggatt. If you come back again you'll maybe find your man was shot by Leggatt's own right hand."

XIII

In The Way of Trade

Throughout the early morning hours rain pelted on the roof; a gale was blowing through the land; the halyard of the pennon over Leggatt's hut would rap at times against the wooden gable like a signal for admission. Half a dozen times did Ninian, alarmed, start up from where he stretched upon the floor with Colin rolled up in his plaid for pillow. As soon as it was dawn enough to see, he shaved himself, and looked about, and came upon a horn of ink, a pen, and paper on the window-sill. With them he was engaged when Æneas, lying on the Captain's blankets, waked a moment, turned upon his side, and asked what he was doing.

"What am I but at the clerking!" Ninian said. "Leggatt will have a glyde-post runner for his letters to the south, and it's well to take the chance to send a line to Inveraray."

"When you are finished with the pen I'll write my uncle, too," said Æneas, and slept again till Ninian shook him up for counsel on a point that gave him trouble. The chronicle he worked at was, officially, for Islay, but the writer knew it had to pass, first, through the hands of Duncanson, and this called for a guarded pen. No word was said of what had happened at Loch Laggan; simply was it stated that the Messenger had reached the scene of these untoward happenings whose scrutiny had called him hither, and already had employed his craft with profit to the situation. The kernel of his story was a vaunt about the smuggling of arms and his discovery of its meaning. "They are hereabouts in loads," he wrote; "brought in like herring by the cran, poor stuff, but seeming good enough for selling. Your L'ship will have mind of my dubieties about your L'ship's notion of a Rising. There is, or I am cheated, nothing in the Air no more than when I had last time the honour to be in these parts on your

122

L'ship's commands. The guns is meant for honest trade. I had the fortune to come on a pickle stored by some Mackdonals, chiefless men, but cunning. The Mackdonals, poor wratches, have not a groat to spare on such cargoes, but will be my endeavours betwixt Badenoch and the town of Inverness to put the bridle on the man that has the purse. Of this I have no fears, *but will get my man*. The one thing that has vexed me most since leaving Inveraray, Wednesday was a week, is that Col Mackdonal, Esquire, Barisdale, his Watch, and sundry others were against my coming from Glen Orchy on. Barisdale is an arrant rogue. Of this I have the proofs. This business I will go into at a more fitting time. But I must say I was ill prepared to have a leakage of your L'ship's private commands to your obed't servant. The whole country, from the Braes of Glen Orchy till this, was seemingly well advertisit of my coming. Your L'ship or His Grace, or Mr Duncanson, will be best fitted to guess who was in a position to give the alarm to the Enemy. I can assure your L'ship it has been a great calculation to me. But I am in hopes to clear the matter before I set my face to Argyll."

So far, his letter put no strain on Ninian's judgment, but the fact that Duncanson would read it in Lord Islay's absence raised a serious question. Should he mention Æneas?

"That's the bit that bothers me," he said to Æneas and chewed his pen. "Duncanson may ken already that you're in my company, thanks to your speckled horse! but then, on the other hand, he mayna. The man may never have jaloused who aucht the horse in the stall at Bridge of Orchy. Ye see the point? I'll leave it to yourself to say if I should mention anything."

"If you're afraid—" said Æneas.

"I'm not afraid of anything!" cried Ninian. "Drimdorran can burst himself wi' ire, for me. It's you I'm thinking of. Since you're in company wi' me, he'll know ye're going to Inverness, and might send word there, stirring trouble over yon bit snuffbox. That snuffbox *will* hang in my mind; give me your hand on it ye did not touch it."

"I told ye so already!" Æneas cried angrily. "My name is not Macgregor, I'm no thief!" and thereupon began to button on his coat. "I wish I never met you!" he declared. "You brought me into murder, and my sleep is spoiled for me with dreams of yon poor wretch I shot, and now you challenge me with thieving and with lying!"

"Whist!" said Ninian, with alarm. "Cry out like that and everything is spoiled; ye'll call attention to our hiding. Sit ye down, Æneas, *loachain*, and never mind my joke. Indeed there's many a queer Macgregor, at the thiefing and the lying too. You'll never hear me mention snuffbox more. But listen, you, to this—the more I think of you and Mr Duncanson, the more I think there's somehing else between ye than the girl."

"He never liked me—that I know!" said Æneas, cooling down.

"The doocot by itself was not what roused him; what it was I'll find out yet. The man was fairly stricken when he looked his desk and spluttered something to himsel' about his keys. He sallowed in the colour like a frosted leaf. It looks to me as if he had some devilish thing in hiding and was frightened ye had found it."

"I know nothing about that," said Æneas. "Write them I am with you, if you like."

"I think, myself, that would be better," Ninian agreed, and took his pen again. "Always it is best to be above the board in matters, and forbye, I'll wager anything Drimdorran knows already."

But then he started up before a word was written, beat his brow, and turned on Æneas a baffled visage. "I canna clear my mind of this," he said with passion. "*Whence came Niall of Succoth on his horse to warn Breadalbane?* Niall's Drimdorran's cousin's man! The shauchle of a fellow that came wi' me to take back my horse from Orchy had a letter from Drimdorran to his cousin. That was in my mind the whole day through the corries."

"I can make nothing of it," said Æneas, impatient.

"Indeed and ye canna!" said Ninian; "it will take me all my time myself," and finished off his letter, wrote another short one to his daughter, and gave up his pen to Æneas, who plunged into a full account of everything for Alan-Iain-Alain Og. It occupied him half an hour, and all the time was Ninian staring slyly from the window in a key of some impatience for a sign of Leggatt's coming back to let them free from their confinement. Nobody was moving in the camp; they could have left it then without an eye upon them, and so thick the vapours of the morning hung above the ground it favoured an escape that later in the day would be less easy for them.

"Mind what ye are saying to your uncle, lad!" said Ninian at last, uneasy at the length of Æneas' billet. "Letters hereabouts go wandering at times. If ye are saying anything at all about Loch Laggan, tell him to be sure and keep his thumb on't."

"I'll see to that," said Æneas. "But tell me this—you promised me a laugh about the muskets?"

"Ay!" said Ninian, "that I did! But wait you till the Captain comes, and we will laugh, the pair of us, at him, together. Whatever o't, it's not a joke for paper; finish you your scribbling. There's nothing in't, I hope, about Drimdorran?"

"Only that I'll settle things with him when I get back," said Æneas.

"Just that!" said Ninian. "Very good indeed! I'll slip your letter inside Janet's, hers inside Drimdorran's; that will save some shillings for the post. You aye be saving shillings, and ye'll make a splendid merchant, just as good's your uncle Alan."

They hunted high and low for sealing-wax, and had not come on it, when suddenly they both were startled by a key turned quickly in the door; Leggatt, dripping from the rain, stepped in, threw down a pair of moor-fowl on the table, and before a word was said, took out a bottle from a press. It held some whisky flavoured with wild herbs like gentian and camomile; he poured the three of them a little draught; "There's nothing better for the morning damp," says he, and gulps his portion. "If I had just a bawbee's worth of snuff, now, everything was right! You're sure you havena any, Mr Campbell?"

"Not one morsel!" Ninian assured him. "What speed came ye yonder!"

Leggatt seized their hands. "My word," said he, "and you

have done the turn for me! I'll not forget it, gentlemen. If you are in the humour yet for going on this morning, half an hour from now must see you started. My men are on the road behind me. I came through the hills and brought you there your breakfast, but you haven't time to cook it."

And then, as if relieved himself from some anxiety, he said rejoicingly, "There's no one killed at all! The man you thought was dead was supping kail when we came on him; the bullet just went through his side."

"Thank God for that!" cried Æneas. "Since I was born I never heard a bit of news so welcome!" He could not sit, he could not stand, at first, for joy at Leggatt's tidings; like one half-crazed he stamped the room, and rubbed his eyes, and gave a little skip or two as if to start to dance. "I'll never fire a gun again!" said he, and took his uncle's letter hurriedly, and put another line to it that told of this relief. The rest of Leggatt's news seemed immaterial to him, but Ninian heard it with a pleasure nigh as great as that the man was living.

When Leggatt and his party reached Druimbeg, the wounded three were all the men to be discovered. The rest had taken to the hills and left the pay-chest with its locks unbroken, hidden in a peat-stack. Terror held the women when the troops appeared, and Leggatt played on it believing it concerned the chest alone, whose hiding-place they showed him on a threat of burning down the township. He had the muskets loaded into panniers when a half-wit boy betrayed the thing that most dismayed the women—two men had been fighting with their husbands and been drowned.

"My notion at the start," said Leggatt, "was to let them think that you were men of mine; it looked the easiest way to meet your wishes, Mr Campbell."

"And a very good plan too!" said Ninian eagerly. "Myself I couldna better it. But you go on about the drownded men."

"My men were quite confounded when they saw the fellows wounded; I had, of course, said not a cheep to them of what I knew, but when I found your gentleman was in a frame for kail—a very different thing from dead—I passed the word that

I would take the credit for his state and the other two you struck. I found them smeared with salve and drenched with whisky."

"Nothing better!" Ninian agreed; "but what about the drowning? That's the bit."

"I'm coming to that," said Leggatt. "But you see my point? By rights I should have searched the hill and taken prisoners, just to give the pack a lesson. But I'm aye loth for prisoners; it means convoys to Inverness, and trials, and a great expense of men and time much better spent in digging. I thought myself the rogues had got enough to be a warning, and (to make the story short) I just let on the two who did the damage to their men were Highlanders of mine."

"Capital!" cried Ninian. "I told you, Æneas, we could put our trust in Captain Leggatt."

"A woman took a sixpence from a bowl, and threw it at my feet when I said that, and swore she would not let it foul her children's hands. I could not make her out, but one of mine, a sergeant of Lochaber, told me she was bitter that the men should take her meat and water when they were on such a business. She said it beat Glencoe."

"It's a great pity, poor body, she should lose the sixpence," said Ninian. "But time's aye slipping past, and we'll be needing to take legs for it immediately. I'm asking ye, by any chance, are we the men that's drowned?"

"That's just it!" said Leggatt, laughing. "The boat was got adrift without her oars and full of water. They never saw you land, and now you're clear of everything."

"Man, that's fine!" said Ninian. "I shoved the boat off, on a chance, in mind of yon that happened on Loch Duich, Æneas, and there's a lesson to ye, now, to aye be taking steps to kill the scent behind ye."

"But that was not the end of it," said Leggatt. "Before we left the place I thought my scheme was foundered. Have you had any trouble with the Watch of Barisdale?"

"My sorrow, but I had!" cried Ninian. "Is that long rascal still in chase of me?"

"It looked a bit like that. Five men of his came up the loch when we were on the point of leaving; heard about the drowning from the women, said they knew the men, and gave your names. They came to me and argued out the point of your identity, and I can tell you they were not much stricken at your loss. I swore they were mistaken—"

"Hoots!" said Ninian, aback, "I wish ye hadna. Far better snugly drowned than yon one on my track."

"They had been looking for you."

"Yes, and now they'll look again! It's time we steeped the withies, lad, and took the road for't. Put the birds into your poke. Will you can send a letter, Captain?"

"A runner goes to Perth on Friday," Leggatt answered, and got wax out from a box. They sealed the letters, Islay's that contained the others, last, and Leggatt slipped it in his pocket. "It will take a week at least," said he.

"That's soon enough," said Ninian, and strapped his knapsack on. "Ye got the guns, then?"

"That itself was worth my while," said Leggatt, opening the door an inch or two and looking out. The rain was driving. Nobody beyond themselves was stirring in the camp.

"I'm glad you're pleased wi' them," said Ninian; "and what are muskets bringing at the market?"

But Leggatt thought the question trivial, or more likely feared delay; he pointed to a hut that smoked across the square. "My man is up," said he. "Keep down the brae until you reach the burn, then up the Road, the banks will hide you."

They cast their plaids about them, and sped quickly with the wind through rushes water-laden, dipping to the burn. The gale was blowing with a great commotion; little of the mountains could be seen for mist. "I think that I could run to Inverness without a stop," said Æneas, still uplifted with blood-innocence, a beaming on his face.

"Ye canna do't! The thing's impossible!" his friend replied with seriousness, and Æneas laughed at him.

"You promised me a laugh about the muskets, but I never got it. I must just be cheery on my own account," said Æneas.

"There's not much of a laugh in it except we have a sodger,"

Ninian said gravely, plashing through the grass. "Our hurry, leaving, spoiled the thing; I meaned to get a scoff at Leggatt; yon's as smart a man as ever put his feet in good king's leather, and has a royal hand at putting round the bottle, but he wants *yon!*" and saying so he cracked his fingers. "I'll wager you he's still of the belief that getting guns is stopping Risings."

"What honest trade do you think they're for?" asked Æneas.

"What for but selling to the Army? Ye've heard of the Disarming Act? Donald wouldna give his dirk and gun for nothing to the king, and so for years the king is paying well for every piece surrendered at a barrack. It cost three thousand pounds last year for weapons handed in at Ruthven by Macphersons—rusted swords and broken dirks, and foundered muskets; no' a decent arm among them! Where do ye think they came from? Straight from Holland! It is not his own good gear at all that Donald gives them, just some merchant trash from Rotterdam. What we got in the chapel yonder, or I'm sore mistaken, is part of a cargo landed in the Forth a month ago. That was what alarmed MacCailein and Lord Islay; when they got wind of it the other day they were assured it meant another Rising, and I was fool enough at times to think there might be something in it, till I saw this rubbish in Druimbeg. The truth came to me yonder like the chorus of a song. Little did I think it was in chapel I would get the key to what this traffic meant— a lesson to us all to go to kirk!"

"Upon my word," cried Æneas, "I think you have the truth of it!"

"Of course I have!" said Ninian, and cocked his bonnet. "Better far than farming! Man, there's money in't! The Hielandman is learning business fast, and that's the New Road for you!"

"But who provides the capital?" asked Æneas. "Yon poor wretches couldn't ship a cargo."

"That's the bit!" said Ninian slyly; "that's for me to find!"

The grouse-cock and his wife were quarrelling among the mist upon the braes within a stone-throw of the roadmen's works, and on a knoll the deer were grazing, with a stag at gaze.

The bottom of a bleak hill showed, and through a cleft of it let fall a cataract that made a din. Steep, lifting to the west, there ran the latest gash of Leggatt, stripped of turf, with swinging engines over it, and carts, and soil high-banked along its sides. The two men rose to it. A row of pegs, with here and there a rag of colour on them, stretched up from the level, swerved but once about a cliff that hid it for a while, and then marched on again until it reached the misty summit, where a flag was waving like an invitation into space.

XIV

Inverness

At seven of the clock on third October, in the morning, and the weather still so good that bees were humming in the withered heather, Ninian and Æneas stood on a hillock looking east, and saw below them, at some miles of distance, steeples of a town, a noble stream that went about some wooded island gardens, and a bay. Ships were lying at the quay; a citadel was on a knoll, and in it pipers blew a rouse; a bridge of many arches spanned the river; upwards from the streets came sounds of men and hammering, and a great fresh smoke of morning fires. Although the countryside was almost void of trees, the winding frith, the cultivated plain, the Grampians beyond them and the heaping clouds of silver, made enchantment for the young man's eye.

"Oh man! Is that not fine!" cried he upliftedly in Gaelic.

"Indeed it's not so bad at all!" said Ninian in that language. And then said he "—to look at! Myself though, always better liked the great brave lands of trees. The like of thou and me are people of the woods. A man would need to move here circumspectly; where would he take hiding with a booty?"

Folk of the wood, indeed, were they since they had climbed on Corryarrick and came down Glen Tarff. They never moved but in the night, or early in the morning while the mists still hung and glamoured; through day they lay in thickets, under banks on water-edges; in forest deeps they made small fires. Their clothing had the smell of burning sticks. The morning they had left the camp of Leggatt they had skirted wide of Fort Augustus peeping at its bastions from behind a clump of brambles hearing on its walls a sentry cry, and seeing on a field beside it redcoats drill. Ninian would not go near it; nothing was to learn there, he maintained, and he was all for places unfrequented. It was this fancy for lone ways aloof from folk that gave him preference for

131

the west side of Loch Ness; they might have easier reached their journey's end by passing through Strath Errick, but that land was thick with Lovat's people, and for Lovat's people Ninian at the moment had no inclination. They took them to the hills and crossed the glens of Moriston and Urquhart in the dark; a land all strange to Ninian, and yet they never strayed,—he airted by the dip of rocks, the growth of timber, sometimes by the run of streams, or by the stars. He travelled by the "feel of things," he said, when vision failed him; always at the dawn they found them coverts where the first thing he would do was aye to start at shaving. There would they lurk while he caught food—a cudgelled grouse upspringing from his feet, one time a roe ingeniously captured, twice at least a fish or two for which he plied a switch cut from the riverside.

The roe was strangely got. They lay one morning in Glen Urquhart, in behind a rock, when passing went a cripple man who bore the deer slung on his shoulder. "A wise-like beast!" said Ninian. "I wish we had a rib," and then upon a thought ran up along the hill, and down upon the track the fellow must pursue, and off a single shoe and threw it where the man must see it. The shoe was sorely worn by travelling, and he that had the deer but looked at it and threw it down again. But half a mile away he came upon the other shoe of Ninian, this one not so bad, and thereupon put down the roe as Ninian expected, and went back to get the other. Ninian took the roe and put it in a hole, and dined that day on venison.

"You would cheat the heron off her eggs, and she with her two eyes on you!" said Æneas in admiration.

"No cheatery at all," said Ninian; "the man's the richer by a pair of bauchles," and put on the brogues he brought from Inveraray in his poke.

But still that dinner cost them two days and a night of skulking on Glen Urquhart edge; the man who lost the deer came on the embers of the fire that cooked it, and brought out his friends to hunt them. They could not stick a head from out the cave they hid in but they saw some figure posted on the hill. Now Michaelmas was past, they ate of nuts and berries; once

132

they ventured to a hovel near the loch and got some milk and bread; their last night out was spent in birches in The Aird.

No wonder Æneas looked on Inverness with quickened eyes; the steeples and the streets, its frank and open situation, promised a relief from all the hazards and the hardships of the week bygone, and—what was even more delightful to escape from—that uneasy sense of menace in the sunniest weather, in the loneliest places, strange airs of ambuscade and plot that followed him and Ninian since they had left their homes.

"Thank God," cried he, "for streets! It's glad I'll be to have my soles upon a causeway!"

The other put his level hand above his eyes and peered across the glittering morning at the town that smoked.

"A town," said he, "is just made up of people. The more folk the more mischief! My father—peace be with him!—used to say for every man that has his sword out for you on the hill, a hundred men are feeling at your pockets in the burgh lands; ay, yes, and following you with hatred and with lies! Give me the grass and heather for't against my foe! I'm far more frightened for myself in Inverness than on the Moor of Rannoch, for it's far too far away from Inveraray and the whistle of MacCailein." He gave that one word "whistle" like a cry from Cruachan.

"There's nobody dare touch us here!" said Æneas loftily.

Ninian twitched the belt that hung his knapsack—"That's to see!" quo' he, and glowered. "Many a nimble lad thought that in Lovat's land, and now his bones are bleaching to the wind or cankering in the dungeon, or he is shivering to the lash in the plantations. Thou and me will better stick together till we're out o't."

They shaved themselves and washed them in a burn, and went down slopes of heather and through garnered fields, and crossed the river where some girls, high-kilted to the thighs, were posting blankets. Everywhere the town was busy: bands of merchantmen were standing at the cross: it was a market-day, and in the gutters of the street poor country folk with webs of linen, scraggy hens, and cheeses, proffered bargains. Some officers in red were hanging round a coffee-house; men of the

Highland Companies who spoke the Gaelic lounged upon the middle of the causeway, every kind of arm except a gun hung to them, feathers in their bonnets, targets on their backs. A ragged woman with her bairns was whining some lugubrious ditty of a sailor lost, and getting now and then a bodle for her song. About the Tolbooth gates some wicked-looking lads were hanging, signalling to folk behind the window bars. The sun shone on the town and made it white as marble; it was mostly built of rubble, harled and washed with lime. Some parts of it were like bastilles, so stern and bare the tenements, with turnpike stairs that led to dwellings over shops; the wynds and lanes were full of playing dogs and barefoot children.

Although they wore the kilt, the two were no way odd to see upon the streets; more kilts than trews were on the causeway, but the sword of Ninian sometimes caught a questioning eye, and at the very entrance to a vintner's inn that he had fixed on for their lodging he was challenged by an English sergeant.

"Friend, what about your sword?" said he. "Have you a licence?"

"Ye may be sure of that, my clever lad!" said Ninian with a twitching eyebrow and a mocking lip. "If you will bring the gentleman that owns you, I will let him read it."

The sergeant had another glance at them; perceived some look of consequence about their bearing, muttered an excuse, and took his way.

They breakfasted on herring and a mutton ham, then sallied out and in a warehouse bought them each a suit of Lowland fashion and a London hat. With some reluctance Ninian left Grey Colin in the vintner's keeping with the clothes of John Maclaren, and put his dirk well down his back between the shoulders, underneath his coat.

"And now," said he, "I'll tell ye what ye'll do. Ye'll go away at once and put your money in charge of him that is your uncle's man. Make you your plans wi' him about your business, and come here for dinner. Myself, I'm going out the town a bit to make a call. Take you your Virgin nut—"

"Not I!" said Æneas, laughing, "keep it till it grows a tree, for me!" and off he went to meet his uncle's agent in the guidance of the vintner's boy.

The forenoon yet was young when Ninian, trimly shaved, a rattan-cane in hand, his guinea hat a little cocked upon his forehead, left the town and walked into the country till he reached a great stark house with planted grounds close by a windy moor. It was the house of Duncan Forbes, Lord Advocate, the man who under God, MacCailein, and Lord Islay, kept King's law at trot throughout the country. Ninian asked to see him, waiting in a stone-flagged hall with arms and cabar-heads of deer in it. More odd to see, there was a gantry, with a cask of claret wine upon the spigot, and a pail beside it.

From out a spacious room, that was resounding with the jovial din of company, the Advocate, a man of middle age, came to him, flushed a little at the gills, a stern official mien assumed that was put off immediately he recognised his caller.

"Campbell!" said he, and thumped him on the back. "You have got through! Have you found anything?" His eyes were lit with eagerness; he licked his lips. He closed the door upon the noisy company he had left, led Ninian round the cask of claret, through a lobby to a tiny room, and there poured forth on him a spate of questions.

"I have found out two things of the three, my lord, that sent me here," said Ninian—"that Hieland Watches are no use at all, or worse than useless, and that guns are very rife in Badenoch."

"I doubted that myself," said Forbes. "Twenty thousand pounds we've spent on them, and still they're pouring in. It looks as if they grew them in the glens like oats. And always rubbish— where's the good stuff lying? What about that cargo to Blackness?"

"I came upon a bit of that," said Ninian, and straightway, leaving out the skirmish by Loch Laggan, told what he had found and what were his conclusions.

"By heavens, you're right!" cried Forbes. "I might have guessed it. Never was such rowth of money in among the clans. That cargo made me anxious; now it's just a joke to laugh at. This is an Occasion, Mr. Campbell; we must wet it from

135

Macneill of Barra's library." He had a jovial eye; a lip that trembled now and then with fun.

He opened up a cabinet of black mahogany in which a dozen bottles, square, with gilt on them, were fitted, picked out one choke-full of brandy, splashed out for himself and Ninian a hearty bumper.

"I thank you very much indeed, my lord," said Ninian, "but I daurna. Not when I'm on business, and I'm thinking I'll need all my water wits in Inverness."

"Very good," said Forbes without demur, and, opening a window, emptied both the glasses on the grass outside. "If some of my gentry in there"—and he jerked a thumb across his shoulder—"were so wise as the Duke's *beachdair*, the office of Lord Advocate was not sometimes so merry, nor my knowledge of my countrymen so deep. . . . Who brings the guns from Holland, Mr Campbell? That's the bit! These tenant bodies havena got the cash."

"I thought, my lord, ye could have told me that yoursel'," said Ninian, twitching down his brows and rubbing at his chin.

"No, no!" said Forbes, a sly smile on his face, "you need not tell me that, Mr Campbell. I know your work of old, and I'll wager you already have your eye upon the parties most concerned. It's not to precognosce the Advocate you're calling on me here. . . . Very well! keep you your news for Islay or his Grace—so long as it gets there it's all the same to me and Scotland."

"Upon the soul of me and on the dirk," cried Ninian, "I'm telling you as much as what I know mysel' for certain."

"Hoot-toot!" the Advocate said drolly, with a twinkle. "The dirk, I see, 's behind your back; it nearly broke my fingers when I thumped you there. It ill becomes a Messenger-at-Arms to carry weapons that way."

"The hills themselves are not more wise than you, my lord," said Ninian with a laugh. "Not every gentleman could guess my backbone was the *biodag*. But faith, I'm needin' it. Since ever I got up the Orchy people have been round me like a rabble, making trouble, and I'm greatly under fear they know my business."

"How on earth, sir, could they? No one knew that you were coming but myself, and Wade, and Islay."

"And still-and-on, the news has leaked, my lord; there's no dubieties about it. Barisdale himsel' was put upon my track."

"Barisdale! Oh-ho!" said Forbes, and tapped upon a snuff-mull, pursing up his cheeks and drawing down his eyebrows like a man who peeped on things behind.

"I saw him lift a *creach*, my lord. The man's a blackguard," Ninian said hotly, and quickly told of tricky Col's device for getting cattle.

"And he was in this very house three weeks ago and borrowed Virgil! A little dipped in drink, but still the perfect gentleman. I'll have to make a study of my classic friend. Say not a word of this to anyone till I turn round."

"Not a cheep!" said Ninian.

"You say that Barisdale was after you. In whose interest?"

"I thought, my lord, ye might have helped me there too," said Ninian, and shuffled with his feet.

"My good Mr Campbell, you thought nothing of the kind. I need not tell you, Mr Campbell, that a man in my position knows nothing—till it's told him with the proofs. I'm much mistaken in you if you do not guess already who could have an interest in hampering you by means of Col Macdonnell."

"I canna put a name on him as yet, my lord. But stop you! I'll find out!"

The Advocate took out his watch and looked the time. "My friends in-by," said he in homely fashion, "are in trim, I fancy, for a chack of meat; you must come ben and join us, Mr Campbell. But first I want to know what brought you here to me if all your news is meant for Inveraray?"

"I thought," said Ninian, "to get a hint from you, my lord. There's not another gentleman in all the North I dare put trust in."

"It's good of you to say so, Mr Campbell, but we'll not, just now, be bothering with the flatteries. Something more impor-tant's in your mind; the sooner you come out with it the better.

137

Just to give a lead to you, I'll ask you who was with you coming North?"

Ninian bit his nether lip, a little staggered. "There's not much hid from you, my lord," said he. "And I was thinking I came yonder like the fox! There must be quicker ways for news to Inverness than over Corryarrick, through the Aird."

"Many a way, and still the best of them a little devious. Wait till we have got the Road! The fox should never hunt in couples; you had never trouble when you came alone before on business, Mr Campbell. Who's the brisk young lad?"

"I'll tell you that, my lord, without a twisted word," said Ninian. "His name is Æneas Macmaster, son of Paul Macmaster, one time of Drimdorran. He came on business for his uncle."

"Macmaster of Drimdorran—let me see now—he was 'tainted for Glenshiel and lost his life about that time?"

"Is that quite sure, my lord?" cried Ninian quickly.

"I have never heard it doubted, sir," said Forbes. "By all accounts the man was drowned in fleeing through Kintail."

"That's the tale, I ken," said Ninian, "but who saw Paul Macmaster dead?"

"It's fourteen years ago," said Forbes, "and it's a strong presumption that he's dead enough that no one ever saw him living since."

"I'm not so sure of that!" said Ninian, blurting out his words with feeling. "A thing befell when I met Barisdale that bothers me—he let slip that he and Paul Macmaster were at fencing once in Castle Dounie when Macmaster had a wounded arm. 'Before he went abroad,' says Barisdale—note that, my lord! Now, Paul Macmaster, as I know, because my father told me, never got a wound in all his life until the battle of Glenshiel, where he was cut across the shoulder by a man of Clayton's Corps—a thing that never would have happened, as my father said, if he had not forgot the first time in his life to take the Virgin nut with him when he went off wi' Glendaruel."

"The Virgin nut," said Forbes. "What haivers have we here?"

"It was a luck-piece in the family, my lord, and came from Barra; I have no faith in things like that mysel', but haivers or no

138

haivers, the bit is that Macmaster was wounded at Glenshiel, and Barisdale fenced after that with him in Castle Dounie. That being so, he couldna have been drowned, as rumour went."

"On that," remarked the Advocate, "there falls one observation to be made—it's not without the bounds of fair hypothesis that Barisdale is lying."

"To what end, my lord?" asked Ninian eagerly. "A lie like that would serve him nothing! Forbye, it came too glibly from him. He must have met Macmaster, for he knew that Æneas was his image. Did ever you, sir, hear of Paul Macmaster in this neighbourhood before the year 'Nineteen?"

"No," said the Advocate, "I think that was his first indulgence in sedition in the North. And what, I ask you, Mr Campbell, was Macmaster doing in—in the place you mention? Lord Lovat at the time was—was loyal."

The Messenger said not a word in answer, only looked from under lowered eyelids, something crafty in his manner.

"You must be careful, Mr Campbell," Forbes went on, himself disturbed a little, fumbling with his watch.

"I never spoke a name, my lord," said Ninian in haste. "It was yourself that named him!"

"Let any name that slipped me be delete. I hardly need to warn you, Mr Campbell. . . . H'm! Your story is a bit fantastic. In any case a tangled hank for fourteen years . . . a little rotten, Mr Campbell! And supposing that Macmaster *was* in Castle Dounie after he went missing. . . . H'm! It's this way of it, my good man" (and here he sat down on a chair and drummed his fingers on his knees), "what's the good of blowing ashes grey and cold for fourteen years? God knows there's plenty to engage you and me and your employers in the rogueries and plottings of today without us tugging at a tangled line that leads we ken not where."

"I see your point, my lord," said Ninian, and bit his finger-nails. And then said he, "I never tug a line, my lord; I have been far too long at fishing. A tangled hank of line, my lord, with any luck at all, can only have two ends to it, and here I think I have got one—that Paul Macmaster was alive when folk were

139

mourning for him! Any wise-like man wi' patience can get clear a tangled hank if only he keeps teasing—teasing." He showed his teeth in a peculiar smile, and made some movements with his fingers—"The thing's to keep the tangle loose, my lord; I never saw a tangled line but I was itching to be at it."

"It seems to me," said Forbes, "the question could be settled by your asking Col exactly when he met Macmaster."

"I asked him, sir! I asked him!" cried out Ninian. "You may be sure of that! I darena ask him wi' the young man there, but got him by himself, and then it was I found his tale was surely true, for he made an attempt to change it. A lie well stuck to looks at last like truth to him that tells and him that hears it; I've often thought myself, sir, truth was just conviction. But when the wild beast of the wood goes doubling before the dogs, ye may be sure, my lord, he's not going home to where's his litter. When I got drawing Barisdale, his eyes betrayed him, and he started doubling. He hummed and hawed, and said his meeting with Macmaster was at Castle Tiorram, old Clanranald's place. And then again, says he, he doubted if the man was Paul Macmaster after all; he feared he had mixed up two different occasions and two different men. With that I couldna push the question further, but bold Col was in my grasp! The story that he told me first was true, and when he found me curious he tried to blind the scent. My lord, he was in fear of something!"

"My learned friend has many sides to him," said Forbes, reflecting.

"The outside is the best of him, my lord; inside the man's as boss as Peter's drum. 'Macmaster went abroad,' I ventured, minding what he said himself. 'He did,' said he, 'and died there.'... That was all, but that did me, my lord! I kent now that the North had a different tale about Drimdorran's end from Shire Argyll. And that itself is mighty queer, my lord."

"My own authority," said Forbes, "was Islay. He had a most explicit story of the drowning, though I sometimes used to hear the other rumoured."

"Lord Islay there had just the same tale as the rest of us; it came from Inverness, but I'll believe it only when I meet a man who saw the corpse of Paul Macmaster!"

The Advocate got up and snapped his watch. "I think I have you now," said he, and blinked his eyes. "At any time you honour me by calling, it is always something else than the pretended business in hand that you are after. I fear you find the Advocate an easy fish to play." He chuckled, caught the other by the arm and gently shook it. "Not this time, Mr Campbell! Not this time! Drumly waters, but I'm off the feed! I'm lucky this time that I got you to the point with less than usual of a circuit journey. The long and the short of it is that you are more concerned with this meare's nest about Macmaster than your proper business, which, I take it, is to find out things concerning guns, and other solid obstacles to law and order. You thought to rouse my interest and get my egging-on in this ridiculous new hunt of yours for dead men's bones, but mind this, Mr Campbell, I'm not in it! And you'll be wiser, far, to limit your official zeal in Inverness to what my lord duke and his brother sent you North for."

"Very good, my lord!" said Ninian, no way hearty in his acquiescence, and the other laughed.

"You rogue!" said he. "I see you're looking wry. You'll do what suits yoursel', I fancy, but there's this I'll warn you of—gang warily in Inverness if you're for stirring stagnant waters. . . . Now then, Mr Campbell, there's my gentry bellowing; come in and have your chack."

But Ninian excused himself on finding half a dozen boon companions of the lawyer were the makers of the din that burst at times in peals of laughter and of disputatious cries from Forbes' dining-room; he pleaded an engagement with his friend for dinner at their inn, and took his leave, confirmed in his impression that retreat was best from joviality for once, on finding in the hall a servant tilting up another claret cask upon the gantry.

XV

The Den

He walked out from the garden leisurely, the Advocate requesting him upon the doorstep to be sure and call again before he left the country. "I sist ye to compear!" cried Forbes, and waved a hand. This leisured step was kept until the house was hid by trees, and then his pace was quickened. Quicker still it grew until the road passed through secluded banks of shrub, and there he fairly ran jog-trot as if to catch a ferry. For nigh a mile he kept at this peculiar gait for one that wore a flapping coat and Saxon hat, and only when he came to fields where folks were toiling put his heels to ground.

When he got to the town his sweat was lashing. Æneas was not come back yet to the inn.

"You'll tell my friend," said Ninian to the landlord, "that I couldna wait for meat at this time. Business, Mr Fraser, business! And you'll say this to him—and mind the way I put it!—'Mr Campbell's compliments, and he was called into the country where the primrose grows.' You'll not forget that, Mr Fraser?—'Where the primrose grows.' Just a bit joke between us; he'll understand."

Ten minutes later he was on a horse hired from a stable round the corner, crossed the river, and rode landwards west. He trotted for an hour, and then came wooded country with a big black ancient castle scowling on a hill, and over it the hoodie-crows loud-clangouring. The frith itself was narrowed here so much, it looked as if a tall-sparred ship that floated near its head was high and dry incongruously in meadows. Fertile fields were widely spread, and here and there dark patches of the pine; high mounts were to the north, the greatest of them broadly-shouldered Wyviss Ben. And everywhere about were smoking houses; everywhere the braes were populous with folk. The high black castle keep with girning crenels looked the master of the mountain and the plain and all therein,—command was in the very reek of it; a king might well be dwelling there.

"It's I like not the look of thee!" said Ninian sourly.

A man with a bare-polled head was in a park beside the road and he was cutting rushes. Ninian stopped his horse and put a question.

"To whom, my lad," said he, "belongs this gallant castle?" though he knew right well the place was Lovat's.

"To whom but to the great MacShimi," said the polled one, using Lovat's patronym.

"That's what I was thinking to myself!" said Ninian. "My soul! but she's the stately one!"

"The like of her is not in Albyn!" said the man, with vanity. "No shadow of a thing that would be for the use of castles will be wanting—even to a herdsman for the geese. Meat of each meat on the board; the barrels of the wine of France as plentiful as nuts; a hundred servants. Great's the man, MacShimi!" And he stood, not like a stot, himself, but like a gentleman, although the shirt of him was all in holes; his head uplifted, hands upon his haunches, whistling soft to show he was at ease.

"Is he at home, Himself?" asked Ninian; "I'd give a cry on him."

"He went this morning to Strath Errick," said the man, and Ninian looked disappointed.

"With any luck at all he'll have a wife?"

"I'll warrant ye! He's never out of them, MacShimi! A Campbellach of Erraghaidheal, a twig of old MacCailein's; money would be with her, you be sure. She's yonder since she came last year a wife to him, and seldom do we see her. They're saying she is heavy."

"*An galar bu mhiosa!*—worst of all diseases!" Ninian said. "Sorrow that that girl should have it, and the world already hotching-full of Frasers!"

He took another turn at riding, passed through shrubbery and garden trees, and round one big old oak with chains hung from its thickest member, chinking in the wind, that on the braeface here was blowing gusty with the salt scent of the distant sea. He did not like the look of those black chains a bit! He never had been there before; the place astonished. It looked more like a fortress than a home, with studded gates about the cobbled yard, and mounted cannons, turrets cloaked with ivy in the which were peering little holes that one might doubt were really meant for windows. In view about the house was not one flower. No sooner had he struck the cobbles than the place seemed swarming like a hive: at least a hundred men revealed themselves from every inlet to the yard, and six came lounging up to hold his horse.

"I want to see her leddyship," he said in English, lordly; "ye'll tell her I have letters."

A gaunt old woman came and led him in and up a stair so steeply pitched and dark he stumbled on it; dungeon airs were manifest—he sniffed them, damp and mouldy; once or twice he put his hand behind his back and felt the poignard.

The gaunt wife pushed a door and gave him entrance to a small, dark, deadly-silent room with hangings and a bed, and there beside a window twelve feet thick in wall he found a lonely woman. She sat upon a stool, and she was sewing, and her thimble wet with tears. Her face was white as one night's snow, and she had great big melting eyes as if with constant staring out for grief. As he stepped in and shut the door behind him she got up and cried.

"Ninian! Ninian! Ninian Campbell!" was her cry. "Oh, Ninian, have ye come to see me?" and thereupon burst out in tears. She took his hand in both of hers and stood a little, fondling it and speechless.

"Oh, *m'eudail!*" he said, greatly stricken, "is this the way of it with you, my leddy?"

"Did you come here to take me home?" she asked then, eager, holding still his hand, her big eyes filled with hope.

"Indeed and I would like that fine!" he said, with a pretence at cheerfulness, "but when your leddyship comes back to yon place yonder that's your home, it'll not be with a poor wee man of no account at all like Ninian Campbell, but a tail of noble gentlemen. And I can tell you that will be the splendid day for sheriffdom Argyll!"

"No, no!" she said with bitterness, "he'll put me in Kirkhill among the rest; he would not even take me home for burial."

"Burial, my leddy! burial!" said Ninian, with impatience, "I wouldna fash my mind wi' burials; it's not the thing at all, and us so young!" His eye fell on two books on edge upon a little table—Baxter's *Everlasting Rest* and Sibbe's *Believers' Bowels Opened*.

"Ach!" he said, "you have been reading Sibbe; no wonder that you're downed! Far better wi' a book of songs!"

She put him in a chair, and sat down on her bed, and dried her eyes, and never after shed another tear.

"Oh, Ninian!" she said, "I'm glad to see you. What was it brought you here? And how is my dear Jennet?"

"The thing that brought me North," said he, and started feeling in his pockets, "is some business of your cousins' that's of no account at all. But seeing I was coming here, my daughter asked me to be sure and call and sent your leddyship a letter. Stop a wee, and I will get it!"

"You must not call me Lady, Ninian; when I was happy I was Primrose Campbell. Be quick, and get my letter! What was Jennet thinking of that never wrote her friend till this? I wrote her twice and never got a scrape of answer. And she my own dear friend!"

"Now that is strange!" said Ninian, and stopped his searching, staggered. "My lass wrote twice to you, and never got a word. There's surely some miscarriage!"

"I might be sure of it!" exclaimed the Lady Lovat biting at her lip. "Now I can understand a lot of things that troubled me. But haste ye, Ninian! give me Jennet's letter."

He felt again his pockets carefully, and showed a great concern.

"Is that not most deplorable!" cried he at last; "I havena got it!"

"Oh!" she cried, and wrung her hands; "and you will fail me too!"

145

He shook his fist. "In all of Albyn there is not a man more stupid or more vexed! Where's your letter but in Buachaille Etive in an inn I changed my clothes in. And I was thinking all the time I had it in this pocket!"

She chided him, not harshly—half in smiles, a little woe-begone, like one too well acquaint with disappointments to lament one more. "At least," said she, "it's always something just to know that Jennet has not quite forgot me, and to see a face from home."

"There is a wise old word," said Ninian, "that will be saying 'Men may meet, but never the mountains!' and it is a very strong true word."

"I do not understand it," said the lady.

"I daresay not, my lady Primrose—no, I daresay not! In faith, it sounds a little flat in English, but in the Gaelic it will break men's hearts to hear. I canna put it plainer in the English but it means that old friends meeting in a foreign land will vex themselves to think the mountains of their home so distant. We canna shift the hills, my dear, my dear! or if we could, a man I ken would bring upon his back to you although his legs would break, Dunchuach! and what is that man's name but Ninian Campbell!"

"Ah!" she said, and turned a ring upon her finger— "Dunchuach! . . . And Glen Aray, and the woods! There was a lass among them, one time, Ninian, was happy. Many a time I wonder if it could be me. No, no! it wasna me! She died, that lass. . . . She was a little wee bit thing and wore a yellow coat, and played wi' Jennet Campbell."

"There's not a printed book on earth that's worse than Sibbe!" said Ninian with conviction, rising up and looking from the little window. He could not see a thing.

At last he turned about and touched her shoulder. "I'm sorry that I have to ask you this," he said,—"it's dreadful low and common in the English; tell me this: is your man bad to you?"

"And what if he was?" said she, still twisting at her ring.

"What if he was!" cried Ninian ferociously, the crinkle on his face. "My God, mem! is there not the cry of 'Cruachan!' "

"A far cry to Lochow!" said she, "and farther still to kin. The thing's beyond redemption, Ninian; tell me about Jennet."

"Jennet can wait!" He stood before her, catching at her hand. "A man," said he, "would need to have a breast of stone to look at you and see you sitting there your lone in this bit closet stitching—you the daughter of Mamore, MacCailein's brother. You might as well be in the jyle! Put on your plaid, my dear, this minute, and I'll take you, though I had to burst through rocks!"

She made a wan attempt at smiling. "What would Simon Lovat say to that?" says she.

"—Or I would take a word down yonder," he went on more eagerly, "and bring the clan. I do not like the colour of this country—not one bit! I'm thinking to myself it would be fine for burning! And what is more, I do not like the colour of your face, Prim Campbell—you were like the flower, and now you're like the cannoch. If your folk thought you suffered they would come here like a fire in heather, and burn out the very roots of Castle Dounie."

"Ah, no!" said she at that; "the roots of it are deep, deep—deep—and many a hole between them like the beeches of Strongarbh."

"Indeed I thought she had a dungeon smell! I like her not, your married home, Prim Campbell! You have wrongs—what are they?"

She sat upon the bed, with folded arms, and clicked her heels—a sound most desolate! "I ken the tune of them," said she, "but I do not ken the words. There *are* no words."

"Well, lilt them to me, then!" he whispered. "Just the least bit whistle."

"Sit down," she said, "and crack. I'll neither sing nor whistle. A bird was in the breast of me a year ago, and now it's dead. And what would be the good in any case? The thing's beyond remede."

For half an hour she kept him plied with questions, drinking up his news like wine until her face had colour and her heart got almost gay. Ninian was deep in some droll story of some folk she knew when suddenly he saw her pale.

"I hear a cantering," said she. He listened, hearing nothing but the crows.

And then there was a shout outside, a sound of scurrying feet, the clattering of horses.

"That's his lordship back," said she; "I hoped he would be later. And there's an end to merriment—the happiest hour since I was Primrose Campbell! . . . Make Jennet write me soon—and not by Lovat's runners next time. You'll have to see him."

"Very good!" said Ninian, twitching at his coat-tails.

"I dare not ask you back!"

"I'll maybe ask mysel'. There's one or two bit things to talk of still—"

"Prim! are ye there?" cried out a voice upon the stairs. "I'm coming up!"

"Take not a bite from him though you were starving, Ninian!" she whispered.

"Indeed and I'm not needing it," he answered. "I had my own good dinner at the inns, and I did nobly."

"Are ye there, Prim? Can ye no' answer me?" Lord Lovat cried again upon the threshold, fumbling at the handle of the door.

"God bless me! Ninian Campbell! Is that you, yourself?" he cried when he beheld his wife's companion. "What mischief are ye after? I never saw ye in my country yet but ye were at your tricks!"

He looked a man of sixty, portly in the form, and bellied, with a great thick neck, and knots upon his forehead, little slits of eyes with wrinkles round them, and a broad cajoling smile. He wore the Highland dress, with trews so tightly cut they showed his legs were bowly.

"Ah!" said Ninian, chuckling, "your lordship's just in time! Her leddyship and me was nearly off together."

"I'm not afraid of that a bit!" said Lovat, leering at her. "Primrose would not leave her Simon." He tweaked her ear and put an arm about her. He might have been her father. She stood as stiff's a crag, and like a tomb for coldness. Ninian's shoulders

148

itched.

"Come away down, the three of us, and have a bite," said Lovat briskly. "How's my lord his Grace, and how's his brother Islay? Have ye letters for me?"

"The only one I had," said Ninian, with shame, "was for her leddyship, and I'm a stupid man that went and lost it. I had to leave some clothes at Buachaille Etive, and just this moment I found out I left my Jennet's line in them."

"Hoots!" said Lovat, "you are getting old! Never put a letter in your pocket, put it next the skin."

The three of them were standing on the floor; they made the small apartment crowded. "Take you a seat, my dear," said Lovat to his wife, and she sat down again upon her bed, and clicked her heels, and turned her ring, and looked at things invisible.

"Ye havena told me yet what mischief ye are after," Lovat said again to Ninian.

"I'll tell ye that, my lord," said Ninian, frank as day. "There's loud complaint of damage to the Road by banded parties; there's a lot of trouble wi' the Watches—some of them are out for plunder; and there's trafficking in arms. Your friend the Duke has sent me up to take a look about me."

"Did he ask ye to come here to see me first of all?" said Lovat quickly, taking out a pipe.

"Well, no," said Ninian, "your lordship wasna mentioned. His Grace and Islay are from home; my orders came through Mr Duncanson."

"Duncanson might have the sense to send you straight to me," said Lovat, querulous, and started polishing his pipe upon his nose. "The Duke, my kinsman, has the proofs of my devotion to himself and to the Government in spite of that it took from me my corps, and then my sheriffship. It must be well kent to you, Mr Campbell, that there is not a gentleman in the North has better means of knowing what is stirring than myself. If you had come one errand's end to me, I could have told you all about affairs and saved you trouble prying. There's not a move among the Jacobites, if that's what my good friends

149

are thinking. It has been a capital year for crops; the lairds and chiefs are rife of money; all the wildest clans have been disarmed—"

"I'm not so sure of that, my lord," said Ninian. "I doubt they're giving up old gear at bonny prices just to buy them better, new. They're landing shiploads in the Forth; if they're no' meant for serious use I'm cheated."

Lovat gave a crackling laugh, deep down his thrapple.

"Nonsense, man!" he said, "I don't believe one word of it! The one who told you that was trying to make a mock of you. It wasna Forbes now, was it?"

"At any rate that's MacCailein's notion," said Ninian lightly.

"And as for trouble on the Road, ye canna wonder at it—what's the good of roads for folk brought up on heather? The Road's no pet of mine."

"Nor mine," said Ninian heartily. "I think it spoils the country. But that is not MacCailein's notion."

"If my Highland company had not been disbanded, by what influence at the Court I'll fathom yet—it couldna be my age, whatever o't; I still could lead the lads—there would have been no trouble on the Road, for I myself would see to it. That land of Badenoch wants the strong firm hand."

"Indeed it does, my lord!" said Ninian. "I had my bellyful of trouble getting through it this time."

"Had ye that!" said Lovat, rubbing with his hand upon his pipe. "It was not Col, now, was it?" he inquired in Gaelic.

"No other one!" said Ninian, reddening for the wife, and on him, there and then, came down a cloud.

"That's the damnedst rogue in Gaeldom!" Lovat cried, and cracked his pipe. He threw its parts upon the floor, and ground them with his heel. "That's what I would do," says he, "with Barisdale!" His face was purple.

"Did I not think," said Ninian, "he was your lordship's friend?"

"Friend!" cried Lovat, choking. "If I will get him in Strathglass again at his old capers with my cattle, I will show the kind of friendship!"

"Well, faith," said Ninian, "he has the turn of telling with great glee what ploys he used to have in Castle Dounie."

"He has not set his foot within my door for years. The man's in fear of death of me! What ploys, now, was he telling?"

"Oh, just a lot of *bòilich*—that is bombast in the English, Lady Lovat—the only thing I mind is that he had a bout of foils with Paul Macmaster here. He said he beat him."

Lovat snorted. "Beat Macmaster, did he! He's a liar! There was no better fencer in the country than Drimdorran, and he beat Col level though he had a wounded arm. Col couldna hold a candle to him!"

"That's what I was thinking to myself," said Ninian, very slowly. "Her leddyship, I'm sure, is tired of listening to my nonsense. I'll be better stepping," He shook her by the hand. "Before I leave the North," said he, "I'll get my daughter's letter, and come out with it myself."

"Be sure you do," said she.

"But you must have refreshment, Mr Campbell," Lovat briskly said again. "Come down the stair, the three of us; I havena had a morsel since the morning."

He led the way, expecting them to follow: Ninian glanced at Lady Lovat, and she shook her head. He groped his way downstairs behind her husband, sniffing.

"Is Prim no' coming?" said her husband at the foot. "Well, let her bide!" He gave the crackled laugh and peered at Ninian. "I'm thinking she's on her high horse the day, Ninian; you and me will just take pot-luck together. What did ye think of her ladyship, Ninian? She's an old crony of yours?"

"I didna get much chance to speak to her," said Ninian, "but I thought her just a little downed with reading Sibbe's *Bowels*."

"That's just it!" said Lovat, crackling. "Far better wi' the wanton plays of Wycherley! But ye see yoursel'—" He pursed his lips and with a droll expression whistled the ground of a pibroch called "Too long in this condition."

"I see, my lord!" said Ninian; "I see!" his gaze between two buttons on Lord Lovat's coat.

"What the devil are ye looking at like that?" cried Lovat,

stepping back.

"I was just thinking to myself I never saw a bonnier tartan coat," said Ninian, and passed his tongue across his lips.

XVI

Dead Men's Bones

A great commotion in the street at ten o'clock that night brought out young Æneas from the inn with some alarm lest Ninian should be involved. A Highlander from France was the occasion—he had raked the market in the morning for recruits, got seven likely fellows, kept them primed with spirits in a tavern, and waited for the dark, to march them to a boat. His sheep had friends who pounced on them when they appeared from out the tavern; there was a squabble; some one fired a gun; a guard of redcoats hurried out and took the Gael of France a prisoner.

For half an hour the street was in a turmoil; then, as in a thunder-plump, the folk ran back into their closes; silence, like a swound came on the burgh. Æneas saw it like a picture, felt it like a song—the whitewashed mason fronts, the surly-looking entries of the lands, high-arched, the glimmer of a window here and there extinguished at a puff, and over all the quiver of the stars. He nursed within his breast a sense of eeriness and wonder.

When he got round the corner to his inn, his friend was standing at the door.

"I thought you had got lost," said Æneas.

"Night, the good herdsman, brings all creatures home," said Ninian. "A bonny night, indeed! Let you and me just take a little turn before we seek the blankets."

They walked the riverside, and Æneas recounted his first steps in business with something of a gusto. Haggling over freights and fish-crops, with Mackay to help him, was, it seemed, to have some spice of fun in it.

"And did ye give Mackay yon money?" Ninian asked.

"He wouldn't take it! He never saw such money in his life

before, and he was frightened."

"Frightened, was he? Well, it's not a wonder; I would be in fright myself to have so much about me, and the world so wide for spending. You be sure and watch your pockets! Did yon man Fraser at the inns convey my message?"

"He did," said Æneas.

"And did ye get my drift?"

"Primrose Campbell;—you were out at Lovat's—"

"Well done, yourself!" cried Ninian heartily. "Ye're getting to your schooling, I'll assure ye! I didna want the Fraser one to know where I was going. If there's a clan in Gaeldom worth the watching it's the Frasers."

"I fancy they are just like other folk," said Æneas, "good and bad among them."

"I never liked them from the start, and neither did my father, and now I'm under vows against them. But never you mind that the now! The way I'm taking you this walk is not for health, for I can tell ye I was plenty on my feet this day. There's things I have to say to ye that couldna well be said in Fraser's inns with lugs about us. Far better on the mountain-top!"

"I must confess I was surprised to think of you at Lovat's. What business had you there?" said Æneas.

"None at all that he kent of, and that's the truth for ye! I had to tell a bonny lie for an excuse, about a letter to his wife from Jennet. Never was a lie so sticky in my throat before!"

"I can't see what you wanted there at all," said Æneas; "my uncle says the man's a brock."

"The brock's a gentleman compared to Sim!" said Ninian. "But I'm the dog to draw the badger! The way to get a brock is not to stand and whistle at a cairn; I had to see him. If you will just stop talking your nonsense about the Frasers being like other folk, I'll tell ye what I did. First and foremost, I went out to Duncan Forbes, a man as deep's a well and clean as crystal. Ye'll know yourself that Duncan is the one man in the North that's worth a spittle. What Duncan does not know is not worth kenning. Now ye'll be wondering to yourself what brought me there in such a hurry?"

154

"I can't say that I am," said Æneas.

"Fie on ye there!" said Ninian. "Always, you, be curious; that's the way to learn. Myself I couldna see a man go up a close but I would wonder what he wanted there. I went to Forbes for three things—first, because I had to, for Lord Islay bade me. Man, yon's the clever, deep one, Duncan! He should have been a *beachdair*! There's nothing that I learned this week back that he doesna know already, but he never guessed before what meant the trade in guns. I think I pleased his lordship there!— oh yes, I pleased him; out at once he brought the bottle! But that was not the only thing that sent me yonder; that could wait: the second thing was more important,—I wanted him to know that I was here, and give him just the least wee hint that I might beard the badger. If I by any chance fell down a stair in Castle Dounie, it would be some comfort just to ken that Duncan might come looking. Do ye think I would go into the den without letting my friends ken? Na, na! And that's the very reason I left word for you about the primrose."

"I guessed so much myself," said Æneas.

"Of course ye did! Ye must have heard of Simon's dungeons. I felt the smell of them! Well, I came back from Forbes, and got a horse, and galloped off, and—"

"But what about the third thing took you out to Forbes?" asked Æneas.

Ninian nodded. "Good!" said he. "I wondered would ye mind to ask. Oh yes, ye're getting on! But never mind the third thing now—just come with me to Lovat. I feared at first I wouldna see him; he was at Strath Errick." He stopped, and stood, and whispered low to Æneas, "Did ever ye see Primrose Campbell?"

"No," said Æneas.

"It was my wife gave milk to her. She's just the age of Jennet. Many a day they played about Glen Aray. You'll no' can mind of that; it was before your memory came to you. She was as bonny as a trout! What woe has come upon that girl? Yonder she was sitting like a ghost, and greeting. Never was there seen a drearier girl! Her room was like a cell for darkness and for size, and in it was a girnal, and a skellet at the grate for cooking. What can ye make of that but that she feeds alone? Duke Archie's niece, you'll mind ye! daughter of Mamore!"

He put his hand behind his neck and gave a tug, and brought his dagger out, and held it level in both palms as one would show a fish.

"*Bheil thu faicinn sin?*" said he—"Ar't seeing that? I never had a flea on me that bit my back the way that *biodag* did when I was standing there with Simon and the girl he spoiled. He put an arm about her—he was like a falcon with a heath-hen in its claws; I picked the very spot where I could strike him just between the buttons."

He was inflamed with anger; cried loud out, all trembling.

"*Cuist!* for God's sake!" Æneas whispered, looking round about him. "This is not the moor; you never know who's listening."

"That is very true," said Ninian, and looked about him too. No house was near. The place they stood on was a haugh where clothes were bleaching. The wind of night was blowing. He slipped the dagger down his back again and more composedly resumed his tale.

"It's not the first time I met Sim: I got the size of him one time before when I was North on business, and this time, like that last, he started out to draw me."

"And little he got out of you, I'll swear," said Æneas with amusement.

"Now there ye're wrong! I told him just the truth—to baffle him. When you will have a rogue to deal with Æneas, in your business, always tell the truth,—it foils the other fellow. All the time Sim fiddled with his pipe and rubbed it on his nose to hide the mouth of him, and I kept half an eye on him. He knew as much as Forbes, and blamed me that I did not come to him the first go-off for information. 'They took my Highland corps from me,' says he, 'but my good friend the Duke knows that I'm staunch and steady.' 'Ye damned old rogue!' thinks I, and aye as cheery as the morn with him, although that poor lass sitting on her bed fair made me think him stinking. 'Ye rogue!' thinks

I, 'stop you, and I will have ye!' And then, my grief, I got a blow! Ye see, Æneas, just to tell ye the truth plump and plain, since ever we met Barisdale, and yon black lad who had the *creach* made mention of some Big One checking me, my mind would aye be running on Lord Lovat. He doesna like the Road; he's just the man to turn a penny troking with the Dutch for guns, and he's the only man I know that might in some way get a word that I was coming."

"Who could tell him that?" asked Æneas.

"That's the bit! I never yet came North but Lovat knew my business. Indeed, that was another reason for my telling him the truth this day; he maybe knew't already. Well, at the last, yonder, I thought I had him, and then, *mo thruaigh!* I got the blow. Ye see I mentioned last of all that I had trouble coming, and thereupon says he, quite sharp in Gaelic, though his wife was there who does not know, poor soul! the language, 'Was it Col?' That fairly downed me!"

"It looks to me," said Æneas, "a very foolish question for a man so sharp as Lovat. To my mind it proclaimed him guilty, or at any rate with knowledge."

"There ye go again! Just think a wee, my lad!—if he had been the Big One in command of Col, he never would have breathed Col's name. Whenever he said that, I knew my twine was twisted just as bad as ever. I went there sure he had put Col on me, and the man who put Col on me was the man who trafficked in the guns, and the man who trafficked in the guns was the man who egged the ragged remnants of the clans to break the Road, and whenever he said 'Was it Col?' I felt a fool."

"But craft for craft!" said Æneas; "if Lord Lovat's quite so cunning a man as all that, might his question not be made so purposely simple just to blind you?"

"Not a bad observe!" said Ninian, with approval. "It might well be that Simon tried the truth too, just to blind me. But na, na! It turns out Barisdale and he for years have been at variance about some pranks of Col with cattle in Strathglass. 'I'll break him like my pipe!' says Sim in fury, and he smashed it with his heel. I thought, at last, like you, there was a chance that all this was put on, so out went Ninian, and took three farm-town dinners, and spent three hours in questioning the country. There's no doubt about it—he could cut Col's throat! Col is in fear of death of him; he has a mortgage over Col's estate, and plays him like a fish. So there, ye see, I'm all aback, and have to start some other way to loose my hank. And Duncan Forbes is on the wrong scent too,—although he never cheeped, I knew he thought the same as I did."

"Well, that clears Lovat, seemingly," said Æneas.

"Of that, perhaps! Of that!" said Ninian. "But I have other things to settle with his lordship. He piped a bit of a tune to me— 'Too long in this condition'—By God! I'll make him pipe before I'm done with him, or my name's not Macgregor. Oh, Æneas! if you had seen—if you had heard yon woman! Brock! brock! Give me his head on a stick! He wanted me to stay for meat— a bite of it would choke me! I had a task of it refusing in a way to shield his wife, but I managed. Now here's a thing will make ye wonder—I'm going back to Castle Dounie."

"I wouldn't go!" said Æneas.

"Ye see, I promised Prim to find my daughter's letter and to take it out to her. It's ill to find a thing that never was, and I'll no find it, so I'll just go out and say so. Although that lie stuck in the throat of me, I'm not ashamed o't: I can use it twice to some advantage. If ever you have need to tell a lie, be sure it is a good one, Æneas."

"I wouldn't go," said Æneas again, "I wouldn't go!"

"What! Not for that poor woman's sake! Is that the man ye are, Macmaster? Just think of her—the old MacCailein's niece, to grow up like the rush on Aray-side and wither like the fern in yon black cranny of the brock!"

"Can she not leave it?"

"Not of herself, nor of her own contrivance. Ye wouldna ask the question if ye knew Prim Campbell—she was like the kings for pride! Her man might hang her by the nails, and she would not give one wee cry to show the world she suffered. She would not even tell myself what ailed her at the brute. And what am I to say to Jennet—that I left her old friend yonder in the falcon's claws?"

"No, no! you can't do that!" said Æneas, greatly shaken. "I see it now; you must go out and plead with her to leave him if it be so bad as you are thinking. I'll go myself with you, if that is any use."

"That's what I was thinking to myself," said Ninian, and clapped the other's back. "It's this way of it, Æneas,—I want your backing-up about her state when I get back to Inveraray, and, forbye, I want ye just to have a squint at Simon."

"That bit of it I know I'll scarcely relish," Æneas said wryly.

"I daresay not, but ye can help me greatly just by giving him the squint. Between us, if we canna get Prim Campbell to give up her man, we'll maybe get a way to take her man from Primrose Campbell. Come you down this way just a bittock, lad, before we turn. I'm like the man of Knapdale—I'm not finished with my story."

They now were well out of the town, and opposite the river's isles whence came above the rushing of the stream the whistling of whaups. It seemed the voice of terrified conspiracies to Æneas. The plumage of the isles was black against the stars; no whisper of the town, nor any light of it, came where they walked through dewy grasses. A goat at tether on the rough bank bleated. Ninian went off the path a bit, and came upon a bridge of wood that led out to the islands. He stood upon the middle of it with his friend.

"Did ever you hear," said he, "of the fox and the fleas?"

"No," said Æneas, wondering.

"When the fox is bad with fleas, he will take a piece of moss into the mouth of him and wade very slowly out in a river just like this, and the fleas will come up to his back to keep themselves from drowning. Then the sly fellow will go deeper in, until they have to take his neck for it. Then he will sink his head below the water, all except his mouth, and it will have the piece of moss in it. The fleas will all take refuge in the moss, like many a gallant tribe in history, and then the red lad lets the moss go floating."

"Very good for a preamble," said Æneas, leaning on the

159

bridge below which went the black Ness rushing. "What is the application?"

"That is a story of my father's; he was a great hand at the stories, and now lies yonder in Balwhidder, all his stories done. He would say to me, 'If I could get a piece of moss was big enough to hold the Frasers, I would walk through Corryvreckan with them hanging on my back.' But I'm thinking Simon would be an ill beast to shake off the snout! When I went out today to Castle Dounie it was with no particular ill-will to Simon, for he himself's MacCailein's kin, and he was married on Prim Campbell. With that I couldna very well be hard on him; I even might have smoothed things over just to please his leddy, unless they were the blackest. But when I saw yon weeping woman of my heart, the marrow of my bones was poisoned at him. I couldna spare him then! Na, na! I couldna spare him then! The very dirk of me was kittling my back and crying 'Kill him!' "

"You're just a savage, Ninian," said Æneas, with pity.

"Am I? God be praised, if that's to kill a rat! Ye thought he was clear of me, did ye, when I proved him an unfriend of Col's? But I had something else against him, maybe worse than trafficking in guns. Many a left-hand business Sim was mixed in. Ye know the way he got his first wife? He took with him five hundred men and carried her away to Aigas Island, where he kept her in a creel and got a drunken minister to marry them. He was condemned to death for that, and lived for years a hunted man, with Atholl for the worst dog on his trail. MacCailein got him pardoned, and ever since he plays the loyal chief. He took his clan out for King Geordie in the year of Mar, and they were out again against your father at Glenshiel. Are ye grasping this?—at no time was he on the side of Paul Macmaster!"

"I'm glad to know it!" said Æneas warmly.

"But listen you to this—I told ye on Loch Laggan-side your father had been drowned: there's not one word of truth in it! Nor was he killed at all in Ross-shire."

"What happened to him, then?" asked Æneas, bewildered.

"If Ninian could tell ye that he would be clever! When I told ye yon story at Loch Laggan of your father drowned I just was sounding ye. Your family might have a different account of him and kept it to themselves. I found ye knew as little as myself, or less. Whatever happened to your father, it was neither in the battle nor the boat he perished."

"I know that he was wounded in the fight," said Æneas.

"That's true; he was. But after it he was in Castle Dounie, and was fencing there with Col. Ye mind Col told us?"

"But I thought that was sometime earlier," said Æneas with agitation. "Oh, I wish these birds would stop their whistling!"

"Never you mind the birds! They are like all of us, and have their own affairs of night-time. It's me that likes to hear the curlew call! Listen now, to me!"

He told him much the same as he had told to Forbes, of Barisdale's equivocations when he questioned him alone.

"And what does Forbes think of it?" asked Æneas.

"Nobody will ever know what Duncan Forbes is thinking about anything, least of all a *beachdair*. But I saw from the face of him he was in bad weather when I brought up your father's end and mentioned Castle Dounie. Ye see, Æneas, Forbes and Lovat are friends—at least, as close on that as a dove might be with a serpent, though, 'faith, there's no' much o' the dove in Duncan when it comes to the hour of battle. Like all good men, he's loth to think his neighbour worse than he suspected, and you and me will get no help from him in prying into this thing."

"But here's a thing that—if I'm to take your view of it—imputes some dark and sinister connection between my father's disappearance and Lord Lovat: is the Lord Advocate not a man to do his duty to the State—?"

"Stop! stop!" cried Ninian. "Forbes, ye may be sure, will do his duty when it's plain before him, but like the rest of us, he's no' going to break his legs running after it if it means the ruin of an old acquaintance. Time enough for him to think of duty when the story's full before him. Just now he doesna credit me!"

"And what am I to do?" asked Æneas helplessly.

"We'll go out to Castle Dounie together in two or three days—just time enough for me not to be able to find yon letter. For one thing, ye will bear me witness that his wife's in misery.

We'll make a point to see his lordship, and what more natural than that your father's name should call for mention either by Lord Lovat, or myself, or you? We've just to start the crack about Col's story; you be very calm, and I'll keep watch on Simon."

"It is a terrible task you give me," Æneas said gloomily; "it is like digging up my father's bones. And what do you think will come of it?"

"I canna tell ye that," said Ninian, turning from the bridge and making for the sleeping town, "but this I'm sure of,—something happened to your father far more strange than drowning."

XVII

Castle Dounie Again

For three days more did Æneas prosecute his uncle's business; then a thing befell that cut all business short and proved that Ninian was right in thinking Inverness more wicked than the woods. Mackay—a sombre, pious, iron kind of man, who piqued himself upon his own sufficiency—had been at first inclined to huff at having this young sprig sent North to help him, and to pry into affairs, but found a Highland way at last of turning Æneas' appearance to his own account. He hinted to their customers of great new plans for wider markets with the influence of Argyll; made out the lad a protégé of Islay's, and ascribed to him a fabulous amount of what he called the "wherewithal." His own importance thus fictitiously distended he took Æneas down Loch Ness, and through The Aird, the Black Isle, and the straths, the lad in ignorance of what tales secured for him a deference he felt was out of all proportions to his years. He met a score of men whose names were known to him as chieftains on his uncle's books,—majestic creatures holding state in gaunt old keeps where pipers blew from turrets, or in shabby barn-like houses sucking life from clustered crofts about them. It seemed at first to Æneas an insolence to mention business to such lordly ones—they were so grandly clad in plaid and lace, such shining buttons and such high-cocked feathers; sometimes had they tails of henchmen, wet-foot gillies, armour-bearers, like a page of story. They dealt with him, to start with, like a scullion, thinking him a Lowland prentice to Mackay, but once Mackay had whispered to them something of the truth (a good deal stretched), and Æneas, unabashed, confronted them as lofty as themselves, they treated him with great civility.

From these proud petty chiefs he got his last illumination of the North as glamoured mainly to the eye of fancy, and a gleam went off the hills for him as slips the sunset off the heather. It was with some dismay, as one finds river ice break under him, he found that just as Barisdale below his leather coat was but a bellows, so these men of family, for all their show of native ancient pomp and ritual, were more the merchantmen than Alan-Iain-Alain Og. They haggled like to fishwives on the price of salt and salmon crops, and pickled beef, and timber: when one—a Major Fraser, laird of Castleheather—followed him for miles along The Aird to canvass a fantastic scheme for cutting woods and opening a furnace, Æneas told himself he nevermore would wear a kilt!

His dream dispelled of a poetic world surviving in the hills, he got malicious and secret joy in stripping every rag of false heroics from such gentry. From some one he had learned that Castleheather was no friend of Lovat; that day in The Aird, as he came with him brandishing his schemes for making money fast for Æneas (with of course a fat share for himself), the young man, in a mood of mischief, ventured an opinion that no Fraser schemes could flourish in that shire unless Lord Lovat fathered them.

As he was saying so, they were in sight of Castle Dounie. "Look at it!" hissed Fraser, boiling. "Tell me did ye ever see an uglier! It's like the man himself; get you into the grip of Simon wi' your money, and he'll squeeze ye like a lemon."

"I'm never hearing but the worst of him," said Æneas. "Surely he has some parts not entirely vicious, or else he was no friend of Islay and Argyll."

"They don't know him!" cried Castleheather, mad with fury. "Yes, by God, they do!" he added quickly. "A man I kent sent proofs to them of what he was,—a letter of Sim's own that showed he had a share in Grange's business and trepanned the lady. They had it in good time to stop his marriage with their niece, but na!—it didna stop it; knowing what they knew, they let him take her! Lovat has put salt upon MacCailein's tail; he'll never want a pleader now in London, seeing that he's married on a Campbell."

"The thing's incredible of Islay or his Grace," said Æneas

stoutly, yet a little shaken in his loyalty, and thereupon the Major, like a man who feared he had been too outspoken, half retracted, saying that at least the thing was rumoured. "Do not breathe," said he, "a word of what I've mentioned; I'm too ill-neighbours as it is with Sim to make things worse by clattering."

Those three days Æneas spent with Saul Mackay brought down on him in Inverness attentions that he could not understand: he never guessed the pious Saul had magnified three hundred pounds into so many thousands. The street folk sometimes jostled him to see if he would chink. A horde of beggars followed him—in fishing-bothies, on the quays, among the skippers, even in the shops. The inn that he and Ninian dwelt in had at times a row in front of it of idle citizens who seemed to find some satisfaction just to look at walls behind which all that wealth—to judge by smell—was supping sheep's-head singed.

With *beachdair* business of his own that kept him less in Inverness than in the landward parishes about it, where he spent from morn till all hours of the night in seeming useless saunter-ing round mills and smithies, hamlets, farm-towns, inns—any place at all in which he could get folk to gossip,—Ninian knew nothing of his friend's celebrity till one night he came home, himself, a good deal earlier than usual, and from some casual talk among a group upon the causeway, grasped the situation.

"They're talking of ye there as if ye had the wealth of India in your belt," he said peevishly to Æneas when he got in. "Your man Mackay's a fool—he has been bragging, or ye have been flourishing your uncle's money far too free. It's something of a pity, lad, ye ever dropped the kilt; they never would jalouse a man in kilts had more than sixpence. Whatever o't, it's close on time that we were shifting home: if we were only done wi' old MacShimi, I'm quite ready for the road, whatever you may be."

"Have you come speed regarding yon!—a fresh light on the business?" Æneas asked: through every hour—through every moment, almost, of his mercantile engagements, that mystery of his father, like a wraith, stood on the threshold of his mind. He knew that Ninian, like a hound, was tracking, yet until that moment when MacShimi's name was mentioned he had curiously forbore to question him, half-fearful that some wild half-daft surmises of his own might be confirmed.

"Not so much a light as just an ember here and there," said Ninian, and took a fishing-line, all tangled in a mass, from out his pocket. They had a room between them, lit by tallow dips; he held the line up to a candle so that Æneas could see how badly it was ravelled.

"That's your father's business," he said, his deep eyes glittering. "Ye see it's gey and tousy—scarce an ell of it unfankled." He dived his hand into another pocket, and produced a line rolled neatly on a stick, with just some yards of tangled end to clear of it.

"That," said he, "is my own affair; I'll get what twists are left, from that, before I'm two days older," and he put it back into his pouch. "But this one here's a far more kittle task to deal wi'; now it's in a knot wi' me I canna loose another finger-length until the two of us have seen his lordship."

He pulled a chair up to the table, sat, and set the twine before him, glowering at it like a man gripped in a spell. There seemed in him some notion of the thing as more than symbol—as a mystery and problem in itself; over and over he turned it lightly with a finger, muttering to himself in Gaelic. Then he took his small black knife, and with its point for bodkin gently pryed the ravelling.

"Tach!" said he at last, disgusted, and thrust it in his pocket. "What's the use tonight? I needna bother. I've been on the busy foot all day like the deer of the mountain ben, and not much gained from it; I'm thinking to myself we'll better beard the brock tomorrow if your business will permit."

Next afternoon they got a fisherman to take them on a favouring slant of wind to Beauly village, and from there went out on foot to Castle Dounie. A string of twenty horses stood at rings along a wall; and pipes were bellowing. Gillies wearing other cloth than Fraser's hung about a copper where a cook made soup, and with them was a slim, young, silly lad in breeches with a bag the gillies took from him and tossed between them till it burst and gushed out letters. The piper of the house, as they came to the front of it, stopped playing, and threw down his pipes upon the ground as if they soiled his hands, and they were picked up by a man who seemed to wait on him for just that purpose.

"It looks to me," said Æneas, "as if we happened on a busy day."

"My loss! we have," said Ninian ruefully. "He's got a company," and then his face lit up at sight of Lady Lovat standing at the door. She had presided at her husband's table whence that moment burst the uproar of his guests as if they were relieved at her departure when the serious ritual of wine and Ferintosh came on. Before retiring to her cell she had come to the door to breathe a moment's cleaner air than was within, and gave a cry of pleasure at the sight of Ninian.

There was no more than time for Ninian to let her know the name of his companion, when Lovat, who had heard her cry, came from the dinner-room with great displays of warmth to ask them in.

"I'm feared ye're just a little late for dinner, gentlemen," said he, and hiccoughed. " '*Post festum ven—ven*'—what is it now?—'*venisti.*' But if ye're in trim for jinks, ye couldna have picked out a better hour. . . . Ye're looking tired, Prim; go you and lie ye down."

She left them like a child admonished; on that instant every doubt of Æneas that kept his judgment in suspense about Lord Lovat's character was gone—he hated him!

"My friend is Paul Macmaster's son," said Ninian. "He's here in Inverness on business for his uncle, and I took him out wi' me to see The Aird. We took a boat to Beauly and go back that way. The pity is I havena got the least excuse for coming here except to tell her ladyship I havena got her letter yet."

Lovat turned his gaze on Æneas and scanned him closely as he shook his hand. "I'm glad to see ye, sir," said he, indifferent about the letter; "I knew your father, as no doubt my friend here Mr Campbell would inform ye. That was a gallant man! And now come you away and see my hoose." He took them by the arms and led them, waddling a little in his gait; the least faint flush of drink was on his face, a sappy kind of fulsomeness was in his manner; he was blithe.

The place he pushed them into was a hall, oak-beamed, with a stupendous fireplace on whose hearth two dozen tappit-hens were ranked like soldiers, warming what was in them. The bottom of the table scarcely could be seen for reek that drifted from tobacco-pipes; it had been cleared of meats, and round it, closely packed, were sitting men at that particular stage of human bliss, where not the trump of Gabriel itself would matter. When Ninian and Æneas stepped in, the room was like to rend with shouting that was slacked but for a moment while Lord Lovat made his new guests known to half the company—the other half was too far off among the smoke and too uproarious to take notice. "Sit ye here," said he, and made a place beside him, Æneas next his elbow. A servant-man in breeches clapped before them tappit-hens, the measures full of claret or canary.

"Ca' canny wi' the drink!" said Ninian, whispering.

Æneas looked about him at a company of whose notables his host gave him the names; at least a dozen of their number were small lairds himself had met that week with Saul Mackay, who flourished with their glasses, pledging him; but for the piper playing outside in the ground again, and Scottish speech and older roysterers, it might (he thought) be Utrecht and the students.

For seeing Lovat play the patriarch the hour was not quite opportune; his friends had lifted anchors and were driving free before the winds of grape and barley. Repeated arguments boiled into wrangles round the table; sometimes with a toast he stopped them, or would shoot a pleasantry that kept his company in hand; he even ventured some high-kilted tales. Himself a good deal soberer than the soberest of them—as Æneas could see—he was at times a little clouded, his crackling laugh more frequent than was called for by the fun; at times he swayed a trifle on the bow legs when he stood. But always he maintained the chieftain—formal in address when names were mentioned; half his guests as "cousins," all the rest punctiliously by names of their estates. No stratagem was wanting to maintain good-humour; he had every wile! And always, as his eyes swept round them, that cajoling smile!

The clamour made all rational speech impossible, and Æneas and Ninian, too late, by hours, to reach that witless level, sat till they were wearied, not a chance arising to bring up the topic of their call, until at last, as Providence would have it, Lovat of himself gave them an opening.

"Is this your first jaunt North?" he queried Æneas in a lull.

"Yes," said Æneas. "Till now I never crossed Druim Albyn. Your lordship has a bonny land."

"There's nothing wrong with it in that respect, I pride myself," said Lovat, just as if himself had been creator; "when I'm away from it, young sir, it's many a time I'm thinking there's no finer in the universe. A little out the world, but none the worse of that." He rubbed a nutmeg on a risp above his wine and looked benignant. "Your father had a fancy for it; he was taken, in particular, with The Aird."

"You knew him, sir?" said Æneas, with commotion in his breast.

"He spent a month wi' me—a worthy man! It was a mortal pity how things fell! I could have told ye were his son, sir; there's a great resemblance."

"So they say," said Æneas, uneasy at the old man's gaze that searched his features with an eye in which a tear of sentiment was hanging.

"And still ye're like your mother too, in some way—it's the tilt-up of your chin; I saw it at the door. I never met her, but he had her picture."

"I've never seen it, sir," said Æneas, with interest.

"Oh yes, he had it with him—very fine! A little of the rebel too, to look at, as he said himself."

A host of questions cried in Æneas; he turned to Ninian, to find he was engaged in speech with some one on his other side.

"It was after Glenshiel that he was here, I think?" said Æneas at last.

"It was. That sorry business!" He looked about him

169

cautiously; assured the clamour of the table made it safe, he leaned to Æneas and whispered, "Between ourselves, I risked a lot by harbouring your father that time. My kindred were against him at Glenshiel, and yet I was myself suspected to be friends with the Pretender—the damnedst nonsense, as my good friend Ninian could tell ye! An old acquaintance of my own and of your father's—Dugald Ross of Keills—came on him blooding like a wedder in Glen Afric from a cut he got that morning in the skirmish; hid him for a week, and brought him here in cloud of night for my protection. I mind that evening well—your father made a dash into my room, and touched the fire before I could prevent him, making sure of sanctuary. Ye know the custom, Mr Æneas?"

"Sound Greek," said Æneas, mastering his agitation.

"Yes, and good Gaelic too; as he had touched my fire I darena harm him if I wanted. I kept him here a month at no small hazard, for he was a man put to the horn, denounced and searched for, and, as I was saying, I was just a trifle 'neath the cloud myself among my enemies. He darena venture home—that much we learned from Duncanson, who sent him money to clear out the country. By luck, three nameless men were drowned on the day Glenshiel was fought; some men of Glendaruel's were of opinion that your father was among them, and said so in Argyll when they got back. We heard of this from Duncanson—this all between ourselves, now, Mr Æneas!—and Duncanson proposed that notion should be nourished. We backed it up, and when the hunt was over for your father, he went off."

"Off," said Æneas blankly; "where?" The toe of Ninian's boot pressed on his own so sorely that it made him wince.

"Where?" said Lovat vaguely, with a hiccough. "Oh, just off! The last of him was riding out of here for Forth. He got from me a horse and saddle, pledging they would be sent back from Perth or Stirling. They never came; I cared less for the horse than for the saddle, that was something of an heirloom, silver-mounted. But I must own he sent their value later on through Duncanson."

Again was Ninian tapping on the ankle, with his nose dipped

170

in a goblet, and the knee of Æneas nudged him for assistance but he paid no heed. "What's next for me to say?" thought Æneas, desperate, and made incapable of guile by feelings far too intimate and solemn, threw his cards upon the table.

"My lord," said he, "what you have told me there comes on me like a thunderclap."

"What way?" asked Lovat sharply, picking up a pipe and rubbing with its bowl along his nose. "Your father paid the horse; I'm no' complainin'. He might have had a score o' horse, and welcome."

"Not that," said Æneas, and his tongue felt in his mouth like pith for dryness; "until the other day I never knew my father had been here—"

"Who was it told ye?" Lovat asked.

"Macdonnell of Barisdale," said Æneas.

"Col-of-the-tricks! Ye came across the country then wi' Campbell? . . . That's a trifle ye forgot to mention, Ninian, last time that I saw ye!"

But Ninian, engrossed in talk with some one on his right, seemed deaf to this appeal, though not too much aloof to give another tap to Æneas.

"Oh yes, my lord, we came together from Breadalbane," Æneas answered for his friend. "I came on Mr Campbell in a change at Orchy. The tale of Barisdale surprised me much. I always understood my father went straight from Glenshiel to where the story went he perished."

"And where was that?" asked Lovat quickly, polishing a pipe he seldom smoked.

"Loch Duich," answered Æneas.

Lovat looked at him, astonished.

"Loch Duich!" he exclaimed. "Ye surely do not mean to tell me that your people took that tale in earnest! We only gave it just to cover up his tracks."

"It looks as if they had been covered up too well," said Æneas. "Where did my father go to?"

"It's strange indeed that you should have to ask me that;—to France," said Lovat. "The thing is almost unbelievable that you

171

should be in darkness all this time. Duncanson sent out his rents to him until he died."

"Where did he die, and when, my lord?"

"I only know it was in France, about a twelvemonth later."

"Did Mr Duncanson ken that?" asked Æneas, and Ninian's hand below the table clapped him on the knee approving, though he seemed aloof as ever.

Lovat showed the least degree of hesitation.

"I'll warrant ye he kent it," he replied. "It was from him I got it. Of course it was a ticklish business at the time, for Duncanson was in the pay of Islay and the Duke, and darena have the name of sheltering your father, but it's queer to me so long a time should lapse before ye hear the truth of it. You must have been a child yourself at that time, Mr Æneas; but surely I have heard ye have an uncle?"

"He knows no more than I do," Æneas said bitterly.

"You're sure of that?"

"I am. He thinks my father perished in Kintail."

"And is he friendly wi' Duncanson?"

"No," said Æneas; "they haven't changed a word since Duncanson became the laird."

"I see! I see!" said Lovat, pursing up his mouth, and looking underneath the chin of Æneas at Ninian, still engaged. "The thing's beyond me!" he declared; "unless—" and there he checked himself.

"The thing's as plain as porridge, sir," said Æneas. "He dare not let it out that he was in a correspondence with my father, and he hates my uncle, so he let the false tale stand."

"It looks like that," said Lovat anxiously.

"Your lordship cannot wonder that I feel concerned. It was a cruel thing of Duncanson to keep us in the dark."

"Indeed I'm all aback at him!" said Lovat. "Put you the thing to him yourself when ye get back"; and then he said with cunning so transparent it was almost silly, "Tell him that it was from Barisdale ye got it—so it was; my name need not be mentioned." In tones equivocal and wheedling he expressed his sympathy, but laid most weight on the necessity for tact in

opening up the story, and tact with him meant plainly no desire
to clash with Duncanson.

XVIII

A Hank Unravelled

Æneas sat like a stone for some time after this astounding revelation. The brawling of the table-foot had swelled again, and Lovat started blandishing a stockish little man dressed in the Highland habit with a scarlet waistcoat scarce more flaming than his face, who was at variance, it seemed, with one who from the first had caught the eye of Æneas—an officer of troops in uniform. Ninian was at a brisk exchange of stories with a big-jowled man upon his right, and hotching to the other's humour. The piper on the sward out-by was playing "Fingal's Weeping" on a sobbing chanter, grief's peculiar note; the pibroch alone was in the key of Æneas, on whom a great resentment came that folk should laugh while through himself went sweeping tides of indignation. In those three minutes' talk with Lovat something staple in his life was overwhelmed. Yet here was Ninian who had brought him there with a deliberate purpose to get Lovat talking, under influence of Lovat's claret, plainly, cracking heedless with a fat-jowled fool.

The officer was one named Burt, an English captain, pay-master to Wade. A peaceable and sober man, he sat all through the dinner, and what Lovat called the jinks that followed, something of a foreigner among his fellows, sipping at his wine restrainedly, and not to be enticed to that more potent beverage, the Ferintosh, that most of them by now had started on. They took it out of stemless glasses, smashed in some former bacchanalia to discourage heel-taps, and the tankard oftenest was at the elbow of the man with the scarlet waistcoat, whom the others called Culcairn. Culcairn, a Fraser of cadet relation to Lord Lovat, had some rankling spirit of resentment still at something that had happened months before—the stoppage of a pay he drew in Lovat's Independent Corps—and sought to

174

draw the soldier out on his opinion of the Highland Companies.

Burt gave them every credit short of discipline and strict concurrence with the aims of Wade. Their knowledge of the country and the folk, he said, was of the first importance; they had been bred to arms and steeled to hardships; nothing could be said against their courage, but he feared they were more loyal to their chiefs and clans than to the crown.

"And what for no?" cried out Culcairn. "My skin is nearer to me than my coat, as we will say in Gaelic. I never saw the king between the eyes but on a signboard, and I ken MacShimi."

Burt gave a little smile. "With all respect to our noble host," said he, "I'm certain he regards the interests of the clan as second to the welfare of the country at large, or else the North was barbarous."

"Barbarous!" screamed out Culcairn, a flaming fury on him, too much gone in drink to grapple with what qualified the word. "It's on a piece of grass outside we could be settling that!"

He jumped to his feet, with a thickened neck, and his black beard bristling; two of his neighbours, laughing, gripped him round the middle; the room was in a turmoil for defence of Burt, who sat composed.

"Gentlemen! gentlemen!" cried Lovat in reproof, his paunch upon the table. "I think the deil himsel' could not keep sulphur to my kinsman's furies; what now in all the earth is wrong with you, my dear Culcairn?"

"Devil a thing but drink!" replied Culcairn with honesty, and laughing now himself.

"It's not the drink, I'll warrant ye!" said Lovat. "Culloden never brewed a sounder tipple, it's your heid that's not the heid it was, sir; in faith, in that respect I fear it's like my own. I doubt, good cousin, we are gettin' old." He gave a pawky smile and passed his hand across his forehead. "Many a tree we scourged, Culcairn, and many a flagon tilted, but we used to keep our tempers, you and me that's off the self-same blood. What ails my robin redbreist at ye, Captain Burt?"

"A point of judgment on the Independent Companies," said Burt. "I ventured to remark to Mr Fraser that they had some

175

faults."

"And very right you are there, Captain Burt!" said Lovat. "Such as they are at present I cannot deny it. Just a useless lot of gillies!"

"But still a dangerous weapon ready for the hands of disaffection."

He could not have expressed a thought more stinging to his host, whose Highland company was taken from him just for such a fear!

Lovat scowled and purpled. Burt saw his error instantly and hastened to amend. "I spoke particularly," said he, "of those upon the Road. Their knowledge ought to make our work as safe as if it were on Constitution Hill, and yet it doesn't."

Lovat with an effort mastered his vexation. "There's nothing in that view," said he, "that my friend Culcairn need quarrel with, I'm sure. The Government that took my company from me took it from the one man in the Highlands fit to keep the peace; thank God, it never fell to me to ward the Road—I have no great regard for it."

"Why not, my lord?" asked Burt, astonished.

"I'll leave it to my good friend Mr Campbell to adduce the reason," said Lord Lovat, turning upon Ninian a waggish smile of challenge.

"Bad for the feet! bad for the feet!" said Ninian readily. "Harder than ever to walk to kirk, it's neither good for men nor horses,"—and the company roared.

"But likely to be very good for business," broke in Æneas, astonished in a moment at himself to be so suddenly and warm the merchant, half compelled by some annoyance at his friend and a repugnance at that spirit of reaction or arrest he felt in Lovat. Between this orgy and the pibroch, plaintive, singing Fingal's sorrow in the glens of Tir-nan-Og, old days remembering, was no single bond!

"Business!" cried Lovat, throwing up his hands. "My good young friend says 'business'—what in fortune's name do we want wi' business? Here is a healthy and contented people bruicking and enjoying every comfort fitted to their state, secure of the invasion of those desperate and levelling ideas that in other places have played havoc with the loyalty of commons, and reduced authority of chiefs. There is no one under the cope and canopy of heaven loves his country and his king—God bless him!—more truly than myself, and I have given the proofs of it on more than one occasion, but as for roads and schools and all that means of stenting and of levying, I'm utterly against them in the shire of Inverness."

"Not schools!" said Æneas boldly, shocked beyond measure. "Surely not schools!"

"Yes, schools!" said Lovat, thumping on the table. "What good are they to Gaeldom? So long as men of family can have their children tutored in what arts belong to their position, either in their homes or furth the country, the setting up of schools for all and sundry of the folk is contrar to the welfare of the State. My people always have what fits them best in their condition—schooling of the winter and the blast, rough fare, the hills to strive wi', and the soil to break. They need no more, except their swords and skill to use them. What do you say to that, Macmaster?"

He leaned upon his arms, swung round upon his hips, and snarled the question in the young man's ear; and Æneas, looking at the face thrust close up to his own, saw in it everything for which he had contempt—unscrupulous craft, and cruelty, and greed.

"It sounds to me," said he, "like blasphemy."

A glitter came to Lovat's eyes; a flicker crossed his face, and Æneas perceived without concern that he had made an enemy.

"Your sentiment about the road, my lord, seems pretty general in Inverness," said Burt. "Poor Leggatt, up on Corryarrick, had a furlong of his work destroyed three nights ago. But as for business, the clans seem wonderfully quick to learn it; down in Badenoch they're shipping guns from Holland."

"Hoot-toot!" said Lovat mockingly, "ye'll tell me next they're for a rising, Captain Burt. I had that news already from my good friend Mr Campbell."

177

"Oh no," said Burt, "we're not alarmed for that; we know now what they're meant for—thanks, I hear, to Mr Campbell. Leggatt has picked up three hundred stands of arms."

"Where?" asked Lovat sharply.

"Somewhere near Lock Laggan," said the Captain, who had not yet got his "chs."

"Capital!" cried Lovat. "I never heard a word of it."

"I only heard, myself, today, sir, when the post came in."

"The post!" said Lovat quickly, pricking up. "I havena seen a post since Monday was a week."

Æneas touched him on the arm. "My lord," said he "unless I'm cheated, he is here. I saw a runner with a bag out-by among the gillies."

"Ye did!" said Lovat sourly. "Ye might have told me sooner, man!" and making an excuse, went from the room.

He was gone for twenty minutes. Burt, for part of that time, kept the rest in tune with more particulars of what had happened on the Road, and then when he was done, the spirit of the company went flat as whey. Ninian alone maintained his animation, cackling like a cobbler with his neighbour; it looked as if he had forgot that such a friend as Æneas was in the world. A clock outside struck seven with harsh deliberation; dusk was fallen, and the room grown dark. "It's time that we were gone," said some one; "Simon's off for his usual sleep."

When Lovat did return, it was to find his guests all ready for departure. Pleading something instant and important in his letters as excuse for his delay he pressed on them a final dram he called the door-drink, cloaking up in drolleries his willingness to see them gone. Ninian and Æneas were the last to shake his hand.

"I'd like to see ye, sir, again," he said to Æneas. "What quarters have ye in the town?"

"Fraser's in the Kirk Street," answered Æneas.

"But we leave tomorrow morning," Ninian added quickly, to his friend's surprise.

"Tomorrow!—bless my heart!" said Lovat blankly. Not another word but that, and turned upon his heel.

The sun had set a while and dark was spreading; a north wind sharply cold was blowing, with a smirr of rain, and they had two miles of a walk before them, into Beauly. The jowled man, who was Ninian's neighbour at the table and had plainly liked his company, was waiting for them at the gate, the tippet of his coat about his head—a crazy figure—set on showing them a shorter way to Beauly than the one they came by. His shorter way, they found, was longer than their own but passed his house, a solitary, sloven place that seemed to crave for human company. He was insistent on their entering, promising a better dram than Lovat's, but they would not stop. Nor even then could they get quit of him; he took a bouat-lamp and trudged through fields and herbage rank and wet until they reached the outskirts of the village, where he left them. His tongue had gone the whole way like the clatter of a mill, with no assistance from the two, who only listened, finding it engaged them quite enough to pick their steps across the wilderness of weed and stubble. When he had bade them boisterously good night and turned for home, they watched his lantern bobbing for a little through the mirk.

"That's the dreariest body ever wore a tippet! My grief, it's me that's sick of him," said Ninian in a voice as sober as the Sabbath.

"You seemed to find his talk engaging," Æneas said dryly. "The two of you went cracking at the table like a bush of whin."

"It's not much depth of crack ye'll get from one so heavy on the dram; the man's fair stoving wi' MacShimi's drink."

He said it with an air of such disgust that Æneas marvelled.

"I thought you werena slack yourself!" said he.

"A *chiall!*" cried Ninian. "Me! Just listen!" He moved upon his feet and made a sound that showed his boots were squirting-wet inside. "That's my share of Simon's liquor. I feel as if I had been wading in the ebb, but better in my boots than in my belly! . . . Oh Æneas!" he said, and put his two hands on the other's shoulders, "you and me are well met! I liked ye from the start, but never better than this night when you drew out the badger—yes, and gave him word for word defiant, like a man!"

179

"My share of it," said Æneas, "was simple as a child's. I did no more than ask him questions."

"That was it! Ye profited by what I told ye—always to be frank when dealing wi' a rogue, and got from him what I could not manoeuvre to get from him in a twelvemonth. It's nothing but the face of ye!—that face of yours, so honest, would beguile the kestrel from the tree. My own is too much like a jyler's; let me just say 'How's the weather?' to a man like Simon, and he backs out parrying, wonderin' where I'll light. My boy, ye have done nobly! Feel you, now, at this!"

The bobbing lamp was quenched by some twist of the track its bearer followed; they were on the lee of bushes, sheltered from the wind that carried from the shore the sound of breakers, and the night was cauldron-black. Something rubbed the arm of Æneas, and he caught what Ninian thrust on him—a piece of stick with a line rolled on it neatly to the very end!

"Oh, Ninian!" he cried, "which is it?"

"What but my own affair! My sorrow! that it's not your father's. Trudging through the grass there with that blether of a man, I kept my fingers and my wits engaged on Ninian's private hank, and got the last twist out of it. That's all bye wi't now,—*I have my gentleman!*"

He said it with a savage exultation, grinding with his teeth.

"Lovat?" said Æneas.

"Yes, Lovat! And he knows it! That man Burt made a botch of it when he let it slip that I was him that found the meaning of the guns. I hadna said a word of that to Sim when I saw him last, and well he knows the reason now. He saw it in a minute—did ye see his thrapple working? It's good for you and me a company was there to see us, and that drunken man to give us a convoy, or we were maybe now in irons, warded in the dungeon."

Æneas was shocked and dubious.

"I somehow hate the man," said he, "but still—but still—I think he may be, in his own way, honest."

"Honest!" said Ninian. "Honesty's not natural to human-kind; it takes a devil of a lot of practice, like the pipes, and Lovat never had the training. Man! ye're just in some particulars a

180

child. Ye're lookin' round about for fairy stories—something that ye saw in books; but I'm a *beachdair* out for flesh and blood. And oh! it's just a splendid world, to have both right and wrong in it, to give the *beachdair* chance! Give me that hank; it's done wi'—let us on!"

He started walking through the dark.

"Are you certain sure it's Lovat?" said Æneas, Still dubious.

"I wish I was as sure of getting home to Inveraray wi' my hide complete. That, now, 's the only thing to bother me. I'm leaving in the morning, whether you can come or no'. Old Sim was staggered when he heard of that. It doesna give him time to set his snares. Ye saw the way he took it?"

"You said that Barisdale and he were foes."

"Toots! Never fash wi' Barisdale. Barisdale it was who led me all astray. Whoever was the man who put Col on to us it wasna Lovat, and whatever was the reason, Lovat's interest was not concerned. I'm thinking to mysel', Æneas, *that's a twist that belongs to the other hank!* We'll let it bide just now. If Lovat's thrapple worked when he heard I knew what meant the guns, he nearly choked when he heard that Leggatt had them. 'Capital!' says he; but he didna think it capital a bit in that way—not wi' a comb in his throat like yon,—rather he was thinking on the capital he lost in that three hundred stands of firelocks. A man like Lovat never should put lip to drink: he fairly put himself into my hands this night wi' yon explosions about roads and schools. It's him that heads the bond of remnant clans to worry Wade; it's him that has been shipping guns from Holland, it's him that knows the Hielan' claymore 's still among the thatch. I'm done wi' him—the rest 's wi' Islay!"

"But still," said Æneas, "I'm loth to think the man who gave my father sanctuary would play this double part."

"That for him!" said Ninian, and spat. "Ye never ken a man until ye drive a spoil wi' him. Did you see yon lank lad wi' the earrings at the table foot? We never got his name from Lovat."

"I noticed him," said Æneas.

"That is one called Patrick Grant, the skipper of a boat now lying in the road off Inverness—my drunken neighbour told me.

Grant's a gentleman of family from Rothiemurchus. I heard of him three weeks ago. The muskets landed at Blackness came off his boat!"

Yet Æneas, all through this, as if a part of him had shed the immediate senses and stood somewhere back in time, saw, mounted on a horse, his father riding into mist!

"You heard," said he, "what Lovat said about my father?"

"You may be sure of that!" said Ninian, standing. "I was two men yonder—one that gave his tongue to nonsense, one that gave to Lovat's least bit word his two good ears, and oh, *mo creach!* I got another blow, for Sim 's not guilty!"

"Of what?" asked Æneas. The rain was on his face, the wind was driving. They stood close up together on a track that led down to the river where their boat was waiting.

"Of half a dozen things, and all of them the blackest, that were hanging in my mind," said Ninian in a gust. "The dungeon—or the tree—or the plantations!"

"My God!" cried Æneas, "I thought of all these things!"

"And well ye might! They have been long the tools of Lovat. But this time he's not guilty. Yon was a true tale that he told ye!"

"I thought it sounded true," said Æneas with agitation.

"As true's the tomb! Your father started off from Castle Dounie. Ye wiled the truth from Sim by simple honesty, and I was there in terror thinking ye would spoil it all by blurting out too soon about Loch Duich. When you came out with that the man was fair dumfounded! I know what, now, disturbed Drimdorran! Ye didna steal the snuffbox, but I'll ask ye this— did you ransack his desk?"

"I did not," said Æneas, gulping.

"Well, it's a damn pity that ye didna! I swear he thinks ye did! In yon bit desk, as sure as I'm Macgregor, lies proof that Duncanson deceived your folk!"

"But what, in God's name, for?" cried Æneas, bewildered. "I said myself to Lovat it might be because he feared to have the name of sheltering a rebel, but, on thinking since, that seems impossible. The thing's blown by long years ago. In fourteen years he surely could have plucked up courage to have told the truth to my father's brother. It would have been a feather in his cap."

Ninian stood dumb.

"Can ye not help me?" said Æneas piteously. "Where did my father go? How did he die? For what did he keep silence there in France with not a word for me or for his brother?"

Still Ninian stood silent, thinking, fiddling in his hands a line all tangled. At last he spoke, with great solemnity.

"Look at the night!" said he in Gaelic. "Hearken to the sea-wave roaring! That is the mind of Ninian—no blink of light in him, and every wave of speculation shattering. . . . I'll have to sleep on it."

XIX

The Trammel Net

Their skiff was lying at the quay, her man sound sleeping, coiled up, like a whelk, in a den decked forward at her bows: they roused him up, hoised sail, and started down the water, Ninian's one lament that there, behind them, in that place he hated, should be Primrose Campbell still in bonds. Until they turned a headland opening up the frith, the wind was in their favour; now it was dead-on-end. It blew out from the east in squalls that scooped the brine and flung it in their faces, stinging them like pellets, rattling in the sail like salt. They were not twenty minutes out when, staggering in stays, the skiff was swept by one great sea that crossed her quarter, drenched them to the bone, and now was frothing through the ballast. They beat into the Black Isle shore where sea-birds cried on ebbing beaches, put about and reached, with little gain, for the bays of Bunchrew, as the fisher called them—wooded land where trees were brawling.

"Far better had we ridden out or walked!" said Ninian at last. "We'll not be there till morning, and I'm sitting in a dub. I canna stand your boats; give me red earth! This skiff is making no more of it than a shuttle."

Two hours they beat from shore to shore, and then, in a tack to port, came close in on a light.

"Is that the ferry?" Ninian asked, his clothes a sop on him.

"It's Clachnaharry," said the man.

"Then in we go!" said Ninian. "We'll walk the carse and save an hour of weaving."

They landed at a slip, paid off the boat, passed through a sleeping village, followed a muirland road a mile, and reached the town upon the stroke of midnight, and the rain downpouring. It was as if they came upon a graveyard! No creature moved; the tenements were shuttered; throughout the lanes the wind went volleying; thatch and slate gushed water noisily as though they had been brimming weirs. And every light in Inverness was quenched, save one that moved about low down beside the river.

Ninian, looking from the bridge, gave out a whistle, and the light blew out as if it had been bitten.

"It's never too late for mischief!" he said, chuckling. "Give you a whistle in the night when folk seem sleeping, and ye'll always hear some skurry. These lads have been at poaching."

Their inn was of the humblest, picked by Ninian—as it proved with shrewdness—on a likelihood that they might have it mainly to themselves: it did, by day, a roaring trade in vintnery, but they alone, since they had come, had been its boarders. It formed part of a long three-storey land or tenement in which it was the only domicile, a bit back from the river, flanked by what had one time been town-houses of the gentry, now degraded into stores on one hand and a lint-work on the other.

As they were coming to it they heard footsteps on the causeway.

"Stop!" said Ninian slyly. "Maybe there's a fish for breakfast, and we shouldna spoil it. These are the lads o' lantern. They're making for the inn."

Clean through the inn went running from the street an entry, close, or pend, high-arched and broad enough to pass a cart. Two men—to judge by sounds; it was too dark for seeing,—laden with some burden from the river, dashed into the close, and Ninian and Æneas loitered. When they reached its mouth the wind was skirling through it, and there came from parts behind the smells of malt and leather. A lamp for usual lit the entrance to the inn, which was at midway through the close, but now as if their landlord had despaired of their returning, it was out.

Æneas was about to rap.

"Stop you a wee!" said Ninian; "I told ye that I never saw a man go up a close but I would wonder. I want to make it sure these lads are in."

He went through to the back, and stumbled on a bundle, felt it with his hands, looked round a green, high-walled, he knew by daylight, and came back.

"Nothing there but their trammel net," said he. "It's fish for breakfast!" and rapped upon the door. Inside there was a scuttling.

"A trammel net!" said Æneas. "What is a trammel net?"

"Oh just a kind of a net for foolish fishes. . . . What is keeping my friend the Ferret? He'll be frightened that we ken the way he buys his fish. Stick from the wood, deer from the hill, and salmon from the linn—no honest Gael took shame of them!" and again he rapped more urgently.

This time their landlord answered, with a candle in his hand—a long-nosed sandy man with bead-like eyes, no chin to speak of, and a whisker combed back to his ears completing that resemblance to a ferret which made Ninian call him that as by-name. Behind him lay the kitchen, dark but for a fire that seemed to Æneas the cheeriest he had ever seen, for he was shivering; the more appealing since the chamber shared upstairs with Ninian had no fireplace.

"We're late," said Ninian in Gaelic, "and what's more, we're wet, and hunger's on us. Fetch us up the stair a halfman of good spirits and a bite of something."

"Whatever the gentlemens say," replied the landlord, peering at them queerly with his head aside. He had some silly notion that more state was in the English.

They took two candlesticks he offered, lit them at his own, and climbed the stair.

"Isn't that the Fraser dirt!" said Ninian, throwing off his coat, all soaking. "A man that keeps an inn should be a gentleman, and that one's but a clout. Look at them two candles!—burned down to the dowp, and they were almost hale last night when we were bedded."

"He might have asked us to the fire," said Æneas, taking off the belt about his loins that bore his money and his pistol.

"Na, na! no fears o' him! And gets him to his English!— 'Whatever the gentlemens say'! I never saw him looking more

186

the ferret! I wonder where he put yon night-lads skulking!"

Fraser in a little while came up with a piece of pickled tongue, the whisky, and some scones. Even to the eye of Æneas was something singular in his manner. He never looked at them but with his head aside, obliquely, and his face was sallow.

"Would the gentlemens like to dry their clothes?" he asked them; "I could take them to the kitchen."

"That's just what I was thinking to mysel'," said Ninian. "But first of all, bring up two candles; this pair's nearly perished."

Downstairs he went again, a little grudgingly; they stripped their clothes from them and changed their shirts and put on John Maclaren's garments, at which the Ferret looked with some surprise when he came back, but nothing said. He lit the two new candles, blew the old stumps out, and put them in his pocket; then bent down and gathered up the wet clothes of his guests and took his leave.

They drank part of the spirits and sat down to eat when all of a sudden Ninian started up and looked about him.

"He's taken away your belt!" said he.

"What odds?" said Æneas. "There's nothing in it now except some shillings and the pistol. I left the money yesterday with Saul."

"It's me that's glad to learn't," said Ninian, relieved. "If only ye can trust Mackay! But that's your uncle's business. Yet, still-and-on, we'll need to get that pistol; never let your wife nor arms sleep in another's chamber. Have ye got your powder-horn?"

"It's in my coat-tail pocket; let it bide!" said Æneas, tired of these precautions.

"Then up she comes!" said Ninian firmly. "Poor is the pistol wanting powder and the pipes without a man!" and going to the door he cried out down the stair to Fraser what he wanted.

"That's right!" he said when Fraser brought them up. "A horn is not a safe thing drying at a fire unless a man is wearied of his mistress."

"She's not at home," said Fraser; "she went out to spend the night at Kessock with her sister," always with his head aside.

187

"Then ye'll be all alone?" said Ninian carelessly.

"Yes," said the Ferret. "Goodnight with ye, gentlemens," and left them, creaking down the stair, his head more to the side than ever.

Ninian sat down at last, began a grace, and had not got half through it when he stopped, and, opening his eyes, looked at the pistol. It lay behind his plate, the flask beside it. With Æneas regarding him, amused, he took it in his hand and probed it with the rammer.

"Was it loaded?" he inquired.

"Yes," said Æneas. "You loaded it yourself this morning."

"Then, by God!" said Ninian below his breath, "there's something wrong, for now it has been gelded!" and he tapped the barrel on the table. A few loose grains of powder spilled.

Until that moment Æneas had looked on the other's fidgeting with unconcern, so much was clamant in his mind of more perplexing things, but now there rushed on him a feeling that the hour was eerie and that something in the air gave to the inn a quality of brooding expectation. Outside, the dead dark of the night was boisterous with wind and the splash of waters, that by contrast made the inner muteness evil. Each time the landlord had come up he seemed more sinister; each time he had gone down it was as though a grave engulfed him—not a sound!

Ninian, with a face of clay, picked up the powder-flask and shook it, then turned down its beak and poured a charge into the pistol barrel. His hand was trembling so, a part of the charge was spilled into his plate; he glowered at it, infuriate.

"*Sand!*" said he. "They've taken out the powder and filled up with sand! My grief! but they've got the twist of us!"

"What does it mean?" said Æneas, with an uproar in his heart; his comrade's face dismayed him.

"What does it mean but that accursed money ye have got the name of! The Ferret and these men are meaning pillage; and they think they've pulled our teeth, but better far for biting old Grey Colin!"

The broadsword hung upon a bedpost next the wall in shadow. He lifted it, and made to strip it of its scabbard. A muffled oath from him filled Æneas with new alarm.

"In the name of the Good Being, look at that!" he said distressfully between his teeth in Gaelic. "Sword of my father, and they have put hands on thee! Colin! Colin! Let me get him that bashed thee in, and I will give thee flesh!"

He showed the sword to Æneas, almost weeping. One side of the basket-hilt had been hammered on the gripe so close a hand could not get entrance, and the weapon was as useless as a wand.

"But no!" said he, "I'm not done yet; I have my fingers, Fraser!" He screwed the pommel off and slid the basket from its tang; put down the blade, and as a man would straighten horse-shoes, pulled the basket bars apart to their old position, every sinew of his hands a wire that might have twanged.

Æneas, in some queer confusion of the senses, chewed a bit of scone to soothe an ache of emptiness that took him in the stomach.

"Stop that! the hour of battle is not for meat," said Ninian, his sword assembled, and he whipped the scones into his pocket. "I'll never say grace in Inverness again until the meat is in me. If there's only three men there, we'll bide and deal with them and then take supper, but if there's more, as there well might be, we'll feed, then, like the gannet, flying. . . . There's my dirk for ye," and he took it from the pillow where he placed it when they stripped; "ye're a quick hand at the pistol, see what ye can do wi' steel!"

Æneas seized the dagger like a truncheon.

"That's not the way!" said Ninian, and showed him how to grip it with the palm held down. "Strike up at all times in a scuffle; ward wi' your other arm and your plaid about it; the thing's to get him on the groin."

In the lock of the door inside had always been a key which they found was now awanting; they opened the door with caution, and heard for the first time mutterings below. At a sound so seeming warrant for their fears, all fears abandoned Æneas and gave place to calculation.

"If it comes to the worst," said he, "we can leave by the window."

189

"And break our necks!" said Ninian.

"No need for that; we can first get on the butts and then jump down."

"Now that's a thing I never noticed," whispered Ninian, "and ye put me to my shame to be so stupid. Nothing beats a back-road in a battle."

They pulled the window open easily and looked out to the back. The rain was still in torrents, and a gutter from the roof was spouting loudly in some barrels close below. From kilns and tanneries in the lands beyond the walls came smells of malt and leather.

Assured that the casks were lidded, Ninian drew in and stared to see a candle flicker to extinction. An inch of it had not been burned, and yet it quickly languished to an ember!

"What's this of it?" said he suspiciously, and fingered at the wick. It came away, a fragment, from the tallow! With the knife that always dwelt below his armpit, he slit up the candle quickly as a man would gut, and found no wick from end to end of it.

"What think ye now of that?" he said, and showed his teeth, then pouncing on the other candle cut it into halves. The only wick it had was the short piece at the top still burning; both candles had been stripped and moulded up again.

"*Mo chreach! Mo chreach!*" said he, "aren't they in the hurry to be at us! No shot—no sword—no glimmer, but the hearty dunt of blows! Mind what I said about the dirk!"

"To tell ye the God's own truth, I'm sweir to use it," Æneas said sadly. "Why should we bide, and there the window?"

"Because I want to see them!" Ninian hissed. "We'll take to the window in time enough. I'll hold them off till you get out, then bolt you through the close out to the street and wait for me. But if there's only two and Fraser—!"

He opened the door, with the candle in his one hand and Grey Colin in the other. Below was now more patently the sound of some disturbance.

"What are you going to do?" asked Æneas.

"Get them all on the stair while the candle lasts. . . . Light! landlord, light! Bring up a candle!" he cried loudly.

There was a moment's stillness, then there burst out from below a clatter of many feet on the kitchen flagstones—muffled exclamations. Followed, a rush, and four men huddled at the stair-foot, staggered for a second by the light, then started climbing singly, brandishing with cudgels.

"Four, no' counting Fraser," ruefully said Ninian. "Bundle and go, my lad, and I'll be after ye!"

Æneas leaped for the window.

The candle Ninian had was flickering, with little life in it; he held it high above his head and stood in shadow, so they could not see his sword. But they were all in light; he saw their sunburnt faces, every man a rogue. They came without a pause, hard on each other's heels, and the first on the landing, one with a fiery beard, lashed out wildly with his stick.

"*Sin agad!*" screamed Ninian, his blood on fire, and thrust him through the ribs.

The man went reeling back upon his followers.

"That's my father's sword and my fist in it!" Ninian cried. And at that moment died his light. Heaped on the stair with the struck man rolling on them, all the others swore in consternation.

"It's a ferret ye want!" cried Ninian in the darkness. "A Fraser ferret! Go back, ye messan dogs, and send him in!"

He backed into the room and clashed the door behind him; dashed for the open window, dropped on the water butt, and reached the ground with the broadsword in his hand. Rain battered still, and the night seemed empty but of wind and water, yet something in the gloom disquieted. He stood for a moment peering, gathered himself together, shot for the close, and fell upon its threshold, netted like a hare.

The men who held the net came out of their obscurity and piled the trammel's ends on him: he struggled in the mesh and gave one cry, loud out, "Oh, Æneas! the net! the net!"

They struck him with a cudgel like the hare.

XX

To The Woods

Ninian, like a bubble, floated up from those grey deeps and
bottomless, that lie below the living world. A while he swung
upon the surface, and he thought himself a fish. His fingers were
in meshes, and his mouth was filled with net. He thought himself
with fins and scales in Tulla, and there drifted through him
notions of a passage from the sea—by sands of Etive and the Pass
of Brander, surging through Loch Awe, and rushing at the leaps
of Orchy. Netted! That ignoble death! And, oh, but it was cold!
He heard the race of water.

Something cleared from off the surface by-and-by as suds
clear from a pool; he shook himself and found he was a man. His
head was aching, but a sore far sharper was the sense of
something wrong, of deprivation; memory was for the moment
dulled but not destroyed.

Now all came slowly back to him—the sea-drenched boat,
the conflict on the stair, his leap into the trammel stretched
across the close, his warning cry to Æneas.

That was what was hurting so within him—where was
Æneas?

Some seal was on his eyes; he could not open them at first, and
wondered was he blinded. Then he guessed the reason of that
tuainealaich in his head—he had been smitten, and the stream
of blood had clotted on his face. When he had got his eyelids
parted, and looked up, he saw the black vault of the night, and
through one hole in it a star. Quite close beside his feet the river
gurgled.

And he was bound!

The net was coiled about him, part of it stuffed in his mouth
for gag; some bights of cord were tight wound round his hands
and feet; he lay on sand.

With a struggle he got up his pinioned hands and reached the knife below his armpit; slashed through the meshes; cleared his feet; stood up, and with the knife between his teeth cut through the last bonds on his wrists.

"Faith!" said he, "I'm early to the river!" and felt his head. "Ah! were ye dunting, lads? Ye were the boys to split oak timber! Thank God I wore Maclaren's good thrum bonnet, and I'll get my knee yet on your chests!"

He bathed his face; cut out a yard of net and put it in his pocket; sliced from the bank a turf of grass and threw it in the river; then went up and into Kirk Street. Still was the night blind-black, but dry.

There were lights in Fraser's inn, and in the close were women talking, their feet unshod and plaids about their heads. It did not take him long to get their story. The inn had been attacked, poor Fraser bound; two gentlemen were spoiled and missing.

"Just that!" said Ninian, with a whistle. "Very good indeed!" and passed into the house where half a dozen neighbours had been called by an alarm from a slattern servant lass who slept up in a garret. Her master had been found, a piteous object, tied up on the kitchen floor, lamenting for his guests whose money was the aim of the marauders.

"And where, now, is the decent body?" Ninian asked, as he looked about the kitchen, all tossed up as if a tide had swept it, but with nothing broken.

"Up the stairs in his bed, poor man!" said an old grey fellow. "Art thou, by any chance, now, one of the worthy gentlemen?"

"I'm thinking to myself I am," said Ninian, "but I have here a head on me that's like a pot that would be kicked round in a quarry. Did no one see my friend?"

Nobody had seen him. Before the alarm had broken out, the spoilers and the spoiled had vanished.

Ninian took the lantern from above the entrance; lit its lamp, and searched out through the close and to the back where, on the ground, without a stain on it, the dirk was lying.

"They've got him!" he said to himself with great vexation. "They shot their trammel twice and got two fish; and now the wits of me and God be wi' Macmaster!"

Then in, and up a stair that had been newly washed, and picked the knapsacks up, and through a lobby to where Fraser lay in bed. When Ninian came in on him he seemed to shrivel; then he sat upright and stared, a tassel on his nightcap wagging. The only light was from the lantern, and Ninian had the naked dirk; it had a glint; his body loomed in shadow like the shade of Vengeance.

"Where is my friend?" said he in Gaelic.

"What way on the earth of the world should I know that, good man?" said Fraser, trembling like a leaf. "They put on me the rope."

"It's on thy neck thou'lt have it next!" said Ninian, bending over him. "Who were they?"

"I never put an eye on them before," said Fraser, and his bed was shaking. "They came in strength and hardihood and mastered me."

"Oh, *mhic an galla!*" Ninian said in fury; caught him by the neckband of his shirt, and dragged him on the floor. "Stand up there on thy legs and look on me! Where are our clothes that were at drying?"

"They took them with them," said the Ferret.

"Where is my friend?" again said Ninian, and gave the dirk a shake.

"*Cuid—*" broke out the landlord in a scream for help, and with a kick at him, but did not get the word completed; Ninian with the dirk-hilt struck him in the stomach and he fell convulsed.

"Take thou that now till I come back!" said Ninian, and deliberately went down the stair and to the street, two knapsacks on his back. He had the lantern with him, and its light seemed all that was alive in Inverness beyond himself. Its beams lit up the lands and inner grime of closes; every street he searched—there were not many,—every lane, and now and then would whistle softly or give out the howlet call that Æneas by this time knew.

He had come back from the cross to near the inn again, when

suddenly from out a vennel leading to the river, some men made at him. The deluge of the night had choked the syvors of the street and left a pond the men must wade through to the brawn, or skirt, to reach him; one started wading while the others ran about the pool, and Ninian bolted from the street between two tenements and into tracks unbuilded on behind the lands. He found himself among small bleaching-greens and gardens, fenced by low dry-stone walls which he climbed or vaulted. But for the lantern, they had caught him, for they followed nimbly; he saw where to leap and what to shun while they came stumbling after him in darkness, clashing into walls and tripping among kail stocks, so that soon he left them well behind. But then there came an end to flight in this direction; up before him rose a lofty tenement with early morning lights already glimmering at a window here and there; he whipped round sharply, crossed a tanner's yard, and through a close into the street again. A bit ahead of him he heard a cheery whistling.

But now the lantern that had been his friend was like to be his enemy; the chase had seen it swerve, and through another close got to the street as quickly as himself, and now was pelting up behind him. He heard their feet.

The whistling came from a boy who at a well was filling water-stoups, as cheery as the thrush, with neither boot nor bonnet on him, and his wee breast bare, and Ninian ever loved a whistling boy.

"Would you like a bonny lantern, boy?" said he, and his ear cocked for the folk behind him.

"Fine!" said the laddie, eager.

"Well, there it is for ye, my hero! Skelp you off for home or these bad men that's following me will take it from ye!"

The boy grabbed at his prize, forsook his stoups, and darted down a lane. Ninian followed for a little, then slipped up a close, to come out again when his pursuers passed like beagles, hot on a spurious trail. A while he watched the lantern darting; then it rose up on a stair and disappeared—the boy was home!

"Now for the woods!" said Ninian to himself, and made at leisure for the bridge.

For more than an hour he trudged, part by the noisy sea, and night was turning to a milky dawn when he plunged at last through breckans into a nut-wood that stretched back for miles on either hand a burn, and changed, to the distant south, to wilder woods and blacker, upon lofty hills. He had made for it as the stag for sanctuary, and the wild mare of the moors in her own time for the place where she was foaled. But once before had he seen it, as a boy, coming down from the Caiplich with his folk, and dogs behind them, and had slept in a cave of Bunchrew till a fine spring morning. The first burn he had fished! The very stones of it were in his memory!

What, all these years, he had thought a cavern deep and spacious, proved, when he reached it now, but a small recess in the bank of the water, screened by trails of toad-flax and the ivy. It occupied an *eas*—a deep cleft of the hill wherethrough a burn went churning, and a plash and gurgle made it pleasant. The steep banks rose high up above the water, bearded with the hazel, dripping; birds were wakened, and the wae wee chirrup of the yellow-yite, the robin's pensive ditty, came from out the clusters of the nuts.

"Now I am home!" said Ninian, putting down his pokes, and did a strange thing there. He plucked his bonnet off, and turning to the east, stretched out his hands. A moment stood he so, and then bent down and bathed his face, and stood again, and chanted—

> Black is yon town yonder,
> Black the folk therein!
> I am the white swan,
>   King above them!
>
> In the name of God I'll go,
> In shape of deer or horse,
> Like the serpent and the sword,
>   I'll sting them!

On his wounded head he rubbed some salve, felt at his

stubbled chin, and took from his sack the razors, but returned them without shaving. He made a fire, and cut a wand, and dropped a maggot in a pool and caught two little fishes. He spitted them on sticks and cooked them, eating them with scones, then lay down in his den and slept.

At noon he woke, the *tuainealaich* gone from his head, and walked back into Inverness, and straight down to the river's bank, until he found the place where he had cut the divot from the grass. The net was gone. He searched about the bank a while, then sought the house of Saul Mackay to find he was from home since yesterday.

At Fraser's inn, which he went to next, good trade was doing, and the wife, returned from Kessock, yoked on him like a vixen for her man's condition; he was still in bed. She clamoured for her lawing, and Ninian, like a wise man, paid the reckoning of Æneas and himself—a trifle, since they paid it daily. Throughout the town he pushed inquiries for his friend, and was amazed to find the town not much concerned about a squabble in an inn and settled on the culprits—three Camerons who had broken stanchions and escaped from a Tolbooth cell.

"There's only one place in the air, or on the earth, or in the deep, or in the nether-deep can beat this town for roguery, and that's the Worst!" said Ninian to himself, and having picked a meal, walked out to Duncan Forbes and told him all.

"Dear me!" said Forbes, "you're looking gash! A body would think to look at you the North was up. Well, what do you make of it; was it the young man's money?"

"It looks like that," said Ninian. "And Fraser hired the gang."

"The Tolbooth's not what it should be for security," said Forbes; "but it's not so ill looked after that a rogue when he likes can pick his robbers from it like a tenant arling servants at a fair. Ye'll find that Fraser himself's a victim of the spulzie."

"But, my lord," cried Ninian, "it wasna the Camerons at the inn! At the very least there were half a dozen—four inside and two at the trammel net. What's more, the Cameron leash of lads were still in jyle when this thing happened; they broke out later in the morning."

The Advocate walked the floor, reflecting, and his hands behind him.

"It puzzles me," said he. "It's not in the nature of native theft. Have you been making enemies?"

"I am always making them, my lord," said Ninian. "It's my trade."

"You talked when I saw you last of a certain gentleman?"

"The two of us went out and saw him yesterday, my lord."

The Advocate stopped his walk, alarmed. "Good heavens! did ye come on bones?" said he.

"Not even a shank, my lord," said Ninian. "I was on the wrong scent altogether. Drimdorran was in Castle Dounie as I said, but he left for France, and died there."

"Thank God for that!" said Forbes, uplifted greatly. "For a little, there, ye frightened me!"

"But I found another thing, my lord—who ships the guns."

"Compared with the other thing that's but a trifle," Forbes said, smiling. "Ye had guessed that much before, and so had I; what proofs have ye?"

"There's a sloop, the *Wayward Lass*, at the water-foot, and Pat Grant of Rothiemurchus is her skipper. He dined wi' Yon One yonder, yesterday."

"O-ho!" said Forbes, and made for a small 'scritoire where he did his writing. "The Blackness guns came off his boat; I'll have her searched."

He dashed a letter down with a squeaking quill, cast sand on it and puffed it off again, and rang a bell and ordered out a messenger.

"And now," said he, "there's your friend to find. The first thing we should do, I think, is to fetter Mr Fraser."

"He wouldna be the worse of it, my lord," said Ninian. "But that's no' going to help us. The man's a clever rogue, and has a bonny story. Yonder he was tied when the alarm broke out that brought the neighbours, and there's only my word for it that he planned the thing. Wi' a jyle like Inverness, my lord, that folk can break like an old wife's henhouse, Fraser's best left in his inn

198

till I get Æneas. Besides, my lord, I want to keep an eye on him. If Fraser thinks he's lowse, he'll some night join the others, or they'll come to him, and then I'll have them all."

Forbes looked at him with comical admiration. "Ye're a great man, Mr Campbell!" said he. "I wish the like of ye were sold in shops; and I would order one to cheer me through the winter. I wonder when I'll get the bottom of your quirks! What, now, is the genuine reason for your wishing me to take no steps immediately with Fraser? Ye may as well confess, because I know it."

The *beachdair* flushed.

"I might have kent ye would, my lord," said he with some chagrin. "There's not much hid from you."

"Not when it comes to the Hielan' heart," said Forbes complacently, and gave in English a Gaelic proverb—"What the heather kens the ling knows."

"The truth, my lord, is that Macmaster was not seized last night for money."

"Now we're getting at it!" said the Advocate. "Not to beat about the bush—ye were at Lovat, whom I warned ye to keep clear of. Did ye rouse him?"

"Indeed he's not in love wi' me, my lord; he knows now that I know his merchant trade and have some news for Islay. I did a silly thing, my lord, last night, when I told him we were leaving Inverness this morning: I could have bit my tongue out all this day to think o't. The men that shot the net for us last night were Lovat's, and he got the Camerons lowsed from jyle to blind the scent."

"I wish we had your like in Inverness!" said Forbes with honest feeling. "Many a bafflement ye could have saved me. Where did ye get your cunning?"

"Where but with my folk—my poor own people, driven from their holds and hunted like the otter. Get you out in the mist, my lord, and be its child, without a name, and every name against you, and your wits must ward your head. There's not a quirk of man I canna fathom!"

He said it with a passion, and no sooner did than laughed.

"Ye'll be thinking to yourself, my lord," said he, "that I'm a boaster. That's what my daughter Jennet says. It was not altogether in the old Macgregor day I learned my wisdom— yon's the place for schooling—real Argyll! It's on the lowland border, and I get both kinds of wickedness to try my hands on."

"You have a daughter then?" said Forbes, with seeming interest.

"Would I be what I am but for a daughter, sir? My heart is in the wilds!"

Forbes, sitting at the desk, looked at him with a curious smile, half mocking and half sad. "I know, Mr Campbell!" he said. "I know! I thoroughly understand! The hearts of all of us are sometimes in the wilds. It's not so very long since we left them. But the end of all that sort of thing's at hand. The man who's going to put an end to it—to you, and Lovat, and to me—yes, yes, to me! or the like of me, half fond of plot and strife and savagery, is Wade. . . . I wish ye took a dram; we could meet each other better upon this. . . . Ye saw the Road? That Road's the end of us! The Romans didna manage it; Edward didna manage it; but there it is at last, through to our vitals, and it's up wi' the ell-wand, down the sword! . . . It may seem a queer thing for a law officer of the Crown to say, Mr Campbell, but I never was greatly taken wi' the ell-wand, and man, I liked the sword! At least it had some glitter."

"I'm with you there, my lord!" said Ninian heartily. "And that's another thing to find—my father's sword, Grey Colin, for the devils took it."

The Advocate took up a knife and started cutting at a pen.

"That's a pity," said he. "It served ye well down yonder at Loch Laggan."

"My lord!" said Ninian.

The other chuckled.

"And they thought they drowned ye, did they?"

"Leggatt has been talking sir, I see," said Ninian.

"Nothing of the kind, sir! I got my tidings elsewhere. Leggatt never mentioned ye: he fathered both your skirmish and your finding of the guns."

200

"That's what I expected of the bonny man!" said Ninian.

"But let us get back to business," Forbes went on more briskly; "what has happened to your friend? I'm sure you have some notion."

Ninian took the piece of net out from his pocket. "I canna tell ye that, my lord," he said, "but they had him at the waterside where I found mysel' this morning. When I got lowse of the net, I cut a clod that I might know the spot in daylight, and I cut this bit of net that I might ken the trammel if I saw't again. I went back today, and the net was gone as I expected. They had a boat, either to cross the river or go down it, and Æneas was in the boat—"

"Or maybe in the river," said Forbes gloomily.

"No, not in the river, sir, at least they didna drown him: that I'm sure of. Ye see, my lord, if death had been their plan, they would have drowned mysel'; they had me there as helpless as a log, and I'm more in the road of Yon One than Macmaster. They wanted us without a mess—without a clabber of bloodshed—if ye follow; their whole contrivance in the inn showed that, and even the net itself. My lord, they've got him planted somewhere! The only thing that bothers me is this—whose blood was on the bank?"

"Blood!" said Forbes.

"Ay, blood!" said Ninian, "and plenty of it! I tracked it through the close, and there it's on the bank, a puddle."

"This is most desperate!" said Forbes.

"I hope it's not so desperate as it looks at first, my lord; I'm in the hopes it's the blood of a man I kittled in the ribs wi' little Colin. Ye see, when they were on the stair I got a skelp at them. I reason it out like this, my lord: their boat was small, and there were many of them. Wi' Æneas perhaps to struggle wi'—for he's a dour one—and a wounded man to carry, they hadna room for me, so they tied me up, put off, and landed them in some place, then came back for me. And a bonny chase they gave me! It was over the walls and through the kail for Ninian, like Hallowmas."

Forbes stood up and his teeth went snap like a rat-trap. "We'll get him!" said he. "We'll get him, if I have to card the North like wool for him!"

"That's what I was thinking to mysel'," said Ninian, "but—"

Forbes seized him by the collar of his coat, and looked through slits of eyes at him. "And now," said he, "what for did ye let me think at first it was just a robbery of Fraser's? Eh? . . . Did ye think I wasna to be trusted to set justice on Lord Lovat?"

"The man's your friend, my lord," said Ninian; "I meant to carry this thing through and find the lad mysel'. It's ill to draw the sword against a neighbour that ye've drank wi', and I have never supped his cup. . . . Ye better leave this to me, my lord; I'm on the slot already."

"Nay, nay!" said Forbes, "give me that piece of net! My drinking never spoiled my sense of duty. . . . Where are ye staying now?"

"In your lordship's grounds," said Ninian composedly.

"My grounds!"

"Not here, sir, but the Bunchrew wood, a bit behind your house." It was an appanage of the Forbes' property nine miles away. "I fished the Bunchrew burn, a boy, and minded of a hollow in an *eas* where I could shelter."

"Good heavens, man! ye're not in woods?" cried Forbes, astounded.

"Where better, my lord? It's there a man can sleep and no worse than himself for company. In Inverness I have not got one friend except yourself."

"Oh yes, ye have!" said Forbes, with great amusement. "I wish that ye were shaved. Come this way, Mr Campbell, and I'll show ye."

He led him from the room, along a lobby, tapped upon a door and opened it, and pushed him in, and shut it after him. A girl in the room stood up.

"In the name of God!" cried Ninian, "what art thou doing here?"

It was his daughter, Janet.

XXI

Janet

She was neither white nor rosy, but a dusk that the sun and wind had dyed her, and her hair like autumn breckans. On a street he might have passed her as a stranger. The clothes she wore were new to her—a camlet riding-coat, and a three-cock hat that let her tresses wander. But more of the unusual was in her mein; though her eyes were dark with weariness, he felt in her a fire. And she had aged a little.

He might have seemed more strange to her than she to him, for she had never seen him hitherto in Gaelic habit nor unshaven, and she hung a moment, dubious, when he entered, this man stained and kilted, with the stubble on his chin; then ran to him, and put her arms about his neck and kissed him.

"*A chiall, mo chridhe!*" said her father, staggered, "what is wrong?" She had not kissed him since she was a child. For the first time he felt old and knew she was at last a woman. She felt at his arms: her eyes devoured him.

"Oh!" she cried, "I could scarcely credit Mr Forbes that you were living! A part of me is drowned in Laggan. I'll never hear its name again but I will shiver, nor drink water but I'll grue!"

"In the name of fortune!" he cried out, "did you hear of that in Inveraray?"

"Hear it!" she said, and sank into a chair, and threw her arms upon a table. "My grief! I heard it! I have been hearing it on every breeze of wind and every spout of water. I can hear it now—Drimdorran's daughter at our door, and her voice a sword—'Your father has been drowned! Your father has been drowned!' "

"Not one word of truth in it!" said Ninian stoutly, "we werena drowned a bit! I'm sure ye might have kent it; hadn't I the Virgin nut?"

He could not have said anything more certain to command her calm; at that ridiculous speech she looked at him, surprised out of her passion, and she smiled.

"You foolish man!" said she, "you have not got it!"

"Indeed and I have!" said he, and started feeling in his pockets with a face that lengthened.

She held the nut out to him in her hand. "There it is," she said. "I took it from your pocket on the day you left—a foolish prank I've rued in bitterness for a hundred and thirty miles."

He grimaced drolly. "No wonder I had bother! I might have kent the luck was wanting. Did I not think I had it always in my oxter? Who brought the news to Inveraray?"

"The first one was a man named Macdonnell, of the Watch of Barisdale. He came to Duncanson, and Duncanson was in his bed, an ailing man, and sent to me his daughter."

"What!" cried her father, "a man of Barisdale's! Out wi' the string!"

He plucked from his sporran the tangled line, and with quick fingers cleared another yard of it. It looked as if he had forgot her presence. His eyes were glowering at the hank; he pricked it with his knife, and teased it with his fingers; gave little mocking laughs, and all the time she waited patiently without a question. That was the way of Janet—she could always wait; she knew that most things are at last explained if we have patience.

"*Drimdorran was the Big One!*" he exclaimed. "And I was blind!"

She waited, silent.

"I'm beginning to see things! He lettered his cousin in Breadalbane, his cousin sent out Niall of Succoth and the Macintyre we met among the corries, the Macintyre passed on the word to Barisdale. . . . What sort of man do you think is Duncanson, my lass?"

"He is that sort of man," said she, "that his hand feels like a puddock to me."

"I have found him out!"

And still she waited, silent, though his words were all a mystery, she had never heard of Niall of Succoth, nor of

Macintyre, nor of Col's chase.

"I told ye from the start that Duncanson disliked my errand; now I know the cause. I clean forgot he was a friend of Lovat's; all Lovat's correspondence wi' Lord Islay and the Duke goes through his hands. I'll swear he knew who broke the Road and trafficked in the guns. He's playing double—one hand in MacCailein's pouch, the other in the sporran of the North. That's the reason for his putting check on me till he could warn Lord Lovat of my coming. But Lovat didna hear from him in time; he had no letters for a fortnight. It takes a gey long time for letters to come over Corryarrick."

"I'm glad I did not come that way," said Janet. "You are the strange father that finds me here four days' distance from my home and never asks me how I came."

He looked at her sideways, shrugging. "I did not need to ask," said he, "because I knew whenever I saw ye. What could ye wiser do, with your father drowned in Badenoch, than make for Duncan Forbes? You are wearing there a riding-coat of Annabel-Alan-Iain-Alain Og's. I saw it once before, on the day she went on her marriage-jaunt,—that means ye borrowed a horse from her man and rode. Ye were not your father's child if ye did not ride with fury, and where could ye better ride than on the Road? Four days? Ye went, I'll wager, through Glen Dochart down to Taymouth—a couple of days and fairly easy; from Taymouth on the road to Ruthven; from Ruthven here—two more."

"A good two more!" she cried, "at forty miles apiece! Do you think I am made of iron?"

"Na!" said he, with pride in her, "of steel! Small are your bones, my dear, but in them there's Macgregor marrow."

"Indeed, and that was just the road I came," said she. "I slept last night at Ruthven, and oh, but I'm tired! tired!"

"Nobody ever died of that, brave lass! Take you a little sleep. Ye werena frightened, were ye?"

"Of what?" she asked, astonished. "Of Gaelic people! There was kindliness, in every face I met, for me!"

"It's good to be a woman, sometimes. And forbye, ye had the nut."

At that she laughed. And then she turned him round and felt his garments, twitching at the belt that held the dirk unseen behind his loins.

"You look like a wild man of the cairns," said she.

"And a man of the cairns is Ninian, I'll assure ye! My home's the gully, and my bed the moss. I'll tell ye later on the reason. That town in-by is not the place for me; there's not much sleep in it. So I've taken my quarters elsewhere, in the woods of Bunchrew."

"I was just going off to the town to look for you," said Janet. "It's less than an hour since I came here."

"Ye couldna have come at a better time to help me. But tell me this—you say the man of Barisdale was first to bring the story; was there, then, a second?"

"There was. That very day a man reached Duncanson with letters from Corryarrick."

Her father stared at her.

"Letters from Corryarrick! Who told ye that?"

"The man himself—a soldier. I heard he had come, and hoped for better news of you, so I sought him out, but got no consolation there; he said there was no doubt about your drowning; he had seen the very boat."

"And his letters were there before ye left?"

"The day before: he came at midday."

"And Duncanson didna give ye any?"

"No," said she.

He stood before her, stunned, and rubbing his hands together till the palms were creaking. His breast was raging.

"Oh God of Grace!" he said at last in Gaelic, "isn't that the swine of his father's pig-stye! . . . Stop thou, Drimdorran! I will make ye pay for this!"

"I *thought* you would have written," said his daughter. "It is all a cloud to me."

"There's never a cloud but what will lift. There's a cloud about yourself this day I canna fathom. What's wrong wi' ye?"

Her hand went to her breast; her eyes showed perturbation.

"What is't?" said he, suspicious.

"Only that I'm tired."

"Na, na!" said he, "it's not the flesh; it's something in you! I canna make it out; ye're different. I left ye there at home a girl, and now ye're like a woman with her fate pursuing. Ye have not even asked me where's my friend."

"What friend?" she asked, in a small soft voice that stammered.

"My grief! Aren't you the stupid girl! What friend but Æneas! You knew he was to join me."

"And I know he did," said she, "and so did everybody else; the man who brought your horse from Bridge of Orchy told us."

"Well? Well?" he urged.

She said nothing at all, but turned her side to him, and looking in a glass, made trim her hair. It baffled him.

"Ye know the lad was with me and ye never breathe his name. There's something sly about ye, but I'll find the reason yet."

And still she never answered, busy with her hair.

"If we werena drowned in Laggan we were very near it; and I was a dead man otherwise but for that callow lad's wee pistol."

"Where is he?" she plumped out, turning from the glass.

"It's high time ye were asking! And now that ye've asked I canna tell ye," said her father, and laid before her all the past night's happenings.

Her face that was dusk before with warmth in it, was now like morning ashes. "And you let them take him!" she cried out. "My shame on you! He went away with you, and what will folk think of it? Who were they who took him?"

"Who but Lovat's ruffians? But I'll get him!"

She burst out in a temper that astonished. "You'll get him! A night has passed and you have not got him yet. *Mo naire* on you, my father! You took the lad in keeping and you've lost him like a button."

"Toot-toot!" he said, amazed at her, "and this is the child I skelped! You are clean worn off your feet. I'll find the lad, if he's dead or living."

"Dead or living!" she cried out, all trembling. "Unless you

207

find him living you need never go to Inveraray. In that place they would bray at you. I could not . . . I could not face his folk!" She gathered her cloak about her with a great determination. "I'll look for him myself," said she.

"What are ye hiding from me?" said her father.

"I'm going to the inn," said she; "if there's a woman—"

"Ye needna fash wi' the inn," said her father warmly. "I put it through a riddle and got all that's in it. I thought that ye were tired?"

"Tired!" cried she, in a turmoil of the spirit; "I have tired three horses, and I thought myself a wreck, but now there's not one tired bit in me! If I cannot learn at the inn I'll learn at Lovat's."

She moved to the door. He stopped her.

"*A rùin!*" he said, "but ye're like your mother; peace be with her and her share of heaven! I always thought ye had a soft and Saxon bosom, but I see the red Macgregor's there! What's wrong wi' ye?"

She laughed in his face,—a laugh a little woebegone and taunting.

"And I thought you a clever man!" said she.

"Indeed," said he, "ye're right to blame me! I thought myself as clever as was going, but I made a bauchle of this business coming by the old ways north instead of by the Road. I should have taken the Road as you did. That you should come in four days on a saddle and be none the worse except in temper is the first thing ever made me think Wade might be right and the Road turn out a good thing."

"Let us not be talking!" she said, heedless of all this. "The hours are flying. Have you no idea where is Æneas or what they took him for?"

He had always the tangled line in his hands, and plucked at it with nervous fingers, absently.

"I can only make a guess," said he, "that Lovat has him."

"Where?" she hurried.

"That's the bit! It's a great big country, Sim's, with many a glen and hole in it, but my mind will aye be dwelling on the vaults of Castle Dounie."

"Do you think he's there?" asked Janet, feverish with alarm; Lord Lovat's vaults were an old theme of her father's.

"At least," said he, "it's the first place to make sure of. And that's the way I picked on Bunchrew for my lodging. It's well on the road to Castle Dounie, and as near as I care through day to venture."

She threw up her hands. "You talk!—and you talk!—and you talk!" said she, "but you leave me still in darkness. What in the world does he want with Æneas? What has Æneas done to him?"

"If ye were a wise-like lass ye would have asked that first," he said to her. "Do you see that hank? There's a verse in every yard of it, like the cloth that women would be waulking. But it's all a fankle, as ye see, and I have only got the start of it. Ye've helped me wi't a bit, and ye'll maybe help me more. It was not only me that Duncanson was frightened for, but Æneas. He was in fear of Æneas prying round in Inverness and finding something out about his father. Do ye ken what we have learned about his father?"

He told her all the story. "And Æneas," said he, "is fair distracted."

"Poor lad!" said she, and her tears were running. "Poor—poor lad!" Again and again she said "Poor lad!" and aye her tears were falling.

"Just fair worn off your feet!" said her father, with distress, astonished at this melting.

"How far is it to Dounie?" she asked at last, abruptly.

"Fifteen miles and a bittock."

"Then I'll go out and see Prim Campbell," she said firmly.

"Now ye are talking like my own smart lass!" said her father. "That's just what I was thinking to myself. But ye'll not can go till morning. By that time I'll have raked the burgh, and made sure that Æneas is out of it."

"And what," asked she, "am I to do till morning? I'll go out with you to Bunchrew."

"Ye canna do that," said he. "It's an inn for single gentlemen

I'm in, and there's no' a looking-glass. But maybe Mr Forbes can help us; stop you till I see him!"

He went out of the room and came back in a minute or two with Forbes.

"And so you want to fly already," Forbes said to her, and thereupon made a proposal which would keep her near her father. It was that she should stay in Bunchrew House kept by his sister. "Indeed," said he, "this house is a little wae for a girl just now, Miss Campbell; I'm a lee-lone widower; my brother the laird came home last night a sickly man and I doubt it's serious. You'll rest a while, and go tonight on a pad with a groom to Bunchrew House, where Mary will make you welcome. I have offered the same convenience to your father, but he'll not hear of it."

"Na, na! my lord," said Ninian firmly. "I'll bed where I can hear the water brawl. It's like enough that I'll be out all night, but ye'll know I'm on the road for sleep, if ye hear the *cailleach oidhche*, Jennet. But the thing that bothers me now is this—you must see the wife without the husband if you're to get any news from her, and how can ye manage that?"

"That's easily arranged," said Forbes with a smile,—"if you make your call, Miss Campbell, late in the afternoon—his lordship's no longer young, sleeps ill at night, and always takes, as I know, what he calls a 'good long dover' after dinner. But the lady is something of a recluse; folk see but little of her."

"She was my foster-sister, sir," said Janet.

"Ah, that I did not know!" said Forbes. "In that case I can enter with a better grace into your father's plans, feeling sure you will not be unfair to her husband's interests. We're perhaps a little hasty in assuming him concerned in this young gentleman's trepanning: I hope it may turn out an error."

"Deil the bit, my lord!" said Ninian. " 'Twas him that did it! I know it in my bones."

"No wonder you feel things in your bones," said Forbes, "if you sleep on the side of Bunchrew burn. It's not conviction, Mr Campbell; it's just damp."

He rallied Ninian on his den till Ninian lost patience and took his leave, with a promise to see his daughter sometime in the night at Bunchrew House.

XXII

By Bunchrew Burn

Next day he sat on the burnside busking lures, for nothing but the fun of it, since he could get what fish he wanted now by guddling. A dozen times that morning had he stretched upon the bank and peered down in the pools to see the sea-trout, lank and ruddy, lying on the gravel. He rolled his sleeves up, plunged a hand, and gently slid his fingers over them, then gripped them by the gills and lifted them, to cheep to them as though they had been pets and stroke their bellies. "Be thou aware," he said to them, "of nets! Keep out to sea or well up in the burn among true gentlemen." And then would he put them back again, unharmed, and seek another pool.

The morn had come with frost and every sense of him experienced the change—chill air, the constant patter of falling leaves, a tinkle in the water, hoar on the grasses, haze among the trees, fresh earthy smells. For most of the night had he been roaming; a fire was crackling behind him, and he had made a bed of the Fenian fashion, with brushwood next the ground, then moss, and a top of rushes. On a stick above the fire a fish was roasting; he had made an oaten cake from seed he had plucked down in the valley, singed, and ground with stones. His bonnet was full of nuts and his face was stained with berries.

It was now late afternoon.

The shilfy piped "fink-fink," and ousels talked among the stones; across the blue strip of the sky went wild geese southward, calling; there was no lonesomeness.

Well down the burn below him were great crags conglomerate whence there rose of a sudden croaking ravens. He dashed for the cave, stamped out the fire, and waited. A figure moved among the rocks.

It was Duncan Forbes with a terrier at his heels and a gun

below his arm. He looked at the embers, at the cake and fish, the Fenian bed, and the shaggy *beachdair* standing in his den, with a whimsical expression.

"I was pitying you, Mr Campbell," said he, "to have no better lodging, and now I'm in the mood to envy."

"Indeed I might be worse, my lord," said Ninian. "Sit down and take your breath. . . . Has she come back yet?"

Forbes sat on a boulder. "Yes," said he, "she has come back," and looked about him. When he had first appeared he was the man of business although he bore the gun as an excuse for rambling; no sooner had he sat than something dropped from him—the coldness of restraint, and he became exceeding natural and human. He had on a *crotal* coat, a good deal chafed, and might have been a shepherd. A robin came quite close to him and looked at him, and chirped a little song.

"*Bi falbh!*" Ninian said to it in fun,—"Be off!—thou'rt speaking to a lord, and thou'rt just a wee bit bird!"

"I have not been here," said Forbes, "for fifteen years, and many a thing has happened since. The climb is steeper, but the place is noway changed. It's hard that men should age and pass, and the burn and the rock be constant."

He broke some bread and fish at Ninian's invitation and drank a drink of water. "Ah," said he, "if we could aye be young, and shun the world, and go a-fishing!"

"What way's your brother, my lord?" asked Ninian.

"Poor John! Poor John! He'll never again see Bunchrew burn. We fished it both as laddies; what things have happened since to make that time seem gold! What is gladness, Ninian? It is to be simple, to be innocent, to think all men are good, and to be a boy, at fishing. But that's all bye wi't now; *eheu fugaces, Postume labuntur.*"

"That's just what I was thinking to myself," said Ninian. "Ye're capital at the Gaelic!"

Forbes smiled at this expression of erroneous politeness. "Men pass," said he, "and old estates. I wish we could aye bide boys at fishing. . . . That's a braw lass of yours, Mr Campbell."

"Ay, and a brave!" said Ninian, eating. "But just now she's

213

not herself. I'm beat to understand her."

"She's naturally put about for young Macmaster."

"No word of him?" asked Ninian quickly.

"Not a whisper! Wherever he is he's not out there and she is much concerned. I never saw a girl more stricken."

"God knows," said Ninian, "what is wrong with her! She gives me the notion of something hidden, and before, that girl was clear as glass."

"I thought her, myself," said Forbes, "as artless as a bird, as frank's a flower. It was easy to guess her secret; she wore it on her sleeve."

"On her sleeve?" said Ninian sharply; "I never noticed. What is it?" And Forbes laughed.

"That's what I'm not going to tell," said he. "I'll leave it to the *beachdair* to find out for himself.... But now, Mr Campbell, let us come to business. I want you to come down to the house to see your daughter, but first I'll tell you what has happened— part for your information, part to redd up things confused a little to myself. She went out to Castle Dounie, as you bade her, and saw her ladyship. It seems she's ailing, and unhappy. Lovat, as I guessed, was at his doze, and I think your girl did marvellously to find out all she learned in the time at her command. He had been out the last two nights till late—you see I tell you all without reserve. But the lad is not at Castle Dounie—her ladyship made sure of that. And now, for the first time, through your daughter, Mr Campbell, I get some inkling of the state of things 'twixt Lovat and his wife, which hitherto I might suspect but had no proofs of. I am sorry to say she loathes him."

"And well, my lord, she might!" said Ninian.

"You see I met the lady only once since they were married, and from his lordship's air I had no reason to suspect domestic trouble. With his former wife, in spite of the curious way he got her, he was all that one could wish for. I had the opportunities to see them often, and I'm satisfied they lived for long not ill-content together. Lovat has some gracious parts; in that rough carcass there's at times a charm that masters reason. Lord Islay and the Duke have often spoke to me of this peculiar quality in him, as if God meant him for a seraph to begin with, and in a whimsy filled him up with clods."

"I ken his history!" said Ninian, contemptuous.

"Yes, yes! We all know that. And yet, with those who knew him best, there has aye been hope that Simon would amend and be a good man for his country. He has long since passed the age of storm and folly; his aims have been attained; he has as much of power as man need ask for, he suffers from a stone, and must bethink sometimes that death looms. I've had him weeping to me for his sins, protesting Grace."

"When I will see a bad man greeting, I will aye be snecking up my sporran," said Ninian.

"I could tell of a thousand generous acts of Lovat's, and his sheltering of this young man's father fourteen years ago 's in keeping. Such things as these have made of us his friends in a kind of neutral fashion. I squirmed a bit myself at his marrying Primrose Campbell; it was not only age and youth, but it was policy, and I'm loth to see a girl put on a ring for policy. Yet I thought—we all thought—this connection with Argyll would keep him straight."

He took the terrier on his knees and clapped it, thinking, with his low lip jutting.

"It hasna! That's the long and the short of it. I've got news today, through your daughter, sir, that makes me sick of human nature. His wife, before she married him, had never realised his character, and she was, in a measure, forced to it by her people. Indeed, let us not make bones about it—she was forced completely! Since ever she came to him she has been confronted with evidence of his duplicity, for he's at times a foolish Machiavelli who brags of his own designs. Now she regards herself as sold to bondage; she is bitter with her folk, but bitterest of all with Alexander Duncanson."

"I'm finding out," said Ninian, "that he's a droll one, Sandy."

"You know that Lovat has been mentioned in the Grange affair? Last year Lord Grange would seem to have got sick of Lady Grange—indeed I'm not surprised at it, for I have seen and heard her to my sorrow!—and she was bundled up one night in Edinburgh, carted over Forth by Hielandmen, and lost to sight since then. The men who thus kidnapped her were, to all appearance, Frasers and Macleods, and Lovat's friendship with Lord Grange gave this a bad complexion. I ventured one time to inform Lord Lovat what was said, and he denied it to the blackest."

"I'll wager ye that, my lord!" said Ninian.

"And all this time—since her very day of marriage, his wife knows that he's guilty—that he planned and lent his men for the trepanning! I have never had the honour to meet your Mr Duncanson, but he seems to be a gentleman worth watching. A week before the wedding there was sent to Lord Islay by some enemy of Lovat's, proofs of his lordship's part in the Grange affair—a letter written by himself in a freakish mood to some one in these parts. That letter, had it reached Lord Islay, would have stopped the wedding. But he never got it. Your Mr Duncanson, who seems to have a sense of drollery as curious as his notion of his duty, despatched it to Lord Lovat as his wedding gift."

"My goodness! Is not that the ruffian!" cried Ninian.

"There were, I regret to say, two ruffians in this," said Forbes. "I might in course of time forgive Lord Lovat for his helping Grange to put the seas between himself and one who was a drunken targe, but I never could pardon him for showing his wife that letter. There are some sins, Mr Campbell, that I doubt if even the Blood will purge, and this, I fear, is one of them. It has turned her, as your daughter says, to ice."

"I knew he was bad to her!" said Ninian. " 'Twas that that roused me."

"Bad?—yes, in the lousiest fashion—that's in being a bad man to himself; but this is what makes her position hopeless. I compliment you on your daughter, Mr Campbell; she surely has her father's art, for she has squeezed the last drop from the situation. Lady Lovat either will not, or can not, do anything to help herself. He has never once been harsh with her nor failed in public or in private in a certain courtesy. But he wounds her none the less; his very presence is to her a blow. Not much matter for indictment there, now, is there, Mr Campbell? And another thing—there is her pride. It seems there's to be a family, and, now that shackle 's on, she darena move."

"Oh man! for a while I thought I had him!" Ninian said with sorrow.

"I wish you had!" said Forbes with feeling. "For I'm in this position that I can do nothing, even in the Grange affair or in the guns; I have no real evidence in either case. And I have entered into this long harangue, Mr Campbell, because I look to you to help me otherwise. It's forced on me, my friend, that the place for you just now is not in the shire of Inverness at all but in Inveraray."

"That's just what I was thinking to myself, my lord," said Ninian. "If I could just find Æneas!"

"This Duncanson of yours is full of interest to me. I say so to you freely since your daughter, who is most discreet, cannot conceal her feelings to that gentleman, and you, it seems, agree."

He pushed the terrier off his knees and shifted on his seat a little nearer to the other, fixing him with serious eyes, and speaking with great earnestness.

"I begin to think," said he, "that some leakages of late of governmental plans affecting us may have had their origin in Lord Islay's secretary. This is not an instruction to the musicians, mind ye, Mr Campbell; it's just a hint. That Duncanson should have sent on that letter to Lord Lovat at a cost so great for poor Prim Campbell, of itself looks sinister. Our old friend, out the way there, has, sometimes, a charm, as I was saying, and it's possible he may have charmed that gentleman. I can conceive of nothing more advantageous to Lord Lovat than that he should have a faithful private correspondent in the household of Argyll. You gave me a clew yourself, though I did not at the time quite see it, when you told me Barisdale had blocked you. I happen to know that Barisdale's affairs are much embarrassed, and that Lovat and your friend have both got bonds on his estate."

"Just that!" said Ninian, and ducked his head. "I'm getting

217

on, my lord! Keep you on wi' your story; I could hearken to that tale of you beside a fire until a stack of peats was burned."

"In these circumstances, Barisdale may very well have been acting in your Mr Duncanson's behoof."

"He was, my lord!" said Ninian. "There's not a doubt of it. I wondered whatna grip he had on Col."

"So much for that! But now there's another point I owe to your daughter's talk with her old companion. It seems you were well received at Castle Dounie till the post came in?"

"That's so, my lord!" cried Ninian eagerly. "I'm listening."

"There was something in that post that startled Lovat,—so his lady says, and she is anxious, for Miss Janet's sake, to help so far's she can to find Macmaster. I am inclined now to share your confidence that the lad was lifted by his lordship's orders, and I am mighty curious to know why. Here now present themselves two possibilities—one that Lovat's change of key and his presumptive capture of Macmaster and attack on both of you arose from mere resentment at your interference in the business of the guns; the other that he had got some disquieting intelligence from Duncanson that called for drastic measures."

"Did Jennet no' have the sense to ask if there was word from Inveraray?" Ninian blurted.

"She did," said Forbes. "There was! A letter of Duncanson's. Whatever it was about it stirred up Simon strangely. In Lovat's ire with you, or in that letter, lies the motive for those singular proceedings at the inn. The motive is, I think, more like to be in the latter than the former, for Lovat is not the man to go to such extremities of revenge on the head of a pickle guns, and he knows you have no proofs as yet against him. I'd give a groat or two to ken what's in that letter!"

He said so with great warmth, and then drew up a bit as if ashamed that a *crotal* coat, and a burnside, and a *beachdair* listener should so much unbend him. "What are you fiddling at?" he said in a different key, for Ninian was twitching at a string.

"A tangled hank, my lord!" said Ninian slyly. "Ye mind I told ye that a line had aye two ends to it, and that I never tugged, but

218

teased it? What am I at, my lord, but at the teasing? The snow's on Wyviss Ben this morning—I could smell it! Before it's melted I'll have cleared my line!"

He started scattering the ashes of the fire; took out his bedding from the nook and threw it in the burn; tied up his garters tightly; scrugged his bonnet. Forbes watched him, curious.

"My father's people never left an ash," said Ninian, "but all of Gaeldom's grey with their smothered fires. Only the weasel kens their dust in woods; we never left a stick! . . . Clan Alpine! Clan Alpine! Ye hear me in Balwhidder? Nor fire will Ninian light, nor sleep in bed, nor loose a latchet till he finds him young Macmaster!"

So saying, loudly, in a fervour of the spirit, he took up the dirk and held it by its blade before his mouth, and put upon its haft his lips.

"And now, my lord," said he "I'm ready. Let us go."

XXIII

Night-Lads

As they were making down the burn for Bunchrew, Forbes withdrawn into himself, and to a mood less free and confidential by that heathen burst which showed how great the difference between himself and that rough spirit only varnished with decorum, they were, at a point well down, among blown timber, brought to a standstill by a whistle. It mocked the curlew's call that is a voice tuned to the wilderness, a plaint from days gone by, but Forbes, who was a hunter, missed some cadence; Ninian knew it in a moment for a signal. It came from edges of a thicket to their left, in which the mist of frost seemed tangled with the branches.

"Mark whaup, my lord!" said Ninian, like a beater.

Forbes, with the impulse of a sportsman, raised his gun, then smiling at himself, restored it to his elbow.

"What bairns," said he, "we are of custom! That's no wheeple of the whaup. What is it, Ninian?"

"I'll soon can tell ye that!" the other said. "Lend me the gun a minute."

He fired it in the air; the gorge roared with the sound that echoed, and re-echoed, clanging back from cliffs like waves from off a headland. "I'll give them every chance," said he; "I never yet shot hare a-sitting," and throwing down the gun left Forbes and dashed up to the thicket.

"Come back! Come back!" cried Forbes.

"Devil the back!" he shouted, furious, and climbed the brae. "Come you up with the gun behind, and see it's loaded."

He disappeared into the wood.

Forbes charged his gun afresh and followed. He had not reached the trees when Ninian came out, his dirk drawn in his hand. "They're off!" said he as he sheathed it. "I got but the one

220

wee glimpse of them."

"Put that away, sir, on the moment!" said the other panting. "Who were they?"

"Who were they but the mischief's own!" said Ninian dryly. "Three men running like the wind, as if their hour was after them. It's good we had our lady friend the musket. That's three, my lord, that have been tracking me since I left Inverness last night. I saw them on the bridge; I heard them in the dark behind me; I saw them on the moor again this morning. I'm thinking now it's time that I was out of Bunchrew. To the Worst Place wi' MacShimi! That arrant rascal needs a scaffolding. . . . But nothing to my daughter, sir, about this business! It would put her much about to know that I was followed."

They hurried down the brae as fast as they could walk, and all the way down Ninian revealed his mind upon the meaning of events whereof the other had part knowledge only.

"It's all against my friend," said he. "I thought at first I was the cause of it, but now I see I'm only in't because I'm in his company, and maybe ken too much. The whole thing's centred in a desk in Inveraray."

"Every mischief nowadays is farrowed in a desk," said Forbes. "But what is this one?"

Ninian told him all about Macmaster's tutoring; the sudden end to it; the wrath of Duncanson; the charge of theft; the part of Margaret; and last of all, the strange complexion given to these things by their discovery that Duncanson for fourteen years had kept the truth of Paul Macmaster's end a secret.

"It's nigh beyond belief!" cried Forbes.

"Beyond belief!" said Ninian bitterly. "The only quirk in life beyond belief is that a man could take the breeks off him by pulling them over his head. I'm too long at the *beachdair* business to be amazed at anything else. Your lordship's right about the letters to Lord Lovat; it was the one he got from Inveraray put him to his tricks. There was that in Sandy's desk, whatever it was, that made old Simon partner in some left-hand business both of them would wish kept dark. They think that Æneas saw it, but he didna."

"I'm more convinced than ever that the place for you is Inveraray," Forbes said warmly.

"I'll go when I get the lad," said Ninian. "But not an hour before, if it was till Nevermas!"

"I have twenty men at search today," said Forbes. "I doubted all along he was at Dounie."

"Since Jennet made sure of that I know now where he is," said Ninian; and took from his pouch a piece of cord quite fresh, that smelled of tar. "The three birds that I flushed up there had a bit of a nest among the breckan, and left this piece of marling. They meant to tie up Ninian, and they're men that use the sea."

"Ah-ha!" said Forbes.

"The thing is now as plain to me as print. They had a boat to bring them up the town; they had a net—"

"I know about the net," said Forbes. "It was lifted from a barking-house at Kessock, and found next morning on the beach with your bit out of it."

"*Sin thu fhéin a bhalaich!*—Well done yourself, my lord!" cried Ninian. "That shows they werena fishers. Between the pair of us and God we'll get him yet! The ship escaped my mind till I got this bit marling. And now I see that the time they left me lying on the bank in trammel was just time for them to reach the *Wayward Lass* behind two oars, and ship my friend, and hurry back for Ninian."

"There's much to be said for your interpretation," Forbes said quickly, "and for once I have forestalled you. I got the sheriff to send out an officer to search the brig today more carefully. The men I sent out yesterday assured themselves she had no guns, except a handful kept in the skipper's cabin for his private use, and these the fools distrained as if he had been poinded. We'll have to send them back and eat the leek. The papers of Captain Grant were all in order, and he had a quite good tale. He frankly said he had shipped some arms from Holland; they were on his manifest, consigned to a man in Leith."

"But they were landed at Blackness!" cried Ninian.

"Just so! Of course the man is lying, but his story's quite

complete, coiled up and flemished down, as he would say himself in his tarry way. The man at Leith, he says, paid extra freight to send them farther up the frith. . . . No, no, Mr Campbell, we may have got the guns, but we're not going to find it easy to get pouther in the way of proof that Lovat shipped them. No loophole of discovery's been overlooked."

"I don't give a docken, my lord, about the guns at present; for that affair more proofs can be got at leisure. What bothers me is young Macmaster. Did your men no' see a sign of him?"

"No," said Forbes, "but then they were not seeking him. It only occurred to me today when I heard of the net at Kessock that he might be on the brig that's lying off it, so I got the officer sent out to see, and he's coming to Bunchrew later on to tell me how he fares."

"Capital!" said Ninian, and hurried on.

They were in Bunchrew House two hours before he saw his daughter, though. Worn out by travel and distress of mind, and dashed exceedingly by what had been disclosed at Castle Dounie, she had gone to rest on the imperative command of Forbes' sister.

"The lass is fair foundered," said that lady to the father, looking at him through great horn-rimmed specs; "ye've made a bonny hash of it, my man!"

"What way?" said Ninian.

"What way!" she snapped indignantly. "What way, but losing a fine young man? Good kens there's no' that many in the country, and it's me that knows! Trailing an honest lad through all the ruffian parts of Scotland on your dirty errands—fie shame on ye!"

Ninian shrugged, and turned his bonnet in his hand like an errand boy. He looked at Forbes, and Forbes took snuff, with a helpless kind of pawky smile for both of them.

"Come, come, Mary!" said he, "you're very hard on Mr Campbell."

" 'Deed no!" said Ninian heartily. "She's just splendid! Dirty work is the word for it, though it wasna me that made the dirt, Miss Forbes; I'm just a scafenger that must be there when the king whistles. And there's every word of truth in what ye say, mem; Æneas was better had he never met me."

"At any rate," said she, less tart, "I'll not have your lass disturbed till she is rested. . . . Ye'll take a bite?"

"Not one morsel, mem!" said Ninian. "I thank ye."

"Dear me!" said she. "What do the Macgregors live on?"

"On anything that's going, mem. They're like the herring of the sea that can live on the foam of their own tails."

"Poor feeding for a girl! I canna get that lass of yours to pick a decent meal. Oh me! but ye've made a mess of it! . . . Duncan, give the man a dram."

And away she sailed, all rustling, and left them to themselves. To Ninian it seemed eternity before she came to cry him up the stair.

"There's she's wakened now," said she; "and for good sake, man, be gentle wi' her!"

It was a daughter woebegone for Primrose Campbell, and sharing all his rage with Lovat, Ninian found. She made him sit before her and tell everything afresh that bore, or seemed to bear, in the flimsiest degree on Æneas' disappearance; sifted the smallest meal of facts himself had thrashed and ground; the strange transforming power of some new passion made her shrewder than himself.

"You're all astray!" she said at last to him. "My dear old father! my dear old father! you're all astray—you and your bits of string!"

"I'm not so very old as that," said he with some vexation. "What way am I astray?"

"Because you chase two deer instead of, wise-like, one. A two-deer dog will never bring down either. First it's Lovat with you, then it's Duncanson; finish off with the one before you chase the other."

He looked delighted at her; patted her on the shoulder.

"Ye're a clever lass," said he. "I'm proud of ye! Indeed, a two-deer dog is not much good at hunting, and I was the two-deer dog too long, but I couldna help it. But that's all by wi'—Sim's affair is settled and off my mind, and now I'm on the race for

Duncanson."

"It's from the start you should have thought of that," said she. "Lovat's but his tool."

"How ken ye that?" he asked her.

"How do I ken?" she cried. "A woman's kenning. If a man has a wall to scale he must go up a ladder; a woman jumps."

"I would like to see ye at the jumping, Jennet!" said her father.

"I mean a wall of the wits," said she. "You are hanging on your ladder rungs and I'm already over; Duncanson is meaning Æneas' destruction."

"Tach!" said he, "ye never had a madder notion. For what should he destroy him?"

"I feel it!" she said; "I know it! Duncanson will stop at nothing."

She spoke like one who knew things that presaged disaster.

"He will stop at that at any rate," said her father. "I'll get the lad before the morn's morning."

"Where?" she asked, a flush across her face.

He told her what led Forbes and him to their belief that Æneas was on the brig.

"What coud they want with him there?" said she.

"Ship him off abroad," said Ninian; "the thing's quite common."

"Abroad?" she stammered. "Where?"

"Where, but to Virginia—to the plantations! Many a body Sim sent there. Ye see, my lass, he's like a king in this regality. He has the power of pit and gallows, and to sell a lad to slavery would bother Sim no more than selling heifers at a fair. He doesna keep them now in vault and salt; he gets so much a head for them upon the hoof. The thing's against the law, of course; he hasna got the right of transportation, but he drives a bargain—either transportation or the tree, and who would choose the tree? In this case Duncan Forbes will have a word to say; I'm looking every minute for a man he sent to search."

She trod the floor like a creature caged; again he felt some secret in her, and he scanned her sleeves, but nothing was to see there that accounted for a spirit so unusual in Janet.

The night was drawing in with suddenness: it dimmed the room. He walked up to the window and looked out. Below him was a garden bounded to the east and west by tall old trees; ahead were shallow terraces, with paths between, which ended at a wall, beyond which lay a great wide stretch of sand, whereon, far off, the tide was breaking. Big clouds were piling on the distant hills; the frith was black; the sands were so immense and desolate they gave a dowie aspect to the scene, that further saddened when a gust of wind shook through the garden and filled all the air with leaves.

He turned away from it, to find her standing at his elbow looking out too at the prospect.

"My grief!" said he, "it looks like the start of winter."

"Winter!" she said, and shivered. She leaned against the wall, her head upon her wrists, and burst in tears.

"Good God!" cried he in Gaelic, "what is wrong?"

"Winter!" she said, sobbing. "It will make things different. I hate to think of winter."

"What!—God's own winter!" he cried out, astonished. "Beloved Scotland of the winter and the hills! 'Tis little that thou'lt get from them, but they will make thee hard and brave!"

He was all aback at these strange gusts in her; about her waist he put an awkward arm and soothed her. "Poor lass!" said he, "poor lass! Indeed it is a bleak night and a bleak land, I wish that we were yont the Spey again, and all was well with Æneas Macmaster."

As if she could no more contain herself, she struggled free and darted from the room.

To him the house was quite unknown; it was not very large, but rambled oddly upon different levels, with confusing passages and narrow stairs that now the dusk made ill to navigate; he went to follow her, and down a stair as narrow as a ship's he found himself in kitchen quarters at an open door. The air blew chilly through it; he looked out on leeks and kail and berry-bushes. No servant was about to guide him, so he walked out round a gable-end to reach the entrance whence he better knew his bearings.

Away out on the ebb were mallards quacking; teals that feed in dark were screaming; there was no other sound round Bunchrew but the pattering of leaves from trees that had their feet already in the pools of night quick-coming like a tide. A bird with a cry of "skaith!" came whirring from them, low above his head with curious twists and twinings; he looked towards whence it came and listened with his hands behind his ears. Beyond the trees a slim young moon was setting.

There was a snap of brushwood, and he moved a little nearer to the door.

A man burst suddenly from underneath the trees and ran to him—a stout-built fellow with a cane, who looked across his shoulder once or twice as if he had been followed.

"Ye're in a hurry, lad," said Ninian. "Are ye from the *Wayward Lass?*"

"Yes," said the officer, "and three men through the wood in chase of me."

"They're friends of mine who took ye for myself," said Ninian. "Silly fellows! Say not a word of that inside among the women. Come you away: his lordship's waiting."

He went in with the man, who, in a sentence, shattered all their hopes. Æneas was not on board the ship!

"Are you sure of it?" said Forbes, incredulous.

"Not one hair of him is there, my lord!" declared the officer. "We searched her high and low. The skipper's ashore and half his crew. I came on a drunken man—a Fraser from Strathglass."

"A man of Lovat's?" queried Forbes.

The officer, who had a broad and honest face, with eyes of darting penetration, smiled at the question slyly. "I think indeed, my lord, he was. At least he was no willing passenger, for he was clapped in irons. A poor young fellow he had stabbed was bedded groaning in a fever."

"Had the man in bed a ruddy whisker?" rapped out Ninian.

"As red's a rasp! Ye could gather a clan wi' him for flambeau."

"Tach!" said Ninian, "that settles it! I'll wager he keeps mind of wee Grey Colin!"

227

Miss Forbes, with trembling hands, put on her specs and looked across at Janet. Ninian looked too, and saw his daughter's face most pitiful. He was himself far more concerned than he displayed, at this last failure of his judgment; Forbes could not hide that he was mortified, and stood without a word, his face beclouded; the girl could not but feel that they were baffled worse than ever.

"A word wi' ye, my lord," said Ninian at last, and left the room.

The Advocate came after him; they stood out in the lobby.

"That's a bad twist, my lord!" said Ninian.

"Indeed it is!" said Forbes. "We're where we were, and I'm getting really anxious. I can't conceal from myself that things look far more gloomy for your friend than I at first imagined. No wonder that your girl's in such an anguish."

"Can ye tell me, my lord, what ails her? There's nothing of her there I seem to know."

Forbes cleared his throat. "It's very plain," said he, "that the *beachdair* business spoils a man for seeing anything but mischief. It might occur to you, Mr Campbell, that your daughter has a tender interest in young Macmaster."

"Is it Jennet?" said Ninian, amazed. "Good lord! she's but a child!"

"She'll never be anything else to you, my man; that's one of the jokes of nature. But other folk have eyes. I'm wae to see her prostrate this way, Mr Campbell."

"Whatever o't, she's in the dods wi' me," said Ninian sadly.

"No wonder, when she thinks you let them kill him."

"Na, na, my lord!" said Ninian, with conviction. "He's no' dead; not one bit of him! They have him planted no' far off, in cleft or cranny, and I'll get him."

"If you're not to sleep in bed nor loose a lace till you find him, Mr Campbell, you'll have to be gey and slippy."

Ninian buttoned up his coat. "I know the way to get him, my lord," said he. "It came to me in a flash in there. There's nothing in your notion about Jennet and the lad, but still-and-on"—

He moved to the outer door and opened it; dead leaves were

whirled into the lobby by an eddy of the wind, and Forbes gave a shiver of cold; he had come from a roaring fire.

"—I like the look of your officer, my lord," said Ninian, "he has a clever eye. It's in the eye of a man ye'll see if he has *yon* in him, and this one has it. To look at the wood ye would think there was nothing in't but crows, and still it's throng wi' mischief. The men I flushed on the hill are there; they're not done yet wi' Ninian."

"What!" said Forbes, "do you see them?" and came to the doorstep.

"No," said Ninian, "but they're there, as your man can tell ye. Now this is the way it will be with me—I'll take a daunder."

"Not one step!" said Forbes, alarmed.

"There's no other way, my lord, and not much risk in it. I'll let them seize me, and your man has but to keep well out of sight and follow."

"It's not a bad idea," Forbes admitted, "but the risk—"

"The only risk, my lord, is that they'll weary waiting on me, or the moon will hide, and that might spoil it all, so here's furth fortune wi't and fill the fetters!"

XXIV

At The Ebb-Tide

Without another word he left the door, and Forbes confounded
on its threshold; gave a turn to the Virgin nut in the bottom of
his sporran, and plucked tight his kilt.

Though he had spoken bravely of the winter to his girl, and
truly felt, for ordinary, some sting in winter that called forth in
him the best of manhood, quicker pulses, keener zests, this end
to autumn, earlier than usual, found him now experiencing that
droop of spirits which had sent his daughter crying. He had not
left the door a moment when he felt as she (he thought) must
feel—an eeriness to think of Æneas amissing in that great cold
country. So long as grass was green, while still the hills were
blue, their passes open, and while yet the birds were blithe, the
lad's condition had not seemed so desperate, nor his own
research so hopeless.

And now a hint of winter altered all!

It was as if a door had clashed on Æneas and left him out from
light and warmth till spring, perhaps for ever. So much had
happened since they left their home, that home seemed all at
once unreal—the woods of Inveraray, pleasant gardens, streets
well-kent and folk one knew. At least it seemed an age since they
were there and heard the reaper's song on Cairnbaan. And now,
he wondered, where was Æneas? In what hold or hollow of this
dreary land? or looking on it through what chink? in what sad
stress?

Already had his scheme begun to look ridiculous.

When, having left the Advocate irresolute on his doorstep, he
went crunching through the gravel round the lawn and reached
the avenue, he turned and looked behind him at the house in
which were lights now gleaming. Already the place seemed quite
indifferent to his quest, and yet behind these black high walls he

knew were fear and speculation. He seemed, himself, shut out; if Æneas was lost for ever like his father, who could face the lasting blame of Janet?

The thin moon, slicing through the mirk of clouds, lit wanly things about him but to make their shapes uncanny. An acre to the westward of the house was laid out trimly, level as a pond, with here and there some knots of evergreen, the myrtle and the holly, under them black shades that had a look of ambush. More solemn shadows, wider spread, more likely to be harbouring the men who sought him, lay below the thick groins of the trees, and spilled at intervals an inky pool halfway across the broad path of the avenue that stretched before him like a nightmare passage. Not life nor living dangers in these glooms compelled him to stand still a moment, half-inclined to turn, but something very old and rediscovered in himself; forgotten dreads of boyhood in wild winter wastes of midnight, and his people breaking from some thicket under moon to see before them spread unfriendly straths and hear the wind in perished heather. The mist it was they cherished—not the moon who made their progress visible; too often had she brought calamity to old Clan Alpine trailing through the snow, a broken and a hunted band, with children whimpering.

The silliest of these old alarms, the ripple of the skin upon his back, this unco evening now restored to him; he felt like one awakened from a desperate dream, aware that nothing is about him but what man can combat, yet bringing from his dream unreasonable terrors all intractable to sense.

He had the worst ill of his race, the oldest—*dubhachas*: he was forlorn, and feared his own forlornness as an omen.

"Tach!" said he to himself at last, and struck out boldly down the avenue, like a man not apprehending anything, yet all the way were his shoulders shrugged, and his eyes on either side of him expectant of a sally from the dark.

Nothing happened. He reached the gate that was of iron; opened it, passed through and made it swing. It had a balance, shutting of itself upon a latch that loudly clanged at every swing before it settled. A bell could not more noisily attract attention.

231

A while he hung about it, peering round and listening. He now had cleared the wood; before him lay the fields, their boundaries vaguely visible, and farther south the rising ground with rocks encumbered, murmuring with the passage of the burn. No other house was near than Bunchrew, not even shed nor sheepfold. Outside the trees a bitter wind was blowing; ice glittered in the ditches. His eyes searched every airt for movement; nothing moved. Nor was there any sound to show the wood was tenanted by other than its birds; he gave out once the howlet call, so natural an owl cried back, but then its grove relapsed to silence deeper than before. Only the breeze in beeches, high in the branches, harsh and dry, continuous, neither hum nor hiss, but a babbling about old things forgotten of the world, remembered by the great community of woods; the creak of boles, the tinkle of dead leaves.

He was surprised, uneasy. When he had entered on this project, driven to it by the blank despondency of Janet, each nerve of him was strung for something instant and decisive. But this unlooked-for absence of the men confounded him: they might be gone for good, so spoiling every chance of his manoeuvre leading him to Æneas, and the moon was sinking.

A clamour of birds out on the ebb gave him a notion that men walked there—they were on the sands and watching Bunchrew from the back; he turned down to the shore.

The tide should now be flooding, but the sea was still far out, and in the bay of Bunchrew every waukrife bird that haunts the shore at night was screaming. He heard the grey goose call; peewits, too late of leaving, ducks and whaups were in a multitude that dinned astoundingly; somewhere an otter whistled.

A more melancholy place for ruffian engagements Ninian, who liked a wood or rock, had never seen, and the moon made worse its dreariness. The bay, for all its birds, was like a desert, and the breeze swept through it like a knife. Far off, disconsolate, the frith was moaning.

On a horn of the bay the burn came down, well-filled, and bordered with rough scrub of thorn and willow on the knolls of

232

sand. Its channel thrust through the sands a bit, then branched in rivulets that rambled awkwardly in Ninian's way, too deep to wade with comfort and too wide for jumping, and he found himself entangled. It vexed him most that nothing had been gained so far by his adventure; wherever the men were gone they were not visible; the wide stretch of the bay was empty save of birds. He peered, he listened uselessly, and then he sniffed, and, on the sniffing, started.

Green sticks were burning! The wind had brought on it the smell of fire.

Without a pause he waded through a pool and sought the channel of the burn, and followed it through stones. He stole across salt grass with caution, parted sauch-tree branches, and looked down into a linn, the last stand of the Bunchrew ere submitting to the sea.

And there he saw what instantly commanded flight.

He had never thought about a boat!

He knew that they were seamen who pursued him, who had followed him for hours the day before and found his covert in the *eas* that morning, but always he had thought of them as severed from their vessel, instruments of Lovat and his vaults. One glance at the linn corrected him—a boat was there in waiting for the tide, and four men round a fire were supping.

They heard him in the bushes, saw his face a moment in the firelight, and jumped. He turned to fly, his plan immediately abandoned in the face of dangers unforeseen, but slipped on the frosted grass, and, falling, rolled to their very feet.

They were on him in a swarm; he struggled only for a moment, then gave in.

"*Thoir thairis!*" said he. "Give over! Ninian's done for." He had not even time to draw the dirk that now was always down his back; he was got without a blow.

When they had done with him, "Well, lads," said he, "this is a warm end to a cold day, whatever," and started whistling a tune with unconcern.

It was a singular company in which he found himself so suddenly—three little men as black in the face as peat with

233

weather, one of them a hunchback; the fourth a man gigantic, shouldered like an ox, with sleepy eyes and an open mouth that gave him a look of helpless laziness. The big one plainly had stood by the boat all day; the others were the hounds. This nook of the burn they occupied was chosen well for hiding. The rocks and scrub about it screened it from the land, and even from the frith it was invisible; a fire might burn in it in blackest night and not betray a glimmer. But for the scent of Ninian he had never found out where they lay.

What struck him as most curious was that they should fall on him and master him without one spoken word. The small men hung on him like leeches, and the big one brought his wrists together like a child's, for all his struggling, and held them with one hand while he lashed a cord about them with the other, but all without a voice. Not even when he was settled with and helpless in their midst was speech from them; they sat them down on boulders and resumed their meat.

The giant had been cook as well as butcher; he it was who stirred and fed the fire and turned the flesh on it; the carcass of a lamb, half-skinned, was lying near; its in-meat, dragged out on the stones, was reeking still, and the knife, yet red, was at the giant's waist.

He was gnawing a mutton-bone; a tooth more brisk about a bone had Ninian never witnessed, and it made him hungry just to see: the last food he had tasted was the fish he shared with Forbes. A lamb at roasting never smelled more savoury.

"If I was in the company of gentlemen," said he, with impudence, "and they at meat, the first salute for me were 'stretch thy hand!' "

The black lads never said a word, nor even looked at him, but lifted cinders from the fire and lighted pipes; the big one never answered, either, for a while, but finished with his bone, and then picked up a rib and held it out to Ninian, and for the first time showed himself not dumb.

"Oh, men and love!" said he in island Gaelic, "but Peter-the-son-of-James is sick of this pursuing! A silly, small man like this to keep us from our sleep two nights, and spoil our sailing!"

At this the other three looked at their friend surprised and disapproving; to Ninian they were like creatures of the tales wherein queer figures not of earth come to a house at night and sit about the gathering-peat, with mould upon their faces and their hair bedewed, so that the children cry. Sailors they were for certain, for their clothes smelled of the pitch, and the hunchback's hair was pleated, but an odder crew, thought Ninian, was never shipped in Scotland.

"How can I eat," said he, "and my hands in bonds? It's not a hen I am."

At that the big one laughed, and loosed the prisoner's wrists, but first he tied his feet.

Ninian drew closer to the fire, for he was shivering, took out the *sgian-achlais*, the armpit knife, and started eating, with a look about him. The boat, a broad-beamed craft of shallow draught, was floating in the pool, with canvas boomed out on an oar for shelter aft. Reeds fringed the water's edge below them; through them went the night breeze, swishing mournful. The burn itself had many voices where it broke on stones, and the sauch-tree switches sometimes gave a little shivering pipe. The pallor of the moon came through them sifting.

Peter-son-of-James, when he had given him the meat and tied him freshly, sat again and propped against a root, and shut his eyes for sleep, with no attention to the questions Ninian poured on him. The brothers sucked their pipes and fidged themselves, or they had seemed like granite. He coaxed them and he twitted; tried them with a joke or two, and even crooned a song; he might have been a merman they had found, without a knowledge of his language; nothing would they say to him, and by-and-by the hunchback took a stocking from his breast, half-made, and started knitting.

At last the moon was gone; the wind went round a point to east; it grew more chilly, and one of the men put driftwood on the fire. He was the oldest of the three, if rime upon his beard was proof, and having sat again, he said, offhand, "It's cold."

He spoke to no one in particular, and no one answered.

An hour went past. Except that every move of Ninian roused

attention, he might not have been there for them, so he picked a bit of wood half charred, and started whittling with the small black knife. He made it like a boat, with clever fingers, stuck two skelfs of mast in it and had it finished when the hunchback broke the silence.

"Were ye speaking?" said he.

He was turning the heel of his stocking, and it looked as if the first man's speech had only reached his understanding.

There was no answer, though; the first man smoked his pipe, and the big man snored, and Ninian industriously whittled, whistling to himself. He knew they waited for the tide.

Another hour was gone when the third man tapped his pipe on his boot-toe, got to his feet, and looked at the other two with some impatience.

"Far too much of chattering!" said he, and started down the burn.

Ninian burst out laughing. "Oh, Peter!" said he to the big man, who had started up, "it's often I've heard of the men of Boreray in the Isles that keep their speech for courting, but I never heard them gossiping before. *Mo chreach!* aren't they the merry ones! No wonder that you're fat, man, sailing with such lads to give you laughter."

The big man gave a grin of comprehension, but said nothing in reply, and looked at the other's feet. The cord, though still about the ankles, had been cut an hour ago!

"I thought better of it," said Ninian, no way aback to be discovered. "I'll go like the lamb with you if you will tell me where's my friend."

"He's on the ship," said the sailor; whereupon the whole night's *dubhachas*, a load of apprehension, fell from Ninian's mind; he could have danced for pleasure.

They did not trouble to tie him up again, but put him in the boat. The tide was now well up; they drowned the fire and pushed down-water, shipped four oars and started pulling. A heavy sea was running into Bunchrew Bay; the night was dark as ink, with only one light visible in all the world, and Ninian knew it for a ship's at anchor in the deep off Kessock.

XXV

The Wayward Lass

From the gut of the frith a wind was belching. They came through jabbled water to the ship that strained upon her cable, heading to the narrows, heaving so that she was all a-rattle. The big man gave a bellowing hail as they went round her stem; a rope was thrown to them, and in the feeble light of a lantern brought to the bulwarks Ninian saw that she was neither a sloop, as the big-jowled man had called her at Lord Lovat's party, nor a brig, as Forbes had said, but a sturdy schooner. Plainly she was in ballast; her sides stood very high above the water.

"My goodness! but the tide's far out on her!" he said with great simplicity, and the sailors laughed.

"It's not much that you know of boats," said Peter in broken English.

"Nothing at all," said Ninian readily, "except that they lie but poorly on my stomach. Where's the door?"

They got him clumsily on board; he stood for a while with some perplexity in the vessel's waist while the boat that had brought him off was being led astern; then groped about the deck, gear-hampered, lit in spots by the lantern that had been left upon the hatch, and by a glow that came from somewhere at the poop. Now that he was shipped his captors seemed prepared to leave him to his own devices, and the two men who had come on deck on their arrival gave but a squint at him and followed the others aft. Had the wind not hummed in cordage, and the blocks been jerking, and a creak gone through her timbers every time she rolled, the greatest peace would have prevailed; she might have been a ship asleep.

He picked the lantern up and stumbled round with a shrewd eye cast on everything about him—battened hatches lumbered up with ropes, a boat on chocks, a coop with hens in it, and a harness cask without a lid, in which salt beef was steeping. The wan glow at the poop, he found, came from the companion of the cabin; looking down he saw a table and a lamp above it swinging, but the place would seem to have no tenant. It reeked with the smell of balsam. He was bending down to look into the cabin when he heard a step behind him; straightened up at once with some confusion to be found so curious, and walked in its direction, to find himself faced by Æneas.

"Oh *ille!*" he said, with a grab at his coat, "is't you that's in it? And I was thinking of you all this hour back dapped in shackles!"

Æneas for a moment could not speak. He looked at the other, stunned and unbelieving. "In all the earth how came you here?" he said at last. "Is it Grant that's got you?"

"Has Grant been on the prowling too?" said Ninian.

"Since morning. He went off with half his hands. 'Ye'll need them all,' I said to him, 'and sharper wits than I suspect ye of.' I could have staked my life he would not get you, and here you are. Oh, Ninian! Ninian!"

He spoke with great distress.

"It wasna him at all," said Ninian, and cocked an ear for the men abaft. "I came with a burly lad called Peter and three dreary men of the poorest conversation; there they're aft at tying."

"I thought it was Grant who hailed," said Æneas, more surprised than ever. "It mortifies the worse to think you should be caught by fools."

"In a way I wasna caught at all," said Ninian; "I let them take me. It was the only way if I'm to get my boots off or to sleep in bed; I couldna find ye otherwise."

He was standing by a mast, with the lantern held up so that he could see the young man's face. He saw it very pale and weary, first, and then of a sudden flushed with feeling. It was as if the morn came to the young man's brow; he seemed transported.

"Tell me this, Mr Campbell," he said, with a shaken voice, "did you of your own purpose submit yourself to these men only that you might join me?"

"What else?" said Ninian. "You may be sure it wasna for a crack wi' Captain Grant."

Æneas caught his arms. "Oh man!" said he, "you make me happy! I could sing! I may be lost to Scotland, but I've found myself again. You canna guess what joy is in my breast to find life better than I thought. I was in a black mood all this day, reflecting on the wickedness of humankind, and sure the world was evil—"

"So it is!" said Ninian cheerfully, "but, man, there's blinks!"

"Blinks!" said Æneas; "you find me like a devil, and you make me like a god! Never again can I think ill of humankind. You came to me—you came to me—"

He could not finish, broken down with feeling.

"Tach!" said Ninian, "there's nothing in't! Ye surely didna think I was going to leave ye with those blackguards. If ye had seen me no' an hour ago on Bunchrew sands, it's there ye would see the sick and sorry gentleman, as frightened as a child because I didna ken what happened to ye. But now I'm here wi' ye I'm quite joco; what is the best of life but strife and two companions?"

"And yet," said Æneas, rueful now, "I'm wrong to feel like this; you should not have come here. You have—you have a daughter. You'll never get off this ship. She's sailing for America."

"Fair wind to her, then," said Ninian; "but one thing's certain—you and me's no sailing wi' her. There's far too much for us to do in Scotland. Two good heads on us to a lot of tarry sailors—it were shame to us if we couldna quirk them! Ye're better off than I expected; the hold was where I thought to find ye, snapped in links."

"In that particular," said Æneas, "I have no complaint. But for an hour that I was yesterday shut up in the beak of the boat with rats and cables, I've only been a prisoner to the ship and free to take the air on her. And not all the time a prisoner to the ship either; today I was ashore for hours with a crew on some pretence of getting water, which I cannot fathom, since our casks are full and we took none back with us."

239

"Just that!" said Ninian. "I see! They knew there would be search, and cleared ye out till it was over. Oh yes! I'm thinking Pat's a clever, clever fellow! Where were ye yesterday when Duncan's lads were searching for the guns?"

"That's when I was in the bows a prisoner. Grant ordered me below when he saw a boat approaching; I had not seen the boat myself, and did not know the searchers were on board till they were gone."

"Whisht!" said Ninian, "here they're coming."

The men at the stern came forward, looked into the cabin through the skylight grating, then made for the fo'c'sle. The big man took the lantern from Ninian's hand and blew its light out through a hole that was in its horn. "It's warmer down below," said he, and gave them a little push, but quite good-naturedly. They all went down together, Ninian stumbling in the dark and knocking his head resoundingly against the scuttle coamings.

Two men were in the fo'c'sle, one of them patching trousers and the other fast asleep with his back to a deal partition that cut the place in two, a doorway showing the narrower part beyond. A cruse that stank of coalfish oil was smoking on a nail and gave a pauper light, but did not altogether drown the smell of bilge. Ninian looked about him for a place to sit.

"In here," said Æneas and ducking his head passed through to the inner den with Ninian following. The only light it had came through the doorway from the cruse, but enough to show a man well up in years, in breeches, with a coat all tattered, stretched upon a chest.

"My fellow-prisoner," said Æneas. "There's no doubt left with him as to where he's meant for. Can you guess?"

"Fine!" said Ninian, and sat upon a keg. "For the plantations." He started speaking to the man, in English first, but found he had no word of it but a phrase of "mich obliged," which he used for everything, most laughably. Of his own tongue he was just as sparing, with a voice like buttered brose; he had been drinking.

"I think he's safe," said Ninian. "I never can trust a Fraser,

but he hasna got the English and he'll no' can understand us. . . .
Oh, Æneas! Alan-Iain-Alain Og, your uncle, little thinks his
man-o'-business is in a place like this! Stop you, though! we'll
get out o't. What happened ye at the inn?"

On either hand of them, quite close, were bunks, and one of
them, it seemed, was Æneas's; he lay on his side in it and set forth
all that happened.

When he had leaped from the window of the inn, he had, like
Ninian, plunged for the close and landed in the net but had
escaped the cudgelling. He fell with a jar that shook his senses;
before he could grip what happened, he was picked out from the
trammel, whipped into the inn, and thrust down in a cellar. He
lay there quarter of an hour, locked up in darkness; then was
taken out to find that Ninian was in the net, lashed up, with his
head split open.

"I thought that you were dead," said Æneas with earnestness.
"I'll never see a man more like it."

"No, nor dead!" said Ninian; "Macgregors are as ill to kill as
Tulla trout. Go you on with your story, *loachain*!"

They had all gone to the waterside, Ninian carried in the net,
and Æneas walking, stupefied at this disastrous end to a night
of terrors. The wounded man walked too; he was the vessel's
mate, a relative of Grant's, and on the waterside he swooned.
There was a boat; when Æneas saw it, he came to his senses,
shouted an alarm and roused some people in a land of houses
close at hand which looked out on the water. Windows opened,
whereupon, in consternation, he and the mate were bundled in
the boat, but Ninian proved too much for her, and he was left
behind.

"That's just what I was thinking to myself," said Ninian.
"Dead or living I would be a handful!"

The boat was hurried off downstream, her men in a frenzy for
escape. They reached the ship and found a furious skipper, who
ordered them back at once for Ninian: in leaving him he swore
they had bungled all; he was sure to follow.

"I knew he was a clever fellow, Pat!" said Ninian. "And they
nearly had me too, but for a brisk wee laddie and a lantern."

241

Four men went back; the ship made ready for immediate sailing. She had ballast only, and was meant to lift a cargo further up the coast. Grant whipped his crew about their duties like a thong—a fiery swearing man with a scorching tongue, but luckily his rage with Ninian who had stabbed his mate was not directed upon Æneas, whom he treated rather with disdain than rudeness. On his ship he was feared by his crew, but not detested like his mate, in whose misfortune all the crew rejoiced, so much that they felt friendly to their prisoner.

"I thought he was a dog!" said Ninian. "Where is he?"

"Aft in the cabin there," said Æneas. "It's nothing very serious by the way he blows his whistle. A hundred times a day he pipes for something. . . . Hearken to him, there he goes!"

A whistle shrilly sounded through the ship.

The sailors, chattering forward, stopped to curse with fervour, and one of them went up on deck. A minute later he cried down the scuttle for four others.

"How many men 's wi' Grant?" asked Ninian, whispering.

"Seven or eight," said Æneas, and the other's jaw went down.

"Good lord!" said he. "No wonder that ye're downed! This boat's a barracks. And when is he coming back?"

"I thought you had been he," said Æneas, "when I heard you hailing. He may come at any moment now."

Ninian was more concerned than ever: he drummed on his keg with nervous fingers.

"I wish we were out of this," said he.

"You should never have come," said Æneas. "The more I think of that the more I'm vexed. At least you should not have come alone. Did any one know your purpose?"

"That's the bit!" said Ninian. "We're on a boat that has been jerqued and nothing found on her. When I made up my mind that seeing I couldna find ye I must let them take me where ye were, I thought ye were on land, and on the land I aye can work a passage. When I saw the boat in Bunchrew burn I got a fright, I'm telling ye! That didna suit my plan at all. It's this way, Æneas—I was with his lordship, and I knew that I was chased. We were at Bunchrew House. I thought to take a walk out in the grounds and let myself be seized that they might take me where ye were. Forbes knew what I was meaning. A man he had—the officer who searched this ship—was going to follow me and watch. Whatever happened, that man made a bungle of the business! Wherever I went I saw no signs of him, and that of itself looked curious. I was sitting there with Peter and the rest for hours and waiting for the tide, and he made no appearance. I doubt—I doubt he lost me! I did the best I could and cut a wee bit boat for a diversion, fitting her with masts, and stuck a rag of my kilt through one of them, and left it by the fire. Unless they're natural idiots they'll know what that means when they come on't in the morning, for they'll look for me, I ken."

"But the thing is this," said Æneas, "we may be off by morning. Grant will sail whenever he comes back and finds that you're on board."

"That's just what I was thinking to myself," said Ninian, and bit his nails. And then of a sudden he got up.

He went forward where the sailor patched his clothes and Peter-son-of-James with great minuteness span a tale of his exploits ashore. A third man in a scarlet shirt, and with a high bald cliff of forehead, hunched below the light and read a Bible like a man apart in body as in spirit. The rest were still on deck. Peter, noway checked by Ninian's entrance, kept his story going for the tailor, and Ninian himself must laugh to hear his seizure at the last put on a droll complexion. He had dropped of his own accord into their hands when they had given up all hope of getting him, and did not greatly care.

"What kind of warlock bodies had ye yonder, Peter?" Ninian asked; "I thought that they were dumb."

The big man roared and slapped himself, his white teeth glistening.

"I thought that that would bother ye!" said he. "Three of the silliest creatures ever shipped. They're brothers with a quarrel, and for years they have not split one word between them. But, man, they're ready with the stick; if you have a head at all you'll mind the humped one."

243

Ninian screwed his face. "My grief!" said he, "was't he that loundered me? The little deil! Man of my heart! but he put dirling in the thickest head in Albyn! and all for a ploy of old MacShimi's!"

"Better for us," said Peter, "if MacShimi's ploys were all on shore; this one of his has spoiled a mate on us, and, what is worse, has lost us two days' friendly wind."

Æneas joined them; all in the cheeriest key, but for the salt who pored upon his Book, they might be a company of friends, and the seamen proved not ill-conditioned, dull, nor ruffianly,—just vagrom men prepared to pull on any rope the skipper bade them.

"Where will I get a drink?" said Ninian of a sudden, stopping short in a banter of the tailor.

"At the scuttle-butt on deck," the tailor said, and Ninian, with a look at Æneas, made for the ladder.

The night was dark as pitch when he got on deck, and the wind had risen freshly from the north, so that the schooner, swung thwart-tide, rolled wildly. Aloft the tackle sang, and the ship was full of noises, not all of her own complaining, for aft the men were speaking loudly in the cabin; he could hear them plainly though the door was slid. No watch was on the deck; he hung for a moment to a shroud and swung to the vessel's heaving, looking ardently at lights along the shore at less than a half-mile's distance—Clachnaharry.

In another moment he had whipped his shoes off; found the scuttle-butt with ease, though a man unused to ships might search for it an hour, dipped in the pannikin quietly and took a drink, and sought again the hatch.

"What was it ye called the thing?" he shouted down.

"The scuttle-butt," bawled back the tailor.

"I'm none the wiser," Ninian cried; "come you up, Æneas, and show me where it is. It's dark's a dungeon."

Æneas came up the ladder. As soon as he stood on deck the other caught him, led him to the side, and whispered, "Kick your shoes off, *loachain*; now is the hour for us if we are the men. There's not a soul on deck of all these swabs that surely have

244

come in by hawse-holes; the boat we came with's lying at our stern. Hie aft!"

Through the truck of the deck he picked his way to the poop as if his eyes were cat's, and Æneas after him in stocking-soles, with not a scrap of faith in a scheme so suddenly contrived.

The wind was lulled a bit, and the sound of speech came plainly from the cabin. On land was some one playing on a fiddle. In the utter dark of the stern, where the tiller strained its lashings, they went stumbling over coils, and felt about the rail for fastenings.

They came on nothing but empty cleats—the boat was gone!

"My grief, we're done!" said Ninian.

He crept to the cabin skylight and looked through the grating, then came back with a great chagrin. "No wonder," said he, "they're at their ease about us! There's only two down there with the mate; the other three are off for Grant and I was a fool that did not think of that!"

"Indeed, it seemed too simple altogether," Æneas said, and his heart went like a drum. "They know we're here as safe as in a Tolbooth."

"There's no' another boat?" said Ninian.

"There's two on shore with Grant, and the only one is that one on the deck," said Æneas.

"On chocks! She might as well be on Ben Lomond. And just you look at Clachnaharry! You could throw a stone! But I'm no' done: I'll have my soles on it before Pat Grant comes back. Come here!"

He caught him by the sleeve and hurried him along the ship to the very bows beside the windlass, with a loud clash of the pannikin as they passed the butt. The cable, like a bar, stretched to the hawse-hole, where it was served with rags to check its galling: some bights of it on the bitts and some fathoms ranged behind.

"Stand back!" said he, with a fumbling at his armpit—"stand back, or it may brain ye!"

With the knife he cut the cable at the serving, strand by strand, all but the very last.

245

"Now on wi' our boots," said he, "and back to that ill-smelled hole; she'll do the rest hersel'."

XXVI

The Escape

They could hear from the Black Isle shore the fiddle playing "Moidart Lasses" with a screech in the higher parts. "That man has a hack on his wee finger," Ninian said as he went down the ladder, drying his mouth like one who had been drinking.

"A bleak night, and a cold!" he said to the sailors. "There's something brewing, and it's well for us we have a shelter."

They scarce were down a minute when the two men from the cabin joined them, with a third they had not seen before, a lowlander who had been tending to the mate.

"If we had just the peats," said Ninian, "we were a *ceilidh*. My notion of a ship and she at anchor would be wind above that had no meaning man could guess, and below, good stories going, full of pith. Didst ever hear the tale of Conal Crovi?"

"*Faoinsgeulachd!*—But emptiness and folly!" said the man who had the Book, and sighed.

Ninian never heeded him, but plunged into a story of a king of England's sons and a tenant, Conal Crovi; marvellous things that happened them in Erin; a wedding lasting twenty days and twenty nights, and hearty work with swords. Never was a man more talented at telling; though in parts the tale was old to them—a story of the peat-fire and the winter, they sat round him, squatting, like so many bairns, and gave themselves to every fancy. "*Sliochd! slachd!*" would he say when swords were slashing; little hurried bits he put in rhyme, and lilted; from isle to isle with him was but a spang, and even Æneas, every nerve of him on edge with expectation, lost at times his interest in the vessel's movements, not for any heed of what was told, but for surprise at Ninian's mastery of himself and of his hearers. It might have been a summer sheiling of the hills; the story-teller played on them as one would play on reeds; he seemed himself

247

transported, clenching with his fists and scowling, whinnying like a horse when it came to Conal's stallions, high head and lofty speech for challenge and the talk of kings, and a mighty laugh for the binding of Conal Crovi. Had the width of the world been 'twixt him and things threatening, he could not have seemed more at ease; but the sweat, as Æneas saw, was standing on his brow, and every heave the vessel gave more violent than usual lit his eyes.

It seemed a tale without an end. The Fraser, who came ben to listen, fell asleep; the lowlander ate bread and onions, but all the rest, enchanted, hung on Ninian's lips, and Peter-son-of-James, his mouth wide open and his eyeballs staring, panted.

What Æneas expected from the cutting of the cable he had no clear notion, only that the strain should snap her tether and the wind, behind her, drift her into shore. As time went on, and still the story ran, with nothing happening to change the nature of her swing, or of the sounds the water made against her hull, he grew despondent, thinking Ninian's plan had failed.

And then there came a lurch that stopped his breath—not great, but still enough to show the ship had sheered. She lay a little over, and the plowt of water altered.

The tailor raised his head. "Slack tide," said he, on thinking; back to his breeks again, and the tale went on more warm than ever.

Æneas sank again; in Ninian's manner nothing fed his hopes till of a sudden something scraped; the schooner shivered, and the cruse swung over.

'Twas not as if she had been stranded, but as though some wizard hand had caught her by the keel. Uprose the floor; below, the ballast rolled; the *Wayward Lass* careened.

"*A chiall!* she's grounded!" someone cried, and they scrambled for the deck. Peter-son-of-James picked up the lantern, lit it at the cruse, and was the last of those awake to follow. They all poured out on planks steep-tilted; Æneas, but for Ninian's hand, would have lost his footing.

"I never was more put to it to keep story brisk," said Ninian, whispering. "I waited for that hemp to jerk the way a man would wait for hanging. But here she is ashore at last and neither her nor us the worse for it."

The ship was grounded eastward of the clachan, on a sandy bottom, where, at ebb, the spout-fish and the cockle might be gathered by the bairns. Between her and the shore the lantern lit a sea that frothed and broke with sounds that, with the piping of the rigging and the crew's commotion, gave to her situation a look of jeopardy more grave than Ninian suspected. She listed to her starboard, broadside to the land that was invisible; a sleet began to fall; upon her lifted parts the waves were thudding; at every thud she shook as if she had been kicked upon the buttocks, and below, loose dunnage made a noise.

At first her men seemed stunned and helpless. The giant Peter, in whose breast appeared some curious fondness for her, blubbered like a child, and cried continually, "The bonny *Lass*! the bonny *Lass*!—she's gone!" as though she were a sweetheart, or the home of his heredity. The rest in stupefaction clung to shrouds and gabbled Gaelic, till the mate, a spectre figure in a shirt, came staggering from the cabin and assumed command.

They searched out somewhere in the hold a rusty chaffer that they filled with wood and fired. It stood upon the bows and lit the whole ship up, and sometimes even gave a glimmer to the shore that looked forlorn and low. They stood together for a little in its smoke and cried out loudly to the land.

The great moods come to us in curious places, in the most unlikely hours, and sometimes we will feel a grandeur that we share, in common things—to see a man plough on the hill against the cloud, or hold his face up to the buffet of the storm. A mood like that came now to Æneas, to hear the sailors cry out altogether for their fellow-men as from a pit, their faith in human aid enduring. To him the sea was strange; he had no share in Ninian's assurance that they might escape; the men's anxiety seemed very ominous, and yet he had no fears. He looked up at the tall spars of the vessel, slanted; at the sloping deck; the chaffer flaming, and the men, a knot together, roaring to the shore; he saw the frith boil round them, hissing, Ninian hanging to a pin, possessor of himself, and waiting, and his heart, that should be low, was high as if with drink. It seemed to him the one keen starry hour that he was born for. Something in him sang.

And then, in a moment, was the mood departed; he was vexed to think a boat was killed.

He crept along the slanted deck to Ninian, and spoke to him. "I feel," said he, "as if we had done murder."

"As God's in heaven," said Ninian, "that is just what I was thinking to myself! It's not as if a boat could hit ye back. And a brave boat would she be, I'll warrant—just like a human body; many a storm! many a storm! . . . I wish I had thought of something else." And then he shook himself. "Tach!" said he, "the boat's no' ours nor of our clan. There's many another boat in Scotland. And she'll no' sink in the sand; she's no' *a brallach*. With any sense at all they'll get her off at spring-tide. If I could swim like you I wouldna bother. There's the shore."

The shore was there indeed, but growled inhospitable; only one light glimmered now in Clachnaharry, and the sailors bawled in vain.

"What better are we off?" asked Æneas, holding to his bonnet.

"Stop you a wee," said Ninian, "and I'll tell ye that!" The men were still a cluster at the bows, but now beyond the chaffer, where the windlass lay. He crept along the deck and down into the cabin where a light was burning; cast his eyes about; tossed up some bedding; searched a chest, and pounced at last upon Grey Colin thrust headfirst into a barrel. "Ah! son of love!" said he with great delight, and stuck it in the belt that held his dagger.

He was not gone a minute, but that minute changed the whole complexion of affairs on deck. When he got back the bellowing of the men had now a menace: they had seen the cable. Though he had cut it underneath the serving, so that any scrutiny might fail to show it had been sundered otherwise than by the hawse-hole's chafing something in the nature of the rupture hinted at the knife.

With savage cries they scrambled aft, the bellowing of Peterson-of-James, who led them, loudest. The mate was in their midst with the lantern in his hand, a gruesome figure, with his white limbs showing; most of them had handspikes, picked up at the windlass. Their whole concern about the ship now seemed forgotten in their rage at their discovery. With the chaffer flaming up behind them they appeared like creatures born of fire. The ship careened so much they could not run, but crawled with awkwardness along the coamings of the hatch, or with one foot on deck the other on the bulwark.

Ninian stood at the cabin door with Æneas and the Fraser, who had just awakened, sober, from his sleep, and come on deck bewildered. They propped, to keep from slipping to the scuppers, with their feet against some ring-bolts, dubious at first what this advance intended and the hunchback, brandishing his spike, was close on them, when Ninian cried, "Down!"

He pushed them to the opening; they fell down half a dozen steps, and rolled on the cabin floor. In a moment he had entered too, and shut the door and shot its bolts. Already was the hunchback pounding.

"They'll burst it into spales, quite easily!" said Æneas.

"Of course they will!" said Ninian, gasping. "There's my dirk for ye, and you, man, Fraser, take this knife. Keep an eye on the skylight window, and I'll see to the stair. I'm a great hand on a stair wi' little Colin."

Again, for a flash, came the mood to Æneas that this rare tingle of the flesh, this throbbing of the breast, was finer than the rapture come of books. There was a pause among the seamen who were cursing loudly, "I'll shell them like the peas!" cried Peter-son-of-James. He went to search for something, and came back and thundered on the door as with a sledge. It burst wide open and he stood beyond it with an adze which he was swinging like a halbert. His body filled the opening; behind him all the rest were snarling.

"For the sake of all thou ever saw, set not one foot within that door or I will broach ye like a cask!" cried Ninian, beating with his broadsword on the ladder.

A handspike, flung like a javelin from behind the giant's back, came flying down and grazed the Fraser's temple. It was the hunchback threw it. The mate somewhere behind them all was hounding on.

Ninian looked such an asp, his sting so threatening, that the big one swithered. He lowered the tool. "Bring here a gun!" he cried across his shoulder.

"If it comes to guns," said Æneas, "we're done for!"

"No fear of that!" said Ninian. "There's no' a gun on board this boat; they were poinded all by Duncan's gallants. And these ones think I divna know."

He had turned his head a moment to say this: the big man put a foot in the companion, where the sleet was falling, melting as it fell, and slipped upon his back. The adze fell from his hands and rolled into the cabin. He turned upon his fours and scrambled, awkward, on the ladder; the others jammed within the opening ready to pour down.

"I have no war wi' ye! Go back!" cried Ninian, and prodded with his weapon. "Go back! I wouldna soil my sword on creash!" He beat with the weapon's flat on the big one's rump: he bore himself like one who herded swine. "If the tail were on ye I would twist it!" he declared, and Peter hauled himself on deck.

Ninian tucked the sword below his arm and blew upon his hands as though they had been frosted. The stubble on his face by now had changed him greatly; he was rough and ruddy as the deer; his eyebrows, someway, seemed to jut extraordinarily, like easings of a house, above his glance that sparkled deep with venom.

"Now," said he, "we'll have a scuffle. Well I ken the sort of Peter! I've marked his breech, and when he finds his pride he'll come again, and wild will be his coming; that's the Isles! Æneas, my lad, take you the eitch and work it like a wright if feet come down that ladder. Give Fraser here the dirk; he's more a deacon wi't than you. I doubt they're going to burst in by the roof."

Æneas picked up the adze and gave the dirk to Fraser, who rubbed the little knife along its edge as if he were a flesher whetting, felt the point of it, and grinned with satisfaction. "Mich obliged!" he said, and took his post on the canted floor, close by the ladder foot.

The sailors had drawn back a bit, and somewhere in the waist were holding counsel. Their voices came on flaws of wind, disputing. Æneas got on his knees, and, stealing up, looked out. The mate had now a blanket on, and half the men were working at the skiff on chocks, upheaving her with block and tackle. Big Peter by himself was loosening the lashings of a spar, a spare one stowed on deck: he plucked its fastenings hurriedly and swore.

"They're going to launch the skiff," said Æneas, coming down.

Ninian shook his head. "That's bad!" said he. "The skiff's our only chance of landing. If they send her off for Grant we're worse than ever. My whole concern is this, that Patrick and his tail may join them any minute."

Æneas crept up again and down immediately.

"They're swinging her over the side," said he, "but here is Peter coming with a plock."

He had no sooner said it than the spar, a great thick boom, was slid across the sill of the companion, and its end thrust in their midst. It reached clean through the cabin to the back.

"My grief!" said Ninian, "but that's the bonny spirtle!"

"What are they going to do with it?" asked Æneas, bewildered.

"What but to stir the porridge! Stand you back here in the corner, it's a man that's cooking!"

He jumped himself, so saying, to the cabin's end below the ladder, where he crouched with Æneas beside him. The spar began to sweep from side to side, the greater part of it stuck far out on the deck, with Peter and two others swinging. It crashed against the bunks and splintered them; a table bolted to the floor was wrenched at one sweep from its fastenings and at the next was shattered into bits. Above, the men "yo-hoed!" and plied the lever; it was like a thing bewitched, infuriate; they dared not stir an inch from where they crouched but at the risk of braining.

Fraser, who had slipped behind the chest and ducked at every sweep made by the spar, was in the greatest danger; its ironed end seemed searching for him, hovering at times above his head or thrashing at the chest. Once he put his hand up, seizing at the butt; he might as well have tried to check the heaving of the sea.

"Come here! Come here, or ye'll be killed!" cried Ninian, and he and Æneas threw themselves upon the stick till Fraser with a rush got in beside them.

"Do ye ken what I'm thinking to myself?" said Ninian to Æneas. "Of that old devil Sandy sleeping in his bed and us like this! And every minute that stick lashes there is lost to us; I'm just in terror Grant will come."

"Can we not put a stop to it?" asked Æneas, as the spar tossed over them and clashed against the cabin's sides.

"Can the whelk stop the pin?" said Ninian, and as he said so, seemed to take a thought. He whipped with his sword at the cord that swung the lamp; it fell, and they were left in darkness save for what of glow came from the chaffer's burning.

On that the stirring of the spar was stopped; a great calm came on the cabin; only the sea outside was thrashing on the quarter; the seamen were withdrawn. Æneas crept up again to see what they were doing.

"The boat is launched," said he; "there's some one going ashore."

"If anybody goes ashore it's us!" said Ninian. "They're not on board her, are they?"

"No, but the big one's putting off his coat," said Æneas.

Ninian crept up the stair and looked; the Fraser came behind them, smelling of some balsam he had found and rubbed his head with where the spike had struck him. More loud than ever sang the wind aloft; the sleet was turned to hail that stung their ears; the boat was tossing, twenty feet from them, close to the fallen bulwark, and the sea between them and the shore was creaming white. Two men were at the fire; the mate lay helpless on the hatch and coughed as if his chest were racking; the others worked at ropes.

"Have ye got the eitch?" asked Ninian in a whisper, and Æneas held it out.

"Then now's the time to travel! There's eight men there, but they havena got one blade among them."

254

"Seven," said Æneas. He had been counting them, with the same thought in his mind as Ninian.

"Na, na, but eight," said Ninian again. "And that's no' reckoning the red one wi' the hoast; there's nothing left in him but water-brash. But ye'll mind there's Peter; a man of the Isles whipped to his pride has the rage of three. *A mach! A mach!*"

He burst from the companion, flourishing his sword and calling out "*Ardcoille!*" the clan-cry of his folk, with Æneas and Fraser at his heels, the Fraser screaming something foul. They stumbled down the deck and swept upon the sailors, who went scattering before them, sliding bent along the tilted hatch with nothing in their hands for their defence. Æneas stumbled on the handspikes they had dropped together in a heap, to launch the boat; he picked them up and threw them overboard. The wits of him were never more his own; he saw the whole thing like a picture in a glass, himself outside of it; his mind was working like a clock; he felt endowed with life eternal nothing could destroy. Had he a sword or dirk his stomach would have risen, but the adze, a tool of peace, seemed like a pen to him; he felt that he could dip with justice in the blood of men.

Two of the seamen plunged down through the scuttle to the fo'c'sle; the rest crept towards the bows; the mate lay on his side and barked, with guttering. Ninian stretched the sword.·

"Cry on!" he shouted, herding them like sheep, and Fraser, like an old grey cat, was spitting.

Of all that ran before them only Peter turned. He had his sleeves rolled up, and in his hands a knife. His shirt was open at the throat and showed a breast rough as a bull's-hide targe; he roared like one demented. It was at Ninian he made, and had there been a hundred still would he have come.

"I have no war wi' ye!" cried Ninian, slashing with his sword at air as though he sheared at breckans. "But come ye nigh and I'll put death on ye!"

The man was no way checked; he gave a jump and swept him from his feet; they rolled together at the scuppers, with Ninian below. The knife was back to strike him when the giant gave a grunt and settled like a log.

Æneas had struck him with the hammer of the adze between the shoulders.

"The skiff! The skiff!" gasped Ninian, getting to his feet, and in a second they were overboard and into her. They fell all in a huddle on her thwarts.

Æneas fumbled at the ropes, but Ninian had a quicker way; he took the adze and cut them at a blow.

The whole affair on deck had taken less than half a minute; the crew had not had time to find them weapons; they gathered now and screamed with rage to see the skiff drift off, and some one threw a clasp-knife.

The three fell to the oars and slipped through broken water to the shore.

XXVII

The Advocate Commands

They were no sooner landed through a sea that wrought like barm than Fraser dropped the dirk, with "mich obliged!" and vanished, making for the ferry. He bade them no farewell, but just took heels to it, and yet no trouble threatened; neither man nor beast beyond themselves was visible; it was a solitary place, grown thick with rushes, over which the spray was borne like smoke. The fire upon the stranded ship was burning clear and high, and now the rain was gone.

"My soul! but we are in the desperate country!" Ninian said. "A man would need to have his wits about him here. I wouldna say but that one's off to stir up mischief."

"Not he!" said Æneas. "Poor man! he's not quite sure of us, and he has little cause to trust his fellow-men."

"What trouble was he in with Sim?" asked Ninian as they walked up from the boat.

"He does not know himself. The sailors lifted him the night they lifted us—a poor old cottar man who has a wife and family across the water and they know not where he is."

Ninian stopped, stock-still, among the rushes.

"I wish ye had told me that before!" he said with great vexation. "If I had kent the sailors took him he would not escape till I learned something more."

He walked a step or two and stood again and beat his palms.

"Toots, man, Æneas!" he said, "ye should have told me! All this time was I not thinking he was one condemned for reiving? What ye tell me puts another colour on him altogether."

"What does it matter?" said Æneas.

"It might matter nothing, but on the other hand it might matter a great deal. Ye make me curious about that man—what was he gathered in with us for?"

"He doesn't know, I tell you."

"Perhaps; but if I had a chance I maybe could have helped him to find out. And this is the way of it now, that I'll have to see that man again before I leave this country. Do ye no' see, Æneas, boy, that if we knew what he was seized for, it might throw a light on what they seized ourselves for?"

"I fear I'm very stupid," Æneas said humbly. "I never thought of that."

Ninian caught him by the arm. "God forbid," said he, "that I should think ye stupid, *loachain*! Ye're anything but that, although ye havena Ninian's practice with the quirks of man. It was a clever man who picked the handspikes up and threw them overboard; if you had not done that we couldna risk the skiff, they would have brained us. And it was no stupid man who struck big Peter with the eitch when I was struggling with him; you and me have now a bond of manrent; after this I'm man of yours although it was against the world. That's twice ye plucked me from the brink of life; I'll no' forget!"

He said it with great depth of feeling, then, as if ashamed, broke off, and with a heather step went through the rushes.

They were only two miles off, or less, from Bunchrew, and they kept along the shore, with Ninian leading. The dark was like a mort-cloth at the start, but by-and-by it seemed less thick, and long before they came to Bunchrew House they saw its light between its trees. Already was the morning old; in Clachnaharry all was dark; the schooner might have burned to ash and not an eye ashore to see her.

Only twice they spoke in all their walking—Æneas asked where they were going, and later on was asked by Ninian if he knew the springs of all this tribulation.

"There's little doubt of that," said Æneas,—"Pat Grant was hired by Lovat."

"Clever!" said Ninian, "but do ye ken the reason?"

"That beats me. I've turned the whole thing in my mind a thousand times and get no light on it."

"Ye might well do that! It's a gey and kittle business. But never mind; we'll fathom it before we're through."

The bar was on Bunchrew House when they got to it, though its lights were burning; Ninian beat loudly on the door, and Forbes himself came to it, with his sister in a wrapper.

"Come in! Come in!" he said with great relief. "I'm glad to see you, Mr Campbell, and your friend, although you've spoiled a night on me."

"Dear me! and is this the wondrous lad?" said his sister, scanning Æneas through her specs. "I thought ye would be something special to occasion all this tirravee!"

Æneas smiled; this tart demeanour was his aunt's: he knew it masked the sweetest nature.

Forbes still stood at the door. "Where's Boyd?" he asked,— he meant the officer.

"Did he come after me?" asked Ninian.

"Of course! Yourself arranged it."

"And I could have sworn that he had yon! The silly man has botched it. I never set eyes on him. The man, my lord, 's no' worth a docken! My friend Macmaster was on board the ship, and no' far off, when Boyd was searching her; if Boyd had any sense he would have tracked the boats."

"Hoots! never fash wi' Boyd; he'll turn up for his breakfast, I'll be bound," said the lady with impatience. "Duncan, you take Mr Campbell in where I have left his supper—and a bonny hour for supper, two o'clock! This way, Mr Æneas, for you, a moment; here's an old acquaintance who'll be glad to see ye."

Now all this time had Ninian never mentioned to his friend the name of Janet. He thought to do so once or twice, but someway baulked at it. Miss Forbes' speech meant nothing, then, to Æneas, who followed, mildly wondering, to her chamber.

Ninian and the Advocate went to the dining-room, and there the latter learned the whole night's incidents, save one particular—how came the ship to drift. On that it seemed to Ninian discreet to keep his counsel.

Forbes listened with the greatest eagerness. "Well done!" he said. "You have been lucky, but you have been wise, too, Mr Campbell. I must confess your plan for some hours back had

259

seemed to me fantastic, and I blamed myself for falling in with it so meekly. With rogues like these heaven knows what might have happened. Now that the ship is on the hard, we'll have a chance to go a little deeper in the business with Captain Grant. Since you went off I've had some news about the fellow Fraser."

"What kind of news, my lord?" asked Ninian sharply.

"He's not from Strathglass at all, as Boyd made out, but from the Muir of Ord. He came to Beauly on the Wednesday with a cow, and got inveigled to a tavern that night by sailors—plainly some of your particular friends. They took him, primed, into a boat, and now the hue and cry is out among his people. There's far more stir about his missing than your friend's, for he's a simple, harmless creature, not a bodle in his purse to tempt such villainy. His sons were here some hours ago; they have not left a yard of both sides of the water but they've searched. I'm glad to know he's clear."

"Do ye ken anything about him, my lord?" asked Ninian.

"I never heard the name of him before this night, but I was struck by the fact that he and you and young Macmaster should be all in trouble on the self-same evening, and all with sailors, so I pried into his history from his sons, but not with any great illumination. He's a cottar on the Muir, and has been there a dozen years, an honest and industrious man, who does not owe a penny in the country, and has not had, so far as I could find, an enemy."

"There's something still behind," said Ninian with confidence. "It wasna for a prank, nor for his sale they lifted him; the poor old body wouldna fetch a guinea in Virginia. I never saw the man before, nor yet, of course, did Æneas, but it *will* stick in my mind he's mixed up some way in whatever lies behind Lord Lovat's variance wi' us."

Forbes helped them both to a little spirits. "That was a point of course I did not overlook," said he. "I questioned every particle of Fraser's history, and learned a lot of useless genealogy, but came at last to this important fact, that up till a dozen years ago he was in Lovat's service. He was about the stables. He joined him in the year of Mar, and was among the

Frasers at Glenshiel."

"They didna have a quarrel?" Ninian asked.

"He quitted Castle Dounie on the best of terms with Lovat, and his lordship seems to have been very good to him in some ways ever since. At this time of the year he got an annual haunch of venison, and on the Wednesday he went missing was at Lovat's thanking him for its receipt."

Ninian sat back in a chair, his chin upon his breast, and brooded.

"My lord," said he at last, "if I could just get half an hour wi' Fraser, I would give the last placks in my sporran. It's galling just to think that I was in his company for hours this night and never thought to draw him! This means I canna leave the North tomorrow, and that thought was all my joy when I was landed from the schooner."

Forbes firmed his jaw; he had a way of snapping up his teeth which left his mouth a slit.

"My good man," said he, "you're going tomorrow! You're going with your girl. My sister has made all arrangements. Unless you want that lass of yours to wither in our hands she'll have to flit before another night like these two last. Your friend can please himself, but if I had my will he would go with you, and I fancy that he'll do it gladly. It's this way of it, Mr Campbell—there are men who seem to bear about with them the seeds of trouble, rather would I put it that they carry with them elements of storm, and either you or young Macmaster are endowed that way. Since ever you came over Corryarrick, I have lived in a continual state of great anxiety. Smuggling of arms, and broken roads, and stouthrief, and kidnapping! You have stirred up or unmasked more mischief than I have experienced in the last three years. I look about the country by day and see it peaceable and frank, my neighbours at their honest business, and yet, since you came here, the nights are all filled up for me with wild forebodings and with rude alarms. This has happened before with you, my good man. It was the same way when you came in search of Duncan Cameron—that devilish business that goes yet like a wail through all Lochaber, though I give you

261

credit for it, who but you could find him in such marvellous circumstances? It was the same when you got the Frenchmen; my heart was in my mouth that whole month that you spent among us. The stormy-petrel may be in the scheme of providence, but I'm not going to have it skirling up just now in sheriffdom of mine; away you back and screech beside Loch Fyne!"

Ninian made circles with his glass upon the table. He had listened with a face that showed no sign but of attention. But now he had a stubborn demeanour and his brow was knotted.

"It's not me that's the storm-cock, sir," said he. "Ye have him here continually, and he wears the pigeon's feathers. If it was for his race I might respect him, but 'tis always for himself, and that was not the way of it in ancient Gaeldom."

"But, my dear sir," said Forbes with some impatience, "you are finished here. You have done all you were sent to do by Islay and his Grace. We'll see, henceforth, ourselves, to Barisdale and this sly traffic with done muskets, and you are satisfied, I think, that Lovat was no party to Drimdorran's disappearance. I ask you—I command you therefore, to depart this shire immediately; whatever dirt you have to stir, you'll find it where you came from. . . . No, no, Mr Campbell! Not one word of mutiny! You'll go tomorrow. That's the way my sister took Macmaster in, himself, to see the girl; she was fixed herself on an immediate departure if you found him, and we thought it best that she should influence him before you made objections. I'm telling you the thing is settled! I've got a chariot—the first in Inverness; the first that ever used the Road this side of Spey. It brought my brother to Culloden, and it's going for a doctor for him, back to Edinburgh. Instead of stalking moors and climbing corries in the way you came, you'll just go back a gentleman, on wheels, and handsel my new coach and Wade's New Road. . . . . No, no! Not one word now, I command you!"

"Ye canna command me, my lord!" said the *beachdair*, and pushed aside his glass from which he had not even sipped. "I have MacCailein at my back; I have my warrant. But whether or no, the country's free to me; my name is Campbell, not

Macgregor of the mist, and it is not the nicest manners between two gentlemen sitting in a room and at a glass, for one to talk about commands. I may be coaxed, I may be flattered, but little ye ken of me my lord, to think ye can command me like a gillie."

"Hoots, man!" said Forbes, "don't let the Hielan' birse get up. That's the worst of ye all; ye find an insult where there's none intended."

"I canna tell what ye intended, my lord, but I ken the Saxon language. The Duke himself would not speak so to me, though I am under his protection."

"Ah!" said Forbes, and shrugged his shoulders. "His grace is wise. He understands a people who put all their silly pride in ritual and quarrel at a word, but eat the humblest pie in other ways.... Well, well, I do not command anything; I entreat you— what is it you say?—*tha mi a' guidhe ort!*—to lose no time in clearing off. I am speaking for your good, and for your daughter's. . . . How came the ship to drift?"

He asked the question with sly meaning in his manner; Ninian was staggered.

"She broke her cable," he replied, but looked uneasy.

"She didn't by any chance, now, slip her shackling?"

"No," said Ninian, "she sundered at the hawse."

"You rascal!" Forbes exclaimed, and shook his fist at him. "You did the deed! I'm sure of it as if I saw you do it."

"In faith that's just what they were thinking on the ship. 'Twas that that roused them. I had to get ashore some way, my lord. . . . It's you that should have been the *beachdair*."

"I knew it! Ninian, ye must be gone ere things become more jumbled. These rogues whose ship ye've stranded will be hotter on your track than ever, and worst of all I'm feared of him who is behind them. *Tha mi a' guidhe ort!*" He gave again his Gaelic with an English *blas*, not quite familiar with the language.

"I challenge him and all his tribe!" said Ninian, and thrust out his chin. "It's not for fear of him and of his plots I'll go tomorrow as your lordship craves, but for Macmaster's sake; I'm only at the start of a tremendous story."

"Now that's a wise man!" said Forbes, relieved. "And seeing

you have fallen in with my proposal, I'll be frank with you and tell you this—I have a personal wish to see you back as quick as possible to where you came from. Tonight I have gone over sundry things that puzzled me for many years; the more I think of it the more am I convinced that Duncanson needs redding up. There's no one else can do it but yourself; it must be done in Inveraray, and I don't want you dirked in my diocese before you leave, though dirking is your fate as sure as God's in heaven if you bide longer here."

"Very well," said Ninian, and took off his glass. "But Æneas must come wi' me, and we darena start by daylight. If you will have the coach a bit from Inverness we'll join it there. I ken what Inverness is—every bairn and burgess in't will run to see a chariot."

"That's true," said Forbes. "I had not thought of that. I'll send the coach to Daviot at gloaming and you'll get it there. In any case you must conceal your movements; not for worlds would I have that sweet lass of yours disturbed, but—"

He stopped, and looked at the other's garments. "H'm!" said he, "ye're not in the grandest trim for going wi' ladies, neither you nor young Macmaster. I'll have to lend ye clothes more seemly to my braw new coach."

"My grief!" said Ninian, with a start, "I clean forgot! The kilt is second nature to me still, for all these years of breeks. These ruffians have our clothes we paid good money for, and two of the bonniest hats your lordship ever saw cocked on a Gaelic heid. I never thought to search the ship for them."

"I'll search the ship and Fraser's inn for them tomorrow," Forbes replied, and then he drew up short again, with a knowing look for Ninian. "Ah!" he said, "I understand! I wondered! The Hielan' birse went down a bit too quick there. I ought to have remembered your way of conceding small things of no account with a generous air to cover up your dourness about things material. What way do you mean to spend tomorrow?—or today, as I should put it, for it's morning?"

"I'll go to the Muir of Ord—"

Forbes raised up his hands, despairing.

"There's no danger, my lord; give me a boat to Beauly mouth, and I'll be back for dinner. I *must* see Fraser or his family; the thing's of prime importance; he has my wee black knife."

"I'm not so dull as that!" said Forbes. "Well, go your ways; I wash my hands of it; but oh! I wish I saw ye out of here!"

"Fraser ran for Kessock; he was making for the ferry; he'll be home," said Ninian, and then he started, lifting up his head. "There's somebody moving outside," he whispered.

Forbes listened. "I hear nothing," said he. "It is the wind."

"The wind doesna wear boots, my lord. It's some one on the gravel."

There came a timid rapping back at the outer door. Ninian went to it, and returned with Boyd. "Here's a good messenger to send for death," said he; "he wouldna hurry back," and the officer looked very sheepish.

"Where were you, sir?" asked Forbes, and Ninian laughed when they got the explanation. The man, on going forth, had come on other hawks than Peter and his friends—on Grant and half a dozen more at least, who chased him all the way to Inverness, and kept him in a siege for hours in a house where he took refuge.

"Well done!" cried Ninian. "Ye served my purpose better that way than the way I planned, for ye took Pat Grant and his gentry out of my way at the very time when I could best do wanting them."

Forbes sent the man off with a servant to get quarters for the night, and in a little Æneas came with the women to the dining-room, and all of them had a belated supper. For Ninian it was spoiled a little by his sense of being out of some general secret understanding; Miss Forbes was archly merry; Janet to himself was warmer than at any time since she had come, but almost coldly formal to his friend Macmaster, who seemed quite uplifted at the thought of leaving Inverness.

XXVIII

The Return

Some hours before the house was wakened, Ninian took a stick, and out in the sun-bright morning went along the shore till he found a boat owned by a man who for a shilling took him up the frith to Tarradale, whence, with a shepherd's stride, he made through grassy land to the Muir of Ord. It was easy to find the croft of Fraser, even in that countryside of crofts and swarming Frasers; the man's mishap had made it notable, and every bairn the *beachdair* asked for guidance told him Fraser had come home. But when he reached the cot, black-stoned and heather-thatched, that had been reft so lately of its head, he found himself set back in all his hopes by Fraser's family. Already they had put him into hiding. Not all that Ninian could assure them of his friendliness, or claim of gratitude for having got the man's release, would move the sons; they had no trust in him. Their mother was more frank, and answered freely several questions he put to her bearing on her man's connection with Lord Lovat, but even she looked dubious and askance at his rough appearance, and would not give the faintest inkling where her husband lay.

Though he might have seemed to miss the object of his visit, Ninian departed not dissatisfied with what he learned, and got to Bunchrew House again by noon. The Advocate was gone to Inverness; already there had come from him the clothing stolen from the inn; it had been found in Fraser's cellars, none the worse except that Ninian's hat was cloured so much it looked an ancient; whereon his daughter rallied him.

"Faith ay!" he said, a little rueful, "it looks a gey old hat for riding in his lordship's chariot."

"Hoots! never mind!" Miss Forbes exclaimed. "The life of an old hat's just to cock it, man!"

The first time for some days he shaved, and in the Lowland garb was once again the proper gentleman. Miss Forbes was quite surprised to see the difference. "Dear me!" she said, "ye're looking spruce! Ye're like the lad—I thought him unco tousy in the kilts for girls to make such fash about, but when he left a little since he was so tight and trim I could have kissed him."

"And did ye no', mem?" Ninian asked, amused.

"Na, na!" she said, and looked at Janet. "I didna dare. He wouldna thank a rudas wife like me for kisses while there's young ones to be had for askin'," and Janet coloured high.

Æneas, too, was gone to Inverness to finish off affairs with Saul Mackay, who had but yesterday come home to find the youth amissing, and distracted, spend a whole night's useless search for him. That afternoon they all foregathered at Mackay's, left John Maclaren's clothes with him to send through to the inn on Rannoch Moor when an occasion offered, and having bade goodbye with Forbes' sister, walked with the convoy of Forbes himself halfway to Daviot, where the coach was waiting.

It stood within a field in which the unyoked horses grazed— a massive equipage which could have held a family, and round it gathered all the people of the neighbouring farms, a horde astonished at this new device to save the toil of walking. They stared at its interior, looking for a fire,—a house so fine, they thought, must have a fire; they crept below the axles curious to see the fastenings of this house which hung on leathers. Children swung on the pole; the splendour of the wheels provoked loud admiration.

"Poor souls!" said Forbes, compassionate, "they never guess the wheel's to master them. The road that will take a coach will take a cannon."

They were almost the last words they had from him; a little later they were on their way past great stone circles standing on the moor, above them plovers crying. Behind them for a mile the children trotted. At gloaming they were in Strath Nairn; in a loch at Moy the stars were steeping; they rolled, some hours, through fir-woods dark and solemn till they heard the Spey loud-thundering. That night they rested in an inn at Aviemore.

So far it might have been a funeral. The road, though still unused, was like a beach on which the great coach swung and jolted with an uproar of its frame that made all speech impossible. For the first time Æneas doubted if the new ways of the world were better than the old, He would have loved to walk the moors, or through the darkening of the glens, this girl beside him; help her at the fords, and share with her a vagrant fire in desert places. Now Corryarrick and the wilds of Badenoch, the Wicked Bounds, and dark Breadalbane's corried hills, seemed preferable to journey through, for all their hazards; better than this humdrum track on which was only that tame pleasure, comfort. Indeed there was not even comfort here; his bones were sore with sitting in the coach, with tossing in it like a dried pea in an infant's cogie.

Ninian and Janet sat before him; sometimes in the dark they were so still he felt as in a dwaam, and, doubting they were present, would put out a foot to feel. He took to Ninian at times a great repugnance. Whom hitherto had seemed the cheeriest of companions now irked him like an incubus; the devil fly away with such a dreary father!

And all the time, though Æneas did not know, was Ninian uneasy as himself—his one relief from weariness was trifling with a hank of twine.

The next day was a Sabbath, and they could not travel, so they went to kirk—a poor, bleak little kirk, with a cold prelection on eternal fires from one who wept enough to drown out Tophet.

At daybreak on the Monday they pushed forward for Dalwhinnie over a wild unfinished weal of road whereon Macgillivray's men were labouring. An axle broke on the slope of Monadh Liath, and they were there cast out for hours beside Loch Insh, a swelling of the Spey where wildfowl thronged. It was, for Æneas, the happiest day of all their journey. The coachmen went on horseback for a smith, and, seeking all ways, failed to get one nearer than Dalwhinnie, whence from the gusset of John Leggatt's road to Corryarrick they brought back a lad who did the welding. While thus delayed, afar from dwellings, Ninian made a fire, and started fishing.

They were among a concourse of the hills, whose scarps were glistening in a sun that gave the air at noon a blandness, though some snow was on the bens. The river linked through crags and roared at linns; all rusty-red and gold the breckans burned about them; still came like incense from the gale-sprig perfume. They sat, those two young people, by the fire, demure and blate at first, to find themselves alone. From where they sat they could perceive down to the south the wrecks of Comyn fortresses; the Road still red and new was like a raw wound on the heather, ugly to the gaze, although it took them home. Apart from it, and higher on the slope, a drove-track ran, bright green, with here and there on it bleached stones worn by the feet of by-past generations. They saw them both—the Old Road and the New—twine far down through the valley into Badenoch, and melt into the vapours of the noon. And something in the prospect brought the tears to Janet's eyes.

"For why should I be sad?" she asked him suddenly, "to see that old track of the people and the herd, and this new highway boasting—boasting—?"

She could not utter more, she was so shaken.

"I think I know," said Æneas, sharing in her spirit. "I could weep myself to think our past is there. Where men have walked are always left the shades of them—their spirits lingering. To your eyes and to mine is nothing on the old drove-road but grass and boulder, but if there's aught of the immortal in men's souls, there's the immortal likewise in their earthly acts. Our folk are on the old drove-road—the ghosts of them, the hunters and the tribes long-perished to the eye, *duineuasail* and broken men. It's history!"

"That's just it!" she cried, "and I hate the New Road—hate it!—hate it!"

"There is something in me, too, that little likes it. It means the end of many things, I doubt, not all to be despised,—the last stand of Scotland, and she destroyed. And yet—and yet, this New Road will some day be the Old Road, too, with ghosts on it and memories. In a thousand years will you and I be sitting by Loch Insh—"

He broke off with a smile.

"Indeed, and that would be a dreich sit!" she said, half-mocking, but it was to hide her deeper feelings.

Her father was far down the water plying a fruitless quest. They saw him trudge the banks, surrendered to his passion; they might be clean forgotten. A squad of soldiers once came marching past as if from Ruthven barracks and looked at them and at the coach with wonder. A fellow with a gun, a dog behind him, showed on the drove-track for a moment, shouted something out to them, and disappeared into the hills. They heard the red deer belling.

To while the time that Æneas would have stay for ever (as he thought) they looked for berries. He was like a boy, so gleeful, searching shrubs, and she so grave even in their slightest chattering. In her was something sweetly wild, like to the tang of myrtle blown across the moor to mingle with prosaic scents—a breath of growths unsoiled, a cry of ancientry that shook some chord in him no other thing in life had reached.

They talked of many things, but most of that bewildering discovery about his father, a score of times she turned to it when he, regarding it as something out of key with other moods within him at the moment, changed the topic, and at the last, to his astonishment he found a new light break on him.

For reasons of his own—or likelier for the want of opportunity—her father had not told him of her visit to Prim Campbell; he was thus in dark about the later evidence of Duncanson's rascality. Till now he had not thought of Duncanson as at the back of this past week's events whereof himself was victim; he had ascribed them all to Lovat's vengeance upon Ninian, the desperate resorts of one who meant at any cost to cloud his knavery. Not once had it occurred to him that Duncanson might have communication with Lord Lovat, and urge on this mysterious persecution. Ninian had not even hinted at the possibility. But this account of letters hurrying over Corryarrick after them, to turn a man not previously unfriendly into an unscrupulous kidnapper, all in an evening's time, upset him greatly.

The Grange affair which Janet next laid bare was also new to him. At first he thought it might account for things, but she dispelled that notion. She had a way of knitting brows and cogitating, like her father, when a problem offered; she did so only for a moment now.

"No, no!" she said, "that is not it!—at least it is not all of it. They had no reason to think you or my father likely to find that shame. The fears of Duncanson began when you left Inveraray and he learned where you were going. It put him on his back; when I left home he was a bedfast man."

"Your father's right!" said Æneas. "There something in that desk Drimdorran thinks I saw, exposing all his infamy."

They had come again back to the fire that cheerily crackled. She poked it with a stick which she had picked up in the heather, nothing saying for a little.

"Was the desk the start of Duncanson's vexation?" she inquired at last, with hesitation, not looking at him.

His heart leaped frightfully. Did she know about the dovecote? Had Ninian told her he had been with Margaret there? It was the last thing he would have her know—that incident, and yet he felt he must seem frank lest she should know already and attach to it a wrong importance.

"The desk is mixed up with the doocot," he said simply, mastering his alarms. "I was there that night, quite innocent, and Duncanson found out."

She reddened; he saw it though her back was to him; that of itself was most disquieting, though she had not hid all further interest in the dovecote. What he had said was trivial, unfinished, like to rouse her questioning, but she passed it by.

"Ah, well!" she said in an altered tone, "the doocot or the desk—between them lies the mystery, it's too involved for me," and seemed relieved to hear the clatter of the horsemen coming back with one to mend the carriage.

From that hour on, the journey home to Æneas was miserable, The very weather changed, as in a humour to depress him more. An inn of Wade's they spent the night in at Dalwhinnie let the rain through its unfinished roof and shook till morning with wild blasts of tempest.

Next day they got to Taymouth, where great woods were blown like corn and fields were flooded; the Road was soft as butter and their wheels ran deep, while, on the drove-track close beside, the folk who came to see them trotted dry of foot. At that was Ninian merry. "There's your roads for ye!" said he; "I doubt George hasna got the bottom though he has the breadth! The old folk werena fools!"

That night they spent in Stirling, where they left the coach, and hiring horses, rode through Drymen into Lennox, and in two days more got home.

The sun was setting on the hills when they got round the bay below Dunchuach; a flag was on the castle tower.

"MacCailein's home!" said Ninian. "It's time for him! He little thinks what crops grow in his absence. Weeds!—just pushion weeds! But I'll put the hook to them!"

XXIX

Candlelight

That night, while it was early yet, Drimdorran walked about his house, with hose untied and flopped down round his ankles like a tinkler man's. In every nook and chamber, every landing of a stair and twist of passage, there were candles burning. He tended them himself. He tended them as though they were his final days. When, sometimes, he would come on one that guttered low, and looked like dying, he would give a crazy twittering cry—most eerie!—pluck a fresh one from a pouch that he had filled with dips, to light it with a trembling hand, and nurse the new flame with his palms about it, labouring in his breath, his bosom heaving. He stared into the lowes of them with apprehensive eyes, but not so fearful as he peered at windows, shutterless, that had the black night squatted on their sills.

Since dusk had fallen had he thus been busy—gardener of the candles, so had he ministered, a week of evenings, to this curious passion. Nobody dare tend them save himself; his household sat down in the stanchioned understorey, whispering, or they lay awake at night and listened to his shuffling from room to room, and ever and anon would shiver at his twittering cry.

He slept, himself, but in the mornings, when the dawn was come, and through the forepart of the day, but fitfully, and all the common duties of the house were stopped to meet a daft demand for candles. He never ceased to cry for candles— candles—candles! They made them in a cellar at the back, beside the brew-house—dips and moulds; himself came down to them a score of times a day to urge them on, to stretch the wicks with them, and slice down tallow. He counted every candle made as if it were a guinea. The cellar's shelves were stacked with them; the moulds were never cool; the tallow always simmered, yet he

273

cried for more.

There was, in this craze of his, for those who had to suffer its inconvenience, some quality of mystery that latterly oppressed the house like fever. His servants were afraid. It was not him they feared, poor man! but the house itself, so monstrously aglow night after night and all night long with no discoverable meaning in its waste of light. They, too, would look askance at windows, cautiously open doors and start up tremulous at a rap. They loathed this riot of illumination, yet were nigh as sedulous as himself in snuffing candles when his back was turned.

In all else save this strange extravagance he seemed rational, though something of a shattered body. He had had, as they thought, a stroke, on the week of Michaelmas; since then he had not left the house except one night when they had found him in the grounds, bedewed and maundering, in his gown. He kept his correspondence going; sat on term-day dressed, in the business closet, lifting rents for Islay with his old alertness; he had the shrewdest eye on all that happened round about him, and would talk on anything, by day, with great composure, even when he dipped the candles; only the night unmanned him, and his craze attained its summit.

They set it all down to a stroke more stunning than the palsy—he had lost his daughter, and had proved himself unfit to keep a ward. Margaret and Islay's son had gone away together, only a letter left behind to say they went to England. It was a blow, undoubtedly; the lass had been the apple of his eye and this precipitation of a union he had cherished ruined all his plans for her, the thing to any worldly eye would seem a scheme himself devised, and Islay, now abroad, would be implacable.

He did not wince, Drimdorran, when he read the letter (so they said), but after that he never dressed nor trimmed himself, but went about the house dishevelled in a tattered gown, his hose slipped down his shanks, his face like parchment, and his eyelids flaming red. No step was taken to discover where the fugitives had gone; he never mentioned them; it was as if he cast them from his mind.

This night, since gloaming, he had sped about the business of the candles, shuffling from room to room with snuffers in his hand, and coming back between each round to quaff at water from a pitcher in his closet. Its window had a tartan plaid tacked to the lintel—something new; for usual it was left uncurtained. No breath of air came in, and with a fire that burned high up the chimney, and the candles stuck around, the heat was stifling.

He had come back to rest him and to drink, and sank down in a chair with elbows on his desk. He leaned his head on hands, and there, as overcome by weariness or woe, sat breathing heavily.

A dog outside began at barking.

He started up, and drawing back the tartan screen, looked out into the darkness. The stars were shining bright above his property; so do they twinkle on the garden and the tomb alike, on trysts in country lanes and men tormented. Beyond the fields, indifferent, sang Aray to the sea.

There came a rattle at the entrance door, and hearing that he gave the twittering cry and skipped about the room and wrung his hands. A voice was on the stair, and footsteps in the lobby; with effort he sat down and put the pitcher to his lips.

"Come in!" he mumbled, on a knock; the Muileach opened; Ninian Campbell entered, still the stour of travel on his clothes.

"My God!" cried Duncanson.

The Muileach left and shut the door. They looked at one another for a moment, Ninian like a gled, his eyebrows meeting, not a word from him. He saw a ruined man.

For twenty years had Duncanson to him seemed made of granite or the whin—proud jowl and haughty eye, trim habit and stiff frame, he had been so when last he saw him. Now was he like curds that shiver in a basin. 'Twas almost unbelievable a man in three or four weeks' time could shrivel so and look so much a wreck of what he was, and yet be living. What most astonished was that he should look like pulp, and yet his knuckles gleam with bone, the veins of his temples stretch on a craggy skull. It is the heart that stiffens, and the heart was gone.

"*Tha 'm fear so air falbh!*—This man's away with it!" said Ninian to himself in Gaelic, and for a moment felt some pity.

"I thought ye had been drowned!" said Duncanson, and every nerve of him was quivering.

Ninian gave a girn; to pity such a thing were folly. "Na," said he, and sat him down, unasked, "but gey and close on't! MacCailein nearly lost his *beachdair* in Loch Laggan. Ye heard of it?"

Drimdorran nodded. It was as if he could not speak. Through white gums parted showed his tongue, extraordinarily thickened, moving, but as mute as wood.

"Ye're not well, sir," said Ninian. "I see that ye have had a shake. They told me in the town."

Drimdorran waved his hands. "I'm an ill man," said he, a husky voice recovered. "It would shake any man, ill or well, to see a ghost." He fumbled in his gown, and got a mull, and drenched himself with snuff, then gave a glance about him at the candles.

"There's no' as much o' the ghost in me as would fright a bairn!" said Ninian. "Ye didna get my letter, then, from Corryarrick?"

"No," said Duncanson, and gulped, and Ninian looked at him with a peculiar air.

"I sent one, then," said he, "explaining everything. It's likely on the road. I only got home myself an hour ago, to find I was a ghost for Inveraray."

"And him that was along with ye?—Macmaster?" said Drimdorran, writhing at his hands.

"I lost him."

"Lost him! Where, man, where?"

"The strangest thing, Drimdorran! Ye see I came on him at Bridge of Orchy, and the two of us went North together. Oh, man, but we had the mischief's time! First the Watch of Barisdale came round us nibbling like fleas in hose, and then it was Loch Laggan with Macdonalds snapping at our heels. We won away from that and over Corryarrick into Inverness, and there the very devil seemed in every step we took—"

"Yes, yes, yes, yes! But ye say ye lost him!"

"I did. He was dragged on board a vessel."

Whatever blood was left in the recesses of Drimdorran's frame now gushed into his face. He purpled at the cheeks; the veins along his temples stood out thick and blue; he swallowed. And his eyes grew big and bright. He put the pitcher to his head and drank from it; its spilth streamed down his chin and soaked his breast.

Ninian watched him curiously.

Drimdorran put the pitcher down and sighed. "Ah!" said he, "I'm an ill man, Ninian Campbell; the least thing staggers. Who was it took Macmaster?"

"A man called Grant from out of Rothiemurchus. Yon's a rascal place, Drimdorran! They make a trade of picking young men up for the plantations; they would have picked myself up too, but for my own manoeuvring."

The most astounding change was come on Duncanson. His eyes were dancing. "A good riddance!" said he. "I'm through wi' him, at any rate! But this'll be a blow to Bailie Alan! What was the young one doin' North?"

"I'll tell ye that!" said Ninian agreeably. "He went up on his uncle's business, wi' pockets full o' money; that's what played the mischief. Yon's no place for flourishing the sporran; and I warned him. Well, anyway, his uncle had great notions of the Road to open trade on; Æneas was to look about and see what business might be done in wintering. There's something in't for trade, perhaps, but no' much in the Road for pleasure; I came back that way, and many a time in coming damned George Wade. There's nothing beats the old drove-track!"

Drimdorran screwed his face up. "That's what I think too," said he, and checked himself; then slyly glanced at Ninian. "I like," said he, "a good thick wall of hills between us and the North. The less we have to do with it the better."

"That's just what I was thinking to myself; for all that, Badenoch's no' canny for a *beachdair*."

"Your girl went off, I'm told, to search for you, and Bailie Alan later at her heels."

Ninian smiled. "Alan mounts," said he, "a good half hundred-weight more beef than Janet. He hadna much o' a chance, wi' that, to run her down. She's back with me; she came to Inverness, and I'll wager the Bailie's still about Loch Laggan dragging for his nephew."

Up got Drimdorran then and seized a stick with which he pounded on the floor. "Ye'll need to have a dram," said he, as cheery as a man new come to fortune. "I'm vexed for young Macmaster, but ye ken he was a rascal."

"Ye mean the snuffbox?" Ninian said. "He never took it. I charged him wi' t as soon's I met him on the Orchy, and he nearly struck me down. *It's in your desk!*"

Duncanson turned round. "Did he say that? Did he say that?" he cried.

"No," said Ninian; "I guessed. Whether it's there or no', Macmaster hasna got it."

"He was in my desk!"

"Not him, Drimdorran! He never had a hand in't."

"I'm telling ye he took a key from out this desk, and opened up the doocot."

"He didna. I'll let ye ken the truth, Drimdorran, though Macmaster wouldna. The whole thing started wi' a cantrip o' your daughter's. She and Campbell werena in the mood that night for lessons. 'Twas she who got the doocot key, and Æneas, looking for her, found her in the doocot."

The old man stood with his hand on the back of his chair a minute, speechless. Incomprehension, light awakening, doubt, conviction, and dismay successively showed in his aspect; last of all, an air of relief that puzzled Ninian.

"Ah!" he said at last, "I have it now! . . . The randy!" He plucked his hose up from his ankles, ran his hands through his whisp of hair, and took a drink. For the first time was his manner like the old Drimdorran Ninian best knew.

"I was all astray! I never dreamt of that! From the start I blamed Macmaster, and she never said a word to change my mind. I was sure it had been him—that he had rummaged. There's many a thing in this desk of mine that's no' for prying eyes—you understand?—the Duke's affairs: there was in't that night some State concerns that, blabbed too soon, would bring

278

confusion to his Grace and ruin to me."

"I see!" said Ninian gravely. "It well might make ye anxious."

"Ye were here yourself that night; ye'll mind I left ye for a little? I saw, from the window there, the doocot lighted, and jaloused. I went to the door of it, to find all dark; but I felt the smell of a smouldered candle, and I knew there was some one there. The thing so staggered me, that I should have a spy on my very hearthstone, I couldna speak, and I left without a word."

"Just that!" said Ninian. "Man, that was a pity! If you had got them to declare themselves it would have saved misunderstanding. Macmaster couldna guess what ailed ye at him; he had done no wrong."

"I see that now, but think of my position! My desk was riped; the siller box was gone; ye would yersel' have been the last to blame a daughter. . . . Ye've heard she's off wi' Campbell?"

Ninian nodded. "Youth," said he. "It'll soon blow by!"

"Na, na!" said Duncanson, with bitterness; "it'll no' blow by. What will his family think? That I connived at his entangling, and him my ward. His Grace came home today—they tell me, furious. I havena seen him yet; I canna!"

He broke down utterly. His voice trailed off to a whimper; the tears ran down his face and he was leaning on the desk, a spectacle of shabby grief.

"For what do we breed children? Is it to plague and torture us? I gave her all indulgence; I moiled and toiled for her, and granted her every whim; improved this property, and starved myself for it that bairns of hers might have some cause to mind their grandfather. I come off a good stock—"

"*Mo chreach!* we all do that in Gaeldom!" said Ninian, shrugging.

"—A good family, though in the money bit of it declined before my time. My grief was that I hadna got a son. But even through a daughter I could make a name to last beside Loch Fyne—Drimdorran. For that I would jeopard life, one time, and sell my very soul!"

He beat on the desk with a bony hand; he was clean swept off with feeling, and Ninian himself was a little moved.

"And now it's done!" said Duncanson. He took the stick and thumped again the floor for an attendant. "It's finished! She has ruined all."

"Indeed and it wasna nice of her to leave the blame on Æneas," said Ninian. "It might have ruined him. The ugliest thing of it all was that damned snuffbox."

Drimdorran sighed. "Had I but known," said he, "the snuffbox cleared Macmaster. I found it two days later in the desk in a drawer where I never put it, so far as I could mind. But still there was the doubt, I might have put it there myself. I see now Margaret did it. She got my keys again."

The entrance of the Muileach interrupted. He came with a tray, a bottle of spirit, glasses, and a kettle; placed them on the table and retired, a customary evening office.

Drimdorran brewed. His hand shook as he filled the glasses. Ninian looked closely at him fiddling round the tray, surprised to see how greatly he had rallied in the last five minutes. The look of doom was gone from him, his back was stiffened, and though the outburst of a moment since concerning Margaret might naturally have left him dull, he actually seemed livened. There are men who brighten at the first glimpse of a bottle, but Duncanson was not that kind, and Ninian knew it. The man was inwardly rejoiced at something. As for himself, he sweated in the chamber's heat and longed for a release. He wondered at this multitude of candles, and the tartan screen particularly commanded his attention.

"And now," said Duncanson, his brewing finished, pushing a steaming glass across the table to his visitor; "take that, and tell me how ye sped in Inverness. I heard ye got some guns."

Ninian half-shut his eyes and cracked his fingers, quite unconscious that he did so.

"I did," said he; "but who could tell ye that?"

Drimdorran for a moment hung; his eyebrows knitted.

"The man who came from Badenoch to tell me ye were drowned," said he.

"Oh yes!" said Ninian. "I see! Of course that would be the

280

way of it. Yes, I got a pickle guns, Drimdorran—three hundred stands in a heather chapel on Loch Laggan-side, They werena worth a spittle—broken pieces out of Holland. But there's a splendid trade in them; George Wade gives a pound apiece." He twinkled. His glance for Duncanson was very sly. "They're the first trade the New Road's brought to Badenoch. I'll have to mention it to Islay, but I'm sweir."

Drimdorran looked uneasy, plowtering with his ladle in the glass that tinkled to his shaking like a bell. The tone of Ninian was much too confidential.

"Are ye sure of this?" Drimdorran asked a little weakly.

"Tach!" said Ninian, and stirred his drink. "As sure as death! I saw Himself; he didna take the trouble to deny it. But he said there was more than him in't."

"Ninian," said Drimdorran, and leaned across the table, "did he mention me?"

"His lordship's quite discreet. He mentioned nobody."

Drimdorran rose and snuffed a candle. He bent across his guest. "There's money in't," he whispered, "both for you and me. And it's not against the law, as ye say yourself. I've known it for a year. There's money in't! There's money in't!" He clenched his fists and shook them.

"That's what I was thinking to myself," said Ninian calmly. "If Wade's so keen on guns, just let him have them! He's just an Englishman."

"I can get ye a part in this. Mind, now, it's deadly private! It would never do to placard Lovat, and his wife a Campbell. Say not a word about it, let Islay think the guns are for a Rising if he likes."

"Very good!" said Ninian, stirring with his ladle, drinking nothing.

And then there came his final opportunity.

Duncanson had got into his chair again and quite a new man from the wreck he seemed when Ninian entered, quaffed his liquor, smacking with his lips, A candle flickered out, and he saw it, but he paid no heed. Now conscious of his flopping hose, he pulled them up, and snuffed with gusto.

"Did ye see anybody else in Inverness?" said he. So far, no sign had come from him of interest in Macmaster's fate, and Ninian felt grim.

"I gave a cry on Forbes."

Drimdorran winced. He could not hide it.

"It wasna about the guns?" he asked with some anxiety.

"I went to him about another matter altogether," Ninian said. "I got the strangest story on my way up North, and I went to him to ask about it. Duncan's a clever man, and not much misses him, but here he was no use to me. The drollest thing took place on the Moor of Rannoch. Col-of-the-tricks came down on us—a man with a leather coat and a boaster's feathers, and what was he on but to stop my passage? Just listen you to this, Drimdorran! I had Macmaster with me. Barisdale had never seen the lad before, and still he knew his stock whenever he clapt eyes on him. That man is just a dirt, and I wouldna trust his word upon the steel, but he said something yonder gave me thinking."

He got up and walked the floor, with three steps up and three steps down like a beast in cage. Drimdorran sat bent forward, sunken at the chest.

"The thing was this. He knew Macmaster's father. They had fenced together. And where should they fence do ye think, but in Castle Dounie? It was after Glenshiel and Paul had a wounded arm. Are ye following?"

The glass of Duncanson upset. Its liquor spilled across the table, ran over the edge, and made a puddle on the floor. A plashing sound made Ninian look down; the old man's heel was drumming in the puddle, out of his control.

"Is there anything in it, do ye think?" he asked, in a queer flat voice.

"There's in it that the man was never drowned!" said Ninian. "He went abroad. We found it out from Lovat."

Duncanson got on his feet and reached for the water-jug. "A dubious tale," said he,—"unless—unless, like the son, they shipped him."

"But the son's no' shipped!" said Ninian. "I got him off, and he's home in Inveraray."

As if the legs were cut from him, the old man dropped. The chair had been against his knees; he plumped into the cushions with a jar that shook the floor, and he gave the twittering cry. And then of a sudden he got up, put his palms across his ears, and shuffled from the room.

XXX

A Search

Ninian stood five minutes waiting his return. In the midst of the house he heard a door go bang. He plucked at the tartan curtain; raised it; opened a window pane and held his face against the breeze.

The desk next tempted him. The key was in its lock; his hand went to it, but some sentiment restrained him and he turned his back on the temptation.

Plainly Duncanson had no thought of returning. His guest took up the glass which he had not drank from, and emptied its contents upon the fire; then out and through the lobby and down the stair in a blaze of guttering candles. He quit the house.

Having walked across the gravel to the grass, he stood for a little, pondering. The house lay in a flood of light; it gushed from every window, even from the attics, very strange to see. In that wide solitary haugh of glen so dark itself, without another house, it seemed preposterous. It might have been a dwelling of rejoicings, only that festive sound was missing. He searched his memory and was beat to recollect that he had ever seen it lit like this before. Since Duncanson had come to it, at least, it had no social gleam; there never had been dancing there, though the parish danced in winter-time in every loft, nor yet a supper for the tenants. Black Sandy, when a younger man, was no way slack at gaiety, and when he lived in town had many an evening ploy in Fisherland, but that all stopped when he became a laird.

For what should a craze take the shape of such silly waste of candles? In a grasping man—and Sandy had always a grasping reputation—extravagance was not the natural thing to look for should the man turn daft. And yet there must be something— Candles? . . . Candles? . . . A thrifty man. . . . What freak of memory in a madman would suggest the candles?

284

The *beachdair* drummed on his teeth with his fingernails, and tried to make himself an old man crazed, and think of things that through the labyrinth of an old man's brain might lead to a candle passion. Though mighty curious, when in the house, to see such blazing round him he had not showed, even by a glance, that he thought it odd. He had not asked the Muileach, when he first arrived, what it might mean. It would not have been good Highland manners to say anything, even though the candles had been ten feet long. But now they cried importunate for explanation.

Instead of starting off down through the garden, he went quietly on the grass about the gable of the house. It had a fosse or ditch, some four feet deep, to light the basement. There were windows in it at the back, some of them built up, but the others glazed and lighted; this was the kitchen quarters. Beyond the kitchen windows, however, was one a bit apart which he knew to be the Muileach's. He picked some pebbles up and threw them at the glass.

In a little the man came out, and up some steps to reach the level. It was because gravel is plentiful, and nights are dark, and human beings will go courting, that stanchions are on basement windows. He thought he had caught the lover of a kitchen-girl, and was quite aback to find the Messenger.

"*Dhe!* is it you that's in't?" he said, confounded.

"Tell me this!" said Ninian, and took his sleeve. "In the name of fortune, what's this great parade of candles?"

"You may well ask that!" said the Muileach. "We're rendering the very kitchen-fee."

"Tach! Never mind the kitchen-fee!" said Ninian, impatient. "Thou needst not want for that so long as the castle jack is going. What is thy master meaning, blazing there?"

"It is aye for some end of her own the cat croons. Myself I cannot tell you; but I wish to fate I was back to the Islands!"

"Is he frightened?" Ninian asked.

For a second or two the man said nothing, his hand on the railing of the fosse.

"There's nothing wrong with him," said he at last, "except at

285

night, and then, *mo chreach!* he's in the horrors."

"Another thing," said Ninian hurriedly. "What does he want with a curtain on his window? He never used to have it, and it's nailed."

"If I could tell you that I would be wise. Day and night it's there, and it's never lifted."

"He's a done man!" said Ninian, reflecting.

They talked for a little longer and then he took his leave.

He went down the grounds; across the fields; took a short cut to the dovecote. The stars were thick as dust. Some young roe-deer were from the hill, he came upon them browsing. They fled before him. To the west Craig Dubh rose black with plumage of the fir, in whose midst were night-birds questioning. There was a little frost.

He had never been in the cote, for his interest lay in the bold and wild, not innocence and pigeons, but he knew its outward features, and even in the thicket's gloom he walked straight to the door. It was locked; he had not expected otherwise. On finding this he went down to the river's bank; walked up the water for a bit, and came on a drifted tree, a thin young birch. With his knife he lopped its branches, then carried it to the cote and thrust it at the window, which fell in. With the tree for ladder he got up, squeezed through the narrow opening, and dropped. He landed beside the bin.

Having struck a light to tinder, he fed it to the lantern; looked about him; opened the lid of the bin and searched it, even below the moulded grain; emptied the sacks of their mildewed corn till it piled up to his ankles. The dust rose round him in a cloud; he sneezed.

When he had finished here he got up the ladder through the hatch to the second storey, and there came on other boxes, a barrel without a lid half full of pitch, and a mattress filled with feathers. He searched in everything; the boxes were the lumber of a flitting, and held musty papers. He turned them out and found them drafts of tacks, which he put to the closest scrutiny. They were read to the very testing clause, and then thrown back; there was nothing in them.

Nor yet was he done. He went to the topmost storey where he stood below the sarking, stooped, his head against the beams. Nothing was there at all but the soil of doves; he turned to leave, then noticed something that had hitherto escaped him—every pigeon-hole was boarded up. In this there was some apparent interest, for he put his lantern down, took out his knife, and cut a skelf from the boarding of one hole, and chewed it.

To get out of the place without the tree to help was not so easy as to enter; he got upon the bin and made a great attempt, gave up at last, and felt in the dark about the door. The bolt of the lock was shot in an iron staple which could be levered out; he thought of the mattocks, groped for one, and putting the pick-point in the staple, forced it at a push. When that was done and the door stood open, he hammered the staple loosely back; whoever should find the door unlocked would think it carelessness. But the door itself, shut to, he jammed at the foot with stones. His last precaution was to take the tree and throw it in the river.

The wind was from the north and stirred the thicket which shed no longer leaves, since all were blown and scattered. They rustled below his feet. He stood a little, and stared at the flaring house. A wild-cat on the Scaurnoch wailed. Dark shapes of cattle moved on the farther bank. The river brawled, but yet above its brawling sounded something to the north that had an echoing beat as if of metal.

As it came sounding closer, Ninian moved up beside the road, and stooped to get between him and the stars the figure of a man who trotted on a horse.

"*Sin thu*, Alan, it's thyself!" he thought, and cried the Bailie's name.

"Is't you that's there, Ninian?" said the rider, pulling up.

"That same! I put a welcome on ye. Man of my heart, but ye ride heavy! I heard ye a mile away."

Alan-Iain-Alain Og got off the horse and painfully stretched his legs; he rode with a short Kintyre stirrup.

His first words were of Æneas and Janet; when he heard that they were home he was much relieved. His own experience had no stirring incident; in that respect he found his journey very different from Ninian's. On the road, with the reins looped in his hands, he gave a brief account of what befell.

He had been from home on the forenoon when the news came from Loch Laggan, and Janet had three hours' start of him, with no clear notion left behind of how she meant to go. At the head of Loch Awe there was no one who had seen her pass, and he was in a quandary, but he reasoned that her goal would be Loch Laggan, and he rode up through Glen Orchy to the inn, where he stayed the night. She had not passed the inn, it was clear now she had gone down through Glen Dochart, but he kept on his way to the Black Mount, eastward by the Cruach to Loch Laidon, whence he turned to reach Loch Treig and up the Spean to Badenoch.

"How long did ye take to get to Loch Laggan?" Ninian asked.

"Three mortal days!" said the Bailie, groaning. "And my skin's not mended yet."

"Janet beat ye! She took only four to Inverness."

He had with him in wallets the key to every pass in the wilder Highlands—some sweetmeats and tobacco, and to give his coming a hue of unconcern he pushed inquiries everywhere regarding cattle, posturing as a dealer. Wherever he went he found folk hospitable: Badenoch came trooping to make terms with the Merchant Mór. In the hamlet of Druimbeg he spent a night in the very house where Ninian and Æneas had supper, and in Druimbeg he learned that they were safe. They had been seen on Tarffside on their way to Inverness.

"I thought of going to Inverness myself," he said, with a lift of the shoulders, "but the snow, they said, was three feet deep on Corryarrick, and I'm too thick in the girth, *mo thruaigh!* to face the drift, so I just came home."

"The best thing ye could do!" said Ninian with conviction. "Yon's no' a place for Christian men."

"It took me two days at Loch Laggan finding out what I was after, for I had to use some caution. They fed me on kippered fish and ham till I was parched so dry I could have drank the loch, and then I took my leave of them and through Lochaber into Appin. I spent last night with the tacksman at Bonaw."

To this itinerary had Ninian listened with an absent air, his eyes on the glowing mansion hung up in the dark where it seemed at times to rise and float.

"Isn't that the great house?" he said when the Bailie finished. "There's a stone of candles burning in't this minute."

"It made me wonder," said the Bailie, looking up. "I saw the scad of it beyond Carlunan. Is there some Occasion?"

"I canna think of one," said Ninian, "except that another man is going to keep his daughter after this." He caught the Bailie by the arm and squeezed it, whispering. "I've just been there. Drimdorran's fey! Ye never saw a man more under weather. The shroud's upon the breast of him!"

"I heard about his daughter and young Campbell," said the Bailie. "That a blow to Sandy!"

"It's not the only one, I'm thinking, nor yet the worst. I gave him a blow myself this night that shook him to the found."

"Ye'll tell me all of that wi' a bite of supper," said the Bailie, and turned for the horse's mane. He gripped it with one hand and with the other caught a stirrup.

"Stop you!" said Ninian. "I've news for ye that's no' for bellowing to a man cocked on a horse. If you will just play legs wi' me, and lead the beast, I'll tell ye something I told your wife a little ago, and it left her dumb."

With a last glance at the lighted house they walked down the road together.

Ninian first recounted how he had got home, with a verdict on the Road as the dullest he had travelled, and then swerved back to the affair with Barisdale.

"I heard about that at Buachaille Etive, at the inns," said the Bailie, "and I couldna make heid nor tail of it. I know that Col's a rogue, but his booty's cattle, or the cess the cock-lairds pay him for blackmail. What could he want wi' you?"

He stopped, with an alarming inspiration. "Ye're no' goin' to say it was my nephew's money?" he exclaimed.

"Na, na!" said Ninian, "it wasna that. The money's safe and sound, though it gave me manys a fright. . . . Keep on! It's better walking. . . . Col was put on my track by a fellow from Glen

Strae. Ye wouldna think they were so clever in Glen Strae? Ye would wonder what a body in Glen Strae would herd a man like Col on to a Messenger-at-Arms for? I never plied my trade in Strae in all my life—I couldna. It was once my people's and their bones are there, and the folk there now are not to blame that we are landless.... Well, well, *coma leat!*—the lad and me took the twist of Col, and got to Badenoch, and ye ken what happened yonder. 'Tis he can flash the pistol! We left some work for women there, and to make my story short, we got to Inverness. It's a bonny town enough if one were looking at it from a steeple, but get to the guts of it and it's a different story. I mean in the quirks of men. There's a spider yonder, hoved up in the belly, sitting in a net that's spread from ben to ben, and has a string the length of Inveraray. The whole time we were there he kept us skipping. We were leaguered in our inn by ruffians, my head was split, and Æneas was carried on a vessel. If it wasna he was smart to swing an eitch I wasna here this night, and he was on the way to Carolina."

"*Dhe!* that's a fearful story!" said Alan-Iain-Alain Og, astonished.

"It's no' a story yet; it's just the start of two. I'm glad ye're home, Macmaster! I'm here wi' a tangled hank that's worse than the search for Duncan Cameron in Lochaber, and I'll want a hand. Ye're wondering to yourself, I'll swear, the spider's name. Who is it throws a web across the North and catches flies and ships them off, and feels a quiver of the net, ay, even as far as Inveraray?"

"Ye're meaning Simon Fraser!"

"Just him! *Trusdar!* Filth!" cried Ninian, fierce. "Oh-h-h man, if he were young and I had just his thrapple!" He grated with his teeth. "But there's two beasts at the web—Lovat and another, and the other glues the strings in Inveraray—Alasdair Dubh."

"Black Sandy!" said the Bailie, stopping his horse. They were in the midst of trees.

"Just him! He might well sit wakened all night long wi' lights; by day he's at the weaving—here a strand, and there a strand;

one in Islay's mailbags and the other up to Dounie; one in MacCailein's castle, and the other among the clans. Give me a besom till I sweep him down!"

Macmaster clicked his tongue. "I never thought much of Sandy, but he's surely no so deep as that?"

"To the very eyes! He thought this night he had me. 'There's money in't for us,' says he: I had him open like a mussel ye would shell! Little does MacCailein know the snake he's warming! This is the way of it, Alan—Lovat is shipping arms from Holland to the Forth, old scabby muskets, no' a belch left in them. They come up the Road in creels, like haddocks, and a widdie of them's dropped off here and there in the slyest glens to wait for market. Beef's cheap the now, but iron's up in price, and more's to be made of iron since ye needna fatten't. When fair-day comes at Ruthven, and Fort Augustus, and Fort William, Donald comes up in the name of the Disarming Act wi' the faithful weapon of his fathers on a string, and gets a pound for it from the English sodgers. It wouldna cost a shilling in Amsterdam! The clansmen get the credit o' being loyal, escape a search that would discover what they have hid below the thatch, and Lovat shares the pound wi' them, and clears a profit on his cargo."

"I don't believe it!" said the Bailie firmly. "He's maybe rogue, but not in that packman fashion."

"Trade, Alan! Trade! What's the Road for, if it's no' for trade? I always thought that trade demanded cunning! But do ye no' see that the packman bit of it is least important? He wants to keep the real stuff in the thatch; he doesna want the North disarmed no more than he wants roads and schools. So long's the North has gun and claymore ready, Simon is king beyond the Spey. It's no' for the money he's in the trade wi' Holland, but it's for his share in the money Sandy is in the pact."

"It's like enough."

"I'll warrant ye! Sim would be a poor spider wanting the help of Sandy. The whole affairs of Islay and the Duke come under his eye: he milks their mailbags, and will whiles send up a cheese to Sim. There's no' a move in politics but Simon's warned; that's

291

the way ye find him first on one leg, then the other. I know now who spoiled many a jaunt to the North for me by leakage. And this time it was him put Barisdale across my track."

"Isn't that the rogue!" cried Alan.

"Oh, but there's more than that! Far more than that! He had his knife in Æneas. It was at his command Lord Lovat lifted us. Barisdale was watching only me. When it came to Inverness, though, Lovat was far more keen on gripping Æneas, and that had nothing at all to do wi' the trade in guns. . . . I want to ask ye this: did your brother go to France? I'm meaning Paul."

They stopped on the road again; the horse cropped stunted grass in a happy world of beasts where is no mischief.

"To France?" said the Bailie. "Yes."

The *beachdair* gave a whistle. "My grief! I never heard of it," said he, confounded.

"I daresay no'; it wasna a thing to flourish in Inveraray. It wasna wi' my will he went I can assure ye! Nobody knew but me and Duncanson who sent him out his rents."

Ninian scratched his head. "Ye've knocked the feet from me!" he said in a voice depressed. "I'm fairly wandered. And did he write ye?"

"Paul? Yes, every month."

"I'm the silliest man in the whole of Albyn!" Ninian said, disgusted, starting to walk again. "I never guessed it."

"Ye see it was a ticklish business," said the other, tugging at the horse. "He was among the Jacobites, and I darena breathe it here."

"I'm done! I was sure I was on the track of everything that happened this past month, and now I'm more in the dark than ever. It's strange to me that Æneas didna ken of this."

"He was but a child at the time."

"But your wife doesna ken either. Surely to God ye wouldna keep a thing like that from Annabel! She thought the story of the drowning was quite true, and so did I; ye've kept it up wi' me yourself for fourteen years."

The Bailie groaned. "I'm just as sore," said he, "as if I had been lashed. I havena slept much in the last three nights; ye put me in a whirl. What has poor Paul's drowning got to do with France?"

Ninian stopped, as if he had been shot.

"When was it he was in France?" he cried.

"In the year 'sixteen. He went in April and came back the following March."

"And ye think he never was there again?"

"No, poor man!"

"That's where ye're wrong! My grief! but ye gave me the fright there, thinking I was wandered! Your brother wasna drowned at all, he died in France!"

"What *cailleach's* tale is this?"

"It's no' a *cailleach's* tale at all; it's the God's own truth. And you have been the blindfold man these fourteen years that never found it out! Drimdorran knew. He feared your nephew might discover, in the North, and he put Lord Lovat on to him. Thank God he did! for otherwise we might have never found the truth."

He gathered into one impetuous burst of speech, without a pause in it, his evidence.

Beside them where they stood, and falling in a pot, a little well was singing to the stars with which the whole arch of the night was trembling.

XXXI

The Man From Gunna

The castle, when they passed, was mournful dark, with no light
in it—at least that could be seen. Its evening rooms looked to the
courtyard; outwardly its walls rose blank expressionless, below
the star-bright curve of night. A breeze fanned through the ivy,
stirred the laurels. The low town, crouched beyond it, lent it
height: the tower would seem to lift gigantically. Bats were
abroad; at times they gave a cheep. To the east, on the Cowal
hills, was a fleece of cloud that hid the risen moon.

The two men and the horse were on a private way that took
them through the policy; between them and the walls was but a
garden border, and they spoke in whispers. It was as if they
feared to spoil MacCailein's sleep.

"Rats at nibbling, MacCailein! Rats at nibbling!" said Ninian.
"The wonder is to me Himself can sleep, even in a turret, with
so many crannies for the rat in Scotland."

Alan-Iain-Alain Og put in his horse at the back of the land
where he had a stable; left a man to groom it, and took Ninian
up the stair with him to find a supper ready. All Annabel said to
her man was, "There you are!" and pinched his elbow. She took
from him the wallets.

He pulled her ear. "Ah!" said he with a smile, "what a fine
enduring woman! Many a wife left to herself would take the
chance to run. Were ye no' feared I was lost among the mounts?"

"I feared for nothing," she answered, happy. "What always
happens is the thing one never thought of, and I took time and
thought of everything that could befall."

Æneas and Janet were already at the table; the girl had not
gone home.

At another hour the spirit of a company thus gladly brought
together would be different, but over them tonight there was

solemnity. The mystery of Paul Macmaster clamoured for solution. They scarce were seated when Ninian brought it up.

"I ask you to excuse me," Æneas interrupted. "Was I a good soldier this month back in your command?"

Ninian beamed. "Ye couldna have been better! Ye did what ye were told, the sodger's first concern, and held your tongue. If I was ever in a corner I would cry for Æneas-of-the-Pistol."

Æneas flushed. "That bit of it," said he, "is neither here nor there. I only ask assurance that I played my part as a soldier should, nor questioned anything you did, nor pushed decisions of my own. I went with you on sufferance; led you into trouble, and I felt the least that I could do was to be the humble private. Now that the campaign's over, and a new one's started closely concerning myself, I must take another rank."

He spoke with great decision, yet without offence, and Ninian clapped him on the shoulder.

"Well done!" he said, with heartiness. "You're a man for the brindled hill, where each man does his own bit stalking."

"With me it stands like this," said Æneas. "I am greatly in the dark about affairs at the period when my father disappeared. Particularly I know little about Duncanson, and instead of working back from that amazing story we got from Lovat, I think it better to begin at the other end. How came my father to have anything to do with Duncanson?"

It was a somewhat lengthy history he got from Alan-Iain-Alain Og in response to this inquiry. The Bailie went into the most minute details. He began with a wet spring day when Æneas was unborn, when a shabby-clad man with a canvas bag and a bundle in a napkin stepped from a fishing-smack on Inveraray quay and asked the first one whom he met where he might find a lodging. The man was Duncanson. He had come from the Lowlands, where, for some years, he had followed the law in an obscure capacity. There were Duncansons in Inveraray; they were a Campbell sept, but long established in their own cognomen. It was thought at first that he was a relation. But there was no connection. In less than a week it was known in the town that his real name was Maclean. He belonged to the Isle of Coll—or rather to an islet 'twixt Tyree and Coll, by name of Gunna. His father had had a croft in Grishipol in Coll, and dealt in swine. He was a man of race by all accounts, declined in fortune—a kinsman of Lochbuie. Coll, at the century's start, was a rebel and unruly island, though within a strong man's hail of the Hebridean garden called Tyree, the holding of Argyll; there was always trouble with it, and the elder Maclean, to escape a prosecution, went over the narrow strait to Gunna and settled there, befriended by the Duke.

If he could not change his blood, at least he could change his name, and he aimed at a continuance of the ducal favour by taking the name of Duncanson, his father being Duncan dubh a' Chaolais. When he died he left a son grown up—this Alexander, who had for some years made a living of sorts, in Tyree or Coll, indifferently, as the season suited. He had the name of a clever lad; the family of Argyll were interested; he was sent to a writer's place in Edinburgh, and there he had been till he came to Inveraray.

His coming to Inveraray was a shift of ambitious policy. In Edinburgh he was lost; there seemed no rung he could reach to in the ladder of success, so he came to the very seat of patronage. In a day, with MacCailein's influence, he was perched at a desk in a lawyer's office; in a year he was indispensable to his master; in three he had bought him out of the business. The money which bought MacGibbon out was a scanty part of a fortune Duncanson fell heir to from a distant cousin; he was now a man of substance, so sure of his own importance that he paid attentions to the lady who was later to be Æneas' mother.

From his first appearance Duncanson had courted Paul Macmaster's favour, even though Macmaster was at times suspect of politics repugnant to that quarter of the shire. Himself, he had no politics that could not be trimmed and twisted to pass with either side, but mostly he avoided disputation in these matters, and with Paul the bond was one of sport. They fished and shot together, and had a taste for fighting cocks which came to an end when Paul took up with pigeons, to whose fancy he was led by the other man. They spent long nights by the dovecote fire, one winter, playing dambrod.

"Stop, stop! . . . By your leave, Sir Æneas! . . . Are ye sure it was in the winter, Bailie?"

Ninian broke in upon a narrative whose interest sadly marred the supper.

"There's no mistake in't," said Alan-Iain-Alain Og; "I've seen the doocot lighted up when I was coming back from curling."

"What light, now, would they have?" said Ninian, but not with a show of much concern. "Besides the fire," he added.

"Oh, candles, of course! Or a lantern," said the Bailie. "That's not of great importance, is it?"

"Go on!" said Ninian, buttering bread. "I only wondered. My mind *will* run on candles," and history was resumed.

Paul's interest in pigeons slackened when he married, and ceased entirely when, a twelvemonth later, his young wife died. He was, thereafter, a homeless man, who could not bear the house of his inheritance. His wife for a year had been its warmth; its stairs (the doctors said) had killed her; he never set foot in it again. The infant Æneas was sent to the care and nurture of his aunt, and his father made the world his pillow. It was a time of great conspiracy with Jacobites; for the first time seriously Paul became involved, and spent both time and money on a cause too easily made attractive to his restless spirit by the guiling tongue of an old friend, Campbell of Glendaruel, a laird impoverished and proscript. 'Twas rarely he came home, and then but for a flash, to see his child, and stay a night with his brother, and meet with Duncanson to audit his accounts.

For Duncanson was now his doer—factor of his land, and always ready to accommodate with money. Moreover, he was tenant of Drimdorran House, with a five years' tack from Paul: he had got married. As well as Paul's affairs he managed Islay's, and in time was Baron Bailie to the duke as well as secretary. The son of Para-na-muic was thriving! Aware of Paul's political engagements, he kept them secret, but in the year 'Fifteen, when Paul was drumming up in France, the knowledge of his doings leaked at home, and but for Islay's pity for the child, Drimdorran would have been escheat, its owner outlawed. It was only a fate postponed. Four years later he engaged with Glendaruel in the rash adventure checked abruptly at Glenshiel. Drimdorran had not been forfeit to the Crown—MacCailein had seen to that— but Duncanson, who had for years made overtures to buy it, stepped into possession.

"I would have fought him! I would have fought him!" cried Ninian, pushing back his chair: their meal was finished.

"That's what I aye said!" said Annabel.

Her husband shook his head. "And what were the good of that?" he asked. "I had no standing. Neither had the boy. Sandy had his ledger and my brother's pledge. I wasna goin' to fight a law plea for the Crown. . . . That's the story, Æneas. Now, what do ye make of it?"

"Nothing," said Æneas. "It leaves me where I was. I thought to get some clew that I might follow through my father's later days and—"

He stopped with a glance at Janet; her eyes were fixed on something in her father's hands. It was the tangled hank, with the free part coiled on stick; the *beachdair* wrought with it as though beside a burn.

"Good lad!" he said to Æneas. "Aye get at the start of things! And what more clew do ye want just now than that Sandy came from Gunna, and a Maclean at that? I never knew't before. *Theid dùthchas an aghaidh nan creag*—the family blood of a man goes down to the very rock! I ken Gunna; I was one time yonder, there! The solan builds in Gunna, and the solan is a bird that gets his fish just where he can; it makes no difference to him, the herring or the saithe."

He rose and walked the floor with short steps, eager.

"Stop you, Æneas! Although ye're in command, I'm no' so good a sodger as yoursel', and must get talking. A man brought up in Gunna between a loyal isle and Coll is like the gannet,— he will take his toll of fish from both. I know the springs of Sandy now—they're envy and ambeetion. Since ever he stood in your father's house a tenant, and looked out upon the fields, he meant to be their laird. He got his wish. What way? By God's goodwill, or accident? Na, na! God has no particular fancy for the clan Maclean no more nor me, and it wasna accident. He got it, first and last, wi' his own endeavour! Your father—God be wi' him!—was the brawest pigeon Sandy ever flew, and then he plucked him. The thing's as clear as day! 'Twas he that blabbed in the year 'Fifteen; the man was in a hurry to sit down, and seeing your father wouldna sell, he must himself be sold. Sandy is like the ptarmigan or weasel, beasts that take the colour of the season; ye may be sure he wasna Whig in private wi' your father, whatever he might be before the duke, and he would egg your father on. He would lend him all the money that he wanted, and never give a cheep till your father was so deep in treason there was no escape. His chance came in the silly splutter of the clans that ended at Glenshiel. Sandy, as MacCailein's man, was bound to know the Government was going to crush that rising like an egg, but he wouldna warn your father. Na, na! Drimdorran he would have! And Glenshiel served his turn, though your father didna perish there; he was good as dead, and could never show his face again in Scotland."

Æneas was aflame. "I think you're right," said he. "It seems a very reasonable assumption of how things were standing. Duncanson was the only man in all Argyll who knew my father was yet alive, and he smuggled him off to France. Then he proclaimed and proved himself the owner of Drimdorran before the estate could be forfeit to the Crown, and he kept him there."

"Just what I was thinking to myself."

"It defies the face of clay to think how any man could be so wicked!" Annabel cried out.

Throughout was Janet silent, listening. In her mien was some dissent or hesitation.

"What troubles me is this," said the Bailie; "Paul was my brother-germain. We were the best of friends, although I quarrelled with him on the head of Glendaruel, and all that rebel carry-on. His son was in our dwelling. I *can not* think that Paul, if he was for a whole year hid in France, would not have sent some word to me."

"I'll warrant ye he sent ye word!" said Ninian.

"I never got it,—not a scrape!"

"Of course ye didna! Sandy would see to that. It was through him he would send you letters; and Sandy, when it comes to letters, has a tarry hand, as Jennet there kens to her cost."

"That, too," said Æneas, "is a very likely thing. He was done with us, and had his own skin to consider. It would never do to have it come out he was in league to hide the man whom himself, as Baron Bailie, had proclaimed."

They stood on the floor, the men, and reasoned hotly.

"Mercy me!" cried Annabel, "can you men no' sit down and come to the bit that pierces me—what happened to poor Paul?"

Her husband clapped her shoulder. "Patience, *a ghalaid*, patience!"

"Is he dead at all? We have no proofs of it."

"But think of it, Annabel! . . . fourteen years . . . and a son of his loins with us. And he was Paul. He couldna keep the silence of the tomb for fourteen years!"

"But he might have been imprisoned. He might, like Æneas, have been trepanned on board a ship. Do ye no' think that is likely, Ninian?"

"Anything on earth is likely, mem, when a bad man mounts the saddle. Your brother may be slaving in the cane."

Janet touched his arm. She had sat with a pale face, looking at him. "No," she said in a curious low voice to him. "He is not there. . . . He is dead. . . . He was killed . . . Duncanson."

They stared at her.

"How ken ye that?" her father asked, astonished.

"You think so! I know you do! And it would be cruel wrong to build false hopes."

"I've never said a word to make you think so—"

"No. It is in your air."

He made a grimace. "The young bird kens the father's chirp! It's quite true, Alan; your brother's dead, and Duncanson destroyed him. I don't know when. I don't know where. I don't know how. But he brought about his end! I wasna goin' to say that till I saw his grave. My hank is still much fankled. He had him killed. There's not a doubt. I've kent it for the last two hours."

"How?" said Æneas.

The *beachdair* gave a flicker with his hands and pouted. "I've smelled it! I'm like the fisher who can smell the herring shoal at sea. A hundred things cry out that Sandy's guilty. They have been pouring on me since we left the North, but tonight the most of all. Æneas, lad, I've seen your foe! Yonder he was in a lowe of candles, and I made him squeal. He thought he had you settled like your father, and I kept him in that notion till I saw my chance. When I told him at the last that ye were here and that ye knew the story of the drowning was a lie, I pricked his liver. I got no more from him, but—"

On the porch of the house was a tirling-pin, which Annabel preferred to knockers. Ninian's speech was stopped when it gave a harshly grating rasp.

"The lassie's out," said Annabel, starting up.

"I'll answer the door," said Æneas, and left the room.

He came back at once with an air of agitation. "Duncanson," he said, "has sent for me. I'll go."

301

XXXII

Confessions

An hour and a half later Æneas came through Drimdorran garden, his hat in his hand, and his coat thrown open to the wind of night, for he was melting from the heat of an outrageous fire in a room where airlessness and his own commotion suffocated. So rapt was he in agitating thoughts he saw at first the dovecote lit, and even stared at it, without his mind's attention. He had almost passed the path that led to it, when its light went out, and thus gave a jolt to his curiosity. The tower had played so strange a part in the revelations lately made and now so baffling, that he was seized with a desire to find out who was in it at so odd an hour, and for a moment he was half inclined to think it might be a repentant girl.

He went through the thicket on his tiptoes, and just as he had reached its heart he heard the door pushed softly shut. For a little he stood hesitant, and then had a queer illusion. It was that all this past month's happenings were a dream; that he had fallen asleep while seeking for his pupils, and that Margaret was behind the door with the lantern-candle smouldering. In the grip of this strange fancy forth he went, and pushing the door ajar, slid in. Again he fumbled in his coat and struck a light. The first sparks showed him Ninian! He almost cried out loud to see that face where should be Margaret's.

"What in fortune's name are you doing here?" he asked, and Ninian made no reply but lit the lantern.

"What notion brought ye here?" he said when the wick had caught. "How kent ye it was open?"

Æneas did as he had done with Margaret when she had asked that question; he pointed to the window.

"My grief!" said Ninian, "I meant to sort that," and he hurriedly stuffed sacks into the opening. "What said the old man to ye? Did ye see him?"

"So much as is left of him," said Æneas, with a catch in his voice. "The man is shattered so greatly I was wae to look at him." He wiped his brow and stared about him vacantly. "I felt in front of him my strength, my youth, my anger, and my hopes a sort of crime. Oh, Ninian! Ninian! what breast of man who likes his fellows could withstand a sight like yon? Can any pang be sorer to our manhood than to see a creature, made like us, with every spark of what ennobles us and makes us other than the brutes, stamped out of him? Everything gone! Health, cool reason, self-respect, and nothing left but a cringing bag of bones and shameful terrors. . . . It humbles, Ninian! It is an affront to the race. I would take the poor wretch, broken, in below a nook of plaid and hide him from the trees and flowers, for they would grue at him. I declare to God I share his scathe and shame; they're mine, too; they're all mankind's. You and I have seen him; for pity's sake and for our human pride can we not conceal him?"

He was wrought up to a feeling that was painful even to witness; his lips were quivering. Nothing in the dovecote caught his eye—the scattered grain nor Ninian's stern demeanour that changed at the close of that impetuous burst to a look that had some hue of tenderness.

"Are ye sorry for him?" asked the other.

"I ache to the very soul with pity for myself and him!"

Ninian puckered up his face. "I can peety, too," said he, "and just as keen as you. I never like to see a broken man: it might be, with a twist of chance, mysel'; for we are like the fir-trees, some will grow up straight and others crooked, and the woodman kens not why. Oh yes, I can peety, too, but I can peety most the man that's wronged, and better than peety in a man is justice. Peety and justice should be like a body's lugs—aye close enough together and both listening, but they never meet. . . . What lies was he telling ye?"

Æneas sat on the bin. "It was just what we thought," he said. "Craft, greed, spite, and cowardice. He has confessed it all, and though he has wronged me cruelly, I have hardly a spark of

303

anger left for him."

"If I was you," said Ninian drily, "I would not let out the light of anger altogether; I would keep a wee bit *griosach* for the morning just in case."

"He admits he urged my father off to France, and was in correspondence with him for a year, and that deliberately he kept my uncle ignorant of the truth."

"What for? What for?" cried Ninian. "I'm sure he's quirking ye!"

"No. The thing is quite patent. He was in mortal terror to do anything fourteen years ago that should expose his own connivance in my father's hiding. Then again he feared that any dispute might arise as to the validity of his possession of Drimdorran. You see he had himself at first believed the rumour of my father's drowning, and before he learned the truth from Lovat, he had claimed the property and quarrelled with my uncle. His greed to keep it when he learned my father still was living prompted him to clear him out the country and hush the whole affair for he felt that only my father's death could justify a closure on the estate. My uncle couldn't clear the debt, he knew—"

"Stop!" said Ninian sniffing. "Do ye smell soot?"

"No," said Æneas with surprise and some impatience.

"I could swear I do," said Ninian. "Never mind! Go on wi' Sandy's lies."

"Do you doubt him, Mr Campbell?"

"Yes, I doubt him, Mr Macmaster! I would doubt him if it was his deathbed and I was his priest. Ye're far too good and simple, Æneas, for a man like yon. *What way did yor father die, and where?*"

"I am coming to that. Duncanson, part from spite at my uncle, as he now admits, but mostly, as he says with abject shame, to stick to what he had prematurely grabbed, never divulged that he was keeping my father abroad, supplied with Drimdorran rents. And just as we suspected, he destroyed my father's letters to my uncle and to me."

Ninian started. "Let me think!" said he, and held his chin. "Well, well! What else?" he said in a little, with a steely glitter

304

in his eyes.

"My father lived a shiftless life in France—" A cloud came over Æneas' manner. "He went about from place to place without a settlement. All Duncanson's letters to him were addressed to the care of a Scot, Macfarlane, with a shop in Havre; and the thing came to an end with a letter from Macfarlane sending back the last of Duncanson's. My father died in Paris—"

"Who saw him die?" shot Ninian.

Æneas wrung his hands, with his visage furrowed. "That is the bitter thing!" he said. "That is—that is what revolts me! I have only the old man's word for it, but he says my father at the last— ... He changed his politics. ... He mixed among the Jacobites, and sent their plans—"

"A spy!" cried Ninian, and spat. "A turncoat spy! Oh-h-h, isn't that the damned rogue!"

"My father, sir?" said Æneas, whitening.

"No, no, no, no! Ye silly boy! But Duncanson! I knew your father little, Æneas, but I knew his stamp and know his kin. There never was a traitor named Macmaster! There, sure enough is Sandy lying. Blow on your *griosach* now, and have a fire; ye never can wrestle wi' a rogue until ye hate him."

"You hearten me!" cried Æneas. "I doubted it! I doubted it! Oh, Ninian, if you could understand what it means to me to have my father's memory clean! It was the last that was left to me of that romance that made the Highlands cry in me like trumpets. And what have I seen?—the ruffian chiefs with their men for instruments, their cunning and their crimes; a land held under bondage to mere names! More poetry is in the life of the poorest fisher on Loch Fyne! But I couldna think my father such a man, nor moved by the springs that actuate such men as Lovat. He must have had some gleam, some vision worth the dying for; 'twas that that sent me North. I went a prince, in a mood of glory, and I came back a beggar, for I saw nothing there I would lift my hat to. There was only left for me the hope that there might, one time, have really been a cause that justified my father's ruin. His story was the only scrap left to me of my old romantics, and the sorest blow I have had in my life was this tale of Duncanson's. He says my father was suspected by his friends and challenged, that he died in the encounter twelve months after he left Scotland, and no one knows now where he lies."

"The lying's up in the big house with the candles in't," said Ninian hotly. "Where's Macfarlane?"

"He's dead, according to Duncanson. He died ten years ago."

"And where's the letters of your father and Macfarlane?"

"That I asked, of course. But they're no longer in existence. Duncanson had kept them in his desk till the day he fancied I had searched it, and then in terror of exposure he destroyed them all."

"My grief! isn't he the master-hand? Ye're in grips wi' the cleverest scamp in Scotland!"

He took off a shoe and shook the grains from it, the mildewed corn was to his ankles. Æneas for the first time saw with surprise the signs of questing.

"What were you doing here?" asked he.

"Seeking. Just seeking what's no in't that I can see—the cause of Sandy's terrors. When you were gone from your uncle's house I took Jennet home and came up the glen to meet you. It wasna altogether to meet you either, but to glisk again through this place. I was here tonight before and put it to the probe like any gauger—Can ye tell me this? Did Sandy leave the house this evening?"

"He did," said Æneas. "He was found in the park two hours ago with neither hat nor cloak on by the Muileach, who missed him, and was sure he was in the river."

"That's just what I was thinking! It wasna the river he was for at all, but here. I left the door shut close wi' a stone at the foot to latch it, and when I came back just now the stone was gone and the door was locked. It didna fash me much to burst it in, for I had loosed the staple. I'm feared he's got the better of me, Æneas; he was here for something that I failed to see. I thought I had searched in everything, but no!—there was something I overlooked, and Duncanson has got it."

He grimaced with vexation.

306

"Of what nature?" queried Æneas.

"That's just what I canna tell ye! But this I'll stake my soul on—the end of my hank was here! It's no' in the desk at all! It was something in the doocot. In the talk I had wi' Duncanson I got that quite plain. Man, I played him like a fish! . . . Did you say oucht about his trappin' ye in Inverness?"

Æneas flushed. "Upon my soul," said he, "I couldna."

"What way?"

"It seemed a trivial thing in the light of what he said about my father. And then—and then he looked so wretched! With a load of such disgrace on him, I felt to add another roguery to his charge."

Ninian shrugged. "Ye beat all!" said he. "But it doesna matter. He ran off from me wi' his hands on his lugs before I got that length. But I got this from him—there was nothing in his desk that night he needed to bother about beyond the doocot key. His whole concern—what put him bedfast on his back— was this, that you were in the doocot. Now what was here that he should be afraid ye might find out?"

Once more Æneas reddened. "You said yourself it might well distress him to think his girl was here."

"I did!" said Ninian. "But I ken better now. He never thought for a moment she was here until I told him so, mysel', this very evening. It was no consideration for his girl that vexed him; it was you being in the doocot, and he thought that ye were searching. If he had not something o' the most dangerous character hidden here, what for should he be troubled at your looking? Tell me that, *ille!*"

"You have found nothing?"

"Not one iota! It was here, I'll swear, when I came first, and now it's gone. I've ransacked over again; there's nothing here now but trash and useless papers."

"What sort of papers?" asked Æneas.

"Oh, just the kind that a man of the law would have—the kind that show men trust each other even less in the days of written sheepskins than they did when they held by swords. I'll warrant ye I looked them, for I'm sure it must be papers Sandy's

307

hiding. It might have been the very letters from your father or Macfarlane! . . . But no!" he added quickly. "There never was Macfarlane! The mind that made your father out a spy made up Macfarlane."

He took up the haft of a pick and beat on the dovecote wall. "Cry out!" said he. "Cry out! Oh, Æneas! if lime had not the heart burned out of it, this place would tell me what I'm wanting. It kens what troubles Duncanson! There's no' a hole in this house he hasna boarded up to keep birds out. It was done when he got the property; the wood looks fresh as yesterday's but tastes of years of weather. What for did he take this trouble? Ninian can tell ye that! Wherever birds are breeding will come folk, and he was not for folk about his doocot. There was here the proof—and not in the desk—that he had plucked your father; ay, and worse! By mankind unbeheld your father died, and that grey rogue is the worst who was ever whelped, who sent Prim Campbell to her cell! But I'm no done wi' him yet; come you away down home, my hero, and we'll see your uncle Alan."

Without another word he blew the lantern out, and this time did not even trouble with the door, but left it swinging open.

But on the threshold he sniffed again, and asked again if Æneas smelled soot. "Ye don't?" he said with disappointment. "I could swear I do, and maybe it's the lantern."

XXXIII

Night-Wandering

Late going home that night, and very late, from Bailie Alan's, Ninian, in the empty street, could not but wonder at the fair face put on life and the aspect of the world by sleep. Here, surely, dwelt the innocent, unconscious: hearts at ease, untroubled heads on feather pillows. The high lands towered on either hand of him, all packed with slumberers, drifting, though they did not know it, like the clouds. Dark windows broke the walls of the lime-washed tenements; the cobbles of the gaping closes might have never known a footstep. Prevailed a smell of peat on fires smothered for the morning. Dead leaves from garden trees, and from the policy, were blown about the causeway; they pattered on before him, crisp, like little living things. Behind him on the walls high tide was beating, and the river made that noise which never changed in it from year to year—so mournful always in the night-time, even with the memories of its pools of fish, so like the voice of time made audible.

His footsteps echoed through the burgh, startling himself a little, like the footsteps of a man whom he had passed deep in the forest hunting-path in small dark hours of morning, once, when searching for a dog astray. The man had stepped out from the dust below the fir-trees suddenly, and come to him, and passed without an answer to his salutation, pacing slow, and melting into shade again, incredible but for his footsteps. That strange night-wanderer in the woods was Ninian's greatest mystery. It was one he never was to solve. Tonight his own re-echoed steps brought up that old experience for a moment; then he heard an infant's cry in some high attic chamber—peevish, as it were with anger that it should be born. Its mother hushed it; he could hear her plainly coax it to its sleep, and sing to it a drowsy strain of "Colin's Cattle." Its whimpering done, the burgh slept again.

Fresh from a long sederunt at the Bailie's, he had a feeling in himself as of a person walking on a crag far up in mountains, looking down through openings in mist at things deplorable, revealed in glimpses—harrying beasts, sin writhing in the depths, iniquitous concerns, greed, pillage, cunning, murderous doings. It seemed amazing folk should sleep at all,—MacCailein's castle or the poorest hovel of the lanes, when the spirit of unrest and evil stalked abroad.

And yet the night, for all its lifelessness, had some wild spirit of its own, in flying clouds that swept across the moon like reek. He wondered. The tide beat on the walls and the river roared; the wind, as it were, blew where it wist, untrammelled; these indifferent to results, though subject to some law outwith themselves. Was it so with men? That they were driven, too, by a force beyond themselves, to make from sin and goodness at the last, far hence, some strong and perfect life, as the life of the *ceilidh* stories?

He felt the weariness of the past week's doings mount on him; he was a little dazed, his mind in a half delirium.

And then of a sudden was he wide awake, with the *beachdair* of him uppermost!

The way to his house was past the Fisherland. It was a tenement of substantial build, with half a dozen families at its southern end where it looked on fields; but at its north with one house untenanted since Whitsunday, when the owner, Campbell of Craignure, took for the summer to his country-seat. The shadow of the church obscured three-fourths of it, but a corner stood blank-white in the light of moon that at the moment fought its way through wrack.

A man was standing on the steps and fumbling at its door, with curious faint imploring cries as if he might be weeping.

At first it was Ninian's notion that some fool debauched mistook the dwelling for his own, and he went forward to explain that this was a house for the time deserted. How great was his amaze to find it Duncanson!

He had on him a greatcoat and a plaid about his shoulders, but his head was bare, and his haffits blowing in the wind

310

disclosed him even before his voice.

A homeless cat was at his ankles, rubbing against his hose; his breast was against the door, and his hands wrought at the upper panels as if to push them in. And he was craving piteously for entrance. He spoke as in a dream; the name of his wife, dead years ago, was uppermost: "Ealasaid!" cried he, "oh, Ealasaid, let me in!" And then in Gaelic said the night was cold and folk were after him. The street was saddened by his cries.

Even when Ninian came to him and touched him, he still leaned up against the door, and craved, disconsolate, paying no attention.

"*A chiall!*" said Ninian, "what is wrong? There is no one in that house, nor light nor ember, Mr Duncanson."

And thereupon the old man turned. The moon struck on his face that was like dry cheese cracked; his eyes were standing in his head.

"It is my house," he said in a wandered way, and looked up at the arch, where a date was cut on the keystone.

It had indeed been his, in the lighter days, the house where he brought his wife, and his daughter had been born; his carefree days, if ever he had any, had been there.

"No more your house, sir," Ninian said to him. "Ye mind, Drimdorran? Craignure has got this place. There is no one there. It will not be opened up till Christmas."

It was then Drimdorran knew him.

"*Tha airgiod ann!*—There's money in't!" said he, with come crazy memory of what earlier in the night he had been speaking of to Ninian, and then as if he wakened from a walking sleep, gave a gasp and shuffled down the steps. He looked up at the house front strangely, then scuffled hurriedly along the street, as if for home.

The wind blew out his plaid; he walked on the crown of the causeway, bent down at the shoulders, dead leaves blown about his feet, and he made no sound, for he wore, not shoes, but slippers. In the dreary street the figure seemed not wholly human—rather a phantom of the mind, an image conjured out of desolation, some symbol of the end of all things,—passion

311

and will, contrivance, cleverness and self-assurance humbled at the last to a slinking ghost going down a high ravine to giddy space where the lasting winds and the clouds had mastery.

Ninian stood watching. There warred in him contending feelings of dislike and pity, utter weariness and curiosity. He guessed at what had brought the old man forth to cry at the door in Fisherland—he sought for peace. It was himself he sought for—an earlier self and unrecoverable, a happier self and better, for whom the ticking clock had no loud warnings. He was not, Ninian thought, entirely mad, but in a fever, thrown back as a man may be in dreams to less-disordered periods of his life.

There were less than a hundred yards to Ninian's house; it was only round the corner; every bone of him was aching for the bed, but Duncanson's appearance in this curious fashion stirred reserves of energy, and in a little while he followed him, and cut through a lane that brought him out ahead of him beside the river.

He left the road and walked the grass, invisible to Duncanson, who padded on till he reached the bridge and crossed to the side his house was on. For a moment Ninian swithered, then made up his mind that his way should be otherwise—on the south side of the river whence, as well, he could command the other's movements with less risk of being seen. Not quite abreast, for the *beachdair* hung behind, they went up the glen where Drimdorran House was lighted bright as ever, and the closer he came to it the more apparent it became to Ninian that he had made an error.

Duncanson was not going home directly; he was going to the dovecote! He went through the thicket, and across the river Ninian heard the hinges creak.

How stupid he had been to place between himself and this chance of some great discovery, the pools of Aray at their deepest!

But he lost no time in seeking to amend his blunder; like a deer he ran back through the grass till he reached a ford, and splashing over the shoes on stepping-stones, he crossed, and along the other bank to reach the tower.

He was too late! The door was being locked by Duncanson, whom, from the cover of a bush, he watched pass through the thicket, then make off across the field in the direction of his house.

It was none of Ninian's concern to attend him further; he had come so far, in truth, from an apprehension that the man might be in flight from perils closing round him, and now that Duncanson was home he felt at liberty to go home himself.

But first he sought the dovecote. For the third time he forced an entrance. This time he blinded up the windows with the sacks before he lit the lantern, still warm from the use of Duncanson. Again he put the building to the closest search, to find that nothing was disturbed since last he was there. But its owner must have seen the evidence of former searching; the corn piled on the floor, the papers strewn carelessly upstairs had a meaning unmistakable, as Ninian had intended that they should.

When his scrutiny was over this time he did a curious thing; he opened up the seed-bin and jumped in, and drew the lid down on him for a minute. That done he climbed out again, went up to the second storey, and clapped down upon the floor and wrought for twenty minutes at the planking with his knife. When he was done the candle of the lantern flickered out; its end was come, its final grease was spilt upon his boots.

In half an hour he was in his bed at home and sleeping like a boy.

The land was bathed in yellow light, and the forenoon well advanced when he got up next day and took his breakfast. Janet had had hers long hours ago; her rest had freshened her, but yet in her manner were uneasiness and restraint. From him to her there was conveyed some influence bodiless and secret—hints and premonstrations in his flattest tones, the twitching of his eyebrows, even in the breathing of his nostrils. His air affected her peculiarly.

"You were late of getting in this morning," she said to him.

"I was that!" he admitted. "It's no' a bite o' the night that'll do for me; I like to make a banquet o't."

"I know where you were," said Janet. "You were in the doocot."

He put down his spoon, laid his two hands flat on the table and looked at her.

"My grief!" said he, "ye're no' canny! How kent ye that?"

"Your shoes were covered with candle-grease," she answered, "and you weren't in any dwelling-house till that time of the morning. Besides, there was grain in them."

"Oh yes!" said he sharply, "that, so far as it goes, is pretty clever of you; but what for should ye think it was the doocot, Jennet? I never was in the place in all my life—till last night."

"I knew," she answered simply.

"There's many another place in the parish where one might come on candle-creash and wade in corn. What made ye guess the doocot?"

She got very red, but this time gave no answer.

"Ye have a way of getting sometimes at the core of things while I am creeping round the outskirts. . . . Do ye ken anything of this affair?"

And then she paled again. "Nothing," she said, and he looked at her with unbelieving.

"This is a strange business," he said, "and of a deep concern to Æneas Macmaster. He has for fourteen years been cheated of his rights. He should have Drimdorran; it is his! The Duke has only to hear our story of it to put that all right—at least a little more would do it if I had just the proofs."

"That's just it!" she cried. "And I know nothing, nothing, nothing!" and thereupon she dashed out of the room.

His own affairs for a week had been absent from his mind; this riddle of Paul Macmaster's fate made the scheme he was sent to frustrate by inquiries in the North of trivial account, but now that he was back he must report. In these affairs he was immediately under Islay's orders, and Islay was from home, but the Duke's concern in the *beachdair* business ever was as close as Islay's, and Ninian made up his mind the report should be for him directly. For hours he wrote at it—a dreary task at any time, but the drearier since his zest was no longer in the business. The name of Duncanson was never mentioned nor a hint conveyed of any difficulties; it might have been a pleasant ramble he had taken to the North.

When he was done he read it through to Janet.

"You say nothing of Prim?" said she, surprised. "Nor the part of Duncanson in her condition?"

He shook his head.

"Na. I'll leave that to another hand. He'll learn of that from Forbes in time enough, if he hasna learned already, and then he'll ask me—"

"But Lady Grange—"

"That's likewise Duncan's business, lass. I'll wager he has nudged the Justice-Clerk already. I never in my life gave out a summons though I'm Messenger-at-Arms, but I would like to have the chance to cleave a stick outside the walls of Castle Dounie and fasten a citation in't for Simon Fraser."

He sent a messenger with his report up to the castle, and spent—a thing unusual for him—the rest of the day about the house, with a snatch of sleep which he explained to Janet by a warning that he might be out all night.

It was late in the afternoon when he sallied forth, and bought in a shop a candle, though he might have had a score from Janet. He bought it from a man who years before had been a carpenter, the one man of his trade at that time in the burgh, and having pouched his purchase, sat on a herring firkin half an hour and talked with the wright who now sold candles. It seemed even to the chandler a singular waste of time.

In another shop he bought two barley scones and a little wedge of cheese, but there he did not gossip. So drolly furnished he was making for the quay when he saw a horse with a boy bare-back on it going down the beach among the shingle. He knew every horse in the parish, and this one was a stranger, a dark bay, *cutach*-tailed, with the rime of travel on its flanks. The boy rode out into the water, splashed about a while to cool the horse, and then came in.

Ninian caught the halter.

"Who's is the beast, my son?" said he, and the boy said it was from the castle stables, newly come with a man from Inverness.

On this went the *beachdair* home, and shaved himself and put on his Sabbath clothes. "It's a man from Forbes," he said to his daughter. "Duncan's stirring! Before an hour ye'll see me sent for by MacCailein."

And he was right; the summons came for him.

He tucked a bundle of papers under his arm, portentous to his girl's amusement: it was his vanity to seem the business man, and the papers had served this purpose often; they were dog-eared farm-stock inventories, quite irrelevant to his commission. "They're like the pipes," he said to her. "A man wi' pipes in his oxter's always bold, and wi' me it's the same wi' papers."

He went to the castle with a fancy that it would be in an uproar over Forbes' tidings from the North, and he found it like a church. The great room he was put in, with its shelves of books, and pictures, iron suits, and banners, had the hush of a necropolis. The only sound in it was when a cinder fell upon the hearthstone. A drum was hanging on the wall beside a window with a silk band round it marked with the names of Ramillies and Malplaquet; he knew it had drummed MacCailein up on battle mornings and he itched to tap it with his fingers. Far off in the house a door was shut and another opened; some one played a flute. A curtain parted, and the Duke came in.

"Well, Ninian Campbell," he said, "I thought before this to hear you barking."

For a moment the *beachdair* hung on the meaning of this speech, and then he smiled.

"I never bark, your Grace," said he, "till I have the beast at bay."

"Come away in here till I speak to you," said MacCailein, backing between the curtains.

XXXIV

Contents of a Barrel

Æneas spent that day in poring, till his eyes were aching, over letters, ledgers, vouchers, fetched out by his uncle from a barrel in the attic where they had lain in the strings that bound them for fourteen years. The mouse had nibbled at them, and the worm; they were thick with dust. They were all that was left of poor Paul Macmaster, of a life once warm and busy, ardent with zeals and animate with youthful passions; wise often; generous always; sometimes—as it must be with us all—a little foolish. Spread out on a clean cloth on the table, musty-smelling, mildewed and yellow, dead things in a world still briskly going on, they solemnised the parlour as a coffin would have done, so that Annabel must feel like weeping, and take her sewing elsewhere.

She could never bear to see them at any time. When Duncanson had sent the barrel home on the death of Paul and the rupture with her husband, she had gathered the unhappiest of the dead man's letters to them—those of his restless years and spendthrift politics, mad schemes and baffled hopes; she had gathered them altogether with the records of factorage and usury from Duncanson, put a sheet on the top of them all as if it were a shroud, and buried them under lumber in the attic. Of all that was in her house, they were the only things not brought out to the green to air in spring.

The Bailie had brought them forth at Æneas' suggestion. He had, himself, repugnance to them. Though he had vehemently claimed his brother's papers when Drimdorran passed to the business man in Fisherland, he had scarcely glanced at them when they were come, delivered one day from a cart for the quay with peats, and like his wife, was vexed to see them now.

"There ye are!" he said to Æneas, as he tossed the barrel over.

317

"Well may Sandy say, 'Let them be clocking, I have the eggs!' "

He helped to place the papers in some order on the table, wiped the dust from his hands, and left the young man to their study.

It was the first time Æneas had seen them since, a boy, he had kept a jackdaw in the attic, and then he had no idea what they were. He saw them now as documents most tragic, not only his father's past in them, but himself (a curious kind of little brother, strange and dead), for every letter to his uncle had some message for the boy, and he could recollect some words of them. They had come from the oddest quarters—inns and monasteries, vessels and casernes; from streets in Leith and Yarmouth; from the isles of Barra and Benbecula; London, Avignon, and Calais; three different houses in the Rue de Richelieu. They guardedly preserved a reticence about the purpose of the writer's shifts from place to place, but Æneas could read between the lines, as doubtless Alan and his wife were meant to do. There breathed in them at times a spirit of elation, oftener despondency. Money had been spilt like water, half the letters groaned at the want of cash.

From the bold and running hand-write of his father, so curiously like his own, as if penmanship were in heredity, Æneas turned, less eager, to the books and papers filled with the scrawling script of Duncanson. The papers were out of sequence, loosely thrown together regardless of their nature or their dates; no letters, but accounts, receipts, and balances, the records of Black Sandy's intromissions with the estate and with its owner. The main book was a ledger, parchment-bound, soiled, and dog-eared as the inventories of Ninian Campbell; it was from it that Æneas could gather easiest the nature of his father's dealings with his factor. A debit, always mounting, stood for years. The rents, such as they were, were rising; but so, it seemed, were the costs of the improvements on the property, and every now and then came in a loan from Duncanson—"to Paris," "to the care of Glendaruel," "to self at Martinmas." On some occasions these had been paid back with interest, after a few months' interval, but otherwise the loans were a constant burden.

Æneas was left for hours at this doleful business. His uncle had a gabbert at the quay with salt, and was at the cooperage, no more preoccupied with what he did there than with poetry; a fury was on him at the mad deception Duncanson had so long maintained, but most of all at this shocking latest accusation against Paul. The worst of it was, he had nothing to confute it! No, that was not the worst!—the worst was that the story might have just a grain of truth in it. It was ill to think of Paul—the loyal, even in folly—so much as turning a sleeve to betray his friends. And yet there were stories of such apostates in his cause—of men who kept up a connection with its victims, selling their plans for safety to themselves, or even for money. Could Paul, in some desperate hour, have played the spy? But it was incredible! His innocence of that the Duke could speak to: Alan would see the Duke and get the truth tomorrow. But the story spoiled his peace of mind today.

At gloaming, Annabel, with her parlour made untenable for her by reason of this resurrection of what she had thought was buried for good and all, left Æneas at his task with a glass of milk beside him, and went round to Janet Campbell's. For Annabel the story of the spying was a trifle, if the men spied on were rogues, as she honestly thought all Jacobites save Paul Macmaster, but she felt it hurt her indirectly through the anguish which it brought her nephew. For her it was more to the point that the father had in some way died—if he were dead at all—in secrecy, with fearful possibilities which left all speculation on his fate a nightmare. She had little faith in the ability of Alan or of Æneas to clear the mystery; what trust she had was all in Ninian Campbell, and her call on Janet was, in truth, a call upon the *beachdair*.

She was a long time gone; so long that her husband went to look for her, and he met her on the street. She was someway roused, a nervousness was in her manner. "There's nothing fresh?" he asked her, wondering.

"No," she said, "but there's a thing that bothers me. It's Jennet Campbell. I canna get over her!"

She walked some yards in silence by his side, as they turned for home.

"Well?" said her husband. "What ails Jennet? She's none the worse, I hope, o' her jauntings? I thought, myself, last night, she was out of trim."

"Deplorably! And she's worse today. I thought it was right to call and ask for her, and learn perhaps what Ninian was doing. I kent he wouldna be losing time at packin' salt or rummaging in barrels."

"Just that, my dear!" said the Bailie. "Ye're in trim, yourself, whatever! And what's the news of Ninian?"

"He's out. He's away for the night wi' a penny candle in his pocket. She watched him leave Carmichael's shop and made an excuse to go there herself and find what he was buying."

Her man heaved up his shoulders. "It's no' wi' a candle Ninian need search," said he. "If it's Paul's concerns he's prying in, he'll need a bonfire. Where was he goin'?"

"It was there that Jennet puzzled me first, for she kens; I'm sure she kens, but she'll no' let on. Alan! there's something at the back of that girl's mind. She's frightened!"

"What for?"

"I canna tell ye that! But as sure as I'm a livin' woman, Jennet Campbell's frightened about something. It's in her eyes! I ken that girl as if she were my daughter; till yesterday her heart was bare to me; she knows I'm friendly to her about Æneas, but for some reason that I canna fathom she's dubious of Æneas, and something's in her knowledge she's afraid that I'll find out!"

"Hoots!" said the Bailie, "it's all in your imagination!"

"Na na!" said Annabel firmly. "Allow a woman! That girl would break her legs for him, and he's just as daft for her; if it wasna that she kens he is, and that I'm friendly, I might think that she was frightened she might lose him."

"But what were ye talkin' about to find this out?" her husband asked her.

"Petticoats! Just petticoats! What widths of bombazeen, and all about tucks and gathers—the lassie's daft! To think she could baffle me wi' her petticoats, and her cheek like ash and her face begrutten! Anything at all but talk of Æneas and his father's business! There's something curious in it, Alan!"

She had got so far when something stopped her—an eager whisper. They had reached their house-front; Æneas lay out on the sill of an open window.

"I thought you would never come!" said he. "I have something curious to show you."

When they got in, he was still in the midst of papers. The milk she had left for him when she went out remained untasted. He had the ledger in his hands, with the back torn off for half its length, and a reading-glass that was sometimes used by his uncle lay on the table.

"Did you ever go through this book?" he asked his uncle.

His uncle stammered. "Well, in a way, I looked at it," he said with some confusion.

"Ye never did," cried Annabel. "Ye just sat over it and grat! That was the way I took the whole trash from ye and shoved it in the garret."

"Indeed I canna just exactly say I studied it," her man confessed. "It had, at the time, too much in it for me. I always meant to take another—"

Æneas clapped it on the table. "It's a blackguard fabrication full of lies!" he cried. "If you had looked it properly you could have found enough to hang Black Sandy! It's falsified! It's scraped, and cut, and built anew to make my father bankrupt!"

He showed them the book's defects. It was only a languid impulse that had made him add some columns up, and in one he had found that a single cipher of miscalculation lost a hundred pounds to his father's credit. With this as a hint he went through the ledger from end to end, and summed up every page of it. He found at least a dozen such miscalculations, all in the factor's favour, and all involving sums substantial. They were all in the yearly balances. But that was not the whole! The wrong summations were not the result of accident; in every case the figures had been altered. To the naked eyes they seemed quite innocent, but Æneas, with his uncle's lens, searched closer, and he found the paper had been scraped. Elsewhere than in the

321

balances, too, he found innumerable signs that a knife had plied.

"My God!" cried Alan-Iain-Alain Og, "was there ever such a robber! I never dreamt to doubt him that way!"

"Ah, yes, but that's not all!" said Æneas, picking up the ledger and turning round its back. "I thought some parts were a little slack, as if a page or two had been cut out. looked all through for the stitching, and tried that way to count the pages in every lith, but it took a lot of time, and, to make it easier, I stripped the back. I was halfway through my counting, and I found some pages missing, but a thing more startling to find was this, and I nearly missed it—!"

He showed a section sewn with black, while the thread of all the rest was white. It had six-and-thirty pages—the last that were written on save a single final page; half the book was blank.

"Do you see what he did?" said Æneas. "That lith of pages covers the last six years of my father's lifetime; they were written after he died—or rather after he disappeared!"

The Bailie took the book from him, and looked at it more closely.

"They couldna be written after he disappeared," said he, "for there, at the end, 's where he endorses—'14th November 1718, found correct,'—poor Paul's last audit."

"But, uncle, look!" cried Æneas. "The whole six years' account as given there is interpolated! The sheets my father audited were cut out, another section was taken from the end of the book, filled up this way and stitched in again before the page my father signed."

The thing was obvious! With the book dissected Duncanson's device of fourteen years ago became transparent, even to Annabel. All he had had to do was to carry a certificate of audit in his own handwriting from the foot of one stitched section to the top of another, get Paul to superscribe it, and effect the change when he was gone. And only his choice of black thread for the stitching had betrayed him! Except to a strict examination the ledger would appear as honest as the day.

This startling revelation sent them now back through the whole mass of papers from the barrel; three hours they spent in checking vouchers with the books, to find at least two-thirds were missing, and they were still engrossed when the big clock in the lobby struck the hour of midnight. Its clangour scarce was finished when the door-risp grated.

Annabel and her maid had gone to bed; it was Æneas who went to the door and let in Ninian.

"I saw by your light ye werena bedded," he said, with a glance at the littered table and the barrel standing by. He was shivering with cold. "If I just had the least drop spirits, Alan—"

He got a glass, which he swallowed at a gulp, and before he could take a seat was acquaint with the knavery of the ledger. He took it all in at a glance.

"That puts the finish on it! Was it you that thought of looking, Æneas?" he said. "Good lad! Good stalking! Give me your hand! I never guessed ye had so fine a barrel, Alan! Ye must agree I was pretty clever in jalousing all along it would be papers troubled Sandy! And ye havena got the half o' them! And ye havena got the worst! Where's the deed that gave him right to grab Drimdorran?"

"I saw't wi' my own eyes," said the Bailie.

"Who witnessed it? What was it like?"

The Bailie clouded; his wife, in a gown, was come from her bed, and standing looking at him.

"Out with it, man!" she said. "I can see ye made a mess of it, Alan."

It was not a deed he had seen at all. There never had been a deed. The bond was one of honour—no more than a scrap of paper in Paul Macmaster's handwriting acknowledging his debt and pledging the estate for its security. But to Alan-Iain-Alain Og, with the consciousness that everything in any case was lost to Paul and to his family, it seemed enough when backed up by the ledger; he had never dreamt to question it. "I see now I was just a fool!" he said, and clenched his fists.

"Indeed and ye werena the man o' business that time, anyway," said Ninian drily. "I doubt Paul never wrote nor signed that pledge! It was the work of Sandy. If the book's a lie, as ye see it is, the paper was a lie as red as hell, and that's what

Sandy feared we were finding out!"

"I'll have him by the neck!" cried Alan-Iain-Alain Og in fury.

"Na, na!" said Ninian soberly. "Ye'll no' have that! There's another twist in the cow's horn, and ye've yet to learn the last o' Sandy's quirks."

"The whole thing goes tomorrow before MacCailein! I'll show him the man he has!"

"He kens already."

The *beachdair* took a chair which Annabel pushed before him. "He kens already," he repeated. "I spent an hour wi' Himself this evening—yonder he was wi' his velvet coat and his pouthered heid. 'Ye havena barked yet, Ninian?' says he, 'I'll bark when the beast's at bay!' says I; but MacCailein didna need my barking, Duncan Forbes had barked before me. His Grace knew all about it—the tricks of Barisdale, the traffic in the guns, Sim's share in the Grange affair, the way we were harassed, and as much as Duncan kens of the roguery of Duncanson. Whenever he got my story he sent a line up to Drimdorran House; I dinna ken what he said in't but it meant the end of Sandy."

He turned to Æneas: "Do ye ken what I asked MacCailein?" he said. "If there was any truth in Duncanson's story that your father clyped? His Grace just laughed at me. Says he, 'What, Paul Macmaster! Never on earth! The Bank of England could not buy him!' "

"I never believed one word of it!" cried Annabel. Æneas could not speak; he was whelmed with a relief that swept away all other feelings.

Throughout, so far, was something latent in the *beachdair's* manner; he had plainly more to tell, and even Annabel could see he wrought up, in what followed, to a climax. She waited for it nervously.

When he had left the Duke, he told them, he had gone up to the dovecote, with his mind made up to spend the night there. He had made his preparations; bought a candle and some food, and knew exactly what he was to do. On the night before, he had thought at first of hiding in the bin, but finally decided on the floor above. With his knife he had cut a hole in the floor, through which whatever happened down below would be under his observation. He was there to watch for Duncanson. That Duncanson would come again he was convinced; the dovecote had some loadstone power and dragged him to it every night. At eight o'clock, then, Ninian took up his post, leaving the lantern where it had always hung below, with a fragment of his candle in it. He lay half dozing on the mattress, with sacks on him, and it was bitter cold.

Hours passed, and nobody appeared. He ventured out to look what time the stars proclaimed. The *Sealgair Mór*—Orion, just was tipping Cowal, and the lesser of his dogs on leash beyond him; the hour was about eleven. Having made the time, he turned to go back to his hiding, and on the threshold looked up at Drimdorran House. The lights were going out! One by one he watched the windows dim, till only three were left with a gleam in them, and then he pricked his ears. In the house there was some commotion; he could hear a woman screaming. People came outside and to its front; he heard the running of a man and a voice cry after him.

"For goodness' sake!" cried Annabel, unable longer to contain herself, "will ye no' come to the bit? What was it?"

"I knew there was something wrong," said Ninian solemnly. "I ran up to the road and stopped him. He was going like the wind. It was the Muileach. He was running for the doctor to his master."

"Ah-h-h! It's not the doctor I will run for but the hangman!" Alan growled, ferocious.

"Na, na!" said Ninian, and shook his head, "ye'll no' get the chance, he's beat ye!"

"He's deid!" cried Annabel, now sure she knew the climax.

"He's all that!" said Ninian. "He died an hour and a half ago, and my hank's twisted yet!"

XXXV

The Portrait

Throughout the night a sudden change came on the weather. Next day there was a fog that hid the mounts completely, narrowed every prospect to a circle of a hundred yards. The loch was blotted out but for a leaden margin; it seemed a scrap of town—the ruins of a fire, still smoking—that stood at the river's mouth with a gable now and then shown through the vapour, gullet of a lane, or figures moving vaguely on the quay. The fishermen were out yet on the water; high above the burgh, in the steeple, rang the bell to guide them in, and on the walls a man kept constant drumming with a drum.

To the child of mist this fog came like a benison. Ninian breathed it like a scent; bathed his spirit in it; felt old powers revive. It was an extra night to him, conceded by Almighty for the *beachdair's* benefit. Many a turn he took that morning through the town and up the glen, unseen as if he had Macreevan's mantle. For once were windows useless to a people who never saw Ninian walk along the causeway, but they looked out after him to see where he was going. With a plaid hung loose about his body and his hat scrugged down, he could pass within a whisper of acquaintances unrecognised.

It would be ill to say what he was looking for; indeed he did not know himself; but as in mists like this his folk, in the years of persecution, found from practice speculation quicker, instincts more acute since all their being was on edge to make up for the loss of vision, and they became as leaves stirred by the faintest air, he hoped the gloom of this lowering day that threw him in upon himself might send him stumbling on something.

That morning he had bathed in ice-cold water, thinly clad himself, but for the plaid, and eaten nothing—not a scrap! It was his father's plan.—"Aye, Ninian, be clean, and lean, and cold, and ravenous when big things are a-doing; then God will come to thee, and woe upon the foe!"

The death of Duncanson last night had been a blow. It was a fox gone into earth just when the grip was on him. And with him, too, had disappeared a hundred chances to find out his secret. No other body knew where Paul Macmaster died, nor how, and it was doubtful if he had left a scrap of anything for dog to fasten on. That had been Ninian's notion in the morning; he had grown more hopeful as it passed. For he had found out how, exactly, Duncanson had died. He had had no warning. There was granted him no time to trample out the embers of his fire the way Clan Alpine did in woods when they heard the *cailleach oidhche* command a scattering. There had come to him a letter, he had read it standing, given out a cry, and fallen in a heap, to die ten minutes after.

In the suddenness of this was Ninian's hope that everything could not yet be destroyed, he was sure it was MacCailein's letter, and at ten o'clock, when he went up to Drimdorran House by MacCailein's orders to seal up Duncanson's repositories, this letter was the first thing that he asked for.

What was his amaze to have the Muileach hand it to him yet unopened, the boar's head still intact on the red seal at its back!

"What's this?" said he. "There was another letter, then?"

And then he heard of Lovat's. A runner had come last night from Inverness, and it was a letter from Simon Fraser that Duncanson was reading when he fell.

"Where is it?" asked Ninian sharply. "Fetch it, Donald, fetch it!"

It changed the whole position, and yet it had less than a dozen lines. "All I have got is the twig the fish were on," wrote Lovat. "They're gone on the road to Inveraray round by Ruthven. And here I can do no more for you. I am beat to ken what your trouble is, but if it concerns Paul Macmaster umquhile of Drimdorran, the lad's papa, they have talked it out with Fraser, for he was shipped with them. I cannot lay hands on him; he may be with them."

With the letter in his hand, Ninian stood in the business closet pondering a while. He sought in its lines for what had crumbled the man who had got it, now lying up the stair, his warfare over. It was plainly not the news of their escape, for that was known to him already; it was the reference to Fraser. Ninian took out his tangled hank and absently began to pluck it, although the keys of Duncanson were there before him on the desk.

The room was sombre, darkened by the plaid still tacked above the window, and only half drawn over by the Muileach to let in the dim light of the foggy day. Ninian tugged it from its fastening when the Muileach left him to his business, and looked out into the garden. Beyond the gravel and a plot of perished flowers was nothing visible; the fog hung over all. From a twig of rose-bush nailed to the ribbits of the window moisture dripped; there was a smell of mould and rotten leafage.

He turned his first attention to the desk. Everything was in the trimmest order. It was a great, deep oak 'scritoire, its drawers filled up with letter-books, accounts, and leases. He started at the lowest drawer, having lit a candle; sat on the floor, and patiently went through its whole contents. There was no need to scrutinise either individual letters copied, or accounts; their character as a whole was obvious: they were concerned with Islay's business. In none of the drawers was a single document of any interest to the searcher.

It was more hopefully he opened up the flap at the top of the 'scritoire and looked at the pigeon-holes within, but, even there, was nothing to reward his curiosity. Bundles of letters and receipts docketed on their backs brought Islay's business down to some weeks ago, among them Æneas's acknowledgments of fees paid for his tutoring of Will Campbell.

Such desks had always in them nooks and slides, with what had long become a mere pretence at secrecy; Ninian pulled at the fluted thick partitions in between the pigeon-holes, and drew out upright drawers that were empty—all but one, and that the last he came on, slyly fastened with a spring it took him long to find.

There was in it a silver snuffbox, tarnished, and a strand of a woman's hair tied up with a piece of tape.

He put the hair back where he got it, and stood up to examine the box a little closer to the candle. When he opened it and saw a portrait on the lid inside, he started. At first he thought it was Margaret, or her mother, but it was neither, and yet the face, in a dim way, seemed familiar.

"*Tha i agam!*—I have her!" said he at last. "Macmaster's wife!" and he slipped it in his pocket.

Beyond this he found nothing with the slightest bearing on the former owner of Drimdorran.

He went along the shelves that lined the room; took out more business books and looked at them; at the back of the topmost shelf he found a plan of the estate, a list of farm stock, and a letter of Paul Macmaster's, all tied together in a roll. The letter he read with interest, and pocketed.

On the desk and on the chamber door he put a seal, and it was afternoon when he went home, his business finished.

To the food which his daughter put before him he did little more than give a stirring on the plate; he fed on cogitations. It was not till she told him Æneas and his uncle had been calling for him that he saw she was, herself, absorbed and troubled, something remote, detached, and apprehensive in her manner. It was plain she had been weeping. What thoughts of her and Æneas had been waked in him by the hint of Forbes at Bunchrew he had stifled up till now as soon as they arose; an awkward shyness made him shrink from prying. But this unquiet anxiety of hers demanded settlement; this time he shook off diffidence, and took to Gaelic, as he must when tender things were uppermost.

"Art a little dipped in love, lass oh?" he asked her slyly, with a bold dash at the point which approached more delicately he probably would have shied from at the last.

She got on the instant in a flame of colour. It was the first time he had ever shown a sign that he expected her some day to be a woman with a life of her own apart from him.

"As deep's Dunchuach!" she said in passion: if she had not said it so she should have lied.

"Tach!" said her father, wondering to find this awkward

329

business so simple after all, "thou'rt just a slip of a lass, and that disease is not enduring. Take sleep and buttermilk, and a cooler day will come, and another fellow. This one's just as poor's the tongs."

"And that's the very thing I like about him!" she cried. "And you would make of him a laird!"

"Well," he said, "that's what it looks like. If I could just get the truth of his father's end—"

"I hope you never will!" she cried.

He jumped to his feet. "My soul," said he in English "wasn't I the *burraidh* not to see it sooner! You're thinking to yourself the house is big up yonder in the glen, and will want a great big moneyed woman. You're thinking that you're good enough to wed the tongs, but too small for Drimdorran. Fie, shame on ye, Macgregor, child of kings! The rock is not more old than us, nor yet the mountain. There's not one blemish on our tree, and you will make me feel a dog that child of mine should think herself not good enough for a Macmaster, even if he wore the banners!"

"Stop, stop!" she cried, ashamed; "you go too fast for me. For all that there is between us—just a word!"

"There's not much need for words at the age of you; it's in the eyes, and I have seen him look at you in yon bit coach of Duncan's till my face was blazing. By God, you'll marry him! And it's not the tongs will do for Ninian Campbell's daughter!"

The upper buttons of his waistcoat burst, he was inflamed and swollen with injured pride. She picked up one that fell to the floor and polished it along her sleeve; she stood abashed like a little child.

"You put me to my shame, father!" she said.

"Yes," he cried, "and you put me to my shame that you should harbour fancy for a lad as poor's a dish-clout, and turn from him with your tail between your legs when you find he's like to be a landed gentleman. The one thing I will not have in child of mine is that she should be humble! I would sooner have you wicked! I would sooner have you dead! My grief! are you not Macgregor?"

"But I am not humble!" she said. "It is because I am proud

I do not want a man to marry me because he may think it is his duty, and he is just the man that, having gone so far, would do it. So long as he was poor I had no doubt of him, and I was happy. I would have followed him across the world, but you are going to spoil him for me, bringing back to him Drimdorran. How am I to tell now that he wants me for myself? I'm frightened, father—frightened!"

Ninian rubbed his chin. "My loss!" said he, "that your mother was not to the fore; she maybe could have understood ye! Ye beat me! But one thing I'm determined on—ye'll marry him! An hour ago I couldna let myself think o' ye marryin' anybody, but now we've got this length my mind's made up,— I'll never rest till I get proof that Sandy killed his father: that's all that's needed now to get Drimdorran for him. He's bound to marry ye! If I clear this business of his father's up he's under an obligation."

"Oh," she cried, and wrung her hands, "that's just what tortures me! I want no man who's under an obligation, or might think he was!"

She flung from the room in a rage of indignation.

He went round to the Bailie's house. Æneas was out; he had spent the whole day calling upon men who had been friendly with his father to see if any one by chance had had a correspondence with his father after he had gone to France. His uncle went to a man who had been skipper of a barque and knew the port of Havre. MacIver was his name; he had sailed for twenty years with fish in their season to the place and knew what Scottish merchants lived there. In all his time he had never known of one Macfarlane; there had been no such Scottish merchant fourteen years ago in Havre.

"I knew it all along," said Ninian, when the Bailie told him this. "It was the lie of a desperate man, no more in it than there was in the charge that Paul was turncoat. Duncanson was lying right and left, enough to make the green rocks cry. He had your brother killed! And he lost no time about it either. Paul never spent a year in France—the thing's ridiculous! Do you think, Alan, the brother of your blood with a boy here waiting on him

331

would not find some means to get a letter to you in a twelvemonth?"

"But Duncanson would burn them," said Annabel.

"Supposing he did? That might work for a month or two but no' for a year on end. When Paul got no reply from you to the letters he sent through Sandy, he would be a stupid man that didna jalouse something and try another post."

"That's true!" said the Bailie. "There was many a way he might have written us. There was, for one, MacIver."

"But he didna write ye. What way? Because he was dead! That flashed on me the other night when Æneas told me Sandy's story. There was never a penny of Drimdorran rents sent into France the second time; your brother was killed as soon's he got there."

He produced the letter from Paul he had found in Drimdorran House. It had come from Leith with bank-notes paying back a loan with interest. They searched the ledger and found the loan still debited to Paul. It was among the very last of the advances made by Duncanson, and the absence of any allusion to a balance showed that all that had preceded had been also paid.

"That's all I found up-by in Sandy's closet that had the least concern with Paul's affairs. The old rogue—peace be wi' him!— made a clearance. Not a scrap is left to help us. But here's a thing—how came the old man to have this?"

He handed Annabel the snuffbox.

She knew it at once. "Paul's!" she cried with agitation, and opened up the lid. "And that is his wife, my dear Selina."

It was, of all they had lost with Paul, the one thing they had most regretted. To him it had been extravagantly precious. And that Duncanson should have kept it from them seemed the most cruel of his villainies.

"But how came he to have it?" asked Ninian. "That's what puzzled me. It's not a thing a man would forget at a flitting nor make a gift of to his factor."

"Never on earth!" said Annabel. "I *can not* think what way that man should have it."

"There was with it a bit of a woman's hair; it was hers, I'll swear. Now what would a man like Duncanson keep these things in his desk for?"

Annabel sighed. "He was one time very fond of her," she said. "Alan, ye remember, told ye?"

"Tach!" said Ninian. "That's a woman's reason, and there's no' much in it. Half the blunders people make come out of thinking life is like a story or a song. It's not! It's grim and crooked! A man like Sandy hadna room in his body for two affections—a dead lass, and a lump of land. He had some other reason for having the box and making such fraca about its loss when he thought her son had taken it. Where did he get it? When did he get it? Tell me that and I'm at the end of my bit string! If Paul had the box with him at Glenshiel we're comin' close on the very hand that slew him. Was it sent from France?"

He gave a start as he asked the question, and beat his breast. "My grief!" he cried, "aren't we the fools to believe one word of Sandy's story when we have proved so much of it is false? *Was Paul in France at all?* Did he ever get out of Scotland? That's the thing I should have questioned from the first! If Paul was killed abroad, and the box in his possession, nobody would think of sending it to Duncanson. What for should they?"

"He might never have taken it with him to France," said Alan-Iain-Alain Og.

"Na, na!" said his wife. "Ye needna say such a thing to me! Wherever Paul went in the body, he had Selina's picture. He kept it like a watch below his pillow."

"Oh, man! if I were only sure he had it in the North!" said Ninian with eagerness, and turned as he said so to the opening door. Æneas entered, looking wearied: he had tramped for hours all round the country, and the first thing that his eyes fell on was the tarnished box he knew in his uncle's hand. He learned with amazement that the portrait was his mother's; he had never seen another.

"That I should not have guessed!" he said as he looked at it again, with moistened eyes. "And now, quite plain, I see myself in her as Lovat did."

Ninian glowered. "What's that ye say?" he shouted. "Did

333

Lovat see this picture?"

"He did indeed, unless there chance to be another."

"There never was!" said Annabel. "And that's what made me long for't many a day."

"Then," said Æneas, "Lovat saw it. He saw it with my father that time at Castle Dounie."

"Are ye sure?" asked Ninian.

"He told me so himself at his dinner-table. You might have heard him. And how, now, comes it in Drimdorran House?"

"I'll tell ye before I'm five hours older!" said the *beachdair*; picked up his hat, and without another word was gone.

XXXVI

The Cobbler's Song

He dashed home, spattering through the dubs, for now the rain was falling; found his daughter absent; opened a press, and got a pair of shoes, his own, much worn. These were each thrust in a deep skirt-pocket of his coat, and away he went to the house of a cobbler near the jail.

"Here's a pair of shoes," he said, "put thou fresh heels on them, just man, that I can walk in grandeur. I want them for Drimdorran's funeral."

The cobbler was an old wee man with grizzled whiskers, and lips forever puckered up for whistling. He was a bard, made ditties, mostly scurrilous, which were sung in taverns. As he sat on a stool and hammered leather on a lap-stone, Ninian set him chanting at a song. It was about a tenant in the glen, and a horse he had neither bred nor bought, yet brought in a cunning way to market; the poet clearly hinted theft.

"Capital!" cried Ninian. "A splendid song! Many a time, I'm sure, it put a fury on Mackellar. It's a long time now since I heard it last, on a Hogmanay. It came into my head today, and I just was wondering to myself did he steal the horse in truth, or was it poetry."

"I'll warrant thee he stole him!" said the bard. "Or else he were a warlock brute got from the waters."

"When was this?" asked Ninian sharply.

"It was twelve—ay, fourteen years ago," said the cobbler. "Son of the Worst! he got a pair of shoes from me when he had drink, and would he pay them, sober? No! I put it before my Maker and was stirred to song. Many a time since then would Mackellar rather he had paid the shoes!"

The *beachdair* left the cobbler in a hurry, and through the driving rain went up to a farm at Tullich. It was Mackellar's

335

farm. The man who had paid so dearly for his shoes was on the hill, but returned in a little while, and Ninian questioned him for nigh an hour.

When he got back to town it was the gloaming. A gale was risen; the woods were rocking, and the rain came down in sheets. It drenched him to the marrow, but he went, all dripping as he was, to Alan-Iain-Alain Og's, and who was come before him but his daughter? Only a desperate interest in his movements would have brought her there.

One word he said when he went in beside them in the room— one word only, in a cry, his face like flint, his hand uplifted.

The word was "Havock!"

Between his teeth it sounded like a snarl.

They stood about him as he dripped; a pool ran on the carpet.

"At last," he cried, "I have him! It's well he has the linen on his chin, or he would squeal upon the trestles! Now I ken what for he did not like the night and must have candles! Your father, Æneas, filled the dark; outside the candlelight, night roared for vengeance!"

"What did he do to my father?" Æneas cried, trembling.

"He did what I said he did—he killed him! Somewhere in this parish lie your father's bones! Sit down the whole of us, and I'll tell ye how things happened. I'll take my string."

He took out the line so curiously employed to mark his progress in unravelling the secret.

"The way to find out what a rogue would do in a given habble is to be a rogue yourself. In every one of us there is the stuff of roguery as well as grace, good fortune to us if we needna use it! And I said to myself, 'Now, Ninian, if you were Duncanson and bogged so deep in mischief, what lengths would ye go to clear your neck?' Duncanson wanted Drimdorran, and when he couldna get it by fair play he tried the foul. For weeks he thought that Paul was drowned, and before he learned the truth he had put his head into the hemp. He hashed and haggled at the books; he forged Paul's name; he grabbed the property. And then, *mo creach!* he got a staggerer! He was no sooner in Drimdorran, laird, and his chair drawn to the fire, than a messenger came one day from the North with dreadful tidings. Paul Macmaster was alive! He was there in the North, with Lovat! He might appear at any hour, though he was papered, and find out how he had been wronged!

"I put myself in his position. 'What's to be done?' I asked the rogue of me. I was there, Drimdorran, at my window, looking out upon my lands, wi' not a crop yet from them, and a letter in my hand, and I saw the scaffold. When a body will see the scaffold he deserves, it's pity him his bowels! there is nothing he will shirk to save him. And I said to myself (for mind ye I was Duncanson!), 'There is only one thing for it—Paul must go!'

"Now, how could this be managed? I thought of Simon. Lovat could have shipped him to oblige a friend, the way he shipped yourself and me, Æneas; but he wasna asked, and that of itself looks black. It meant that Duncanson could not feel safe with Paul alive, even though the ocean lay between them. He must die! Lovat is a bad man, and some day he will suffer for it, but he's not the one to risk his neck in a dirty murder for another man, though he'll stretch a point to do kidnappin', and Duncanson must do the deed himsel'. Your brother never went to France, Alan: he meant to go, but first he meant to come to Inveraray. For a while it puzzled me that Lovat should be ignorant that Paul came this way, but I think that now I have the reason. Paul couldna trust him. No man wi' his wits about him ever sat wi' Sim a day without seeing he was a quirky one. Paul would look at that sly face and mind old Lovat's history, and say to himself, 'This man runs double; if he thinks I'm venturin' home he'll inform, and they will watch for me.' So he never said a word of Inveraray."

"But all this," broke out Bailie Alan, "is but speculation! What makes ye think Paul came to Inveraray?"

"He would never pass this door without a cry on us!" said Annabel.

Ninian shook his head. "That's the very bit!" he said. "I thought of that mysel'. Here were his kin and offspring, and his heart was warm, and he was going to banishment. Would he go past this house at night and not come in? . . . He never passed!

337

The whole thing lies before me like a strath seen from the mountain-top: your brother came down the glen, but never got any farther. . . . Have ye a bite of bread? I've tasted nothing all this day, and now I'm like the wolf."

Annabel put bread before him and some milk.

"But are ye sure, Ninian, that he came this way at all?" the Bailie asked, still doubting.

"As sure as I hear the wave beat on the shore, there! When he left Castle Dounie he made straight for here, and met with Duncanson. How did Sandy have the box? When ye told me, Æneas, that Lovat saw the picture with your father, I knew the worst—that Sandy had destroyed him with his own hand! I knew then what the letter meant that Lovat wrote to Duncanson and brought the death to him—he was afraid of Fraser. That man in the Muir of Ord knew something. He must be shipped with us, if Duncanson would sleep.

"Now, I had the good sense to ask the wife of Fraser for his history. Fourteen years ago he was a man of Lovat's. He carried letters. I thought, when she told me that, of Duncanson, and asked if her man had carried letters to Argyllshire. She told me he had once been there, and it was to Duncanson, with a letter from a gentleman Macmaster. He brought an answer back, and she knew the very day and date, a child was born to her that morning."

"Ah, the poor body!" said Annabel.

"Well, I thought to myself, 'What was that letter? And what for should Sandy want that man trepanned?' I looked at it like this—Paul had affairs with Sandy; he was going abroad; he wanted money; he wrote to Duncanson, his doer, and asked for it. But the thing was far past money with Duncanson; the crying need was death. Oh, man! I saw it all like print! Duncanson said, 'Yes, ye'll have the money; come and get it.' And your father, Æneas, never doubted Sandy. He came to Inveraray! He darena come by day, for his name was at the cross and on the doors o' kirks; he came down that glen in dark, and he met with Sandy under cloud of night. Where did they meet? In Drimdorran House?"

338

"Never on earth!" cried Annabel. "Paul wouldna put a foot in't."

"And that was a thing I thought of, too. They met, I'll swear, in the glen! And then I ask the rogue of me what happened. The scaffold loomed for Duncanson. He had got a property by crime. Here was the only witness, nothing but his breath to make him dangerous.... He killed your brother, Alan, there and then!"

"I canna believe it!" cried the Bailie.

"I'm just as sure as if I saw it! It's what I would do myself if I were him. Consider, Alan—search yourself for the savage in you,—here is a glen in dark and loneliness and a hunted man condemned by law who may bring ye to the scaffold. What for have we got pistol or the dirk except to use them for our own particular skins? . . . Somewhere in Glen Aray, Æneas, your father died! That box was taken from your father's corpse; to keep it was the worst mistake of Sandy."

"You have still produced no evidence that he came here," said Æneas, who was pallid.

"But I have plenty!" said the *beachdair*. "A dead man can be buried, or thrown in a linn with a stone tied to his neck, but a horse is not so easy hidden. Your father borrowed a horse from Lovat and never sent it back. What happened to the horse? . . . You ken the tenant in Tullich—Ellar-an-Eich? It came to me this day, that his by-name came from a song made on him by the cobbler. I knew it but in parts, and I went to the cobbler and made him sing it. It all rose out of a horse Mackellar said he found astray, and nobody believed him. So I went up to Tullich. 'Fourteen years ago,' I says, 'a horse was lost. You sold, about that time, a horse at Kilmichael market and I'm curious to ken just where ye got it.'

"He told me there and then. What he said from the first was true—it was a wandered horse and he found it on a Sunday in his corn, a wise-like, well-bred saddle-beast, without a strap on. He put it in his stable for a fortnight, with never a word to any one about his find. It was the very week Paul rode from Inverness; a fortnight later came Kilmichael market, and

Mackellar rode it there in night-time—thirty miles, and got twenty Saxon pounds for it. Of course the thing came out; the whole land kent of it; the cobbler made his song, and the droll thing was there was never a cheep in the shire of a missing horse!

"There's no mistake about it, Alan; that was Lovat's horse, the one he lent your brother! And here's the copestone of it— Lovat told ye, Æneas, at his table, that your father, later on, through Duncanson, sent the value of the beast. Your father never did, poor man! The money came out of Sandy's pocket, and he little guessed that after fourteen years the lie would rise against him. Sandy heard, like all the rest, that a horse was found in Tullich, but he never said a word. Yet he paid the value of the horse to Lovat! . . . 'I didna hear ye bark!' MacCailein said. If Duncanson was living now there would be barking, for I have everything except the corp of the man he killed. I see the whole thing but the blow! Was it the dirk or pistol?"

"I canna follow ye!" said Alan-Iain-Alain Og, confused.

"Then I'll make it plainer for ye, Alan, and I'll start again wi' Paul in Castle Dounie. He knew he must henceforth stay abroad, and the quicker he was gone the better. Of all the realm of Albyn this parish was most dangerous for him; let him show in Inveraray and his kail was cooked. But he was bound to come here for two things—first to see his child, and next, for money. He wrote to Duncanson to fix a meeting; Fraser took the letter, and brought back an answer. The place of meeting and the hour were fixed. It must be in the night, ye'll mind! Paul darena venture here in daytime. And I wouldna say, when I think of it, but Sandy warned him no' to give his plans to Lovat; that's what I would do in plotting murder. So Paul set out on the borrowed horse wi' the silver-mounted saddle.

"He came over Glen Aray in the dark, and his foe was waiting. It was somewhere in the glen; it couldna be Drimdorran. He took Macmaster unawares, with dag or dagger, and I'll swear it was the dagger in the back, for that's the Clan Maclean! Then he riped the dead man's pouches; got, with other things, the snuffbox; lest earth or water should give up the body he must leave no single thing on it to show that it was Paul's. What he

340

did with the body God Almighty knows, and the woods are wide and thick, and Aray deep, but he put with it the harness of the horse, and lashed the brute back on the road it came. It went into Mackellar's corn that morning, and good for us it did, and that the cobbler made a song!"

All this the *beachdair* gave in gusts that left no chance for question; he was like a man possessed. The steam rose from his clothing; a flush was on his cheek-bones, and his knees were trembling, Janet stared at him with a face white as the cannoch.

And none of them for a while could speak.

Æneas was first to find his tongue in a stifled way.

"I'm thinking of the doocot," he said, and Janet flinched, with her father's eye on her.

"I'll warrant ye I thought of that, but there's nothing in the doocot, and it stands on rock."

"It's just the very place that Paul himsel' would fix on for a tryst," said Alan. "Many a night they spent beside its fire."

Ninian gave a start. "That's just what I was goin' to ask," he said. "Ye talked before about a fire, but fire was never there unless it was a chaffer."

"It wasna any chaffer, but a fireplace and a chimney; I've dried my feet at it when I was at the hares; ye'll see't unless you're blind."

Ninian jumped to his feet. "Blind, indeed!" said he. "But I have my nose! Æneas, did I no' tell ye I could smell the soot? And now I must go up and look again."

"Let me go with you," Æneas said.

"Na, na! You'll just take Jennet home, and I'll come back again. I'll not can sleep till this is settled."

XXXVII

Dirk

Of them all there was no one more disturbed by Ninian's story and the stress of his emotions than his daughter. She was so wan and broken when he left them, Annabel took pity, motherly wrapped her up in a hood, and made Æneas convoy her home. It was nine o'clock; rain teemed; the street was quite deserted; melancholy drenched the night. And there and then, as they went through it, she with a hand on the crook of his arm, it seized on Æneas that all of steadfastness for him, security, and faith, were, in this vexed and mocking world, dependent upon her. All else was meantime reeling for him, he walked on quicksands; every hour brought some new consternation, and now he had a fresh one—he was not so sure of her feelings to him as he had dared at times to be. Like Annabel, he scented doubts. Could the horror of the crimes her father tracked have influenced the change in her?—she was aloof, evasive and yet, two nights ago, she stood surrendered in his arms!

"What is it ails you?" he asked her suddenly. They were come to her doorstep; another moment and she was gone unless he acted quickly.

"I'm tired," she said. "I'm in a stupor. This dreadful business—"

Remorse took hold of him. "I know, my dear," he said; "I know! It would shake the rock, and I am a fool to think you could be calmer than myself. Just for a little, there, I had a fear that I was grown distasteful to you."

His hand was on her shoulder. A fanlight on the doorway dimly lit the porch from a lamp within. The gale blew up the lane with noises of the sea; they occupied a privacy of storm. The crimson hood was slipped back from her head, and her face was wet with rain. Her eyes were troubled; she was dumb; he drew her close to him; she leaned against him for a moment, and he felt a wild heart-flutter, and then she shrank back from him, pushing with her hands against his breast.

"No, no!" she whispered; "that is by with! My far-too-clever father has put an end to that!" and Æneas was dismayed.

"Has he, faith?" he said, and bridled. "I feared what *you* might think, but I never dreamt your father would let that affect him."

"What!" she asked in wonder.

"This—this nightmare in my history, my father's downfall; this appalling mystery. What blame have I? Am I the worse a man for it that you or yours should shun me like a plague? It's not what I would look for from Macgregors—God knows your people, like my own, have died in ugly ways. But I'll have it out with him! This thing is far more vital to me than his search for bones."

At this she changed immediately. Distant no more, she nestled to him. "Æneas," she whispered, "you know my father just as little as I knew you till now! Forget what I said; it was all in error."

Her face was cold and wet; the rain was in her hair; his own face, burning, found in their contact, in their moisture, in their chill, a delight that was almost aching. It is in fires that love is withered, but not in fires that keep a surface damp and cool with clean night-air and storm, and Æneas with his lips on her, drank bliss.

"How *can* we—how *can* we be happy?" she gasped at last. "At such a time! Are we not wicked?"

"No," said Æneas gravely; "the world must aye go on. Weeping may endure a night for death and wrong but love's the morning; we begin afresh. And you will think me a strange man that every fresh discovery of your father's makes me the sorrier for that poor wretch who surely never knew what love was, and can never learn it now. It was not my father's life was marred, but Duncanson's; my father's death was glorious compared with his, even if it were as your father thinks. It's for the sake of that poor clay I hope it wasna."

"You may be sure my father's right," said Janet quietly. "This time he'll find what he is wanting."

"In the doocot?"

She nodded.

"Tell me why you say so."

"I know! I have known it for a week."

"But how?" he cried.

"For not one reason you will listen to, Æneas, but the foolish first was that I loathed the doocot. I hated it since ever I guessed that you were there that night with Margaret, and when my father told me how your troubles started there, I seemed in a flash to see what Duncanson had done. My father might talk about France and your father dying there, but someway I could think of nothing but the doocot, and Duncanson's cold fishy hand. Believe me, Æneas, that's where your father lies!"

He soothed her agitation; she was shaken like a leaf. "You should have told your father what you thought," he urged, but gently.

"I daren't!" she said. "I was afraid. I hoped he never would discover; my happiness looked like depending on his not discovering. And you need not ask me now for why; I'm too ashamed to tell you. Some day—"

"Ah, never mind!" he said in a gush of sudden pity at her turmoil.

He had no faith in her intuitions, and even from Ninian's search expected little. When he got back to the house, he found them there of the same opinion—that the *beachdair's* reasoning had gaps in it patched up with mere surmise.

But the first glance at Ninian's face, when he returned, confounded them. It was grey as ashes. He looked at Annabel strangely, and she left the room.

"Well," said Æneas, sick at the heart, "did you find anything further?"

"*Mo croach!* I did, Drimdorran!" Ninian answered. "Sit you down; my hank's unravelled."

"Was it there?" cried Æneas. The name that Ninian gave him was portentous.

344

"No other place!" said Ninian, solemn. "The first thing you will do, Drimdorran, is, destroy that tower. Leave not a stone of it upon another!"

He sat with his hands on his lap and stared at the fire; the gale whooped in the chimney.

"One thing I overlooked," he said, "and it was very stupid of me. It never crossed my mind that Duncanson could build, though I kent he had some skill with the saw and hammer. It was his own hand blocked the pigeon-holes. The only wright about the place at the time was old Carmichael, and he never knew the place was boarded up. And Duncanson it was who planted trees about the doocot; would he no' be better just to pull it down? That's a thing I should have asked mysel' to start wi'. Another mistake I made was not to trust my nose that I smelled the soot. When first you talked about a fire, Alan, I thought ye meant a chaffer in the middle of the floor, for I saw no sign of chimney or fireplace in the walls—"

"But the fire was there! I know!" said the Bailie.

"Of course it was! I found it half an hour ago. He had built the fireplace up! I found the very trowel he had used to spread his mortar! He built it up with rubble, pushed the bin against the place, and locked the door for fourteen years. But, my God! ye canna lock a door on time or terror! No wonder he kept the plaid tacked on his window in the latter days, with yon tomb before his eyes, a monument o' the man he murdered! . . . I took a pick, when I found the place, and broke the wall, and the first thing I came on was a rotten saddle."

He held out his hand on a sudden; on its palm was a piece of metal.

"I cut that from the leather," he said; "it's part of the silver mounting—a buck's head wi' a motto—Lovat's crest!"

"And—and was there more?" asked Æneas, parched.

"There was," the *beachdair* answered. "At least your father may rest at the last in good Scots clods; it was what I said—the dirk!"

345